Gregory Day's debut novel, *The Patn*
Australian Literature Society Gold Medal in 2006. He has published two
subsequent novels, *Ron McCoy's Sea of Diamonds* and *The Grand Hotel*, which
make up the highly acclaimed Mangowak trilogy. Gregory's short story
The Neighbour's Beans won the Elizabeth Jolley Prize in 2011. He lives on the
southwest coast of Victoria, Australia.

GREGORY DAY

ARCHIPELAGO OF SOULS

PICADOR
Pan Macmillan Australia

Author Note

Although the research that has gone into this novel has been extensive, it is a work of the imagination and should not be read as history. Some scenarios triggered by factual ingredients have been rearranged or relocated. The depiction of the legendary John Pendlebury in this novel, although once again based on research, should nonetheless be read only as my invention.

I am grateful to Sue Fisher and the committee at the King Island Museum & Archive, to Costas Mamalakis in Heraklion, to Alex Craig at Picador, to Jo Butler, Emma Rafferty, Deonie Fiford, Antony Beevor and Peter Thompson. Thanks also to Mary Andriotakis for bearing witness on behalf of her family, and to Nick Andriotakis for his ongoing and practical help. The loyal friendship and intellectual support of Simon McLean, Patrick Mangan, Antoinette Hanna and Ian Chater has been crucial to the completion of this book.

First published 2015 in Picador by Pan Macmillan Australia Pty Ltd
1 Market Street, Sydney, New South Wales, Australia, 2000

Cataloguing-in-Publication entry is available
from the National Library of Australia
http://catalogue.nla.gov.au

Typeset in 11.5/17 pt Garamond by Post Pre-Press Group, Brisbane
Printed by McPherson's Printing Group

MIX
Paper from
responsible sources
FSC® C001695

Australian Government | Australia Council for the Arts

for the hidden ones

Alone is the swallow and costly the spring
For the sun to turn it takes a lot of work
It takes a thousand dead sweating at the wheels
It takes the living also shedding their blood

Odysseus Elytis

One

Days of Butterflies

One

Days of Butterflies

I

BENEATH SHEOAKS ON A SLOPE ON A HILL OVERLOOKING BASS STRAIT is the grave of John Lascelles, a man commonly thought of by the people of this island as the finest you'd ever be likely to meet. It's pretty amusing that for so many years I would have been the last person to reckon that of him and that it fell to myself and Leonie in the end to bury him, but bury him we did, not with full military honours as he may have dreamt, but with a typically odds and sods gathering of people who'd known him both short and long, and who respected him with a deep though often dry-witted affection. Some placed wattle boughs in his grave, some stepped forward to whisper a few words, others offered the traditional hand of ground. Leonie threw in a nectarine. Lascelles would always bring a delicious offering from his garden when he visited us in the warmer months; and believe you me, growing stone fruit is not always an easy task in the weather we get out here on King.

For myself, I posted a letter into his grave; well, a sealed package actually, addressed in cuttlefish ink containing events and feelings written in the same. These were the last of the pages I'd written many years before to Leonie, and which, like all the others, I'd planned for

3

Lascelles to personally make sure she received. They were pages no one bar Leonie was ever to read, pages I know Lascelles himself would certainly have loved to have seen, but which I'd stubbornly refused to show him. Mind you, I did very nearly paraphrase their contents one night over dinner here at Naracoopa, in the pleasurable years of my final thaw, when I no longer saw him as a phoney or a threat, but as a kind-hearted and doggedly loyal friend of above-average intelligence. But no, I could never bring myself to do it, to share with him the words as I'd written them down, in the packages I'd sent through to Leonie with his assistance in those days after the war when he and his father ran the post office. And even Leonie didn't know for sure that the last package had survived, for I'd held it close since the day it had come back into my possession, like a good luck charm, it being the only one that hadn't gone up in the fire at Wait-a-While.

That's where we buried Lascelles, on the block at Wait-a-While, on the levelled site of my old hut, and right alongside the plots where Leonie and myself will eventually be lowered down. I caught sight of her face on the other side of the grave, her skin ghastly white with the easterly and the sadness of it all. She was facing into the molten glare of the water far below but looked down at the open soil as the package fluttered out from my hand. She'd recognise it anywhere, I knew she would even after all these years, and I saw the surprise in her face as it dropped in a slant and then seemed to hover for a moment, before landing with a light *thsk* onto Lascelles' coffin lid.

With respect to gossip on the island, I was thankful that the envelope landed sender upwards, with only my own name in my younger hand legible to the sky and the eyes around, though you would have had to be really looking. People have joked to me since that I needn't have put a sender's address on a letter to a dead man and I've laughed along with them, relieved at what other story they might have drummed up if the package had twisted the other way and landed with Leonie's name face up. Oh, I can imagine the conclusions they may have come to, about the frustrated passion Lascelles had for her and how the only evidence of it would be buried with him. Yes, I can well imagine some of them thinking that. Especially given how close the three of us eventually became and also given the fact that Lascelles had never married. But they would have been wrong. It was a lucky turn for us all that Lascelles, whose life was so pure and thoughtful, died without any hint of such a scandal, though even if he had it may not have phased me, given my own betrayals, and those of others against me, which have so directed the course of my life.

The last time I saw Lascelles alive he'd parked his Cortina back near the jetty and walked the rest. Trying to keep his old body fit. He seemed healthy enough when he showed, his colour was good, and he propped on the couch in his customary green slicker and cords with his pipe and a mug of coffee. As I remember it we had a pleasant chat, mainly about rumours of the scheelite mine re-opening, but when he left and I watched him walking back out across the grass in the direction of his car there was something in the quality of his solitude that caught my attention. Dear old Lascelles. The colours around little Councillor Island in the bay beyond were switching off and on under cloud. Silver, blue-black, green. As usual his tread was tentative – it took me years to realise it was due to the sheer size and openness of his brain that he walked the earth, even in peacetime, as if it was a minefield – but as I watched him go the whole atmosphere of sky and sea seemed to adjust its curvature and hover auspiciously around him. When two days later I found him slumped on his old back porch above the harbour in Currie, with a cold pot of tea, a fallen book, and a honey sandwich covered with ants at his side, it seemed the most natural thing in the world. We are all getting on after all. What rocked me was not so much that he had died, but rather the fact that I, due to the last persistent residue of an obstinate ocker pride, had withheld so long from him the one vindication he so richly deserved.

Leonie and I felt his loss greatly, although I, unlike her, felt it guiltily also. I recalled the day years before when Lascelles first came to visit Naracoopa on his father's shiny old Velocette. We sat out on the garden bench near the rows of agapanthus (they're all gone now), he with his post-office visor still on his head, and he lit his pipe. The thought of what I could have said to him then, and didn't, is a part, I s'pose, of the engine that drives my pen across this page. The good-natured man had built an official RSL Memorial Reading Room on the island and nobody used it. He spent his time off from the post office alone in that reading room, dusting the shelves, writing away on letterhead for new catalogues, unit histories, personal memoirs, photographic records; listening out for a footfall. His benign dream, his *theory*, that diggers needed healing, time to nurture their scars by reading and writing in order to reflect on the trials of their wars, was seemingly disproven. Time and again he watched the King Island SS – my cheeky name for the soldier settlers – trudge past through the squalls to the pub or the club. To drink. To bend their memories with beer and away from vexation. Lascelles knew that theirs was a version of the talking cure. Only it was self-medication. The shrink was no one specific, just any ear who'd listen – not to the gangrenous facts of the jungle or Tobruk, but to the avoiding of them.

Yet out on the east side of the island, here was I, Wesley Cress, a living testament to the rightness of Lascelles' theory. And this is what I withheld from him. What I couldn't say. How he had unknowingly filled my life with love. I can see his discomfort on that day near the agapanthus, as he sat fiddling with his pipe. I can almost see the thoughts in his mind, like a slide show whirring, clanking, re-arranging. I can remember my own thoughts too, that his problem was – there was nothing he could ever do about it – that he never saw action. Simple as that. His keenness and curiosity about anything to do with the war used to cheese me off, though eventually I learnt to have a laugh, even at the thought of it. He would always narrow his eyes when I did that, as if to ask indignantly: '*What?*' But in my weakness I could never say, and all I can think now is how sad it was that something inside of him still envied me my burden.

I crunch the last of my breakfast toast between my teeth and leave the kitchen saying I've gotta set the record straight. Leonie says from where she's reading the newspaper at the table, 'the record's never straight', and before I've even had a chance to walk the gravel path I've been sent way out towards an ever-receding horizon. Truth, by its nature, cannot be clean and straight. It is not the events or the memories of the events creating my condition but the conditions of this island creating them. The life we've lived since the war. The two islands I inhabit. And I'll say in reply, '*ex nihilo?*' She'll nod. Our little erudite joke in my schoolboy Latin. Out of nothing?

Nothing comes out of nothing.

So I walk the gravel path looking straight ahead at nothing. Out over the grass, over the narrow road, the rocks, the sand, out across the ocean. If there's a cargo tramp or a crayboat there I hardly see it. And when I turn with the curl of the path, flick that latch and walk through the bungalow door I somehow think of Captain John Pendlebury doing the same. As the heat rose back in '41. Entering his messy office in Iraklion. Picking up his glass eye from where he left it on the desk and calmly inserting it back into its socket.

II

DURING THE SLAUGHTER, THE SCREAMING DAYS WHEN THE GERMAN pilots would use the piercing sirens fixed to the undersides of their fuselages to rattle us – quite aside from the terror of the bombs – we treated a little house just south of the Iraklio airfield as a hospital, a hotel, and a church. Uncle Tassos our host would say to me, as we hauled in the wounded, 'Mister Wesley Cress you are making the mountains of *Kriti* burst with wildflowers.' Or he would shout to Vern, above the strafing in the air, 'Mister Vernon Cress, your family are forever welcome here.' Once, as we sat out in the courtyard under his trellised vines at dawn, having endured a terrible night of bleeding and inadequacy as Ken Callinan gave up the ghost, Uncle Tassos said: 'You brothers and your friends are here with us for all time. The living and the dead. We are all brothers now. Do you understand?'

Even before we got onto the island we'd had a terrible time. Outnumbered by German and Italian forces on the Greek mainland we'd been forced into a ragtag retreat south after a ferocious and freezing Easter at a place called Vevi. Our instructions when they came were to get to Crete. On any boat we could find. When finally our little band of stragglers, myself, my brother Vern, Mug Wylie and Ken, gangplanked on the island at Souda Bay, we were exhausted. We were told to expect local attention and to respect it as our ally and by the time we'd hauled our kits from Souda across the north coast to join our unit at Iraklio we'd learnt it wasn't so difficult to do so. The very next day, after our first fair dinkum sleep in a while, the four of us wandered off from the unit camp for a look-see. As it happens Tassos had sent his niece Adrasteia to pick two or three of us out for his own purposes, any two or three would do.

We all saw her coming, the dust in her dress and bare feet, her hair stowed away but her brown arm brandishing two plump chooks in our direction. We licked our lips. I took the chooks from her but handed them straight to Vern and he to Ken and then to Mug. Pass the chook, we joked, embarrassed by her beauty. And then she took them back from Mug and we followed her – how could we not? – for at least a half an hour along a creek bed and up a ridge of olive tree rows to the house.

Any one of us could have rung the necks of the chooks that day but we chose Mug to do the honours. He politely stepped outside the rough courtyard wall of the villa and up onto the little dirt lane amongst the oleanders. Started to rip into it. Feathers went everywhere, floating up in the sea-breeze above the wall. Uncle Tassos was impressed. He had good English from labouring on the nearby archaeological digs at Knossos but showed us he liked the way we dealt with the bird by smiling and wringing an imaginary neck in the air with his hands. Then, when Mug had finished, he started to talk. To begin our education.

He told us about their island boys, the Cretan unit of the Greek army, how they were stranded up on the Albanian border leaving Crete to fend for itself, without the prime of its fighting youth. Then he went on about an archaeologist named Pendlebury, a Pom – 'Mister John' he called him – a captain and a friend, who spoke all of *Kriti's* dialects.

He told us how far this Mister John had walked, before the war, from east to west over the island's four high massifs. He laughed as he drew quite the figure for us: a tall Englishman, with a glass eye from a child-hood accident, travelling on foot, with a *katsounas*, a shepherd's crook, in pursuit of romantic adventure and Minoan shards. Now, according to Tassos, Pendlebury was plying the same high plateaus and snowy passes, the cut gorges and barren southern shores to anticipate the Germans by preparing resistance networks. To link hundreds of small villages in the mountains with the villages of the coasts, to set up signalling patterns and strategies, lines of communication, and also to coordinate heavy work like hefting boulders onto potential landing areas to obstruct German aircraft. So *Kriti* would be ready when the Nazis came. 'And she will,' said Tassos, giving us a defiant stare.

Tassos had a big beak, and long thick side whiskers of salt and pepper that seemed to stand to attention as we talked to him, particularly Vern, in the rough-as-guts Greek he'd learnt out on the farm alone when we were kids. Some of what he'd learnt had paid dividends for us only a couple of weeks before at Vevi, when he'd come up with a nickname for the Italian soldiers – *makaroniades* – and as we'd fallen back into the chaos of our retreat the locals just fell about laughing at the joke. Now, in easier circumstances, Vern's gifts were impressing our Cretan host. Uncle Tassos kept correcting Vern's scraps of Greek, converting them into his dialect, but his black eyes were wet with pleasure, his whiskers bristling with excited sociability, and meanwhile Adrasteia kept shimmying in and out through the door in the courtyard wall, with vegetables and a copper pot she was filling with the feathers Mug had scattered in the street.

Of course we'd all fallen for her but Vern took the inside running when the pot of feathers she was carrying changed later on to a heavy load of juniper logs. He didn't exactly have his tongue hanging out but, by the look on her face as he held out his hands to help her, she thought he was a try-hard. I dunno, maybe his mangled, patched-together Greek sounded pathetic and Tassos had only been polite because he knew he could use him. Well, an ordinary shitkicker Vern definitely wasn't, yet as he put out his arms to receive her basket she handed it over with an astonishingly assertive look. Then, quick as the wind, as soon as she'd handed over the basket, her expression changed to one of pure play and amusement.

In the courtyard we roasted the two plump chooks on the juniper fire. What a lark! Sitting under Uncle Tassos' vines it seemed some kind of miracle that Vern, myself, Ken and Mug had found a local enclave. An island within the island. A clear pause. A place where we could remember normal things, like the feeling of a full belly and the relief of the sun in our bones.

~

The Kiwi General, Tiny Freyberg, was in charge of our Cretan forces and day by day he folded his huge burly frame into a jeep to visit the units scattered across the north coast to the west and east of Souda. Our bush scholar Vern gave us the heads up that Tiny Freyberg was not your average type of Kiwi, not even your average general. He'd been a hero of the first war but even more than that he had certain flash associations. For instance, the best man at his wedding was Peter Pan, or at least the fella who'd written the book.

We sat amongst the trees, smoked uncut Players, and listened to the general, sizing him up in the light of that info as he spoke in front of the Union Jack, which he'd draped over a walnut tree. I looked across to Vern and noticed how attentive he was as Freyberg gave us the rundown, such as he knew it. A German landing by sea, a tough fight, a sure victory. In truth the general was issuing us all with boots of clay – the complete bloody opposite of Peter Pan's light step – but he seemed to have no idea.

Afterwards Vern and myself had our first chat about Adrasteia as we traipsed the dusty path back to Uncle Tassos'.

To my surprise, Vern seemed all of a sudden indifferent to the girl. The proximity of Freyberg had got to him, that's all I can put it down to. The big general in the grove was like a thing Vern had imagined before things got real, a bookish vision of a classical war. He admitted Adrasteia's beauty when I remarked upon it – well, it could hardly be ignored – but then he said, 'You're keen on her are you, Wes?' which was like asking if you'd prefer to have no fleas in your armpits, or that the *makaroniades* hadn't invaded Greece in the first place, or better still that the war was over and we were back at home fishing on the lake. How could any bastard with a healthy rustle in his pants not be keen on her!

To this day I believe that it was Freyberg who turned Vern's head inside out, with his flash associations, the way he stood genial but upright with the occult flutter of that Union Jack draped over the walnut tree behind him. Vern had grown up isolated, held back unnaturally at the farm after the death of our mother, while I was away at school. But he was the bright one and while I was away struggling through *amo amas amat* he'd spent his time escaping into books, into classical dreams of legendary islands like Crete, and reading the poetry of people like Rupert Brooke, people who, he'd now informed us, were Freyberg's friends. He'd dreamt himself deep into the lines of all those books he'd read, played out his own mythological roles on the slopes of our farm's volcano, so that as the general put over the prospect of the battle's importance it sounded like literature to him, something already written.

13

As we walked the spiny track back towards Uncle Tassos', I said: 'What, has this bloody war done your head in, Baby? You sure you're seein' what's right there in front of you?'

We'd always called him Baby back home, and now he just laughed, the beautiful features of his face flung back, as if he knew that I, his run-of-the-mill elder brother, was finally and forever more to take the golden family seat he was vacating. You see in his mind he'd been raised up, ill-starred already, by the prospect of the triumph ahead. When he stopped laughing he put his hand on my shoulder affectionately. Then he took it away, looked straight ahead of him down the track as we walked and said, as if to no-one in particular, 'It's the things you can't see that you've gotta see. That's what's gonna matter in the end.'

After that conversation, Vern and I never mentioned Adrasteia again. She was simply in our lives during the build-up to the Germans' arrival, cooking with her uncle on the courtyard fire, sopping down the benches, playing knucklebones with her little cousin Nicko, eavesdropping on as much English as she could, gathering sticks with the donkey by way of reconnaissance for her uncle's always burning and fiercely independent fire.

~

By the middle of May we'd been hard at it for a couple of weeks with the others in the vicinity of the airfield, wiring in, digging weapon pits, dressing up decoy sangars whilst building decent camouflage for our real positions among the rocks. There were two small hills about a hundred yards apart right next to the airfield which, when the boys of our unit first marched in off the lighter, they'd nicknamed The Charlies, due to their uncanny resemblance to a woman's breasts. A couple of days after we'd arrived Vern had dreamt that we'd run a string of barbed wire from one nipple to the other of The Charlies, with the idea of knocking out any Bavarian Stuka comin' in low from the east to strafe the town. It was only a dream but in the light of day it also seemed to stack up as a good idea. It was like something a child would conjure up; that was its beauty I s'pose. When he brought it up in the camp over breakfast and a few of us agreed that it actually wasn't such a bad idea he began to get excited. 'I'm gonna let the brass know about it,' he declared. We all thought he was joking of course but when someone actually remarked that he had Buckleys of getting the CO's attention he flicked away his cowlick and smiled broadly. 'I bet ya dinner at the new Australia Hotel I can get 'em to do it.'

Some of the blokes scoffed but Ken Cal took the bet. 'I'll have a bit of that spread at the Australia,' Ken said. Vern became even more het up then. Straightaway he was up on his feet and weaving through the camp. Soon he had the idea passing along the grapevine and up to the cave in the chalky cliffs above the airfield that served as HQ. Lo and behold, next day the word came right back along the vine and the idea was given the nod.

This was some feather in the cap for Vern, but it being a dream we laughed that this time he couldn't really take any credit. As far as command in the cave was concerned however it didn't seem to matter whether you dreamt something or thought it up dry, and the strategy was actually advertised for the sake of morale as Private Vernon Cress' idea. The young private had proven that with the right attitude to our preparations for what lay ahead, you never knew what you might contribute. And if that wasn't enough, it was also made known, as a kind of further nod to lift our spirits after what we'd been through on the mainland, that Vern and a few of us blokes who were his best mates were to be given the actual responsibility of rigging The Charlies.

Together we worked hard in the sun to set what we now were calling 'the booby-trap', to wire in the ends and winch it tight enough from nipple to nipple to work. I can see now how all this must have reinforced the course Vern had set for himself but it was bloody difficult going dragging that wire on foot through the rocky ground in the heat. Still, we had a fair old time regardless, despite the trial and error, knowing pretty much everyone's imagination had been captured by our task, with plenty of speculation flying about the peccadilloes of the giant young maiden we were trussing, and the blue sky and sea also helping to buoy us along.

Eventually, after a whole day and a half, we had the deadly tripwire strung taut in the air. Vern's dream had come true. Given the Australia Hotel was twelve thousand miles away he and Ken Cal decided instead to make a celebratory visit early that afternoon back to Uncle Tassos' villa for some local R&R (rest & raki). Mug and I however liked the look of the water and took the chance to go down into the town for a swim first. Plus from down there we would see if the wire could be spotted from the mole in the harbour where the resemblance of The Charlies was at its most obvious.

We headed down past groups of Black Watch blokes, who despite the warm weather were still in their kilts and tam-o-shanters amongst the coolness of the freshly dug weapon pits. A few of them joked to us about The Charlies as we passed. Mug and I were tickled pink with the attention, and I was especially proud of my little brother. We walked happily down past the fishermen's moorings and the sponge divers' piles, out under the swifts circling above the Venetian fortress by the sea.

By the time we got out on the mole we were boiling and straight-away stripped off and dived right in. The water was pure heaven and we dipped and skited like a pair of dolphins. With our heads bobbing we looked back east across the harbour on The Charlies. There they were, a jocular trap dreamt up by my brother in collaboration with the ancient island itself. We were happy to see there was no barbed-wire lingerie visible from that angle.

Afterwards we lay on the stones of the mole in the sun and smoked. There had been German flyovers by this stage but nevertheless Cretans of the old town wandered past us, defiantly continuing their daily constitutionals. I started a letter home and Mug threw in a handline with some hooks he'd got his hands on when we'd landed at Souda. After an hour or so the sea breeze was luffing the water around Mug's line and we were drawling happily away. It was a sweet little interlude, and remains so even in recollection, one of the sweetest I remember of the whole war.

By the late afternoon Mug had caught what looked to us like a decent sea bream and was looking forward to presenting it in gratitude to Tassos up at the villa. We set off by way of the streets of the town, until we wound our way back down off the heights beyond the old southern gate and into the scrub towards the villa. But as we came up out of the creekbed, climbing the narrow lane and rounding the white wall into the yard, it was immediately clear there would be no grand presentation.

We found Vern and Adrasteia in the little courtyard under the grapes, with Uncle Tassos quietly stoking the painted stone mouth of the fire nearby. Nothing was said. With the scissors from my kit – I could see from the shapes of gluey tarnish on the blades they were mine – she was cutting Vern's hair with great care. It had become like straw by then, filthy, first matted by the long retreat from Vevi then dried out by the roll in the leaky caique across the water and the recent salt days in the sun. He sat on a rush-chair with her standing behind, his face in mottled repose from the leaves on the trellis above, his eyes shut, and occasionally with her slightly pudgy hand he would let her turn his head this way or that to get the angle right.

We had stepped lighthearted, with the sea on our skin, as if into the grip of a spontaneous but solemn rite. The rasp of the scissors was loud in the stillness. The air was thick with what was about to be unleashed upon us. The walls of the house, recently whitewashed for Easter, borrowed blues and yellows from the sky.

Mug laid the fish on the grey stone border beside the fire. I remember looking at smoke curling from the fire mouth. I remember Mug's face, watchful but a little confused, like a child in church. I remember that rasp of the scissors in my brother's hair, the solidity of Adrasteia's hips in a dark green and black skirt, her belly pressed tight against Vern's back.

I remember thinking these people had always known we were coming. Us boys. I also remember wondering how it could be that Uncle Tassos seemed as old as the twisted knots of the overhead vines.

When the atmosphere changed, Uncle Tassos covered the fish with herbs and placed it into the fire mouth on a metal paddle. It cooked quickly, we drank strong raki, and a group of locals suddenly appeared as if drawn by the smell of the dittany. These in fact were men who had already come to be known as Pendlebury's thugs. *Andartes.* A large man, a doctor called Dimitris, played a miniature lyre in huge hands like those of a woodchopper, and his elder brother, Nickos, with a black beard surrounding bright red lips, sang. These men all wore the traditional garb, strides we called 'bog-catchers', *vakres* in the local lingo, with coloured cummerbunds around their waists. They had flourishing, outlandish moustaches, and their music was a great exhalation.

Knowing nothing as yet of the historical misery and pride which they were singing of, we danced with a liberation only the Cretan dance can bring. The intensity of Vern's haircut was released into one magnificent piss-up and celebration, histories were explained on both sides of the ledger, and in the course of it all Mug Wylie was heralded as a natural fisherman.

I talked to Adrasteia that night as we came together during the dance with great ease. In my relief and happiness I attempted to tell her about the old volcano and lake back home, how much plough-twanging scoria was scattered through our paddocks – as much, I said, as the ever-present rubble of Crete – and I described the walls that, like the people of her island, we built from it. I explained how in our country the south was cold not warm, and how the arc of green slopes and the buckled crater walls of our farm meant we were experts in fat lambs. I took pride that night in my lineage and my fathers' farming acumen but told her how I'd been sent away to school whilst Vern had been kept back on the land with Dad, and how it should have been the other way around. And she said simply: 'You are so far from home.'

That night Mug, Ken and I slept in the upstairs room of the villa, while Vern with his newly cropped hair fell asleep like a young prince in his clothes on a bench of gypsum by Uncle Tassos' fire. He'd hardly touched a drop.

III

To Leonie's father Nat Fermoy I was just another damned remnant of the war when I first washed up here. He'd seen them the first time: wandering, stooping, limping through the biffo of the weather; narrow-gutted, half-shickered, spooked, stopping only to thumb a coin for his little girl, his motherless Leonie, who seemed to be attracted to these misshapen ghosts. There was nothing Nat could do to stop her roaming the island – she was as much its child as his after all – but if he came upon them at some rare junction of the roads, a one-armed wretch stooping like a reed over her own small figure, he'd quickly drag her away across the flatness of the land. 'You back off,' he'd say, on the cart going back home to Tuck White's old block in the north-east and she'd stay silent. 'Those men are dangerous. They could hurt you,' and she'd pull her duffel coat around, thinking that kindness isn't dangerous and danger isn't kind.

So when I first showed up over twenty years later, and plonked myself down between the campfire and a patch of ten sheoaks on the aerodrome road, I was nothing particularly new. More like an old piece of furniture, in fact, another round of jetsam from the nation. Only difference was that I wasn't on the lookout for free land, though I s'pose you couldn't tell that just by looking.

It is my actual belief – take it or leave it – that most Australians are not joiners. A mistrust of institutions is not an inability to love, I used to tell Lascelles. A liking for solitude, or even loneliness, is not an enemy of compassion, I'd say. I already knew by the time I'd arrived on King that any kind of real independence is impossible. Just bullshit. I wanted nothing to do with *Australia* or its handouts but not because I thought I could be free. My notions of freedom went down in a not-quite-hollow ship. But what I hadn't learned by the time I washed up here was the infinite nature of love. Not the romantic love of one man for his maid, not even deep, abiding friendship or the tidal love of a parent for a child, but the vast well of universal love from which all these affections come. Love like the ocean and bigger than any of us. Love like the weather. Brutal love that can change and recover. After loss. After loss and after it's been slung and filleted on the bare rock of the world.

~

On the day that I arrived here on King, when I first caught sight of it from the crayboat as we approached, it was the height of the paperbark stands that made an impression. Also the way the cloud, the *lenticular* they call it, just hovered there above the island, like some meteorological parachute attached to the body of the land with invisible strings. I'd caught a ride with the Shirley boys from Lorne, who were over for the big summer crays, and from the plunge of their deck I could see the strata: white surf like the foam of beer against the kelp-lipped rocks, the low rise of the coasty hummocks and pastures, then the paperbarks, then the parachute of the lenticular hovering there.

But almost as soon as I registered the cloud it started moving, from west to east right over our heads.

A part of me already knew that the things I had to surmount here would be, like the weather, hard to come to grips with. There one minute and gone the next. So for a moment, as the boat bumped in and the decky put out his smoke and readied the ropes, I panicked. Even out here I wondered where I would hide, with no one left and nothing still or solid to hold onto. A surge of giant bull-kelp over the side expressed it too. Humbled I felt. *Again.* Unlike Crete, this island is a raw and level place, and I, like the paperbark trees, felt I'd be sticking out like nobody's business.

As I said goodbye to the Shirleys, disembarked from the boat and walked up the hill from the ocean, I soon realised I could take the roads alone but never get beyond the sound of the roar. Mum had told me coming out of mass in Colac as a child that just south of us, over the Otways, in the waters of Bass Strait, there were islands rife with snakes. We'll never be taking you out there, she'd said with a smile. But somehow, in my little head, I imagined those islands in a way she didn't intend: as places where guilt was present but easily accounted for. Where its deadly venom (which I knew well, from the sermons in church) was standing to attention. Where no matter who they were or what they'd done, people could cop it sweet and still survive.

Up in the northwest here, at Phoques Bay, there's another tiny island out on the water that's a fair dinkum Celtic lace of snakes. Black tigers. And so it was uncanny that when I finally stopped on that first day, and made my bare camp by the ten sheoaks on the aerodrome road, that Leonie Fermoy came cycling by, and without really even introducing herself, leant her bike into the whispering of the sheoaks, sat down by the fire, and started telling me all about it.

She seemed almost as tall as a paperbark herself, and thin; she wore trousers in the manner of a man and had a mass of ropey white hair that stuck out at the back like a spoonbill's bob and fell across her face in the wind as she talked. She had no idea of the pictures in my head. Or so I thought.

Two Chinamen took on that other little island, like Chinamen will, she told me, and she reckoned Chinamen didn't fear snakes. 'They have a *relationship* with them,' she said, as I rolled a smoke and observed what I thought was her rather articulate use of the word.

'But I have a *relationship* with them too,' I eventually said, a little sarcastic.

'Yeah, you and the sharp end of your shovel.'

'No,' I said. 'I'll never get rid of 'em, just like they'll never be rid of me.'

'Well,' she scoffed. 'We all have to die somehow.' I remember thinking about this, then thinking about Vern, and sizing her up even further. 'Yair, but not from guilt,' I muttered, licking my Tally-Ho.

Leonie finished up that curious first hello of hers; she stood up in that bare spot by the ten sheoaks, got back on her bike and cycled on without so much as a wave let alone an explanation. I was left alone to wonder. But before I had a chance to work it out that other face came through my mind again, from the night when the stink of sulphur faded: the way she too took me unawares, how light I was, how I needed to be light, not as a feather but as an act without consequence.

IV

MORNING LIGHT CLEANSED THE SPARTAN ROOM. I STOOD UP OUT OF my blanket, flicked my dog tags round and crossed to the window. I looked north across the island towards the water and saw The Charlies beside the airfield, the string of wire between them still invisible from that angle. All this was true and yet, as in a dream, I can only presume what it was that I saw.

I stepped away then, back into the room, and over Ken and Mug to the plain shard of mirror hanging on the painted stone wall.

The morning's heat had begun to rise but my whole body went suddenly cold. In the mirror before me were new eyes. They'd been brown as soil until that moment, reddy-brown like the scoria, sometimes browny-black like the Barwon, just a shade away from black itself. But they were brown no longer.

Swimming in the clean marine light of that second storey my eyes had turned green. Brightly, unmistakably so. They stared back at me, acidic, wide, and terrified.

It seemed that, like Vern, I had been bloody well possessed. Wesley Cress had green eyes. As if born for a second time, to a second mother, a second sky, a second sea, to another world beyond the likes of Mug and Ken lying there in their kits on the floor.

V

NOT LONG AFTER HER FIRST VISIT TO MY CAMP LEONIE FERMOY SOLD me a sausage roll in the co-op in Currie. Wearing a shiny dubbined leather apron that almost seemed too heavy for her frame. The land agent Bill Murray was waiting outside for me in his Standard Tourer, so I didn't say much, thanked her I s'pose, and went off to look at some ground.

The land agent was a quiet chap. No blarney there. Which was just as well, given the mood I was in. We drove round the island in silence that day, looked through the fences at what turned out to be Fermoy scrub up north-east of Egg Lagoon, but they wanted too much for it. Which meant they weren't selling at all. Bill Murray told me they rated the island higher than most, the Fermoys, rated themselves for that matter, and fair enough too. Old Nat Fermoy Senior had come in off an American whaler in the long ago. The family had gone nowhere ever since. It made complete sense to me that the woman who'd parked her bike by my fire was one of them.

Though it was slow going I persisted with Bill Murray who, although he never talked much, knew how to keep you on the hook. He'd drive me round, to meet the folks, if you like. We'd sit in island kitchens down south towards Stokes Point and up north at Wickham, drink tea and eat scones with people who didn't want to sell, or didn't know it yet. But soundings like that seemed accepted, a part of life, and we were company too. You can't play cards with the pheasants after all. And everyone understood Bill's position. He had to do his duty and, given the fluctuating price of beef and lamb and such, the vagaries of the barge-transport, well you might just decide right there on the spot, right there with a jawful of jam and cream and scone, that you wanted to sell after all. Though it was unlikely.

In truth, I was getting a tour of the island. And when I wasn't I'd sit in my camp and read and try to work out what to do about Vern now that I didn't have any family left to shelter from the facts. That was tough and by god I was flinty about it all. They were the days when everyone wanted to forget the war, especially the embarrassing bits. Time and circumstance had cast their lots, and there I sat, exposed by a blowy fire in the roadside camp, vulnerable on all sides but one to the powers of the strait – the ten sheoaks being my windbreak in the southwest quarter.

I'd smoke. Read Vern's old copy of Epictetus the stoic, which I'd salvaged from our abandoned house on Corangamite when I first came back. Dad had died while I was away, having had the telegrams that Vern and I were both missing in action. I was the only one left, apart from Uncle Den, who filled me in and helped me sell the farm when I made it clear I wanted no part of it.

For no reason that I could make out Leonie began showing up at any odd hour, muddy or clean, with burrs and animal hair through her suedes and corduroys. She started bringing me things: a folding canvas chair, flour for damper, and neatly cut kindling. Until Bill Murray could find me something, it was all I had, my little camp, but she was fast becoming my host. That much was bloody obvious. It was her island. Her father's island. Nat Fermoy. And his father's. Old Nat Fermoy. So, like tit for tat, I started to tell her about our place, about the farm and the lakes.

But – it was uncanny again, just like the snakes – she had relations on her mother's side, the Burrows, who I'd known as a kid. From just northeast of Colac, at Ondit, ten mile or so from us. She'd actually gone there as a child, across the strait on the crayboats and over the leechy wet ridge of the Otways by horse, right past our gate as a matter of fact, and there was nothing much I could tell her about it that she didn't already know. Except for what I found when I'd returned to the farm: the stock all gone, the windows smashed, and some old swaggy from Skipton asleep on the scoria under the pittosporum.

Probably to put some flesh on the bare bones of my situation she began to speak herself. She told me about her grandfather's arrival on the island. About the way he got his land. Then about how her father came to use it. Then her mother's arrival, the marriage to Nat and her own birth. It was like the flippin' family deed, I remember thinking at the time. But that was the start of her letting me get to know her. That was her way. It was an old ballad, each generation of Fermoys had its own verse. But once she got to the point where she was born, the music stopped.

Bill Murray the land agent might have been having difficulty finding me a spot to prop but it seemed Leonie's grandparents, Old Nat and Patsy Ballyhoura, had no such trouble. And they didn't have to spend a penny. Arriving right here at Naracoopa in Nat's curagh in the 1800s, they were told if they went over to the west side there was land near the Yellow Rock river on Phoques Bay where no one would object to them knocking up a shelter. It turned out true, no one did seem to mind them propping on that cloud-ramming stretch in the maw of the westerlies. And for Nat it was a pretty good compromise between life on sea and land. He learnt how to snare wallabies, and from Yellow Rock he could look out towards twelve and a half thousand miles of unbroken water, most of which he'd rolled over in various boats searching for oil and ambergris. Anyway, as Leonie told it, by the time Grandmother Patsy had given birth to Leonie's father and Uncle True it was fairly well accepted that the spot where Nat and Patsy built the house, and the spread of wattle and paddock dune around it, was the Fermoys'.

She carried on then by the smoky fire, about her dad, Young Nat, as he was known, and how he was an abstemious wind hater who crossed to the opposite side of the island as soon as he was old enough, and how he'd no interest in the sea or skins but as a kid got a taste for farming beef and had hitched himself to a fella called Tuck White who was the first to bring Angus cattle onto King. This fella Tuck White had never credited a Fermoy with having a clue about stock and land but her dad persisted as a young bloke and never let up until Tuck White couldn't avoid the use of him and had taken him on.

And then, unnerved as I could so easily be in those days by the unbidden edge of brother Vern's voice calling again in my ears, I said: 'And you've got no one else to tell all this to?'

Her face went plain, even paler than it already was, her skin translucent, her cheekbones catching the light. She'd been right to imagine I'd been comforted by her yarn; even more than that, it was a reprieve she'd brought, the way she'd roll in with her bike and her kindling. But as her ballad had wandered on something had cast me back, into the bitterness of things, and suddenly this young woman on the other side of the fire, with her high-boned face and all the time in the world on her hands to tell a stranger her legacy, seemed nothing short of balmy.

Pain hollows us out, you see, kills the kindness. Less than a minute later she was pedalling back to the turn-off and I was alone with the smoke again, smouldering. My brother's voice was calling, the mythological seas around Crete he'd so much looked forward to were hissing at me, full of tragic water.

VI

BEFORE THE TRUE HORRORS OF THE GERMAN LANDING ARRIVED WE did have info of what might be coming – *intelligence*, the nobs call it – and we certainly had fears, fears which were part-mocked and part-exacerbated by Lord Haw-Haw's 'Germany Calling' broadcasts, which sometimes we'd gather round a wireless set in a *kaphenoi* in Iraklio to hear. I remember the night when through the crackle and static we could just make out the plummy propaganda voice announcing that Hitler had a bullet for every leaf and a bomb for every olive on Crete. And another night in particular when, much to our cocky amusement at the time, Haw-Haw ridiculed us Australians specifically, and went on to pronounce *Kriti* as an island of doomed men and sunken ships.

On the day my eyes changed colour in the upstairs room all such conjecture came to an end. It was late in the afternoon, around five o'clock. We'd been down at The Charlies all day, running a second string of wire between the nipples, just like young scallywags setting a square hook. This time though the shock came not from a snap freeze in the weather, as it had at Vevi, nor from a shard of the mirror, but from the open sky when hundreds of coloured brollies of the *Fallschirmjaeger* suddenly appeared over the water.

From that moment on, hell ruled the island. Tiny Freyberg had expected the Germans to come by sea but instead from the air the brollies came down, in a slow, insidious drift. Were they dots in front of our eyes, a mirage of the heat? No, they came and then they began to land, to become indisputably real. They fell into quarries and fountains, onto beaches and spits, into lanes and backyards and into dried-up riverbeds. We found maps on some of those poor buggers later. They couldn't have known how imprecise their task would be because it had never been done before. Truth was, no matter whose side you were on, the whole joint became a human abattoir from that deadly drop on.

I remember running through the dusk back to Tassos' villa, where we'd set up anti-aircraft guns on the roof, in anticipation of German air support for the ships we'd been told to expect. Vern was already ahead of me, sprinting. Before we could even begin to work out what was possible a disquieting squall descended, the loud *whoosh* and shadow of an enormous orange parachute slanting down into the scrub beside the little lane above the house. A few days previous Vern had traded a bottle of Tassos' wine to a bloke from Black Watch for a fannie – a lethal British Expeditionary Force combat weapon: half-knife, half-knuckleduster – and I watched as he pounced on that Bavarian like a half-starved roo-dog set free on the chase. The bloke was caught up in his strings and wires with silk ballooning all round him. Vern leant deep into the colour and with one swipe of his Corangamite forearm slashed the Kraut's throat. He pushed him back like a ragdoll into the oleanders, the paratrooper's serrated curtain of blood falling onto the flowers. Vern didn't hesitate. He kept tearing on up the road. My brother. Our baby bush scholar. His destiny had obviously arrived.

~

I had a sense Vern was headed for trouble but my search for him over the next couple of hours bore no fruit. And for the next nine days the north coast of the island became a deadly shemozzle. Any pre-ordained notion of strict lines, front or reserve, or strategic cohesion was soon destroyed by the brolly drop. Our structures, all set for the sea invasion, were blurred, by lunchtime of the following day. No one knew what the hell was going on. The night had been murderous, with stray Germans roaming everywhere and the locals quickly rising to the occasion. You could turn a bend on an empty looking road only to find a single German paratrooper shucking off his heavy kit in the moonlight, and in that moment he could simply raise his Mauser and shoot.

As a result, Mug and Ken and I found ourselves using the high ground of Tassos and Adrasteia's house as a kind of base, and also as a place to drag the horribly wounded and the suddenly dead, whilst Vern was god knows where.

During those terrible days Tassos was often elsewhere too. He fell immediately in line under Pendlebury's command that first afternoon but had to range beyond his ken when the legendary Englishman went missing the day after. As we came and went, our ears splitting under the noise of the Stukas, I would see Tassos only occasionally and he kept assuring me that everything was under control. There were German corpses in piles by the road, he said, they were hanging from the trees where they'd been tangled in their parachute wires as they fell.

Almost all the Cretans in the Iraklion area, not only those like Tassos and Adrasteia who were already involved with Pendlebury's networks, had risen to take whatever they could find and gone out into the landscape to kill. Just as Tassos had said they would. In the dusk of that first terrible day, in a low cutting by an old stone watermill, only two or three miles from the Morosini fountain in the middle of town, I saw a pot-bellied priest with a long salt and pepper beard struggling with all his might to retrieve an antique-looking sword he'd driven into the guts of a dangling Kraut. I hid warily, at first confused then actually embarrassed by what I was witnessing, until the horror of the paratrooper's cries flushed me out. Springing from the bushes I wrested the carved handle from the old priest in a rush and wrenched it out midst the yowls of the dying Kraut. As the long blade came free of his *Fallschirmjaeger* tunic he went limp, and silent. The priest and I looked at each other, as if questioning whether we should do something right by the body. Or that's what I thought we were doing. But then through the small gap in his beard the priest made a brief intonation, just a small sound, a *heh*, out of buried lips. He grabbed his sword from my grip with a look of disdain, turned and walked away. There was no sympathy, no thanks of course, and no remorse. He didn't even wipe the blood-smeared sword on the ground or against his robes.

Personally I was reeling by nightfall of the second day. There were no longer cul de sacs. Only deeds to destroy a lifetime. As the blood kept spewing out under the heat in those first few days, boiling and spluttering in different calibrations of surprise and confusion, the German dead behind our lines were piling up and beginning to stink, some just rotting in the sun by the roadsides, some flung misshapen into the dry trunks of the ilex, some grouped together at designated points for mass burial in shallow graves. The problem was the rock-hard ground, it was difficult enough trying to bury your own shit, let alone a six-foot German. And given that we needed cover from the relentless fire overhead the best that could be done on most occasions was a rushed scratching roughly eighteen inches deep, barely covering the victim, and in most cases not even sealing off the smell of his decomposition.

It was around this time that, between forays out into the field, I began helping Adrasteia and others as the injured were brought in for treatment at the villa. I didn't like staying back there, there

36

was fighting to be done and I was also terrified that the next one to be brought in would be Vern, but when she asked I couldn't refuse. I would work by her side for a few hours at a stretch, take orders from her, and marvel at her readiness for the task, her coolness under pressure for one so young, and the way her practicality never erased the tenderness and sympathy that meant so much to those in trouble. We worked well together, in extremely difficult circumstances, and I quickly put aside my own feelings of inadequacy as a nurse.

In the middle of that second night, or perhaps it was the third, a badly injured soldier was carried into Tassos' courtyard on an old wooden door by two Cretans. Out of the corner of my eye I noticed him being laid down for Adrasteia to attend to. The side of his skull had been sliced open, his ear had somehow been dislodged, but on closer look, with his head propped up in her hands, I saw through the gloom that the smashed up soldier was our mate Ken Callinan.

I rushed in, plunging my hands into the mess to try and reorganise his features to at least resemble the fella I knew. But it was no good. He was struggling, beyond pain it seemed. Eventually Adrasteia laid the mess of his head back down on her thighs and he seemed to go somewhere far away from us. As desperate as I was to do something for him there was no question of it. I had to surrender. And so no doubt did he, in a manner of speaking. I watched as his struggle disappeared, he was miles away, then an eternity. For a moment, more than anything else, I was stunned. Then the screaming of Stukas recommenced above our heads and it was clear the battle would stop for no-one.

VII

THE DAY AFTER I'D INSULTED LEONIE AT MY CAMP BY THE TEN SHEOAKS, I spent another morning and afternoon waiting unsuccessfully for some news from Bill Murray, and with ideas of retribution coming thick and fast and repeated like the squalls and knots off the open water – ways I could get back at the world, ways I could get back at the Poms, how I could continue fighting now that fighting was illegal, how I'd redraft Vern's 'missing in action' telegram that was delivered to Dad out at Corangamite – yes, it was with fronts and affronts such as these furrowing through my head, as if the weather had intentions like mine and that's why it was so cold, so persistently damp, yet abrupt and inhospitable to my camp, that without warning I found myself, and with equal intensity, wanting her to come back. But she never showed and, by the time night fell, I lay compounded in the darkness on my swag, craving her company like sunlight.

The next day Bill Murray's Standard Tourer pulled up early and the top was down because the sun was momentarily out. He hadn't ordered a soft-top, he'd told me when I first suggested that King Island was a strange place to be driving a convertible. The Tourer was what had arrived on the barge from Melbourne and he hadn't been bothered to send it back. He took his chances when they came and had grown to like the feeling of having the top down. But in those weeks when we were visiting the island kitchens together we were forever having to stop to concertina the rusted spokes of the old black hood back over again. In the state I was in it nearly drove me screwy.

Where he took me that day was to the Robinsons' on the Sea Paddock Road down south near Pearshape, and the first thing I noticed as we pulled in through the shadows of the paperbarks was her pushbike leaning against the post and rail.

I was there to make a good impression but straightaway things became confused. Bill Murray got out of the car and naturally expected me to follow. But I was ashamed and had no more room, none whatsoever, not even for a hint of humiliation.

'So are you right then?' he said, looking back to find I hadn't moved from the passenger seat.

We heard the sound of a tractor coming our way on the other side of the driveway trees, and then the farmer himself was steering through an old pony run to park beside the sawn-off wood tank on the half-painted southwest wall of the house.

As Brian Robinson hailed Bill Murray everything seemed exposed in the light, especially me not getting out, sitting warped behind the glossy reflections of the trees on the Tourer's windscreen.

Brian Robinson giddayed Bill with a rigorous handshake. He seemed cheery as the morning sky and something about the uncomplicated nature of his manner finally drew me out of the car. As if I didn't want to be responsible for ruining the break in the weather.

We went inside, into a dining room of unsealed boards, which I remember well because of a spring lamb curled up in a similarly raw apple box by the fire. We sat in a large windowed recess, not a bay window proper but there was a round table topped with lino and full of the sun. Behind us, through a plastered arch and beyond where the lamb lay sleeping in front of the fire, we could hear women's voices in the kitchen.

Brian Robinson whistled through his fingers and a tanned looking woman with lots of black and grey curls appeared through a swinging door. She seemed as happy as her husband. We greeted her politely then I looked away. Through the window I could see what looked to me like wire ferret cages, stacked back behind tea-tree craypots, and the bicycle leaning a little way off against the fence. I found it odd to see the cages as there's no rabbits on the island.

Mrs Robinson said she wouldn't chat, she had 'Leonie Fermoy in the kitchen here to see about the wounded'. So we said yes, we'd take a whiskey with our tea. 'Aah, that's good then,' said Brian, clapping milker's hands to complete the transaction as she went off through the swinging door.

The land agent was quiet as usual, next to useless as an intermediary in a situation like that, so Brian Robinson started to strike up with me. Asked me straight out where I'd served and then why the bloody hell I wasn't takin' 'em up on the soldier settlement scheme. I said something snooty like I don't take charity and he scoffed loudly.

'Charity!' he said, sending spittle flying. 'That's not charity, son. That's a fuckin' prison sentence. Have you seen the blocks they're offloadin' onto those poor mongrels? Shitty ground, full of tare and widow-makers, tarted-up swamp. I was in the hotel recently and some poor bastard was askin' what to do with that type of bush. So I told him straight out. "Do what the government does, mate." And he says, "What's that?" And I said, "Give it away."'

Bill Murray started chuckling at the joke and I smiled too.

'Yair, I dunno about your logic there, Wes,' he went on. 'It certainly ain't charity you're refusin'. I'd say someone's lookin' after you coz you're better off out of it. You'd sink like a stone.'

It's true that some people have a gift for conversation and a way of placing people at their ease. The settlement scheme couldn't be all bad but Brian's approach was making me feel better. As he chatted away and his wife, Rose, brought in whiskey and tea and a boiled egg each – on account of the fact it was Brian's morning tea-time and he always had an egg – I relaxed, the persistent nausea lightened, and we ranged over the topics of the farm and what was possible.

As it turned out the Robinsons weren't interested in selling the land down there near Pearshape, but another sixty acres they had back up above Naracoopa. It was too small a block for there to be much serious interest and it was too far up the island now for Brian to bother running sheep on it like he had. His tractor was his only motorised vehicle, and he'd decided after bumping into Bill in town that it might suit us both for him to offload the sixty acres onto me.

While we got into the meat of what was on offer I heard a door slam and then Mrs Robinson and Leonie were standing right there in the yard outside the window. They had their backs to us, discussing the cages. I remember Leonie had a green and white beanie on, with her hair falling out the bottom of it like the leftover wool hadn't been tied off. Bill and Brian just carried on, arranging for us all to walk the ground near Naracoopa later that week, but I was only half-listening. I wouldn't even have admitted it to myself at the time but in truth I was wanting to catch her eye, to give a sign that she should at least pedal that pushbike back along to my camp sometime, that despite what I'd done she was welcome.

She walked forward with Mrs Robinson and they pointed at various cages. Then Leonie leant in, picked one up and opened the wire hatch.

They seemed to agree on it and so they turned back for her to strap it onto her packrack and be off.

It was as she turned that Mrs Robinson pointed us out: three blokes eating eggs and drinking whiskey and tea there on the other side of the window.

Leonie stared, as if any surprise she might have felt was doused by a passing amusement. A smile snuck into her face. I dunno but surely she wasn't finding it funny that we were eating eggs and drinking whiskey at ten o'clock in the morning. Brian Robinson helloed her with a thick pink palm and Bill Murray nodded and I put down my grey spoon. I didn't want to be a laughing stock.

But then I too raised my hand, not the friendly hand of a hale islander but a hand which, with a single sunlit gesture, confessed my need to give and receive.

VIII

I WAS OUT ON APEX HILL, FROM WHICH WE'D FOUGHT BACK THROUGH the German lines over the previous few days. It was the ninth day of the battle and we were in control, but news had just come through, first as a rumour and then as official decree, of our surrender. Jeeps and motorbikes roared back and forth spreading the news, saying that we had lost the Maleme airfield near Souda Bay in the west of the island, which meant the Germans were free to re-arm. This meant that, despite the fact that we'd been winning the fight around Iraklio, we were strategically stuffed and had to go.

Mug and I agreed that surely someone had got the wrong end of the stick. It was as if a bogus bulletin from Lord Haw-Haw was somehow being treated as fact. For the next few hours everyone was in a scramble trying to get verification that it was a hoax but it never came. And by late afternoon it seemed the surrender was deadset. We were leaving. Running away. Again. Just like we had at Vevi. To the west, hordes of other units had already begun the long march to the south coast for boats, but we were instructed to hold tight, to await ships that would take us out from Iraklio harbour at night.

A terrible surging feeling. That was what was caused by this in most of us, a fair dinkum resentment against what we quickly concluded were the blues of command. As Mug and I were marching back to Tassos', in the hope of more info, the air was charged with bitter pride and blokes had started going a bit berserk, sticking in harder than ever, pummelling the mortar shells and anti-aircraft fire from positions we'd worked hard to establish in the previous days.

There was a blind madness to it all. Enough was enough. My eyes were peeled for Vern as we passed groups of soldiers. I never saw him but I had a fair idea what his attitude would be. I noticed some of the blokes had already started drinking. Drinking as they fought. Swigging from local bottles and demijohns. I sometimes wonder what would have happened to any stray Bavarian caught out during those hours. In the minds of many of us who'd copped it over Easter at Vevi if we were being forced to surrender it wouldn't be without a fight. If that makes any sense at all. Which of course it doesn't.

When Mug and I got back to the villa there was no sign of Vern but Tassos was there, stoking the fire in the courtyard as if nothing extraordinary had happened. We began to rabbit on to him about the surrender but he looked unimpressed.

I could hear Adrasteia talking and the sound of an injured soldier moaning from upstairs. Tassos bade us sit as he tidied his teeth with a prunus sprig. He made it clear the fight had only just begun. When we said no, it's about to end, we were to be evacuated from the harbour, he just sprigged his teeth some more and stoked the fire.

I wanted to know where Vern was. Tassos said he'd seen our boys on the grog. His implication was that Vern was amongst them. I thought he had a higher opinion of my brother than that. His face was drained of its typical enthusiasm, he had a deadpan, if not cynical, look. This was almost as terrifying as the German fire overhead as I'd come to anchor myself in his unshakeable confidence over the previous days.

He shared the scanty meat he was roasting with us, we ate snails and Adrasteia brought out bread and meagre leaves of salad and potato. Then, when night had fallen and we had eaten hungrily, Tassos suggested that Mug go out looking for Vern. This also was confusing as it would have been more natural if I had gone. But when I protested, he insisted.

As soon as we were left alone his face relaxed and his voice assumed a business-like tone. He began to outline in great detail his work for Pendlebury. And now that Pendlebury was dead and his body stowed in a secret place where no prying Hun could deface it or prise his glass eye out as a trophy, he and his 'thugs' would redouble their efforts.

'It is now, on the day of defeat, that we are at our most powerful,' he assured me.

Some time later, with no sign of Mug's return, we drank some raki and Tassos continued his accounts of the *andartes'* plans which would swing into action in the following days. He made the terrifying tasks ahead of his fellow Cretans sound attractive. It was noble to fight for freedom and your homeland, especially by comparison with what seemed the hapless failures of our own armies so far in Greece. As he spoke I watched the juniper coals in the fire mouth glow like miniature burning cities under the command of his stick.

Adrasteia sat across from us, on the other side of the fire against the courtyard wall, where she had cut Vern's hair only a few days before. Her eyes were trained intently on her uncle.

We heard shouts and rifle fire in the near distance. Tassos raised his hand for quiet and listened.

'Your friends are going mad,' he said. 'They are twice betrayed. By the Germans *and* the British.'

We leaned towards the sounds a while longer, trying to make out what it was we heard. And then, as if his island was all there was in the world of right and wrong, as if an old man's wisdom was the ideal complement to the beauty of a young woman, Tassos made his surprising appeal, not to my desire for revenge or to my pride in persistence, but to its opposite.

'Life doesn't have to be like that. Find a place to put down your burden. Take a walk with my niece, into the olives. Let her be your guide.'

She stared straight at her uncle, but did not rise from her seat. As if a spell was being cast I sat motionless also, until on the other side of the courtyard wall the shouting and gunfire eventually died away.

IX

I DIDN'T SEE LEONIE AGAIN TILL A FORTNIGHT AFTER THE MEETING AT the Robinsons' and by then I'd walked the 'Wait-a-While' acres with Brian and decided it'd do. It was fenced for stock, had an outlook east across Sea Elephant Bay along the ridge of higher ground, and a nice slope away from the ridge at the ocean end for a dwelling. There were two creeks running through it but it was a plateau really, not sedgy country like Brian said the settlement scheme would have offered. We agreed on a price. Bill Murray took his slice, a nice thick slice I'd say, with butter and honey, but that was fair enough given all the tea and scones and cream I'd had because of him. Brian wanted a fortnight to move his sheep for sale down to Grassy Harbour, he offered me the lean-to hayshed, and the hay, and we shook on it. So I was dropped off back at my camp for the last time by Bill Murray and my days of touring the island in the soft-top Tourer were over.

I had a fortnight to whittle away but it would be accurate to say I temporarily felt a lot better about things having purchased the land. I even got to thinking in a proud kind of way about it, which was perfectly natural although I kept an edge sharpened even with respect to that emotion. Nevertheless by beating the settlement scheme I felt proven in my self-image as a man for whom the scales had fallen from the eyes.

Given her smile in the yard at the Robinsons' I half expected Leonie's bicycle to come by my camp at any moment. Of course I had fresh news now, not just haunted looks or sullen silence and I was keen to share it with someone. She was the only someone there was.

But she never showed. One day around lunchtime I trekked into Currie with the idea if I bought another sausage roll from the co-op and she saw my face it might spur her on to cycle down to me after her shift. But when I got to the co-op there was no sign of her. And I didn't feel like eating anyway.

I loitered around under the Norfolk saplings, hoping she might turn up. I patted a border collie who lingered about and decided when I got onto Wait-a-While I'd get one. Someone other than her to talk to. But I never did get that dog.

Eventually I trudged back along the flat road to my camp. Once again I sat in low with my back to the sheoaks' whisper and waited in the weather for nightfall, my fire buckling in the patchy rain and wind. Night came to the rock in the sea, I had no nightmares back then, it was all when I woke. A mixed blessing, I s'pose. Anyway, the next day the light was pewter, I had a can of beans and some bacon on the fire for breakfast and was huddling like a heron in my grey coat on my perch, when she mercifully appeared.

Straight-off I noticed a green cake tin on the packrack of her bike. She told me later on that she wasn't going to open it unless I deserved it. Well, as far as I was concerned, she was simply an abatement coming in over the water. She opened proceedings with a crack about there being good red meat for sale in Currie that wouldn't give me the runs like tinned beans. And, from I know not where, I managed a tasteless joke about having got used to the smells of my own solitude.

Leonie lit a cigarette and as I took my beans off the boil and dished them up there seemed nothing much to say. She didn't get up and leave, which I took as some kind of sign, though I wasn't sure of what. So, by way of thanks, I s'pose, and to ease the difficulty, I asked her straight out if her old man had ever kicked on and got a herd of his own Angus beef.

Her head pushed back as she took a prolonged and stern sighting of me from the other side of the fire. Draping one leg over the other on the stump where she sat, she fished out a cigarette packet from a pocket somewhere in her riding jacket and offered me one, and a light from a guttering flame on a twig she pulled from the fire.

Our bodies hunched and extended as pockety fronts passed over between snatches of sun. She unwound a long story about her father's early trips across the water with Tuck White in pursuit of Victorian cattle breeds, and how they'd resulted in him meeting her mother, whose own father was selling ahead-of-their-time Brangus hybrid heifers that nobody else wanted at the saleyards at Colac. She was very detailed about the breeds and how Nat had managed when still a teenager to bring the unwanted Brangus cows back across the water to King where they had famously flourished. And then, with me well and truly on the hook, she wound it all up with the oddest thing: a strange family dream her mother's father, Warren Burrows from Ondit, had had on the night Nat had married his daughter.

They'd married in Beeac, as it happens where my own parents were hitched, and set out on horseback to cross the Otway ridge for the boat at Lorne straight after the wedding. That night Warren Burrows, back in his single cot beside his wife's in the flat paddocks at Ondit, with his two sons already laid down in the soil of France, dreamt of a massive leviathan, so big it was biblical but nevertheless palpable, breaching out of the waters of young Nat Fermoy's Bass Strait, bellying high over the Otway ridge and, in a sky the grey colour of wood-duck down, flying over the farms towards Colac town where it eventually, and no mistaking its target, came crashing down in a gargantuan organic bomb, right on top of the newly completed war memorial in the Murray Street civic gardens. The memorial stone, with its plaques and columns, was obliterated, the sacrificial humpback blubber flew, hundreds of squelching gouts of leviathan flesh and oil and grease and ambergris and other innards bespattering the town. To Warren Burrows the message of the dream was clear. The unforeseen meeting of the young sweethearts at the saleyards, and the coming betrothal, was both a sacrificial and satisfactory event.

As Leonie recounted the strange dream her grandfather had had on his daughter's wedding night, and as I, who'd kicked a football as a kid in the shadows of the Murray Street memorial on family trips to the town for provisions, listened, the very sea around us seemed to grow rich with a buttressing wisdom against what I believed was the violence of human society. So then, as if to celebrate, Leonie was getting up from the canvas chair where she sat, walking over to her bicycle where it leaned against a tree, and unclipping the tin from her packrack. She brought it back, prised off the tight lid, lifted back the wax paper and held it out to me. An offering. A reward for my good behaviour, for my listening and my lack of spite and also, as I would later learn, for the period of relative contentment I also represented for her.

It was shortbread in the tin, ridged and buttery. Despite the strange intimacy created by her telling me the dream she was still not what you'd call overly feminine, in her workmanlike clothes and with her vague smell of iodine and creatures. The homeliness of the shortbread came as something of a surprise.

Perhaps if I'd been more resistant that day, more caustic, if I'd not needed to just sit and listen to another voice, a woman's voice, she would have chosen other things to tell. Things she's told me since.

Like how when Nat and his bride, and the eight Brangus they'd been given by Warren Burrows as a wedding gift, had reached the bottom of the hill at Lorne the day after the wedding, he'd driven them straight onto the beach by the Erskine river mouth and cut digestible strips of kelp for them to chew on. And how, as a result, people in Lorne felt sorry for him – the poor young island groom trying to kill his odd-looking wedding cattle on seaweed – and how this sympathy made sure he got a ready passage back to King via Melbourne on the first available ketch, the *Serenade*.

But no, that day the storyteller and the listener were in an unlikely type of tuning, on either side of the roadside fire, as clouds went by seeking the east, and airy florets of moisture anointed them as they passed, the solid ground they were on as brief a reprieve as life itself from the sea of deeper time.

Crumbling the shortbread between my teeth I wedged the billy into the fire and said: 'I know that bloody memorial in Murray Street. Gave me the creeps. As a kid. Gave most of the town the creeps I'd reckon. Strange things . . . often right next to where children play.'

X

UNCLE TASSOS WIPED THE SLATE OF MY EDUCATION CLEAN. HE WAS writing a new story for me now, a true story on the slate, not with untethered colonial ideals but with the stink of death in his nostrils, the rocks and plants at his disposal.

I sat as he cooked and talked, cooked and talked, holding me to the spot even as my mind wondered about the whereabouts of the others, holding me there with his ruthless wisdom and the meat. So that those hours preceding the evacuation became a deadly conversion. And a consummation, when I finally followed Adrasteia out through the gap in the courtyard wall.

I drank the raki Tassos gave me but only in sips as he recommended. 'There will be a time for that,' he warned. 'Tonight will be long whatever you choose.'

Occasionally I heard a sound over the courtyard wall, footsteps, voices, and hoped it was Vern and the others returning from their bitter shenanigans; but no, just some cat probably, a dog nudging a corpse, knocking over a pot in search of food, an ibex tiptoeing into the human habitat from the pure disorientation of cacophonous days. Each of these night sounds became like the tick of a clock, I became aware of time passing, imagining the wild fighting, or our units gathering on the headland, scanning the sea for a sign of the RN ships that were expected to bring us off.

Uncle Tassos only encouraged the flames, and his voice continued: 'If they were promising to take you home . . . but they will take you up from here, your work half done, to some other place where people who are strangers to you like we once were will be slaughtered in their beds. If you go . . . any tears you will cry for them, or for yourself, will sting with pointlessness. Do you see?'

By midnight we were drinking coffee, for courage and energy, Tassos said, for what choices and consequences lay ahead. Still there was no sign of Vern or Mug, and between the old man's offerings of food and advice, I began to worry.

Take a walk with my niece, into the olives. Let her be your guide.

An hour later Adrasteia and I made our departure. I followed as she got up and made for the gap in the courtyard wall.

But Uncle Tassos also rose from his stool beside the fire to stare at me as I went. And suddenly all the hurt and sadness of his world was there, in his eyes.

Adrasteia passed through but her uncle and I stood looking at each other by the gap in the wall. Black pools of sadness. Glinting in an ever deeper black. What indeed was the point of life when we are denied the opportunity to give? One stone burden to another. The things we have worked and fought so hard for are the very things we need to give away.

But this, *this girl?*

Her hand appeared in the gap, she took mine in hers and pulled me through into the night.

~

Adrasteia. A new moon shone on the surface of the olive leaves and on all the abandoned and busted equipment around us – the spent cutlery of war's blood-hungry feast. As we moved through the night I was half spooked: there were trunks in shadow and the trees were like souls, writhing, twisted, tortured. Despite all that, she held my gaze. Her eyes were pale green, deep as the leaves in daylight, but flashing too like their lighter undersides in the dark breeze.

Under the canopy of the groves, deep inside the skin of the battle's end, we walked and walked in silence through the abandoned German positions, until finally we agreed to rest under branches on a rise back from the sea. The night had grown calm, the dying breeze was a brush and the screaming sky almost a memory now in the darkness. The Stuka pilots were resting, unaware of the gnawing insecurities their victory would bring. The air felt suddenly beautiful and warm like it had in those days of butterflies before the brolly drop.

We began to talk briefly about the war but then about how she had lost her mother, and why she'd come to be living with her uncle. It was difficult with my lack of Greek but she managed to tell of how her mother had died when she was only small, how she'd never known her really, but was considered to be the image of her. She also said that with her father away on the Albanian front she was grateful to call Uncle Tassos' her home.

As if as a consequence of the loss we shared, and the comfort it gave us, our mood lightened, we began to joke around a bit, laughing in particular about the obsession poor old Mug had had during the build-up with catching himself a fish down at the harbour. We sat in the grove, our arms occasionally touching, as we retold the story and laughed all over again at the memory of Mug's face when he'd turned up with the fish at the villa.

Gradually the brushing of our arms, the thrill it gave, became a thing we sought, and we laughed more quietly as we began to touch, and then to kiss. It was time itself then that was evacuated as the taste of her lips lingered on my own. To my great amazement she pulled away and lifted up her blouse and there was no rigging underneath, just beautiful curving skin, and it was clear by her grin that she was proud as punch of her inheritance. She offered her nipples with cheek and an instinctual sense of carnal naturopathy. Right then they seemed like the whole point of the war.

Despite the slaughter of the previous days, and all those who'd met the most violent of ends and gone wafting up and out of their skincases, souls freshly released (or we'd like to think so) – despite all that, it seemed the island was not exhausted. It was a disgrace, I laughed, nothing had ever felt so easy, the ease of it was *criminal*. She laughed along with me, with star-bright teeth, then she sat back against the trunk of the tree and let me touch the soft muscled walls of her. I'd never known anyone so confident, so strong and open, so healthy and wet and robust. I touched her and was kissed and then we deepened again and cried together. We cried for a motherless world, the things we'd seen, for Ken Cal and all the others who'd died, the bond we felt in each other for that moment. For this uptight son of Corangamite it was some initiation. All that had been withheld from me, all that I had refused for the sake of what I thought was my duty, as son and soldier, was now offered. I groaned from the relief and the pleasure. My reedy strine was given depth. A richer note.

I had strayed. Strayed from my unit, strayed from recordable chaos into the blind reality of all unspeakable stories.

∼

I don't know how much later but delirious from her touch and not prepared to return with her to Tassos in such a ripened state I scrambled and stumbled, the taste of her in my mouth, up and away from what it seemed the earth itself had just offered me. Eventually I sprung out of the groves on the west of the creekbed and onto the headland beside the town, as if someone had splashed my face with water.

Just a short time ago there'd been blokes strewn about the streets and slopes and waterfront in a celebration of disgust, Italian rifles in one hand and bottles of Cretan wine in the other, their pockets full of *Fallschirmjaeger* grenades and *Waffen* playing cards, their hearts coarsened by a need to disbelieve and discredit the evacuation orders on one hand and the emphatic beat inside their chests of all nihilisms confirmed on the other. Now there was no sign of anything, only the blue night and wreckage everywhere: army cars with their front-ends stubbed out like spent cigarettes, Bren guns akimbo in various stages of dismantling, strewn field telephones and cables lying like black spaghetti all over the place. It was as if a great arm had appeared out of the sky to backhand the lot to oblivion.

As I stumbled away from the bomb-torn town I realised the enormity of what had happened. It was in my nostrils and in the taste on my lips. I'd been left behind. I'd missed the evacuation. Drifting out onto the headland immediately below The Charlies, I sat on the rocks and began to shake, to panic. It was clear. I had passed no one, heard nothing. Everyone – Vern, Mug, my whole unit and all the others – had gone.

XI

ON THE DAY OF MY MOVE, AS I TRUDGED ACROSS THE ISLAND FROM THE ten sheoaks towards Wait-a-While, a strange flock of swallows flew around me. In another mood, in another bloke, perhaps a bloke who could never, and should never be reassembled, a bloke who would sit around in a bout of coddled reckonings, as if exempt from the world's whack, I would have guessed they were my magical consorts. But in fact I was a scarecrow barely animated, clinging to a sliver of spirit but nevertheless spilling needles of straw as I went, falling apart, any trail I was leaving resembled a nest undone.

The birds didn't seem to notice, or if they did they didn't seem to care. Perhaps they had come to torment me, they certainly had me ducking and flinching at times with their daredevilish skill. Regardless, they followed me all the way across, me with my sausage bag, my billy and tarp. All the way along Fraser Road they came, right along through the paperbarks into the east, then down a little dip south as the road runs next to the Fraser River, the tiny swallows proving that the cliché generated around Phar Lap, about the heart's dimensions being a guide to loyalty and determination, was clearly bulldust. And when I got onto Wait-a-While, in a clutch of light rain passing over, they banked to the left, tight in a group towards Naracoopa, before they disappeared altogether, indistinguishable from a tiny travelling squall.

Leaving my kit to speckle and tap in the patchy showers, I walked the high clearing and down the eastern slope a way till I felt the westerly couldn't quite get me. Further down, the grass gave way to a tangle, and gullies of wattle and gum trees continued, broken only by sideways creeks, until I reached the last stand of giant paperbarks overlooking the eastern mutton-burrowed shore and then the ocean. To the north and south of this sheltered spot the bush crept up on either side as far as the plateau, so that there was a little buffer in both of those directions as well.

That was it, I decided, and after returning for my kit I began to set up in this U-shaped clearing, with its view of Bass Strait out east over the slope-away treetop tangle. The ground wasn't level but I would sleep with my head above my feet for once and with no sheoak counsel needed to protect me from the prevailing winds. For the time being it would do, until I got to know these acres and worked out exactly where was best to build the permanent dwelling I intended.

Of course it was a far more isolated perch than the roadside camp so the getting and storing of supplies now required more planning. I couldn't just pad into Currie for a sausage roll whenever I felt like it. Grassy was a good ten miles south, and not an easy walk across the bush. I could fish down at Naracoopa but it was quite the climb back up, so I'd have to think it all through. Which, when I did, over the next few days of tinned beans and milkless tea, led to my decision to get my hands on a bicycle.

No doubt impressed by the way Leonie got around, it seemed the natural solution. And given that the Robinsons' farm was not a terrible way south from Wait-a-While – a lot closer than town at least – I decided to set out there and make some inquiries.

Knowing as I do now that Brian Robinson's late father Ray, or Doc Ray as he was known – he being the island's doctor in his day – had chosen pedalling over galloping as his preferred mode of professional transport, this idea of mine in regards to transport seemed a little tinny. I got the whole history too, from dear old Brian, who, when all's said and done, was a bit of an ear basher. Standing in his tractor shed beside his trusty and lean HV McKay were half-a-dozen Malvern Stars, their handlebars rust-speckled from the salt on Doc Ray's Hippocratic travels, but four of them in perfect order. I soon learnt that the bike Leonie rode was one of the Doc's, a fact which made me feel both connected and a little shadowed. But that's the small circles of island life, ever decreasing, especially on King which has no upthrust of mountains to divide the population. It's as if everyone here can see clear across to everyone else; the longer the family has been here the more braided like a mooring rope their lives will be.

The Malvern Star was a big advantage and made a significant difference to my life on Wait-a-While. Without it, I would have struggled, but with it all that I had to do seemed manageable. In the right wind I'd ride across to the Currie co-op for food and gear or down the hill here to Naracoopa to fish. The bike even had a working light – no doubt for Doc Ray's emergency calls – so I could fish right through when the flood tide came on at dusk and have a lighted way to walk back up the owl-studded hill. I grew expert at riding one-handed with timber in my other arm as I scoured the island for suitable materials to knock up my dwelling. I moved blocks of stone for the hearth on a flat trailer I rigged up behind the bike, and roofing tin strapped crossways. All the riding was making me fitter too, my muscles having been gnawed away with all the stewing I'd been doing. I could feel the pistons of my calves expanding, and my lungs clear. And on those days when I couldn't be bothered shovelling out the level space in the slope for the building, or getting down on my guts to scoop the rainwater and frogs out of the four-foot holes I'd dug for the uprights to be concreted into, I'd go for roaming rides up into the island's north, exploring Wickham and scouting around some of the places Leonie had touched on in her stories: Yellow Rock, where her Uncle True lived in Old Nat and Patsy's original house; Penny's Lagoon; the wreck of the *Neva*; not so much hoping that I might bump into her but wondering when I would.

It was thanks to my new mobility that I first encountered her Uncle True, who I came across one day stogging the beach for sandworms in front of the old Fermoy house north of the river mouth at Yellow Rock. He offered me a swig from his bottle of rum, which I declined, but we did share a cigarette and a strange conversation. Indeed, Uncle True seemed a one-off, he had a certain individuality about him, though he was not exactly a beachcomber, if that implies a casual air, for he nailed me straight out for not accepting land under the SS scheme (it seemed everyone on the island knew about my business), dropping his sand pump at his feet to say that his yard up behind the house was full of the sea's charities and that it was as much of a trick to learn how to receive as to give. He made a slurring reference then to what I must have been through as a soldier but I cut him short, and as I was pedalling away he shouted with some anxiety in his voice that if I saw Leonie I was to tell her to come and visit her uncle.

It was only a couple of hours later on that very same day, thanks again to the bike, that as a result of this request from True, I first met Lascelles. I'd pedalled upwind into Currie, ostensibly to follow a lead Brian Robinson had given me regarding flooring for my hut. Lascelles was coming out of the pub, and although he was in his civvies he caught my eye because of the mint condition slouch hat he was wearing.

I stopped in my tracks to watch him move across the road with his unusual prodding gait, until he disappeared into the co-op.

By this stage, and unbeknownst to me, Lascelles was already in the foothills of his campaign to raise funds for a putative King Island Memorial to the diggers of the war. There was a cenotaph erected near the town hall after the first war, but now with the larger settler scheme proposed for the blokes of the second, he'd had a bright idea. Not many others were that keen on his idea, only Lascelles, and I soon learnt that he was rumoured to wear the slouch to bed, in the shower, even when he was swimming! It's awful how petty small communities can be. Anyway, he'd nearly served in New Guinea near the end of the war but had never got off the beach in North Queensland. By the seemingly untarnished nature of the illusions he got around spruiking you could have been forgiven for wishing he'd got his chance.

I had nothing against a slouch hat as such, though my own was long lost and irrelevant to me. So when Lascelles came out of the co-op again only a couple of minutes later I had no more reason than usual to be unsettled.

He spotted me leaning against the bike next to the Norfolk saplings lower on the road. So he prodded on down and introduced himself, complete with battalion number. I didn't have to say a word in reply; he, like Uncle True and no doubt everyone else on the island, already knew who I was.

Lascelles was small, rover size I'd say, but although he whittled down in the later years of his life his frame back then was stout as a bottle-tree. He was, however, even as a younger man, always gaunt in the face, a tad concave you might say, an odd effect on a thick trunk like his but somehow symmetrical with the way his legs stabbed at the ground as he walked. Once he did arrive to shake your hand, the first thing you noticed was the way his eyes constantly darted about the place, as if he was still expecting the mortar shells he never encountered. Back then I found it bloody unnerving.

'So, Wesley, how are you settling in on the island?' he asked. 'Got everything you need?'

'Yairs. Thanks.'

'It's a nice quiet place to come back to, eh. Where did you serve?'

'Middle East. Greece. Crete.'

'Yes, well. We got there in the end, eh.'

When I didn't reply his eyes darted about like billy-o and he began rummaging in his pockets. Eventually he pulled out a packet of Minties.

'Here, have one, Wes.'

'No thanks.'

'So, they tell me you bought some land over east. From Brian Robinson.'

'That's right.'

'You're plannin' on staying put on King?'

'I'll see how I go.'

'Look, Wes, I wish you all the best with it. There'll be more blokes coming over in the months and years to come. With the settlement scheme and that. You've heard about the scheme have you, Wes?'

He knew bloody well I had. I didn't answer, just stared at him. In actual fact I was trying to figure out why he was talking to me as if I was an invalid. Somewhere he'd got the idea I was to be tiptoed around.

'Yes, well, there'll be company anyway,' he went on. 'And assistance from the Agricultural Bank: fencing, a house, and to get some stock up and going. You'd be from a farming background, Wes?'

'Yairs.'

'You'll know what you're about then. Do you plan on taking the Settlement Board up on the offer, Wes?'

'What offer?'

'Well, the offer of some land, you know, some grass of your own to get you going again.'

'You're from King?' I asked then, partly combative, mainly though to avoid the question he'd asked me.

'Yes, as a matter of fact. My father came over to run the post office in '37. I came to give him a hand. When my mother passed away.'

I nodded.

'We used to run the PO in Sandringham, in Melbourne. Then, when Mum passed on Dad was so upset he wanted a change.'

'I see.'

'The island has its challenges, of course, but weather-wise it's hardly Kokoda, eh, Wes. Or the desert.'

I said nothing.

'Well, what I mean is, it's in some ways quite similar to Melbourne in that respect. Just to the power-of, if you see what I mean.'

He spoke with a Pommy clip.

'Whereas the jungle. That can be so *unfamiliar.* This is a picnic really, by comparison of course. You can always keep warm if you've got enough clothes. Cooling down's a different matter. Not to mention the malaria.'

I wanted to ask him if he'd had malaria but didn't. Then from the corner of my eye I spied Leonie parking her bike against the co-op wall.

Lascelles noticed my diverted gaze and turned to see what was there. Nothing much. Two wagtails sitting on the back of a horse outside the hotel, a tired old mutt loping across the road, a bike leaning up against the co-op wall. She'd disappeared inside.

Turning back to me, Lascelles said: 'Well anyway, Wes, I'm in the PO most days with Dad if you ever want a chat. Perhaps you'd like to come over for tea one night at our place? We're in digs behind the PO you know. We're just up the hill there before the road turns to roll down to the harbour.'

Lascelles thrust out his hand, awkwardly. 'Nice to meet you anyway, Wes,' he said.

I nodded, with no camaraderie and no info, waiting for him to move off. Which he did, swivelling like a marionette to prod carefully back across the muddy slant of the road.

I wheeled my bike up the street and leant it against the co-op wall next to Leonie's. I went inside. She was behind the low counter in her leather apron, checking off ration coupons. By the time she looked up I was standing right next to her.

She didn't look pleased to see me, she didn't look displeased either, she just looked. Then she said: 'You'd be hot in that coat.'

I was still skin and bones, I s'pose, and found the overcoat handy on the bike. Cycling around King can get chilly. But she was right, it was a mild enough day outside. She herself was only wearing a white blouse under the leather apron, with no cardigan.

'I've got a message for you,' I said, inwardly triumphant at having an excuse to talk to her. This was not about me, my isolation, my harrow, nor was it anything to do with needing her company. It was a perfect ruse, and at the time even I believed it.

'Uh-huh?' she replied, flicking through the tickets on the counter in front of her, though slower than she had been.

'I met your Uncle True on the beach,' I told her.

'What beach?'

'Never mind. He said to tell you to go and visit him.'

'You been up there at Yellow Rock, sniffin' round those old days I told you about?'

She shouldn't have said it. With my nerves already strung tight I was shocked, ashamed, the blood drained out of me. I turned and hurried out of the building, stomping in anger by the time I was passing out through the door.

I grabbed at my bike, knocking hers to the ground in my haste. Its guards clattered against the wall as it fell. Not stopping to pick it up, I tucked up my coat, wheeled my bike round to face downhill, and pedalled away.

I was fuming as I rode out along the aerodrome road. I hadn't asked her to come and sit by my fire, I'd been quite all right with ten sheoaks for company. And I certainly hadn't pried into any stories of her life. It was all her doin'. And now she's on about it as if I've chatted her up. As if I've been the one, sniffin' around like a fuckin' bitzer. And every island galah will be given the same impression, every whacker like John Lascelles'll be talkin' about how I'm hangin' around her spots. The pity will pour. For the soldier-shag alone on his lovelorn rock.

'Bugger that!' I fumed, as I turned right and headed southeast, clattering past my ten sheoaks roaring away on their Pat Malone. Off I went towards Wait-a-While.

XII

I STOOD IN THE DARK ON THE HEADLAND NEAR THE SEA THAT NIGHT OF
the evacuation, alone, amongst rocks beside the hulk of a charred
Junkers fuselage. The world had changed, it seemed to tilt, until way out
there in a flash of light on the water I saw an outline of a ship, akimbo,
like a broken fence, going down.

Even now, amidst the bungalow walls and the light of this silver desk
lamp there is another startling blaze in my mind and once again the
ship is lit up briefly in my vision. It's one of our destroyers, but where
its decks should have been crammed with men leaving the island it is
empty and still.

It was if everything had come to an end. Not only the battle but the
war. Not only the war but the world itself. And now I am beginning to
shake. My fingers can hardly hold the pen. In a last halo of acid light I
hear the ship hissing water like a pained and dying beast. Flames dissolve
and darkness surrounds me. Silence. I look behind but I cannot see The
Charlies, let alone the wires we strung between them. I shut my eyes
tight and in desperation reach for sounds out of the long ago, sounds
to fill the silence. The notes of our mother's piano, echoing from her

71

bedroom as she willed herself from the death bed where little Vern lay beside her. Sweating in her dressing-gown she presses the music out of the keys, in an attempt to lift her spirit back towards life. I am outside, always outside that room, huddled on my own amongst skinks between the house and the lake, shivering from the notes ringing out, echoing through those farmhouse walls, until they travel beyond me and die out over the middle of the lake.

The sea becomes the lake. The ship falling into it. Images too, going down, pushing into the darkness. Screens of childhood, Vern and I, with rabbit nets and sacks of ducks, the week after Mum died, the morning our cubby was strewn over the lakeshore by vicious gales coming straight across from Pirron Yallock. The way we were not beaten, the next cubby we made, out of the rocks scattered all around us, the cooled local lava, how we built it dry with Dad's help at the shore end of the yard, having learnt from the weather now the right way to build in the place. To endure. I see little brother Vern, our Baby, crosslegged in shorts at the entrance, his tongue poked out the corner of his mouth in concentration, the smell of our mum still dying about him, as he's plucking a plover I'd shanghaied.

Then I'm there again, alone and in shock on the headland. The sea is the sea, the ship on fire in my head.

You are so far from home, she said.

Eventually my eyes dropped from the sight of the flames, my head falling into my hands, which smelt not of our mum but of Adrasteia.

XIII

'WAIT-A-WHILE' IS ACTUALLY AN OLD BASS STRAIT JOKE DESCRIBING the way life on the islands moves only at the pace the weather and sea allow. No matter your expectations, your ambitions, or the head of steam you work up, everything out here gives way in the end to the gusting fronts and Antarctic gales ripping over the water, to sudden sand shoals and saw-tooth reefs. Well, true submission is often only learnt in tragic circumstances but, as it happens, my land had been given the moniker simply because of its awkward distance from the Robinsons' farmhouse and sheds. It was that very distance from things – almost a feeling as much as a reality, it is a small island after all – that made it perfect for me. In actual fact, the north of the island is where the real distance is, the towns Currie and Grassy being south of its centre, leaving Cape Wickham, Egg Lagoon and Yambacoona isolated from the misinterpretations and lamingtons of town. That northern end was all Fermoy country in my mind now, and therefore not an option. It had even occurred to my suspicious mind that Leonie's telling of her story, going right back to the days when Old Nat learnt the art of scrimshaw on the whalers, was just pure territorial. By telling me all that she'd successfully barred and contained me to the island's more domesticated southern half.

My conclusion, from this distance at least, is that she chose to tell me what she did for practical reasons that had nothing to do with laying out her scent. The island does hold smells in glasswort gullies and behind hot dunes, but not like other places. The wind is a constant mail boat that comes to pick up that particular correspondence. We undergo a perpetual scouring, a scrubbing and washing. Eventually it wears away not only our scent but our flesh. We are wind-whittled. Human sticks in a shallow strait. Until, like Lascelles, they lower us into the ground, but even the soil that holds us will blow away eventually. When the sky truly will be scattered with an archipelago of souls.

Slowly, but surely, I built my hut, an L-shape of slabs, sticks and hessian in the U-shape of the clearing on Wait-a-While. There were three rooms: a bedroom in the proud southeast face of the 'L', the washroom and laundry behind it, and in the space horizontal to the view of the strait a living area fronted by a corrugated iron bullnose porch. I could sit in the shelter of this porch, with not only the rising mound behind protecting me from the westerlies but now the buffer of the hut as well. I could watch the sunrise over Naracoopa and the strait, and also the fronts passing over and into the east. I had two forty-four gallon drums for collecting water and planned for half-proper plumbing. And as I constructed all this around me, like the carapace of a slow-breathing ocean turtle, there were moments of mindless industrial contentment when it felt as if I might just about live as long as they do.

The closer the hut came to completion the less I relied on the people of the island. I'd had help from Brian, of course; from John Sanders down at Surprise Bay, who had the bullnose awning for the porch; from the blokes at Grassy Harbour who'd clued me in on shipping bits and pieces from the mainland, like the tap fittings, the mantle and the windows (there seemed to be no glass anywhere on King, no windows stacked away in sheds or down the sides of houses, it was as if as soon as its usefulness had expired any glass would spontaneously smash in the westerlies); but now as my construction tasks diminished, once again I saw less and less people.

So this was when the coals really started to be raked over. During those long solitary nights at my dining table (a fair slab of macrocarpa pine sitting on two kero boxes), beside the Tilley lamp, my brown teapot repeatedly cooling, the crumbs of the Cretan bread I'd baked sitting on a chipped yellow plate, I began to reflect on the spell that had been cast. Not just on Vern or me but on us all. Krauts and Eyeties and Allies alike.

I was smoking fifteen to the dozen as I nutted this all out at Wait-a-While and tried to focus on the monster in the labyrinth. Did the Germans know what would happen, knowing Crete historically so well? Did they wait on purpose before sending the Junkers and the paratroopers in, to allow us recovering diggers time to be seduced by the dancing light? How many others amongst us, like Vern and myself, like Mug and Ken, found themselves transfigured during those days of waiting in May? How many others fell headlong into that ancient Mediterranean chimera at the heart of the war? Hundreds? Thousands even?

It was during this period, this intense period of my first real still-ness on King – a stillness whose underneath was roiling like a creek in deluge – that there was a knock on my door.

I opened it to find her standing with her back to me, looking out from the high crown, over the straggly messmates below to the sea. She didn't turn around at first, something out there had caught her eye. I looked at her back, the dark brown suede coat, her long thick hair even paler than usual, white as beach bone in fact and wrought in a bleached knot at her shoulders.

I looked over her to the sea. A green crayboat with white trim was beating south for Grassy. I looked back again at the complications of her hair, the weave and wickerwork of her, as she stood not saying hello, not even turning around.

It was not only the first I'd seen of her since clattering out of the co-op enraged, but her first visit to my hard-won hut. And suddenly I wanted to step forward, out of what I had built, and to put my arms around her in the clean openness of the air. But I knew it would bring the pain out with me. I felt that. I would sob at the very touch, I would collapse and be gone.

'See, that's the Abernethys comin' in,' she said, her long finger pointing out over the water.

And then, finally, turning to look at me. 'Uncle True went as decky. Been three weeks. He's made it back.'

With sky behind, her face was clearly delineated. All around her left eye was storm blue bruising and welt. She could still open it but the lids and brow were swollen, gleaming with the stretching of the skin.

I said nothing, just stood to one side of the doorway for her to walk in.

She said nothing either. She entered, and I nervously fumbled for the handle to close the door.

The day shut out, she stood in the middle of the room, with her back to me again.

'This is nice,' she said. 'Better than the camp.'

I paused, adjusting.

She turned for the second time, the eye not quite as dramatic in the second light, but still undoubtedly there.

The knuckles of her left hand resting on the bare wood of my table. She stared at me. I realised. She was trusting me. Trusting me to see, and not to ask. But why?

I felt a pressure then, behind my temples, the memory of a natural shelter, the whisper of ten sheoaks, and wished I was back beside them.

I stepped away from the closed front door and around the table to my kitchen sink. She pivoted, slowly on her resting knuckle, to watch me as I went.

'Would you like a cup of tea?' I asked, touching the hob of the wood heater with my fingers to test its heat. 'I've got a proper pot now.'

The brown teapot sat in the centre of the table. Not far from her hand. She nodded slowly, but in a satisfied kind of way. Around her eye socket there was the faintest tint of egg-yolk yellow, the bruising was beginning to come out. The wound was two or three days old.

Fishing around in the sink I lifted out an abalone shell, gave it a wipe with a rag, and brought it over to the table. I knew she'd want to smoke.

'Take a seat,' I said. 'I've baked some bread. Greek style.'

She pulled back one of Brian Robinson's bentwoods and sat. The chairs had once been brown but I had sanded them. There was still the odd fleck though and I saw the recognition in her face.

She began to roll her smoke. The paper tinkled where it hung from her lip. She really was a sorry sight.

Under the window on the northern wall of the room I had set up a second smaller table with a piece of green baize, a squat vase which I kept fresh with white correa, wattle, daffodils or dandelions, and Vern's volume of Epictetus, which I'd found could well temper any mythologising I was inclined to. Not to mention the wallowing.

Leonie now nodded towards this table under the window and commented on the flowers. 'You read much?'

I took the teapot from the table and headed for the door. 'I s'pose,' I said as I went. 'Well, I did, early on during the war.'

I opened the door with relief. The light was welcome, its possibilities endless. Stepping out from under the porch I threw the leaves over the ground I'd cleared. I watched, as always now, to see what kind of mark they made.

I returned, closing the door behind me. She'd finished rolling her smoke and was now rolling mine. She saw me notice. 'Do you mind?' she asked.

'No, go for your life,' I said, in as blithe a voice as she would so far have heard from me.

'I never read,' she said.

I nodded, from back at the sink, struck by the plainness of the statement. I watched the kettle and spooned in the Robur from the packet.

There was silence, as she was rolling my smoke, hers going out on the ashtray. Suddenly, with a jerk, I needed desperately to climb back out into the light. I looked up, the tea slipped from my hands and I dropped the whole packet. Closed my eyes and swore.

Grabbing the brush from beside the kitchen-tidy, I unfolded *The Argus* from the bench onto the floor and brushed the leaves onto it. I scrolled the newspaper and poured the tea-leaves back into the box.

'Thing with tea is,' she said, 'it's hard to pick from mice droppings.'

A droll smile. Even more so given the state of her eye.

'There's no mice in this hut,' I said, defiantly.

'Yet.'

'Well, that's the advantage of a camp, I s'pose.'

'Of keeping on the move, more like.'

'That's probably true.'

The kettle boiled, I poured the hot rainwater into the pot and brought it to the table. Then I dug out the bread from the wooden box I'd made for it and put butter down beside. Then two cups, throw-outs from the hospital, both Mother Mary blue but with one orange and one floral saucer.

She'd finished rolling my smoke. 'So what's the story with this bread?' she asked.

I picked the lumpen slab up and broke off a piece for her with my hands.

'I learnt how to make it on Crete,' I said, beginning to put on the butter.

'There's rosemary in it?'

'Yes. Normally you'd make it with thyme, whatever you've got really.'

She might have already known where I'd been – I had, after all, relayed bare facts to others on the island – but she didn't seize it as an opening. A thaw of gratitude passed through me.

I poured the tea. Christening the pot with her company.

'I lived with a family for a time,' I said, now buttering my own bread. 'Well, with a couple of families actually. This isn't a patch on their bread but they taught me some of what to do, first while we were waiting around for the Germans to arrive and then again when we were trying to get rid of them.'

She chewed, drank her tea. Her eye was looking nasty again, now that I'd readjusted to the inside light.

'Well that's one good thing to come out of the war,' she said. 'It's tasty.'

Our eyes met briefly. And in that look something came to me. As if I almost knew how to reach back, to locate the ancient source of wounds like ours.

So I talked. Talked some more there in the hut. About the difference in the breads from one part of the island to the other. I talked about Tassos Kavroulakis and his niece Adrasteia, but not about the night of the evacuation, or what happened afterwards. No, only about the days we spent in sunshine, waiting for the Germans. And then eventually about the day they came falling out of the sky. It felt easy enough to say that it was a bit like a duck shoot for a while there, except the ducks were fighting back, I joked, falling whether you hit them or not. It was even easy right there and then to hint at the days of slaughter that ensued. The disorientation. The cowardice, and the mettle.

Finally I joked how in the end it may have been the homemade bread of the south coast that turned me from an average soldier into something truly useful in the war.

For the first time some of the events of May '41 comprised a story passing through my lips. Briefly, it seemed natural. The world's burden was not only mine to carry. It was as if her own darkness had brought mine to the light. She was still in her listening, as if she could have sat there for a thousand years, till I'd told the whole lot, till even her eye and the anguish behind it had healed.

But less than an hour later she was gone from Wait-a-While, down the hill on her bike, riding through the trees like a porpoise through water. Breathing it in and blowing it out.

It was all too much. By eight o'clock I was in bed, utterly exhausted. My guts had begun to churn, any reprieve seemed over. I drifted off into a sleep as porous as flywire and dreamed her black eye had grown worse rather than better. She sat, her smoke going out in the abalone shell, her head in her hands. The black eye was not from any physical blow and it was I who'd made it worse. If I was to continue recounting my story in the same fashion it seemed I may just bludgeon her to death.

I came in and out of wakefulness appalled, getting up to dry retch into the sink before slugging down pints of water from the tank. What had seemed restorative had suddenly become awful. I should shut up once and for all, as I'd always intended.

What was I thinking, talking about shooting Germans like so many ducks on the lake?

It was madness from right before dawn that next morning, flying in the face of all advance; the increasing buffet of the wind a perverse voice from the east. I sat out on the porch as in some kind of penitential site, before grabbing the bucket and a handline from the nugget box and walking down the long hill to the jetty to fish.

As I say, madness, in a wind like that. But against any reasonable expectations I caught a few whiting quickly and returned up the hill with the morning still new and the wind finally petering out.

I sat back and brooded under the bullnose. In the stillness I considered taking her some fish but almost instantly I was up and out of mind, crazy, gnashing over the clearing in untied boots, the bucket clanging, and throwing those fish into the trees.

I slammed my body back down onto the bench. Facing a world flinging back onto itself. I was an evil wave hissing up onto the sand. Leaving its shadow on the beach.

If she ever returned how would I explain myself? In truth, she could probably cope with what I had to offload but something within me knew that throwing those poor fish away was a blasphemy to her.

And then I was up again, clawing through mildewy trunks, retrieving them one by one.

XIV

Eventually I raised myself up from the headland below the airfield and, not knowing what else to do, turned to cut through the night back to Tassos' villa. The fatal calm of that night, the absence of killing itself, was frightening. I faltered again. This time it was not a ship in flames but suspicions about the villa, about Adrasteia and Tassos, that filled my head. A puppeteer's strings tugged at the filth of my uniform. I was not in control.

That's when the stone watermill sprung into my mind. Where I'd seen the pot-bellied old priest on the battle's first day, struggling to retrieve the sword he'd driven into the guts of the dangling Kraut.

I headed north, using the looming Mount Juktas behind town as a bearing, but it wasn't until dawn that I managed to thread my way to the vicinity of that mill. Relieved to find it, and to find it unoccupied, I stumbled down into its cold rocky shadows feeling like I had no friend in the world.

That was a long day, a day of close heat where I hid like a frightened mouse instead of heading out to investigate possibilities. The Stukas came in overhead as usual a couple of hours after the sun, and not long after I was joined by a pair of goats to whom the mill's old timbers seemed to serve as a regular shelter. All day I stayed cooped up with those goats, unnerved by their stillness as they stood motionless amongst the weedy rubble in the opposite corner of the mill, staring straight at me. In lulls between Stukas they wandered outside, only to return when the sky began to scream again. They'd resume their staring in the ear-splitting noise, as if I was to blame for the violent interruption to their lives. But I was none the wiser, lurching as I was in my mind between doubts about Uncle Tassos back at the villa, and remembering the sweet power of his niece's body, as we lay together on the night-slope, amongst the silent wreckage of the war, only hours before.

By the late afternoon the Stukas had taken an early exit, the goats no longer appeared interested in me, and it began to seem likely that there had to be others in my situation, blokes who had missed the RN boats and were now hiding out in the sector. But how would I find them? And would Mug and Vern be amongst them? The local resistance networks were my best bet but, quite apart from my suspicions, I also felt too embarrassed now to return to Tassos' villa.

As I sat wondering what to do, the goats grew agitated in the stillness. The larger one started to move about, to scratch at the dirt, and to bow his head and dip his nose between the back legs of his friend. As the light of the day weakened around the mill their hooves began to clatter in the dust and they started circling each other in an unmistakeable way. Thoughts of my immediate future cleared, as the big goat grew increasingly excitable, the she-goat alarmed, until amongst the scrabble of weed and gypsum the front hooves of the billy goat rose to clamp down on the hinds of his reluctant mate. The jutting began, she refusing to stay still, he moving them all the time around their end of the mill, her forelegs stumbling, and buckling too, as he thrust and grunted rapidly.

I felt sick at the sight of it, as if a cruelly unadorned version of my own crime was being acted out before me. On and on the billy goat thrusted, the female beginning to yelp from the savagery, until my throat became tight, my breathing shaky, my pores oozing sweat, and I could bear it no longer.

With true night descending I scrambled out from the mill, desperate for air. I stood, in the clearing where the paratrooper had been run through with the sword, gasping, completely at a loss. Finally, as the agitation in the mill behind me quietened, my own breathing slowly levelled.

Once again I took stock. With no solutions I made my way through the bed of the creek and up towards the villa.

~

On the lookout for Krauts, I stood in the bushes by the lane opposite the villa but couldn't bring myself to go in. I watched as a group of four men came and went through the same gap in the courtyard wall where Adrasteia and I had left. *Andartes.* Was it possible that these people had planned for me to miss the boats? Was it they who'd cast some kind of magic over me?

I didn't know, but despite, or perhaps because of what I'd shared with Adrasteia in the groves of the new moon the previous night, I felt incredibly naive. Virginal in fact. Stupid too, and lost.

Paralysed by confusion I waited in those bushes for hours. Eventually it was the smell of food cooking on Tassos' fire that got me moving. But not towards the house. I went back down into the creekbed and made a beeline for The Charlies and the airfield, where I knew there were rows of orange trees newly ripened by the sun. I found the trees, peeled the fruit and ate it hungrily, looking around at the breech blocks and other destroyed equipment our boys had left behind. I could see now the barbed wire of The Charlies hanging limply down off the nipple closest to the town but the whole episode of us wiring the booby-trap, including the feather the commanding officer had placed in Vern's cap for having come up with the idea, seemed to reassume its prior status as a dream.

Stuffing extra oranges in my kit I walked further on towards the water. I popped out by the charred Junkers fuselage on the headland where I'd been the night before. There was no one around. Or so I thought.

I sat down on the rocks and ate two more oranges, thinking of how we were warned against too much citrus back in Palestine. Well, there was no stopping me now. I looked across to the streets of Iraklio sloping down towards the harbour to my left, the cordial factory still burning under starlight.

I began to revisit the eerie visions I'd had on the rocks the night before, remembering the flames somehow crazing upwards from the water. My head fell into my hands once more as I felt the burning at the edges of my nostrils, though this time the smell of Adrasteia had been erased by the juice of the oranges.

I heard a sound at the water's edge below. I raised my face, instinctively hopeful rather than wary, and listened out, like you might for chestnut teal.

But this was a human sound, a cursing.

With what now seems a senseless disregard for the fact that the island was officially German-occupied, I called out as if for a native companion.

Coo-ee!

The silence grew even thicker as the call died. The darkness curdled around me like black yoghurt. Until finally there came a reply, barely audible, a weak voice from the beach below.

Even now I can just make out the glow of the shore's edge in my mind. I switch off my lamp, but the memories continue to glint. I put down my pen and close my eyes. I am heading for the water. Scrambling through the bushes until I find the towpath down.

~

There was a small and narrow lump on the shadowy grey beach, a soldier, bootless and foot-bright, wet to the bone, sitting compact by the edge of puny waves, his shivering arms bunched around drawn up knees.

Up close he was blowing hard. In the dark his face, like his feet, was whiter even than the waves.

He was muttering to himself. 'Gawd,' or something like that. 'Gawd.'

I sat down, to his right. We knew each other, by sight, before Greece. We'd sat smoking with other blokes on the stone of unction in Jerusalem, we'd passed each other in the chaos of the previous ten days too, might even have seen each other taking hurried shits in the roadside flowers, carrying moaning stretchers on ghost-strewn paths, but neither of us knew the other now.

I offered him a smoke. He was grateful but didn't look at me as he put it to his lips. The toking calmed his breathing a bit. Eventually he uttered his name, but strangely, in the rote cadence of reveille, as if I was an officer, as if having found him qualified me as somehow in charge.

'Private Peregrine Coghlan, 2/4th. Wireless Operator.' Then he added: 'From Tumut, sir. On the Murrumbidgee. Shit scared of the sea.'

I lit up as well and managed to congratulate him on surviving whatever it was he'd been through. But before I could question him about what the hell had gone on, he was into it.

'What in blazes . . . why're they tryin' to kill *us* . . .?'

A pint-sized bloke, even smaller drenched to the bone. A whippet's bow to his back in the tight hunch where he sat, narrow-gutted from recent deprivations, a long Riverina face. It was clear by his whine that even in his anger he was no hero, no hard nut or man well met, just a shy soul the world had washed up. He took a fierce drag of the Players.

'Noise, sir . . . like you wouldn't . . . woke up in the . . . smelt *somethin'* . . . looked around . . . no one, sir, the whole bloody ship to meself.'

Perry Coghlan sucked air of razor blades back through his nose and turned now to take a good sighting of me. As he peers through the night I open my eyes again here and feel for my pen in the darkness. Out in the strait the winds are searching. I sit for a while, thinking about him, until I flick on the light. I see him twig. He starts to shiver then, a badly idling engine about to stall.

'Launched meself up onto the deck . . . our own guns . . . *boom!* . . . bloody right at us! The whole front 'arf hit an' the fuckin noise . . .'

With the help of the cigarette his voice steadies, though it's more like a wave of clarity has come over him, in order to register astonishment at his own courage.

'I was up the back, in me socks. Been sleepin' off the grog we got into while we were waitin'. Looked over the side and shit meself. I just bloody jumped. Can you credit it? This horrible screaming of metal, and hissin' . . . started listin' then . . . one side fucked and goin' down. Then split, an almighty noise, almost clean in 'arf. Didn't stop to look back. Just bloody got a wriggle on.'

He flicked his glowing butt, lowered his head. There was a pause before his narrow shoulders began to jut up and down. He was sobbing.

I remember looking away, out to sea, half out of respect and half from a terrible mixture of embarrassment and guilt.

XV

WITH THE WHITING IN A BOX ON THE RACK AT MY BACK I PEDALLED west along the middle road, letting my muscles revivify me further. Gangs of pheasants, feathered twos and threes, made way for me as I passed, in a way the wind didn't. The wind had changed of course, as it always did, tilted and twisted in instants and moments, a trauma suddenly normalised and coming from the west. Just a headwind like I was used to, not that inverted mocking easterly which the morning had dished up.

I travelled between the woolly paperbarks. Up ahead a dark blob across the bright strip where the light hit the road. A stray jersey cow which, unlike the pheasants, remained unmoved as I approached, though somehow seemed perceptive of my state of mind. It stared while I rounded with my wheel among the stones, it was watching me with a mixture of sagacity and disdain: a crouching spirit, with legs going up and down too fast, borne away on a clattering contraption, not touching the ground either, not bothering to walk, too pent up, a scarred stick in a flapping coat.

As I rattled on beyond the cow I looked back to see it still regarding me, silently chewing on the folly of motion in a world that's never still.

Pulling up in the main street I leant my bike against the co-op wall. I felt gaunt, like my cheekbones were driftwood sticking out through my face. Were they catching the light? I wondered.

She was there and I must have looked as if I needed to see her because she put down the big squash she was preparing for the scales and came straight out from behind the counter.

Her shiner was barely noticeable now, just the faintest custard colour in the underlid, and I sensed she almost wore that proudly, as if enough time had passed to prove that once again the future would be brighter than the past. She certainly moved that nimble way as she came out onto the shop floor proper, and with a confidence too, not even a hint of challenging why I came.

When I mentioned the fish she laughed like I was local. By that, I mean she knew me well enough for my traits to seem repetitive and incorrigible, and the laugh was unfettered, in its openness as full and replete as the wet brown stare of the jersey cow.

We stepped back out through the door to the bike. I opened the lid of the wooden crate on the fish lying wrapped in *The Argus*. I'd chucked them into the bush below the crown of my hut and so they shared the filth of my shame. I hadn't intended it but the fish were another layer in my showing. Like them, I was not clean.

'Anyway, you shouldn't give me all four,' she said.

'Well, I thought, your old man . . . I'm on my own . . .'

Her tongue clicked in her palate and the sound grew sharp as it bounced between the tin overhead and the close-rendered brick of the co-op wall. 'Oh, that's nice. He'll be more interested in the newspaper than the fish though.'

I shrugged, nervously. Feeling now like a kind of suitor. Finding out something of what her father would like.

She inclined her neck, checking the articles on the paper. I remember seeing death notices, and something about a butcher wanting to sell on a puppy he'd found in his back lane. Mainland details.

'I can take 'em back and wrap them in another page,' I said, dryly.

'Mmm,' she said, a gentle levity gathering amongst the echoing tails of our words. 'Not this time. But next use the saleyard results and he'll be grateful. Might even invite you to tea.'

Suddenly I was prickly under the collar of my coat. The ghost of shame I'd been, so tenuous as I cycled into town, had now put on some threads of flesh and blood.

~

That night, alone on Wait-a-While, I began for the first time to write the pages I would send through Lascelles, though those initial attempts at putting things down were nothing more than rehearsals for my completing the tale I'd begun to tell Leonie. And yes, I was partly unsettled into this writing by romance, as if every phrase I was to utter had now to be scaled and gutted, filleted and floured, perfumed with Minoan herbs and dished up with classical wine and song.

That's why those first pages were destroyed.

Nevertheless I can look back now and see that a fresher spirit was ringing through me, a warmer song, leaving stoics like Epictetus aside. What I now claim fully as the richness and renewability of love gave Vern and his plight some air on the pages of a lined exercise book, as well as laurel crowns and golden status, with myself the courting chronicler. I can smile as I write how Vern was trussed up by my pen, but doubly so, as written by Homer on his wine-dark sea, which was actually hued with blood. By midnight I was so invigorated I went walking on the earth as the jersey cow had seemed to recommend, swooning that owls were hooting just for me, that frogs were croaking their approval, and imagining the island not as Naxos but as a penultimate realm, precursor to the lofty lenticular cloud of the conjugal chamber. The moonlight seduced, just as earlier that morning the day had made me sick, and to be sure I was a laughable remnant of the war, a thirsting man instantly drunk on his first sip of communion.

Morning came. I got out of bed feeling flattened by my writings and saw the pages on the table as I passed to heat up the water for the washtub. Already they were like leaves of another planet's tree.

After washing I sat with my pot of tea and, I am happy to recall, had a good dark laugh. Oh for pity's sake, the difference between day and night, it is relentless. By lunchtime I was chopping wood round the side of the hut to purge myself of poetry and in the dusk by the little table under the northern window I reached again for my Epictetus, to bolster and provide continuity through to nightfall.

That next night I didn't write, or walk, and the charge as we'd opened the wooden lid by the co-op wall began to fade a little, just as the whiting eyes would be dulling if Leonie and Nat Fermoy had not eaten them yet. I sat in shirtsleeves and woollen vest at my main table, smoking Escorts, a bottle of stout at my elbow, my memories pulling me down, on a burning rope from a blue-prowed boat, with not only me but the shade of my brother's bloated body on the end. With hands on fire I slipped back from Leonie's seasoned replies and patient observation, back from the complex figure she cut in the streaky air, towards a goat song of foreign myth, where soldiers have their cocks sucked by nymphs as their brothers die.

But still the image of the two of us by the co-op wall, the leaning bike, the bricky echo of our voices, came on again to right me back to a kind of centre, my elbows on the table, bottle by my side, my hut situated on what felt that night like a hill the surrounding winds had steadied into existence.

By Tilley light, one on the kero boxes by the sink, one hanging from the unoiled rafter overhead, the stove door open, with the coals of the wood I'd cut earlier in the day to cleanse me of my bullshit. Epictetus had this to say:

They who have taken up brave theorems immediately wish to vomit them forth, as persons whose stomach is diseased do with the food. First digest the thing, then do not vomit it up thus . . .

And I realised, sipping at my beer, that myth itself can be a bare theorem, though one shaped to the nature of longing for reason in the brain; and I decided to take a leaf out of Leonie's earthy book and burn the pages of the night before, and with it the idea that Vern and I were players in some second-hand bookish labyrinth.

I placed the prehistory of these bungalow pages through the open door of the stove that night and felt something suitably beyond description.

The burning of those pages was the first layer in a type of composting. These words I write now are the new green shoots.

~

For three nights I dreamt of Adrasteia. It was how we touched that mattered, not what we said or what we thought. It was enough for me that my days were normal and plain as my hut, the completion of which kept me righted. I chopped wood, built a fence and gate at the gap of the paperbarks onto the road, and looked out to sea. And the sea was plain too. At that distance, in a temperate brace of weather, it was as level as my table. I could have placed my book upon it, my teapot and my ashtray. In a giant's life. In another world.

It had been implied that Leonie would visit me again sometime soon, if not by a spoken arrangement then by the nature of what we'd shared, and by what we both knew now remained to be told; but she never showed. And so I entered a pensive and fractious zone where the name of my land seemed nothing but bloody droll. If it was a test, yet another one, sent by her or whoever, maybe even by her father in some traditional courtship ritual, I failed it miserably. Not that I succumbed to visiting her, my instability wouldn't allow for that, even though I wanted to so badly.

It seemed that all I had was yet another questionable encounter on my mind. No physical seduction took place, but I was left alone regardless. And now, as the days went slowly by on Wait-a-While and she didn't show, I copped the full southerly brunt of it.

In training in the desert we had been taught how to handle the Tommy guns, how to wire in, to advance and fall back in formation, the importance of equipment maintenance, how looking sharp and being neat and clean could save our lives. But we had not been taught how to wait, any more than we'd been taught how to watch our best friend pulsing out gluts of blood before he dies with a terrible absence of emotion. We taught ourselves. How to while away hours without killing each other before we even got to the Germans or Italians, how to count butterflies and play knuckles and two-up and poker as we hung around Iraklio in the spring. Well, at least we had each other; whereas now, in 'peacetime', I was still waiting, but this time on my Pat Malone.

And just yesterday, thinking of those days after she had knocked on my door with that storm-black eye, I had the liberty to compose this thought:

Trauma finds its companions, just as happiness seeks out joy.

When I showed it to her this morning she screwed up her face before saying: 'Is that a reference to you and I?' As if to say, 'I thought you were supposed to be setting it straight about Crete, not what's happened afterwards.' And I said, 'But is it true, do you think?'

I saw then how her mind went straight to companion planting, how certain plants will thrive beside others until they all run across the ground in a unified field of tiny flowers and leaves and tufts that draw in the spinebill, the honeyeaters, the landrail. And she finally said, 'Be more specific', requiring that I rewrite the sentence again, or at least elaborate, implying too that if I was to be true to the phrase I would make something less smooth, something more difficult, something endemic to my life.

And so, internal life be damned, I must now recount how a tooth flared up in my soul, something as sharp and well designed as one of old Nat Fermoy's pilot-whale teeth on the wall at Yellow Rock, as if to mock my nebulous pining for his granddaughter, to blight me again. It was my left bottom molar, and bit by throbbing bit it grew like a hard running tide through a common Bass Strait cold, until I winced and whined the days alone amongst the hessian and newsprint walls of Wait-a-While.

If I could have ripped it out myself with pliers I would have taken up the whaler's scrimshaw craft with glee on my very own tooth but all I had for it was alcohol – the last of my whiskey, and when that ran out bottles of Brian Robinson's homebrew stout – and hot compresses I made of wads of rosemary and parsley wrapped in silverbeet, which I thought might help but didn't. My pain was a geologic strata: at the root my grief and guilt and the official injustice, on top of that my self-imposed exile, above that the want of Leonie, not only her face and company and tone but my need now to help with her problems and to continue my account; and then, on top of it all, the final strata of the external reality you would see if you had the chance to peer into my hut on Wait-a-While during those days: a man in a dirty singlet grimacing and sighing, gripping his furniture with the pain of a toothache.

For one who'd been through such layers of difficulty I got myself into quite a state: knowing I should cycle over to Currie, at least for alcoholic relief at the hotel if not to seek out a dentist, but at the same time ensnared by not wanting to miss Leonie if she came.

A full week went by since the tooth started to play up, I was braising rabbit and also a wallaby I'd caught in a necker-snare near the house, hardly sleeping, drifting back and forth between what these days the hippies would call hallucination and in the Old Testament lamentation. An old black woman came to the door one morning to say that a dentist from Melbourne was on the island for a bird-watching holiday, you could tell him by his large brown field glasses, she said, his monogrammed Gladstone bag, and that he was lingering up near Cape Wickham. If I was quick I could catch him before he left with the next boat out of Grassy. I could cut him off on the Pegarah road. She left with a gaping but girlish laugh, in a mouth without one single tooth. After much effort and traipsing through bright yellow canola fields (there was no canola on the island back then, and never has been since) I eventually found the ornithological dentist drinking rum with Leonie's Uncle True at Yellow Rock. He made me lie flat on the big log table in the kitchen, and took out the instruments from his bag. Telling me to concentrate on his birding results, the statistics of which were written in copperplate all over the kitchen walls and even on the salt-streaked glass of the big west-facing window, he began to jiggle and snick and tinkle around in my open mouth. As I read his elegant count of black-browed albatross, storm petrels, sea eagles, stints, chats, Cape Barren geese and sooty oystercatchers, I was relieved there was no pain. He was certainly busy with his instruments and it seemed he was a master. Or was it the interest of the bird names and numbers that was sufficiently distracting my mind?

I came out of this delusion writhing and cursing for it seemed that all the while the dentist had been etching a flock of nimble dotterels onto my tooth. The hallucination ended with him pulling the tooth, and bearing it off to show Uncle True his artwork. Such was the perversity of my distress.

I lost track of days until finally it occurred to me, in something like a cloudbreak of the mind, that I could die of the infection. Also, that it might have already been months since I'd seen Leonie off at the gate. Such was my disorientation, the sanity of the prospect of infection merged effortlessly with my wonky reckonings of time. Later on I found out that my delirium was one week long and no more.

I straddled the bike, rugged up against the westerly I'd be riding into. I was weakened, despite my feral thereabout stews, which I'd eventually boiled the life out of to save chewing, and don't remember much of the ride. But I know I arrived at the hotel because after a couple of whiskeys served up by Jerome Sleeves over the bar I began to gather my senses. The pain relief that the alcohol brought flooded me with a half an hour or so of long-sightedness. I felt my body's exhaustion but was convinced I was in no danger. I could see the effect the woman had on me, how she had reduced me to this. There was probably bugger-all wrong with my tooth, I reasoned. I took another slug of whiskey and looked around the bar.

Jerome Sleeves, the publican, was an average-sized man, with the close grown curls of a bird-dog and a mildly stoic disposition where he stood polishing glasses behind the bar. On the bench under a window looking out onto the street, two red-skinned craymen were sitting, beers in palms, having a quiet yarn. One of them dished out a deadpan stare as I glanced across, but then a belated nod. On a table with four chairs in the middle of the bar between where I sat and the window's bench, another man sat with a glass of portergaff, reading a letter written on blue airmail. He was engrossed but every now and again one of the craymen would ask him for his opinion about something they were discussing. And on the other side of the bar from me sat Lascelles, chewing assiduously on the counter lunch of curried sausages in front of him.

Perhaps Lascelles had said g'day when I first walked in and I hadn't noticed. I couldn't be sure. But now, with his slouch hat resting on the bar-towel beside his plate, having just broken my fever and dulled my pain, I could almost have done with a chat. Even with him. I was so relieved to have ended the week of nightmares alone on Wait-a-While.

The man reading the airmail at the table eventually finished his letter and looked up towards the bar with a pleasant expression. Our eyes met and we acknowledged each other, again with a nod. Jerome Sleeves took the cue. 'Another, Keith?' he asked, or something like that, and the man at the table, folding the letter and slipping it into Harris tweed, said he would.

Getting up from the table he drained the last of his portergaff, and walking over to the bar set it down for Jerome Sleeves to refill.

'So how's he gettin' on?' Jerome asked him, pouring out the beer from the tap before he topped it up with stout.

The man who'd read the letter nodded easily, with high, satisfied eyebrows. 'Her father's given him a go on the farm. Famous potatoes apparently, they've got what used to be the manager's house, which Teddy says is small but snug. So all's well.'

'Well, I expect everyone's settlin' into things again well and truly now. Gettin' some normal work done,' said Jerome Sleeves.

'That's what it sounds like. I don't think we'd be expecting him back anytime soon.'

As Jerome finished pouring the portergaff and the man put his coins on the bar, Lascelles swallowed the last of his lunch as if perfecting a technical assignment. Finally he looked up from his plate.

'Pretty island, Jersey,' he said, nodding, and wiping his chin. 'From all accounts. How are you anyway, Keith? Keeping well? You're certainly looking fit.'

The bloke called Keith took up his glass but didn't return to his table. 'Struggling on, John, you know. Feeling tip-top now though, thanks to the postal service, eh.'

At his corner of the bar Lascelles almost blushed, but just as quickly regained himself. 'And you, Wes,' the postman now called, careful as always to do the right thing. 'How's the new digs coming on? You're looking well.'

Looking well? I couldn't but snigger rudely, after what I'd just been through.

'It's coming along,' I managed.

What ensued then was, it has to be said, an enjoyable conversation between the three of us, especially so for me, I s'pose, due to the way the grog had backed off the pain. As the chat went on I could feel a dull throb in the molar, though more just a tidal pulse than what you would call genuine discomfort.

It seemed Keith, who subsequently introduced himself to me as Keith Brimacombe of Quarantine Bay, and who was a long lairdish but genial type of chap with plenty of hair, had a twin brother Teddy who'd fallen in love with a nurse from Jersey in the Channel Islands during the war and had settled there. Keith and Lascelles chatted amiably, mainly about people I'd never met, but also a little about what Teddy had to say about postwar life on Jersey and how he was getting on as a farmer with only his faraway southern knowledge. There followed a brief discussion about the nature of island life, in part prompted by Teddy's letter but driven also by Lascelles' impressions since he and his father had moved over from Victoria. Lascelles remarked that island living seemed to give people their bearings and Jerome suggested that each island was a world unto itself and therefore often riddled with ignorance. Keith Brimacombe recounted how much his Teddy had felt a stranger on Jersey, and how he figured it was because of the unique limits of each island's life. This got me thinking and, perhaps prompted by the slow thud of my molar, I began to observe myself there in the bar, as if looking down from the ceiling, holding forth on Crete.

Before I knew what I was doing I'd suggested that islanders are habitually patronising to all outsiders and inveterate liars because of it. What was I thinking, mainlander that I was, having been saved and comforted so many times by the kindness of islanders on Crete? But on I went, between the throb of the tooth and sips of the whiskey, until even the red-skinned craymen at the window bench began to show an interest.

There is some kernel of truth in even the worst of delusions, the world often revealing itself in such contrarian ways, but this errant rant of mine also set in train a further and even more extended ear-bash on how islander eyes equate their horizon with the end of the world, and thus with death, and therefore prefer to stay at home in order to stay alive. To this Keith Brimacombe countered with the argument of British colonisation of the far and wide, including the ground where we talked, and Britain all the while remaining just a small island in the sea. I said of course that in everything, including military responsibility and moral accountability, the Poms were often the rare exception, and on and on we went. Eventually, to their undivided interest, I recounted the Minoan hoax of old Arthur Evans, how he had gone to such lengths to weave his archaeological myth of ancient pacifism on Crete, and how the Cretans themselves had played along with it in order to enter his employ, knowing full well that they were about as pacifist as the bulldog Churchill himself. Their inscrutability was yet another example of an island culture's amorality towards outsiders.

Jerome poured us all another drink and said that as far as my theory on Poms was concerned he agreed but that my theory of the horizon representing death didn't apply on King because of the constant looming and roughing of the horizon due to the ever-developing weather. This may all be true, I agreed, but by this time my die was cast. I had shown my hand in a way no one saw coming and in doing so destroyed my prior identity as a lonely mute.

As it turned out, with my toothache slowly reorganising its attack, I had set out on a forty-eight hour bender amongst the locals there at the pub. By the end of that first night I was in no state to ride, and after holding forth on the type of island individual who is the exception and wants to leap over the horizon even as a child – an idea concocted I'm sure from my own mood of wanting to leap over the pain of my tooth – I had taken a room upstairs for convenience, and it was there I stayed in a state halfway between convalescence and further deterioration for the next two days.

They were in fact the days when I first grew more friendly towards Lascelles, in part because of his sympathy towards the soldier settlers that until then I had loathed. Working at the post office nearby he was often in the pub for one reason or other, and certainly every day for the nutrition of his curried sausage. When I finally emerged in the bar just before lunch on the day following my arrival, with a hangover pounding now more than my molar, which was still no slouch nevertheless, he shouted me a tomato juice and helped me decide on a course.

I still remember the coppery gong of the old clock in the bar, which like so much of the better style of furniture on King was salvage from an early shipwreck. As it rang out for midday sharp I had found Lascelles and Jerome yarning in there alone and blurted out that I was in need of a dentist. Pushing the tomato juice across the bar Jerome assured me with a grin that there was one 'due any day'. Even the earnest Lascelles had a laugh at that joke. It seemed as though the history of dentistry on the island was about the same as the history of saints around the lakes back near Colac: there wasn't any. Or rather, as mine host was at pains to point out, dentistry on King involved a tradition of communication between species. Apart from the infrequent visits of the 'school dentist' from Launceston, whose foot-operated drill was the stuff of nightmares, it was a matter for Jim Robbins the vet.

'Either that or you wait for the next boat to Melbourne. I think that'd be the *Princess* in a fortnight.'

I had immediate visions of horse teeth the size of house planks being pulled by tug ropes while a spare bone-saw lay ready in case it was needed. I downed the tomato juice in one gulp, and must have looked bloody awful because Jerome immediately served me up another.

Jerome, who ran the pub until the '50s when he settled with his horses on land near the racetrack, now began to tell me of all the troubles teeth had caused in the island's history, going right back to the *Carrick* which had wrecked in perfect weather near a creekmouth on the east side when the skipper, apparently tormented by toothache, had lost his bearings. That was in the 1890s and, just like the ship, the island had struggled for dental expertise ever since, with at least a handful of people succumbing to torturous infections and actually passing away. One Moira Jones, Jerome informed Lascelles and myself, had gone under from an infected tooth as recently as '42, right about the time of the Jap air raids on Darwin. Her twin sister Jean could still be found across the road working as the bookkeeper at the co-op.

Well, this was a pretty mess I'd got myself into. I'd never considered, when I opted for the Roaring Forties as my place of exile, that I'd end up dying of toothache.

Lamely, I slumped onto a stool and pushed the second tomato juice away. 'Give us a beer, would you,' I said to Jerome, in a tone without much going for it.

Lascelles' counter lunch was brought out about then and he wasted no time in pushing his serviette into his collar, removing his postal visor, and tucking in. Jerome Sleeves, obviously a bit stymied by my slough of despond, reverted to his red ledger of accounts, which lay open by the telephone lectern on his side of the bar. So the three of us sat in our own preoccupations, Lascelles' cutlery clinking efficiently as both Jerome and I toted up our respective damage.

When he'd finished his lunch however, pushing away his gravy-smeared plate with a grunt of satisfaction, Lascelles got up from his stool to come and sit beside me. I groaned, but, in actual fact, I had only myself to blame: I had cycled into town and opened my trap, and followed up that morning with a hung-over confession of my pain. For Lascelles, this turn of events, which he never could have predicted from our previous meeting, when I'd been so curt, was both a boon and a monty.

'Wesley, if I may. Do you know what Dr Freud says about the dreams we have when our teeth are falling out?' he asked.

I think I just stared at him. Perhaps I said, 'Beg your pardon?'

'Yes, I am interested in the principles of modern psychology and, as an approach to dental difficulties here on the island, I think there's a case to suggest it could be of practical use. I know it's proving a great success in the treatment of shellshock in England and can't help but wonder, given what Dr Freud says about these dreams of teeth, whether it could be of some use in your case.'

I shook my head slowly, half in flabbergast and half because I didn't want him to register my interest too keenly. And pointing at my jaw, I said: 'This is no dream, Lascelles. You can take my word for it.'

'No, no, no,' he exclaimed, patting his visor nervously where it sat shining in his lap. 'I didn't mean to suggest that. But if Freud is correct then by inference a little dissection, not of the tooth but of the . . . *state of mind*, may help alleviate the symptoms. Just given the fact that Jim Robbins works better on beef cattle and in the dairies than he does on you or I.'

Lascelles guffawed, sending spittle flying as he did so, very pleased with his joke, perhaps even more so by the fact that he'd been able to make one.

'So what does Dr Freud have to say then. About teeth?' I asked.

Lascelles checked himself. Perhaps he was surprised at my readiness to inquire, or perhaps, like myself the night before, he felt he'd been tricked by the naturally convivial atmosphere of Jerome's bar into an uncharacteristically fair dinkum display.

'Well, it's just a thought you know, my way of assisting a soldier settler in need.'

'I'm not a soldier settler.'

'No, well . . .'

'I'm far from settled.'

There was a pause then, in which he reverted to type, fingering his visor, not knowing how to proceed.

'That's why I'm interested, I s'pose,' I added, to help him out. 'So what's the go with Freud?'

Lascelles took a breath. 'He says the dream of teeth falling out is the dream of repressed desire.'

At this Jerome turned, gave us a slow, thinking look, and said: 'But your tooth hasn't come out has it, Wesley? It's stuck in there, isn't it? Bet ya wish it would fall out.'

I looked to Lascelles and he nodded in compulsive jerks for at least ten seconds, rapidly thinking it over.

'Yes, yes, Jerome, of course you're right. But I suppose my point is just that the teeth can symbolise the field of desires, and be affected as such. Do you see?'

Jerome frowned, scratched his curls, and with a hint of bemusement at what John Lascelles was attempting, turned back to his accounts.

'So what do you suggest then?' I asked dismissively, but betraying the rightness of the chord Lascelles had struck with his courageous approach.

'Well, oh dear, I don't really know,' he replied, smiling humbly. 'I presume you've already had a lot of time to yourself, time for reflection. I have an idea that writing helps. Anyway, it's something to think about. The body sometimes lags behind the soul.'

'What do you mean by that?' I said, thinly.

Lascelles smiled, suddenly more relaxed. He sniffed with satisfaction. 'Well, it's a bit like the mail,' he said. 'More often than not it's a letter that announces a change on the island. But the actual person who brings the change comes later, the physical body on the boat, having firstly prepared everyone by post.'

'Go on.'

'Mmm,' he said. 'It's just that the mind leads as a rule. Thoughts and words. And the body has to follow. That's what separates us from the apes.'

I thought back to the day when Lascelles and I had first talked beside the Norfolk saplings out on the street. How I had noticed the intense deliberation in his movements. Every footstep a decision made at the end of a long debate. But what had appeared as a nervous affliction back then was now something different. He was a thinker this bloke, some kind of intellectual in exile, a cerebral man attempting to help. He had surprised me.

'So yes,' he said, 'perhaps your body's struggling to keep up with your feelings. And it's all coming out in your teeth.'

I spent the rest of the day drinking to ward off the throbbing but when I woke up the next morning in the hotel, I was surer than anything that the alcohol was just a short-term fix. And given that I was not prepared to submit myself to the calving tongs of Jim Robbins the vet, I had to take an even bigger risk. Even through the fug of my hangover, Lascelles' approach to the problem now sounded true. So true, in fact, that it outweighed all the tales of tooth-deaths on King that I'd first heard from Jerome, which were followed up and embellished by various drinking partners in the evening. My sad-sack spree in town was over. I had to get back to Wait-a-While and work it out for myself.

It was in the days following, as I sat on my arse under the bullnose staring out to sea, that I registered consciously for the first time what a single image in the mind can do. I took a glimmer on the water on an otherwise nondescript Tuesday morning, a soft brief streak of light offset by a hue of crowding clouds, and used it as anaesthetic, drill, and forceps combined. And once again the truth of this, like any truth of the earth, was deeply stratified. As quick as I saw this glimmer in the east and had applied it, I saw Leonie's solitary face, in my mind's eye, hovering like some angel out over the strait. And in the time it took for that crowd of clouds to cruise and occlude the emblem, I had accepted my medicine and set to administering it.

I rubbed that streak of soft light into my gums, I gargled with it, and lay it out in front of me, a shining silver road to walk on. I had to accept the possibility of a future, and, even more, I had to humble myself to the possibility of a destiny ahead. Or die. The tooth could kill me, if I let its furnace spread. Or, I could take that beautiful balm out there on the eastern sea, with its mass of ropey white tendrils, its quiet wisdom constantly switching like the wind in my mirror-mind between human love and elemental light, between lips I could kiss and an ocean streak, and I could live.

At the time it seemed the wildest risk in the world. The wildest risk, just to live. And then, would she accept me? Could she, with all that must be taking place in that bruising farmhouse surrounded by Brangus beef?

Lascelles was right, the body sometimes lags behind but conversely the mind can too. Whichever comes first, the fumbly words of desire or the throbbing tides of pain, they must find a way to be unified, in this life at least, on this earth.

It came to me, in my state of relief and the lessening throb, that I should try again to write down the details of the night of the evacuation and beyond, to lance the wound, so I didn't lug that tragic burden into every meeting I had with Leonie. If I ever saw her again – for at that time it seemed possible that I mightn't, that her father had warned her against it, or that she herself had backed away with fright – she would want to know what ensued in the tale I'd begun to tell her. This way I would be lighter in the telling. And, if it came to it, I could hand her the pages and she could read about it herself.

And so I sat at the raw wood of the table in my hut on Wait-a-While. I began to write it down, not as romance this time but as a true-feeling record, unbeknownst to me beginning this habit, this necessity of telling, that has returned again like an ever-replenishing zephyr in my sails since that day when we buried Lascelles.

Two

Fire in the Cave

XVI

I N THE END THERE WAS NOWHERE ELSE TO TAKE PRIVATE PERRY Coghlan. Nowhere else to go myself. There was no sign of Vern and Mug. No sign of anything but the aftermath of battle and evacuation.

We picked our way back through the creekbed to the villa. Eventually, in dry clothes – a black collarless shirt and Cretan bog-catchers, also black – Perry Coghlan and I sat by Uncle Tassos' fire in the yard drinking heavy coffee. Adrasteia was nowhere to be seen.

Perry was telling Tassos how there'd been hundreds snaking silently down to the harbour and along the mole earlier that night, hundreds milling at the embussing point. But due to the turps the evacuation when it eventually came had pockets of mayhem. There'd been a couple of 'man overboards' as they climbed the scramble-nets up onto the ships. One broken leg. Eventually, after most had been ferried out to the cruisers waiting offshore, Perry himself got on one of the destroyers, not long after 1 am. A furphy was out already that the ship he got onto, the *Imperial*, was damaged when it had come under fire during the day, on the way over from Alexandria.

As soon as they boarded the ships a lot of the blokes were hit with the exhaustion they'd been keeping at bay with the grog. Perry was one of these blokes and he headed straight below decks with a mug of RN kai. He fell sound asleep to the burr and judder of the engines.

Next thing he woke in queer silence. In the murk below decks there wasn't a soul anywhere, and when he found his way up top there was no one on deck either. They were way off the coast but going nowhere. And hundreds of men had vanished into thin air.

Last thing he'd known the *Imperial* was motoring off, hand in hand with the others, crawling with men: Pommies, Black Watch, Aussies, Kiwis, in all states of disrepair.

'What the hell happened?' Perry kept asking Tassos and I, swatting away the smoke of the fire.

I already knew that Tassos had mysterious sources on the island but how could he know what happened at sea? And yet now I saw Perry's surprise at Tassos' accomplished English, as he calmly offered a possible version of events.

Most likely, he said, after being strafed on the way over from Alex, the *Imperial* had stalled in the bay. Perhaps everyone had to jump onto another ship and leave the *Imperial* behind. They blew it up before they left, rather than leave it in enemy hands: a perfectly good RN destroyer which, with a bit more time under different circumstances, would be easily recommissioned.

But Perry wouldn't hear of it. He would have woken, he said, with all the movement, the engines of the other ship drawing up alongside, and how do you get hundreds of men from one boat to another in the middle of the night without making a racket? That was fair enough. Also – I recall this clearly now, what he said, so early in the piece – he wasn't the only one asleep in the bunks down below, so why was he the only one to be left behind to sink with the ship?

Tassos pursed his lips, as if in agreement. We smoked in silence. A shadow passed across the open doorway leading from the courtyard back into the kitchen. She had returned. I felt immediately nauseous. I peered towards the doorway, but Tassos' smoke got in my eyes.

~

With the shock of the cold night sea, the physical effort of his daylong float and swim back to shore, the jolt of what had happened, Perry Coghlan wasn't handling things well.

His face kept contracting into the same long and angular wince. He was a thing folding in on itself, his face agitated with a nervous tic.

I wanted to pick his brain about which units were on which boat, in case there was any news about Vern or Mug. But when I asked the questions Perry muttered only that he couldn't remember. His thought process was shot, his memory jammed. Tassos encouraged him to eat but each time he refused outright.

It wasn't too long before tints of a new day began appearing in the sky beyond the courtyard wall. I suggested Perry get some sleep. The little soldier from Tumut shook his head. 'Nah,' he said. But Tassos left no room for argument. The tough old Greek hoisted Private Coghlan up from the bench by his armpits and led him upstairs to lie down.

I remember when Tassos came back sometime later the birds were singing. But he was frowning. Sitting by the fire mouth he began stoking it furiously, feeding it with juniper sticks, so that any smoke disappeared into a spitting bright orange flame.

'You want breakfast?' he asked, gruffly.

I nodded, tired, knowing I wouldn't sleep.

He pulled his cast-iron pan off the hook on the trellis above his head and set it in the fire mouth. From the ammo box where he kept his food under the bench he miraculously pulled out four eggs and set them on the wooden plate next to the fire. From his trouser pocket he drew a handful of thyme and flung it into the pan. With a small brown amphora he poured the oil. The pan crackled and spat like the flames beneath.

'He is lying,' he said.

'Lying?'

Tassos shrugged.

'He can't be,' I said. 'You didn't see him on the beach.'

He gave the spitting pan a shake. '*Ohi*,' he breathed. 'You didn't lay him in his bed. He wouldn't stop crying.'

'I saw the ship going down myself,' I said.

Tassos turned to face me. I'd been with Adrasteia when the ships had set off, he knew what I had or hadn't done.

'From where?' he asked, threateningly. 'From where did you see the ship?'

'From the . . . shore,' I said, faltering. 'On the rocks below The Charlies. When I went back to join the embussing. But I don't know, maybe I . . .'

My voice trailed off. I wasn't sure exactly what I'd seen, or whether I'd seen anything at all.

Tassos said nothing, turned his attention back to the eggs.

Above our heads the vines hung in silence. He coaxed the eggs in the herbs and oil. He set the coffee pot on the heat next to the pan. When the eggs were cooked through he splashed wine across them before folding the omelette over and then cutting it in half. He slid one onto a plate for me, keeping his half in the pan, which he was accustomed to eating from.

After a few slow mouthfuls he turned to me again and said: 'All right. I believe you, Wesley Cress.'

He set the pan down, poured the coffee, and said it once more, but with his emphasis changed, perhaps to buttress my dawn-struck mind:

'I believe *you*.'

He had branded Perry Coghlan a liar, but as events began to slip from the grasp of any straightforward eyewitness account, he said it again: 'I believe *you*.'

As if it were the facts themselves he mistrusted, as if intuitions and myths were his only creed.

~

With the strength of the new morning any bridge between night and day had retracted and folded up behind us. The world was made less of glimmers now, more of hard light and shadow. On the courtyard wall a lizard splayed itself in the rising heat, a prehistoric figure yet at the same time alive. With its right foreleg higher than its left on the stone wall it was making progress but also perfectly still, surviving as if on a substance outside the realm of time.

By mid-morning neither Perry Coghlan, Adrasteia, or any of the other *andartes* had appeared, and Tassos and I sat on amongst fluctuating tendrils of light-pierced smoke. One might have expected a continuation of the mood of aftermath. Instead the air was full now of a strange portent, the quiet around us filled with the slow echo of the dearth of mercy on the face of the earth.

From time to time, with involuntary shudders, I considered how I'd crowned my own disaster with Adrasteia on the night-slope. The aftershocks were starting up in my body, each tremor cutting right through me. I'd been sober yet out of my mind, with the bold life of the girl. But now her beauty had been displaced by the exposure of the sun, and in her absence what we had shared became like the abandoned ship: a thing adrift, cast off from reality's secure anchorage.

Like Perry I wanted to wake from a dream but I wouldn't submit to the sleep that would allow it. And, of course, my host was a champion insomniac. He was waiting for messages, he said, waiting for the *andartes* to confirm the next step, the course of the days ahead; and as he waited, as if to delve further into the quandary of Perry Coghlan's arrival on the shore, and my unlikely vision of the *Imperial* going down, he produced the relic from the mauve rag in his tunic jacket. Pendlebury's eye. The talisman from the archaeologist *kapetan*.

It seemed like a key to a puzzle, proof that I had made the right decision in coming back to the villa, that I'd be best served to trust him. Without his power, I had no choice. Without his knowledge, no map. Nor did Perry Coghlan.

As Tassos closed his fingers around the relic, wrapping it away into the mauve rag, his dark hands secreting it back under the serge flap of his pocket, we heard sounds through the window of the upstairs room. Before long Perry appeared in the kitchen doorway like a frightened bird, a spirit squinting in mortal light, self-conscious in the black Cretan shirt and ballooning trousers.

Tassos stood up, and to my great surprise, bowed deeply and ceremoniously in front of the soldier. It was a formality I'd not seen in him before, and with all that I learnt in my subsequent travails, and in all that I have thought about on this other island since the war, I understand now that it was triggered by the informality he witnessed when he'd put Perry to bed the night before. The wild sobbing. With the German reprisals to come, with all that the island and its defenders had ahead of it, it was not the time for losing your nerve. Weak impulses must be ruled out, or at the very least reined in, harnessed into the discipline of dignity.

Straightening up, he said: 'Come over, Boatman, and have *kafe*. To start the new day.'

I watched as he thrust his fingers under the flap of his breast pocket once again, retrieving the mauve in readiness, the glass eye wrapped up in its rag.

I remember Perry strining 'g'day' to me as he walked over. The greeting sounded odd, like some immensely primitive code. We were comrades by dint of a far-off land, but as our eyes met there was no avoiding the fact that we'd now been anointed, not by flag but by experience, by being left behind.

Tassos put a cup of coffee in Perry's hand, bade him sit down on the bench, and, calling him 'Boatman' again, asked him how he slept.

'Yairs,' Perry said quietly, bleary-eyed, unwashed. 'Fairly well I think.'

Tassos took the marble silica out of the mauve and held it up between his fingers to the light.

'I want you to look at this.'

Nonplussed, Perry Coghlan blinked, turned to look at me for guidance.

'It's Pendlebury's eye.'

His face screwed up, in disgust.

'Uncle Tassos was one of the burial party when Pendlebury copped it,' I explained. 'He helped carry the body out west of the Chania gate, helped dig the grave in secret. He lifted the eye.'

'*Jesus.*'

Perry's own eyes cleared, re-set, peered again. He was recalling the legends of the archaeologist that were often told in the days of butterflies leading up to the battle. I too remembered the stories of how Pendlebury, officially the British vice-consul on the island but actually working to set up the local resistance networks in preparation for invasion, would leave the eye on the desk of his office in Iraklio, to let everyone know he was away in the hills.

Under Perry Coghlan's gaze the glass eye now shone in the courtyard with an added lustre. A sealstone from Knossos recovered by Pendlebury himself would have seemed terribly distant by comparison.

Tassos said: 'You see here, what is left of *him*. *You* have survived. A blessing to your family, your life. Your *kafe* is good?'

Perry sipped, winced again, but without shifting his gaze from Pendlebury's eye. 'Did you know him?'

Uncle Tassos smiled. 'I steal from the dead, not from strangers,' he said. 'There are stories the eye cannot tell. Justice comes in the afterlife, the lives of our children. We fight today for peace tomorrow. We will never know it ourselves.'

He clasped his palm shut over the relic. Crow's feet danced around his grinning eyes.

Eventually he began searching his teeth with a green wick, his open mouth a clutter of wonky teeth. Unsuccessful in the pursuit of whatever was stuck in his gums, he threw the twig into the fire and said: 'There are days when man becomes half animal. Everything is at stake, we become simple, like plants, with no choice to be other than what we are. You see? To be good requires freedom. You can recognise evil by the way freedom is hurried out of the room, even the hope of freedom. Also the good. Man becomes a plant pushing his head through clay, with no possibility to be otherwise.'

I was smoking then. I'm still smoking now. And listening. Suddenly he spits. 'Who makes the rules, the rules of war? Who makes them really?'

Perry leaned forward on the bench, his face stricken. He looked into the flames as Tassos vigorously prodded them with his stick.

'The big problem is this,' Tassos concluded. 'You carry a god inside who will not put up with a life without choice. This is your feeling here.' He pointed to his stomach. 'When good is no longer possible, when the choice you face is between two things which terrify you, the god becomes a prisoner kicking and scratching at the walls. Is that not so, Boatman?'

But Perry was still a shard, just a scrap of jetsam floating on the night water.

Yet I felt the words. With the force of premonition. The hairs on my arms stood on end. The image of God, not as the crucified figure on the walls of the church by the lake at home, but as a figure in a cage, a wild animal kicking at the walls of war, burst through the darkness and printed itself onto my soul.

~

Later that day we heard the first reports of Nazi intentions now they had officially taken the island. Any Cretans known or found to have assisted the Allies would be executed. Adrasteia's cousin, wiry little Nicko with the enormous ears, came in the afternoon to tell us that such recriminations had already begun. Sixteen civilians had been killed at Tsalikaki, to the west of the town, just because the *Fallschirmjaeger* were angry. They had also shot Yannis Manolakis, the son of Nickos who had sung for us at the villa, as he made his way along Agiou Mina Street back to his house. Yannis was not armed. They had shot him from a British military car, without even stopping. And a man named Christos Leppas, his wife and her old mother, had been shot in their home behind 1821 Street that morning.

So the punishment for resisting the invasion was already clear. Standing in the courtyard with his young face inflamed, Nicko parroted

the words he'd overheard – Christos Leppas' old mother never hurt a
fly. As her son had come and gone with other *andartes* from her kitchen
during the days of the battle, she'd holed up in a room at the back of the
house, and that was where the Germans had found her, and where they
shot her dead, sitting at her loom in the middle of her spotless stone
floor. The old woman's brains were scattered and caught amongst the
strings of the loom. Like oysters hung out to dry. With his already high
young voice stretched into incredulity, Nicko said the German soldiers
felt no need to justify what they had done, other than to say, in English:
'There will be more,' and, 'This is just the beginning.'

We sat around the fire discussing what to do. Tassos was expecting
friends to arrive soon but, either way, for Perry and I the course was set.
We would have to leave the villa. As soon as it was dark, Tassos told us.

If we had to leave I needed to see Adrasteia before we went, but
in truth I wanted more than that. The wild god caged within me was
roaring to touch her all over again, even in the midst of everything. Even
a god needs to feel the balm and mercy, the absolution of unhitching
the wire of war for a few moments, to suck those honey breasts, her
smile shining with pride above them, her teeth sparkling, as she lifts up
the front of her blouse like she did on the night-slope. I longed to feel
those plump fingers round me again, her lips upon me, coaxing me out
of myself, priming me for a role in the island horror.

Meanwhile Uncle Tassos' voice was lowered. He was discussing our
options in the corner of the courtyard with three musty-smelling men
I'd never seen before. They listened with grave faces, dark-skinned rural
men who seem to be under Tassos' command. After an intense and, it
seemed, satisfactory exchange, Tassos gestured to little Nicko, who'd
been watching with Perry and I on the bench by the fire. The boy got
up, bursting with pride at being involved, and in smoky whispers the
men gave him directions to a meeting point, from where he would be

led to a cave further north in the vineyards near Mount Juktas. When the grape farmers had left, Tassos explained that that was where Perry and I would be stowed away. Loyal villagers would bring us food until the right course was set.

While all this was being confirmed my eyes keep darting to the possibilities of the doorway back into the house, until Uncle Tassos turned and told me sharply to concentrate. She and a neighbour had left hours before on his orders, he said, in case the Germans appeared while Perry Coghlan and I were still at the house.

These are difficult truths. As Nazi troops strode angrily on the burning streets, their officers sanctioning a wanton revenge, I spent those last hours in the upstairs room of the Kavroulakis villa pretending to catch some sleep. Lying under a cotton blanket, my tears spilling from the events of the previous days, I shed layer after layer of tension and desire. When I'd rubbed myself raw and was finally done I could hear Tassos downstairs, detailing his strategies in both English and Greek, laying out plans to a still stunned Perry Coghlan and to a small group of *andartes*.

The sun rode high over the villa. The official battle was over but a new and even more lawless battle had begun, a battle of mongrel leftovers, Allies, locals, shepherds, cave-dwellers, mufti and otherwise, against revengeful invaders, their dark recriminations, their raping and ransacking and set-jaw firing squads; their wild sense of entitlement on an island never won.

~

It wasn't for nothing that the mystics of yore liked to dwell in caves such as the one our grape farmer guide led us towards through the dusk and into the night. Costas spoke in rasping whispers and had little

English – he knew the word 'dog' I remember, as there was constant barking far off in a village below. After farewelling Nicko and trekking inland for most of the night we climbed through the bushes of a creekbed, scrambling at last up to an outcrop where Costa showed us the cave entrance with the aid of a salvaged *Fallschirmjaeger* torch. Tassos had informed us that, because the road from Iraklio to Knossos had been captured by the Germans early on, the area immediately south of there was already a Nazi stronghold. We would have to be very careful as we travelled but we would be safe in this cave, he had said, looked after by proud *pallikari*.

Any doubts we had about being hidden near a region controlled by the enemy were erased when Tassos told us about the church made of milk. In the days of Turkish rule local villagers had found a holy relic on a lower slope of their town. They had applied to the sultan for permission to build a Christian church on the site. The request was granted, with the condition that they were forbidden to use the village water in the church's construction. It was a sarcastic decree, typical, according to Tassos, of the disrespectful Turk, for how could you build a church without water for mixing cement? The villagers, however, found a way. Instead of water from the village cisterns they had used milk from their goats and sheep. And the church was built, much to the sultan's displeasure. That was the calibre of the *andartes* in the area, Tassos told us. They were also the best winemakers in *Kriti*, he added with a grin.

I slept surprisingly well that first night in the cave, despite the smoke from the badly ventilated fire. I dreamt too, of bright milk running over grass so green it nearly blinded my eyes to look at it. There were lake reeds glinting in the dream, lake water marbling in the daylight at the edge of the milk stream, the smell of silage from our childhood paddocks by the lake was in the air and herons were browsing in the swales beside Dad's glowing Polwarth lambs. It was the kind of heightened rural reprieve that a fair dinkum life on the land almost never provides, until gradually the blinding green of the grass became the strange acidic colour of my vision of the ship in flames. Now the pure white milk seemed to run with the express purpose of washing the violent colour out, and I watched fascinated in the dream as if at a battle between my prior and present selves.

Perry hadn't slept as deeply as I. When I eventually woke to the determined Cretan light reaching into the mouth of the cave he was sitting in the cut of the cave mouth like a bag of bones, his rusty curls backlit by the morning. I managed a husky greeting but got no reply. The poor bastard was still out of sorts, there was nothing about his mood that inspired me to get up for a chat, and so I rolled over and just lay there, my mind running back over events, trying to make sense of how on earth I'd ended up marooned in this badly ventilated island cave.

I saw the Junkers again, the German troop carriers from the battle's first day, coming in formation over the sea towards Iraklio. Plane after plane caught alight from our fire, exploding in midair. I saw a Kraut paratrooper dangling from the tail of a plane, until it droned back out over the water and shrugged him off and into the drink. But soon enough the sky had filled with hundreds more of them, falling at the mercy of Iraklio's regular afternoon sea breeze.

Rolling back over in my kit in the cave I looked out past Perry's huddled figure towards Mount Juktas. They say the profile of the mountain represents the face of Zeus looking skyward from his tomb, but I was no more successful in making it out from where I lay than I was at fathoming how I'd come to be there. Suddenly my throat seemed full of razor blades. The prospect of a hot drink had me out of the swag of cold shadows and joining Perry in bright, circulating air.

We sat on our packs for a time, letting bones thaw. The heat was beginning to rise, and I for one was thankful the coolness of the cave seemed guaranteed by stone and the trickle of water that fell constantly onto a slimy rock in a recess at the cave's back-end. Relighting the fire, we began discussing our prospects, agreeing things were delicately balanced between our duty to get off the island and back to our unit at the first reasonable opportunity, and the already impending conse-quences of what threatened to be savage reprisals against the villages. Removed as we were from immediate danger we would rely on intelli-gence from Tassos, Costas the grapefarmer, and the local networks. For now there was nothing we could do but wait for the next morsel of info.

In the mouth of the cave, and with nothing to be done about our immediate future – unlike Vern and Mug and the rest, who I was hoping would have been issued with new orders in Alexandria by now – we were condemned to reflect on the hell we had just experienced, the battle that had been botched and somehow lost; free also to darn our socks and to wash our hair in the mineral trickle, and, in my case, to think of Adrasteia.

So why not, I thought, in the fresh cast of mind brought on by climbing out of my kit, why not distract myself by concocting a legend to entertain poor Perry, the story of the sultry nymph who derailed so delectably my campaign? As Perry toyed with the sticks of oak in the fire I was just about ready to cheer him up with the tale. Ready to unravel my boast, as if we were at some cricket club turn with an eighteen and a niner. But when I looked up from my smoke and peered at him more closely – the way he was quietly, almost studiously, arranging the sticks and examining the flames – I thought better of it.

He was about my age, Perry, but he looked barely seventeen with his freckles and his pale skin. I could see that even without the shock he'd endured he'd be a worrier. He'd cried on the beach, of course, and I'd guided him back to the villa without word or question when the tears had stopped. We'd shared something then, and now we shared this. So, arranging myself so that I was lying on the ground beside the fire, my head on my kit and my face looking up through the gap between holly oak fronds to the sky, I began, in order take his mind off things as much as anything else, to tell him the less hair-raising story of how Vern and I, Victorian brothers from a farm near Colac, came to find ourselves enlisted in the New South Wales battalion of the 2/4th.

I reckon I began with something like: 'Yair, so it's funny the way things work out anyway, eh Perry. Take my brother Vern, for instance. Growing up the last thing you'd think was that he'd shine as a soldier. Least of all with a whole bunch of nongs from north of the Murray. He was windy of guns as a kid, you see, got it in his head to turn vegetarian when he was thirteen, shirked the hardest work, hated fencing, always hard to get up of a morning for milking. Drove my old man mad with what he wouldn't do. "Bloody Vern. Where's bloody Baby?" the old bloke'd always be shoutin'. We called him Baby, you see. Whereas me, well, I s'pose the old man always kind of took it for granted that I'd turn out all right. He could see the country round the lake suited me fine. When I went off to boarding school Dad was worried about how he'd cope, so he kept Vern back to give him a hand. And he's not what you'd call the greatest encourager, the old man, it's not like he would have shepherded our Baby along at all. I'd come home for holidays and Dad'd expect me to be straight into it, to make up for lost time. We'd be cutting hay on the slopes down near the pines on the lakeshore, or picking the scoria off the paddocks he leased at Cundare, and he'd be paying out on Vern for my benefit. It wasn't as if Vern wasn't capable, he could ride a horse like Captain bloody Moonlight for Christ's sake, but only to go look at a field of groundsel or round to Vaughan Island to spy on the pelican nests; or he'd gallop to the top of Red Rock for the view, you know what I mean. Anyway, I was the one as far as the farm was concerned, Baby was headed for the priesthood, Dad reckoned, which scared the life out of the old man who'd only become a Mick for Mum's sake. Yairs, it was the seminary for Vern, either that or he'd go school teaching like Mum, and Dad didn't like that idea either. That's one of the reasons why he never let him follow me to boarding school. Kept him back, to make a man of him, he said, though it was all caught up with Mum I reckon. Her passing away. Anyway, it's bloody unusual the way it's turned out.'

'How do ya mean, bloody unusual?' Perry asked.

'Well, I just wouldn't have picked him to stand out like he did with his relish for the blue here the last couple of weeks. Never showed any real sign of it beforehand. Not up on the mainland at Vevi. I mean, he was there, and more chuffed than any of us to be in Greece, he survived the arse-whipping like we all did, if we were lucky, hey, but aside from his nous with the lingo and history, stuff he'd taught himself back on the farm, he was just another footslogger like us, you know.'

My thoughts were beginning to stretch out and it was a relief in a way just to talk after the days of screaming planes. Beside me though Perry was still pent-up, and the more I spoke, the worse he seemed to get.

Perhaps infected by his mood I soon too went silent for a time. I upturned a tin of bully beef into the pot and had the depressing thought then as I stirred the tucker that we had only to collect our thoughts and energy here before setting out sooner or later for the next cock-up of the war. And with that a shiver went through me and, dishing out the sludgy beef in the mouth of the cave, I tried to brighten up, hoping to stop myself, and Perry, from stewing any further.

I circled back to the yarn, about how Vern and I had ended up as the only Victorians in a New South battalion. I told him how a few years after our mum had died our Uncle Den had Vern and I sent to Dad's sister's in Manly in Sydney, to give the old man a break. It was '39 by this stage, and if anything, with Vern fully grown, Dad was getting worse. Aunty May's was a godsend for Baby. With her husband Jack she ran a big hotel, the Ivanhoe, on the Corso. Vern felt finally free of the clutches and enjoyed helping out and chatting to all kinds in the bar. With his gift of the gab and good looks he became very popular too with the clientele. We'd been there three months, our time was nearly up and he was dreading coming home, when the war broke out. Aunty May said we should go see Dad first but Baby wouldn't hear of it and we wrote the old man a letter. It was Uncle Den who wrote back saying Dad was all right with our decision. Tim Mangan from Ondit was helping him on the farm and she'd be right. We took the ferry straight into town, then the train straight out to Ingleburn, and joined the 2/4th. As I joked to Perry, we'd never heard the end of it since. We were always copping guff about being the only Vics in the unit.

Pretty soon though these tales of Vern and I petered out like the fire. Perry and I settled back into a silent, smoky companionship. If you could call it that. He obviously didn't want to speak and I wasn't about to pester him. We sat around all day listening to the mozzie-whine of the far-off Stukas, and the barking of village dogs, and around dusk I pushed my way through the oaks on the outcrop in front of the entrance to peer out over the swale of olive lines below, the parched and stony folds towards Mount Juktas.

There were not many signs of life. A distant figure, tiny down there in a stooped black suit and black cap, walking a pack-donkey on a narrow winding path. A small huddle of goats, their bells clonking, browsing at a lower slope of Juktas. A black hawk out in the air in between, pumping his wings like mad for the hover, getting itself right to attack the reptiles on the roasted ground below.

I pushed back through spiny bushes to find Perry had moved further into the cool gloom of the cave. He was lying on his back in his swag, his eyes open, staring at the coagulate of rock overhead. He was wound up tight all right, and I wished he'd snap out of it, just for the company.

After another pretty lousy attempt at conversation, this time about the pros and cons of Aussie Rules versus rugby, I decided to leave Perry to his own devices. A couple of hours before nightfall I fished Zane Grey and also my army diary out of my kit. I wrote and read into the darkness.

Eating oranges again after dark, and olives, and also some more of the rock-hard bread. Perry says he still isn't hungry, we don't want to light much of a fire because of the smoke, and so we set fire to a few small sticks and he drinks hot water and choofs on the German Korfu Rot we found in the sack from Costas. With no conversation forthcoming I move in right over the tiny fire so as to read by the warmth and for a time lose myself among the mesas of the Yukon. Perry sits not six feet away, but it may as well be eight miles. He smokes and mulls things over, is always polite if I ask him something but is as distant as the man I saw walking with his donkey far below our cave during the last heat of the day.

I turned in first that night, leaving Perry to the flux of smoke, the inner heat and outer chill. When I woke next morning he was back out in the mouth of the cave again, but standing not sitting, with his back to the fire pit and a ciggy on his lips. I sang out to inquire if he had been to bed. He turned to face me and said he had slept, but woke early and thought about re-jigging the fire. But he said he heard Stukas in the distance and saw three in the sky far off towards Iraklio. In a worn-out voice then he called them 'evil bastards' and 'dogged arseholes', 'ruthless cunts', and said they were probably bombing all the poor bastards who Tassos had told us were headed south through the western mountains to Sfakia. Which would be against the Geneva Convention, he said, 'but that's all useless now anyway'.

I was just happy he was talking, though he looked drained and his voice was as thin as a reed. Rolling over in my swag, I tried to visualise Adrasteia but felt sick at the attempt. A rat was crawling through my stomach. I saw instead the flash again of a ship going down in flames. That weird moment of telepathy, which haunts me even now. Pure contagion of the war.

~

Sometime around the middle of the day I'd knocked off the western and, like a dissolute child, was annoyingly bored. I remember I began to nag Perry for not eating. Once again he was terribly polite. I wasn't picking up the signs. Then I turned to chastising the darn fleas, the blisters on my feet, then to assembling a woodpile for the days ahead, and eventually to writing letters home. I told Dad about our Baby's magnificence in the battle and how it was stupid me who'd missed the evacuation and was stuck here on the island with a bloke from Tumut who had a touch of shellshock. I asked Dad questions about the farm, about the lambs and the pigs, the water levels in the lake and the stock prices at Colac, questions whose answers I knew would be well redundant by the time any reply he composed ever found me. But I had to ask these things, didn't I? As if I was just up the Beeac road a way doing some milking.

All the writing got me going though and by dinnertime – oranges, olives and dried bread from Costas' sack – I was regaling Perry with further tales from the lake, whether he liked it or not.

He never told me to shut up but it would have been torture for him: my descriptions of Mum's long illness, of how Vern shared the bed with her for the whole last year, about how she died on his birthday, and how later on some poems he wrote got him the scholarship to Geelong and how it caused such a row coz Dad wouldn't let him go, and how in lieu of school he was always running those poems by me on the holidays as if I cared, which I did but not perhaps as much as he imagined. I considered myself to be keen on everything actually: the farm, sport, poetry and fishing included. But Vern's idea of *everything* wasn't so thinly spread as mine, his was like deep soil in a narrow paddock, and it didn't include all the rocks around the place that Dad needed a hand with while I was away at school.

Whether he wanted to hear it or not (and I hate to think now of how it must have tormented him) I told Perry how unnerving it was the way the old man kept Vern back, trying to teach him how to build a decent drystone wall and making him ride his mare into Colac to school rather than take up the carrot in Geelong. Perhaps he figured it was now or never to straighten Baby out and give him some of the fundamental nous of how to work with his hands. But, of course, there was more to it. I'd come home on the winter holidays and there Vern'd be, the scholar in exile, sitting by the ferret cages reading Lord Byron or some such. He never held it against me but he'd roll his eyes at the mere mention of the old man. We'd spend the holidays plugging walls or drenching sheep and I'd get to pick his brain. He'd recite a list in the sleep-out, the books for me to bring home when I came again. We got on better the longer this stupid arse-about arrangement went on, even despite how my mind was emptier than his, or at least more on the land and the quality of grass, not as insightful or bright as his was. I always felt protective of Baby and I can say now I loved him dearly. Since Mum had gone even more so. And I knew that if I was him I wouldn't have handled it. Being kept on the farm like it was a prison. I would have taken off years before we were sent up to Aunty May's in Manly.

Perry just listened as I rabbited on. I was sensing something drastic was amiss but I fought hard to quash my inklings with the old memories. The sun went down behind Mount Juktas.

I got him nibbling on some dried bread that night but nothing more and after a while it was clear once again that he'd prefer it if I shut up. I considered broaching the subject of his dive from the *Imperial*, in order to bring him out of himself, but something deep within me didn't want to know. The scuttled ship, now lying on the bottom of the sea, felt like a no-go zone. So I lent him the Zane Grey by way of a gesture and dug out my army diary again for myself.

~

When I woke the next morning to see Perry hunched in his usual position by the fire I was relieved that Costas was expected with supplies that day. He'd have news, something to tick things along. A few more days of Perry Coghlan's mood and I'd go screwy.

Once again the sky was cloudless and, as I say, Perry was locked down in his own cogitations. Both of us had fleas but he started to scratch at a spot on his left forearm a lot, and to flinch nervously for no apparent reason, and he had a mad dog look about him.

As it turned out no one from the village showed on that day. We had water from the trickle at the back of the cave and food to see us through if we weren't so free with it, but it was slim pickings: olives, walnuts, oranges, dried bread, we'd polished off all the M&V rations, and as the day wore on with a heavy heat I hadn't ruled out the possibility of trying to shoot a bird. But when I ran this idea past my distressed mate he fired up and made me promise I wouldn't, in case anyone heard the shots and came to flush us out. When I tried to protest that the ridge was safe and that a bit of roast pigeon or partridge would hit the spot, he panicked, saying we couldn't be sure now where the enemy were and exactly who they were in pursuit of. In the cold light of looking back, this seems fair enough, far more sensible than firing a shot into all that silence; but the way it was dished up to me, with Perry pulling at his curls and his eyes bulging like a possum's, I didn't want to see my way clear to the sense of it. I s'pose this is how mistakes happen, how madness creates more madness. Sooner or later, trauma becomes an infection circulating in the air, affecting everyone in reach.

Perry remained by the fire throughout the day; we had to keep it at a low smoulder on account of the smoke, so he just sat prodding, toying with it, dragging on the Korfu Rot, and scratching away at his arm. By late morning, though, he started berating the scenes in his head with frenetic whispers. Around the middle of the day, after the sound of German planes through the morning, a surprisingly thick woollen cloud stretched out over our outcrop and Mount Juktas, making the day uncomfortably close and sweaty. I asked Perry if he would please knock it off.

'Just relax would ya, mate. You're off the boat and you ought to take the time to freshen up for whatever's comin' next.'

He gave me a cowering look, rubbing his stubby little nose vigorously with the heel of his hand. 'Yair, sorry, Wes. Forgive me.'

Well, there ya go, I remember thinking, that wasn't too hard; but within a few minutes it was clear I was no miracle worker after all. Once again he hunched low over the fire pit, his back to the cloudy world above the bushes behind, his eyes boring straight into the mouth of the earth as if he'd not only seen a ghost but decided he might become one.

I couldn't take the ragged edge anymore. Walking over to my kit, I picked up my rifle, detached the bayonet, and began to give the barrel a wipe down. I could feel Perry's eyes on me as I jacked the carriage open and began to load it so as to go and find a bird.

I lay the Enfield down against the boulder in the centre of the cave and took my flask over to the trickle. As the water slowly filled the flask I watched Perry in the gloom. He was staring at my gun where it leaned against the boulder. He didn't take his eyes off it and suddenly it felt as if we were hurtling at a hundred miles an hour into danger. I stoppered the flask not even two-thirds full and strode purposefully back and picked up the carbine. I held it across my chest and planted my two feet into the earth.

Perry turned his head away like a kelpie who'd been kicked. I moved out of the shadows and said I was going to get us some dinner and that by the time I got back I wanted him to have snapped out of it.

~

Out in the clear, I stopped to catch my breath and calm myself down. The air was humid and I headed to a higher part of the ridge above the cave that was just a further tangle of sharp stones, wild thyme and prickly holly oaks. Was I going mad or had I really just dodged a bullet?

Roaming the ridge for quite a while I began to enjoy the stretch, and even the sweating under the close cloudy sky. I was careful to stay away from any obvious *kalderini* – that's what they called their old drystone paths – leading back in the direction of the village. Perry might have been terrified of the consequences of me firing the gun but I was more concerned with bumping into a Kraut on the track. Plus, Tassos' orders held sway over me still, in a way no CO had ever managed since I'd joined up.

After what must have been a good couple of hours of combing that spiky ridge for edible birds and finding none, the day seemed heavy to me again, and deathly quiet too, as if anything capable of sound or call had been silenced by the humidity. I began to make my way back through the thick perfumes of the scrub to the outcrop and the cave, but as I followed my own footsteps back, down the loose scree of the slope past the branches I'd broken as I'd gone out – a form of blazing which ensured I'd find my way back – I met Perry scrambling up the slope towards me.

Despite his emaciated state he was sweating like a fat man in only his singlet, his shoulders pink to the heat of the day, his dog tags jumping round against his pale hairless chest like two mice in a maze.

'Wes,' he said, gasping, as he saw me coming down with the rifle towards him. 'I'm bloody glad I found you.'

'What's up? Has Costas arrived?'

'Arrived?' he said, looking confused as to what I might mean. 'No, no . . . no . . . aw, but hell, I'm so glad I found you.'

My spirits sank. After two hours of solitude and scouting on the ridge I was back in the nuthouse. I felt bugger all for Perry Coghlan at that moment. All I could do was close my eyes and pray for the *andartes* to get a wriggle on with our fresh orders.

In a shaky voice, Perry said: 'You loved him, didn't ya, Wes. I know ya did.'

'What's that?'

He turned his lip up, like a sour taste had rinsed through his mouth. He's bloody' balmy, I thought. I couldn't for the life of me work out what he was on about.

'I'm talkin' about Vern,' he said then. 'Your brother, Wes, on the *Imperial*.'

I waited, thinking, my turn to be silent, as silent as this room where I sit, on the rare occasions when the weather stills. I can feel now the way my toes clamped hard in my boots. And my jaw sets, as I listen out all over again for the mad bastard's clarification.

In a hoarse voice but with that apologetic tone he'd taken on the other occasions when I'd berated him, he said: 'Do you mind if we go back?'

I saw the pigeon then, the one I'd been looking for all afternoon. Flustering up from right beside us, climbing the air madly then swooping away on the diagonal from the high ground behind, before sinking smoothly through the sky of the valley between us and the tomb of Zeus. I watched, and it was gone.

～

'He was on the ship all right. And I was with him beforehand. We were drinking together all that day . . .'

Back by the fire, both of us squatting tensely. Perry had on the sanest voice I'd heard since finding him on the beach. It scared the shit out of me.

'Go on.'

'We'd pissed it up. Your brother stood out. He had one of those local belts around his waist. Had his shirt off. I saw him come down the cobbles towards the fountain in the square there, in the smoke and the stink and that, in Iraklio. He had a bottle in one hand and a bloody meerschaum in the other. Singin' too, at the top of his voice. And recitin'. He was wild with it, deadset. He had a few mates too, coming along with him. But he stood out. This big Welsh bastard told me he'd never seen anyone take it to the Hun like Vern had. Beyond the call, he reckoned, a one-man battalion. And now he was leaping into another mission, just as a way to . . .'

Perry Coghlan winced again, the sour look rinsing once more through his features. He went quiet.

'Well, go on,' I demanded.

'Yair . . . well, anyway, me and a few of the blokes I was with got
hooked up in it . . . and we propped outside this *kaphenoi* near the fountain in Iraklio, with your brother and the rest, and went at it. We had
flagons of plonk and bottles of raki and that, and well, we hit it hard,
yair. None harder than your brother.'

'How do ya mean?'

'Well, he was fairly out of control, Wes. I mean, I seen him climbin'
up the side of one of the bombed buildings there, right up to roof
height, ya know, and walkin' a ceilin' rafter left hangin' there, like
he was in a fuckin' circus and didn't care. The building was stuffed,
the timber of the rafter wasn't gonna hold, but he did it with his bottle
and the pipe, and singin' and carryin' on at the top of his voice about
that "fuckin Pommy bitzer Tiny Freyberg", even though we all knew
he's a Kiwi. He was recitin' stuff, all this stuff I didn't know, except
"Charge of the Light Brigade" which I did, and then he'd call out at the
top of his voice, no words, just a wild roar, like the whole war was a mad
piss-up and the fun was done. And then he'd throw his head back with
a lurch and all of us below'd be whooping him on but at the same time
we were fair dinkum worried he was gonna fall and break his back on
the rubble and glass below, and then he'd laugh his head off and shout,
"Time's up! It's stumps, gentlemen. Last ferry's leaving. Time *please*,"
and he'd almost screech the *please*, and he started repeating it over and
over, and he's steppin' bit by bit along this space where once the roof
was and the chant just built and he was screechin' it like some blasted
cockatoo as he crossed and twistin' his body about with no thought for
fallin' and "Gentlemen, *please*" became bloody drunken meaningful the
more we said it, Wes. It was as if he knew we'd all had enough after the
way Wavell spoke to us in the desert when we first got out here, and
then what with the freeze up at Vevi and the retreat back down and then
we came here thinkin' . . . well, we took 'em on despite the fuck-ups, we

watched the Junkers burn and now we were lettin' off steam coz the whole show was a joke, Wes, you know that, and your Vern certainly did and his "Gentlemen, *please*! Last ferry" and all that was like us all cryin' out, strikin' up the band, lettin' out one almighty head o' sarcastic steam and we were bitter, laughin', swiggin', full of poison and then eventually he made it to this zigzag scrap of wall on the other side and stepped off the rafter onto the wall with his arms out wide and then he pulled 'em back in and just stood puffin' on that meerschaum as cool as a cucumber. I'd never seen anythin' like it.'

'And the chanting stopped?'

'Yair, the chantin' stopped and, I dunno, he got himself down somehow and we all continued on down the lanes. But I'll never forget . . . Vern up there. None of the others would either. He was conductin' the orchestra.'

Perry reached for his dish where it sat in the dust and ash beside him. He ran his hand through his curls and looked panicky again. The bloke had two heads and now I knew that his trouble was about to become mine.

'So, what next?'

He looked up at me, startled.

'Aw, shit,' he sighed, as if he'd just returned from some other country. 'Aw shit, I dunno. It was late. But it wasn't long then, the word got round the navy had been sighted comin' into the bay. A few blokes took off down the hill straightaway but others hung back as long as possible. Some blokes were still settin' Brens, with strings you know, strung between the triggers and whatever they could find, water cans, door knockers, so they'd fire and cover us leaving. I dunno about Vern, I lost touch with him then. But it would have been only an hour or so, I reckon, before we were all headin' out onto the mole and up the bloody scramble nets.'

Perry Coghlan made a hissing sound, sucking air rapidly back through pincer teeth. Then his mouth opened but no sound came out. His head went back in a grimace, like he suddenly had a bad stitch.

Turning away, with full foreboding, to the flicker of flames I'd rustled up in the little circle of rocks, I said: 'You right there, Perry?'

'It's what I'm tryin' to tell ya, Wes.'

'What? *What, mate?*'

He hissed again, like a rib was broken. 'Well I dunno . . .'

For a long minute or so we were silent. Then: 'On the way out past the fortress there, it was bloody chaos I know that, but I dunno who was where or what.'

'Yair?'

'But, aw . . .'

He exhaled, a slow breath, putrid with regret. He hissed again, this time wetly, like a black snake, and finally managed to speak.

'I saw him when I woke up, Wes. You know, when the ship was hit. I didn't recall I saw him, not till we, you and I, were back at the villa . . . and you mentioned him . . . and then I twigged . . . the Cress brothers . . . you two, the Victorians . . . I'd heard you mentioned but I didn't put two and two . . . didn't know who you were. Thought you were a friggin' officer at first. And then I saw him . . . in your eyes.'

I waited now, threw oak on the fire, not caring about the smoke. It could cloud us, cover us for all I cared, cut us off in a stone world where a truth could finally be told.

He'd begun, he would finish, things were about to get a whole lot clearer.

'I woke up like I said, below decks, and didn't know what the fuck was happenin'. It was dark down there, Wes, the ship was shudderin' like a stuck bull, the sound was crashin' about but there was this single light on the floor just along from me, I dunno how it came to be sittin' there . . . but as I got up from the bunk it was enough for me to see the way and, as I went up, and I had no fuckin' idea where I was really, or what was happenin', you gotta understand, I saw two or three blokes on their backs in the hammocks near where the light was on the floor. And one of 'em was ya brother Vern. He had his arms thrown up behind, for sure it was him, no shirt, the belt around his waist . . . and anyway, I got meself up the stairs and through the hatch up onto deck and I saw the other friggin' destroyer off to starboard and then it fired again and *whack*! the whole thing lurched. I tried to wrap my wits around what was goin' on. Me ship had no one on it and was coppin' it from what must've been the *Hotspur*, about half a mile off . . . and then, well, you know what I did, I already told ya . . . I went over to the edge and looked, and then I realised there was nothin' else for it and I climbed the gunwale and . . .'

His voice trailed off. He'd climbed up onto the gunwale and dived into the sea.

He turned away from my gaze to the flames, took a moment, the fire mirrored in his eyes, then turned back. Lookin' straight at me.

The facts settled in. Now spoken.

Then he says, 'I was up on the edge, Wes, lookin' into that black sea, needin' more courage than I had. And you know what got me to jump? I thought of your brother up on that rafter back in the town just a few hours earlier. The sheer balls of him. His chant went screech in my head again like a fuckin' cocky, "It's stumps, gentlemen. Gentlemen, *please*!" and Vern lurchin' about and jumpin' down onto that zigzag wall, and I just shut my fuckin' eyes on that, crossed myself and I jumped . . .'

It took only moments to form. The picture. Like a bullet in the guts. What he'd done, and what he'd slowly come to realise he'd done. Why Uncle Tassos had said he was lying.

Inspired by our Baby, our Baby who rode like Captain Moonlight and read Lord Byron to the ferrets. Our Baby who'd kept Mum company in the long dark months of her dying bed. Perry had left him to sleep off the war for all eternity.

~

I got up from the fire and walked slowly out through the bush tangle on the outcrop. I stood right on the edge above the valley. The island of Crete looked suddenly more ancient than old; drier too. The longer I stood there alone on that outcrop, with Perry's news in my head, the deeper the silence seemed to be. I felt like a foreign scrap in my own hurtling dream. A stranger. On an island beyond our care.

I don't know how long I remained out there, staring off into the air between the outcrop and Mount Juktas. I now recall a kind of fisting in the body, a damming of tears and sobs, as the truth of Vern's death rose within me. And soon my wall was built. I began to coolly dissect what Perry had said. This was no official telegram to Lake Corangamite, no glorious death in the thrust of the conflict. The first sparks of my rage began to burn.

I turned in the dust and clawed my way back through sharp leaves in search of Perry. He would pay. My fuckin' oath he would pay.

I found him stoking the fire like a frightened animal, the little cunt who'd said my brother was killed while asleep in the bowels of a retreating ship, sunk by his own navy just as the whole pointless stoush had momentarily slid into the hiatus of his dreams.

When he saw me, Perry raised his shoulder in trepidation. But he would have needed more than a shoulder, or even a claw or pelt, as I came crashing out of the bushes.

I went straight at him, as if to restore our Baby's voice and breath. Grabbing him with my left hand by his throat and my right hand by his hair, I grew quickly catatonic at the touch. I threw his guilty little frame like a puppet onto the fire and then, holding him down with one hand on his neck and with my knee drilling into his kidneys, I fixed him to the scalding spot. Roaring now, in a voice I'd never heard out of my own body, with no regard for my own left hand which was also in the heat of the fire, I pressed him further and harder into the embers and coals until his squealing and screaming merged into breathless groans from the foothills of death. This satisfied me, the punishment beginning to align with the irreversibility of the crime, and so, blind to anything other than my own volcanic core, I screwed him down harder, grinding him even further into the heat. Then, as I released my clutch on his neck in order to re-grip and stamp this fire out once and for all with Perry Coghlan's worthless uniform and flesh, he managed to twist out of my grasp and roll off the coals, languishing on the dry dirt of the cave.

I was panting, crouched, ready to leap. He rolled his body away from both myself and the fire, which at that moment were one and the same thing. In cooler air he began yelping, and then rolled over and over to put out any flame still biting at his flesh, right back into the shadows of the cave.

I stood still, taken aback by his escape, shocked by the image of terror in his eyes. I felt my own hand sting and a thick pall of smoke and confusion surround me.

Perry came to a whimpering halt on the cave floor between the huddled lumps of our two kits. Slowly helping himself up on the boulder in the middle, he stumbled further into the cave, making for the trickle of water. I grabbed my rifle from beside the fire and held it with both hands across my gut to steady myself. My burning hand seared against the sun-baked gunmetal. I, too, wanted to make for the trickle back in the cave but didn't. Instead I gripped tighter on the barrel of the gun and kept my eyes on Perry.

He was shedding smoking garments as best he could, trying to slap the water over himself with his hands, which had not been burnt like his torso by the fire. The trickle was not ample enough for him to get right under, so those unharmed hands were his valuable tools. Eventually he stood naked, the flesh of his ribs and hips blurred ash and pink, raw, the red hair of his thighs singed off in strange designs where the pressure had been brought to bear. He was wincing and calling out with the pain. Even in the gloom at the back of the cave I could see he was scorched.

I stood with eyes stuck fast. A hot rope of urine shot down my trouser leg. I began to shiver and gripped the rifle even tighter. The pissing went on and on and on and when it stopped it occurred to me, out of some sane reservoir of thought and training, that I should have saved some of it for my burnt hand.

~

I sit here at the desk and once again put down my pen and switch off the lamp. On the other side of the window the eastern sky is deep and goes on forever. It is strafed not by *Messerschmitts* but by gales of rain. Behind me, a few well-grassed paddocks, clutches of paperbarks, a small racetrack, a shipwreck, and then twelve thousand miles of open ocean. Those vast waters are akin to my memory now, reaching all the way back into the west as they do, all the way back into the past.

I sit on a log beside the smouldering fire but far enough away not to be tormented by its still radiating heat. My Enfield is trained on the silhouette of Perry back in the slimy recess. We are like coves of different countries, creatures of different species, but caught, for strange reasons, in the exact same lair. As he continues to slap the mineral water onto his opened flesh, moaning and soaking his singlet and squeezing it out like a sponge onto himself, I sear internally at the brutality of what he's told me.

Not a word is spoken. At least not to each other.

~

Minutes passed, then the hours; by dusk I had relaxed my grip on the rifle, I no longer trained it on Perry though it was still by my side. As night once again began its creep over the island he told me in one pained but clear sentence that he felt *crook*.

All I felt in response was my own hand burn. I wanted a share of the trickle. I told him he should move his arse over to his kit and put on his second clothes. This he immediately did, though with difficulty walking, and when he slumped down amongst his things I picked up the rifle and made a beeline for the water.

I stood shivering in the darkness of that freezing, slimy wet back of the cave, my bad hand resting against the cool rock, letting the trickle run over raw wounds. With the soothing of the water I began to breathe a little easier, but the dousing of the heat in my skin was exchanged as if directly for my emotions. I saw Vern's face, its grim expression as the sea filled his body and my memory of it. Torpedo blasts repeated over and over, the flames out on the sea began to roar in my head. Hot tears began to run stinging out of my eyes, until they were streaming down my cheeks. My soul, or whatever it is, rose up, in a silent cry.

Not twenty-five yards away Perry lay squinting, and making a mess of applying his one remaining bandage round his searing guts.

~

The sun rose machine-like the next morning. Before long we heard the familiar mozzie-whine in the distance. I crept out to aggressive light and felt like walking down into the village and handing myself in, so as to obliterate both Perry and I, and by consequence yesterday, and all the other yesterdays that had carried us to this malevolent lookout. I sighted a far-off Stuka but just as quickly it was nowhere to be seen, and before long the sound of it was gone as well.

I soon grew sick of the way the oppressive silence seemed to amplify the awful sadness I felt. To break the power of this spell I began talking fourteen to the dozen, telling Perry what I was thinking, how I'd throw his body off the outcrop after I'd shot him and no one except some rectangular-eyed goat in starved need of a half-charred carcass would be any the wiser.

'There's forgotten bodies lying all over this island after the last two weeks,' I said. 'What's one more? As far as anyone knows you'll have gone down in the boat yourself, rather than bailing like a squib and leaving others there to drown.'

And so, tormented, I became a tormentor, and through the whole rest of that day, and the next, I carried out this task as if born to it, punishing an already punished man until he could bear it no more.

~

Eventually Perry began to plead with me to shoot him dead. At last, after long hours of unbridled wrath, this bald request from a fellow Australian made me check myself. For God's sake, Perry Coghlan was just a normal bloke, the same as me and Ken and Mug. As a rule, the Australian go is to take things as they come, with the underlying presumption, born from the first days of the convicts, that mankind's basically a bastard. Once you accept that, everyone can get on with things and feel a sense of common justice in most predicaments. On any farm and by any river in Australia you'll find men and women whose hard slog and dry humour is driven by such cynical logic. There was something whittled back about Perry Coghlan's terrible pleading that reminded me he wasn't any different.

So, with a quick pulse of thoughts by the fire, I told Perry to cut it out, that things would not be concluded that easy.

He fell back on his gear, went silent. Gradually, a tentative mood of mutual reprieve filled the cave.

For the first time then, and not for the last, I began to take myself into the events on the ship, to contemplate having done myself what Perry had chosen to do. We were volunteers, we'd been trained hastily in the desert and were drilled to always commit to the objectives of our companies and battalions, but it wasn't till we entered the fray that we had any real idea. It was Vevi that had marshalled our alertness to a fine point. Every choice to leave cover, to shed ammo, to help an injured mate, had been taken with the daily hate whistling about the ears, with death summoning us to come. And though some of us were lucky enough to make it down through those deadly passes, it remains to be said that there are plenty of bodgy decisions made in the heat and panic of war, with very uneven consequences.

But, even as I reflected on all this, wincing from the pain of my blistering left hand, I smarted nevertheless at Perry's decision. To abandon Vern. And the others. For Christ's sake, just how many other blokes were below deck? Mug, for instance, would surely have been near Vern. And how long would it have taken that little prick Perry to bolt back, squeeze himself down through the hatch, and shake them awake? He would have only had to rustle one of them for the rest to get the picture.

A deep part of me ground with friction against the facts. Vern was drowned, and I'd seen it coming. The vision I'd had of the ship akimbo returned now as reality, his cause backfired, his face got at by a ravenous knot of moray eels.

~

Eventually Costa arrived to find the two of us slewn on our backs about the cave. He came scrambling up the rocks to the outcrop, brandishing the same Mauser revolver he'd left us with, a black cloth cap on his head, another unevenly dyed crimson sack, almost bigger than himself, slung over his shoulder.

In broken English the grape farmer said hello and made straight to Perry, who was suffering amongst his kit. There the little bastard lay, in boofy shorts, a dirty bandage loosening at his gory midriff, his other burns also exposed to abrasive grit riding on the air. The *andarte* was startled and, through his eyes, I saw how much weight Perry had lost in such a short time.

Costa gestured 'why?', 'how?', needing an explanation, but Perry said nothing, turning gingerly from his position to ease the pain.

Costa turned to where I sat in the light of the cave mouth. *Don't ask and you won't need to be told.* My look said it all. He was confused, but only for a brief moment. He turned to his sack of supplies and fished deep inside with the whole length of his arm. He pulled out a fig and threw it in my direction. Catching it in my good hand, I took a bite of the sweet fruit. I then watched as Perry Coghlan, fellow soldier, fellow demon amongst men, refused to do the same.

As I sunk into the fig, Costa told us, as best he could, the news he had. Already German reprisals on the villages had been catastrophic.

In the nearby village of Skalani terrible vengeance had been enacted. There were rumours that such things were also happening in the western sector of the island.

From his pocket the grape farmer produced a leaflet, dropped by German planes, addressed to the soldiers of the Royal British army, navy and air force, advising us to give ourselves up immediately if we wanted to be treated in an honourable way. It talked of the harshness of the winter to come and was signed by the 'Commander of Kreta'.

Both Perry and I took turns in reading the leaflet. 'You must stay,' Costa said. 'Stay for one more month here.'

'What about a boat?' I asked. 'A boat to get us off?'

The farmer shook his head firmly. He had this one order and was determined to issue it. 'Tassos says stay.'

Perry turned his hips and groaned quietly. I found myself speaking for him. 'Coghlan here might have to see a doctor,' I said. 'A *doctor*,' I repeated for the Greek.

Costas shrugged his shoulders, as if there was nothing, given the precarious circumstances around the village, that anyone could do.

'A *yitroz*,' I said, suddenly remembering the word from when Adrasteia and I had nursed the wounded at the villa during the battle. 'Tell Tassos Kavroulakis the Boatman needs a *yitroz*,' I said. '*Ne?*'

Now the *andarte* nodded keenly. 'The Boatman,' he said, with a broad smile. And then in English: 'The Boatman needs doctor.'

'That's it,' I said. '*Yitroz*. The Boatman needs a doctor.'

~

Perry slept, with his arms behind his head, as if tempting me to shoot him in the same state in which he last saw Vern. In the late afternoon,

I walked from my post by the burnt-out fire to the new food and began to pick amongst it.

With the cool skin of an orange in my burnt left hand I looked over at where he slept, not six feet from me. His face was pained, and I could see how badly his bandages needed to be changed. There was even, I fancied, a smell coming from his wounds; before long he could be in strife without the right medical attention.

For a brief few moments I sat on my haunches amidst the pile of provisions and considered shooting him after all. I had not been brought up to sit idly by and watch a creature suffer and that's how, in this disturbed hour of my existence, I viewed the situation. I was back on the lakes smithereening an injured eagle. I got up, went to the rifle where it lay against the bough-seat I had dragged in near the fire, and took it back to where Perry lay asleep. I stood over him, looking down and breathing hard between saying Hail Marys, would you believe. Raising the gun to my shoulder, I sighted his head, leaning slightly to one side with his unburnt upper arm as a pillow. Peering down the barrel, I pointed it right into his downy little earhole.

When she was sick our mum used to joke that our ears keep growing even after we die . . . so Vern, if you can hear me: I looked right into his ear, so pink and young, muttering fragmented prayers whilst that Corangamite eagle kept skelting above your shot-up ship.

Coghlan was half Boatman, half eagle, a bandaged bird . . . and then the next thing I just buckled, my legs went out from under me and I tumbled to the ground, quivering and calling out indecipherable things, bawling for my brother, my mother's Baby, for the smell of her dying bed and for simply being where I was, so far from what was real. And I sobbed out a version of the whole history, of us and all mankind, I reckon, all wrapped up in myself in that hideaway where all veils shields stalls drystone walls drywitted tarps against the truth of man had been removed.

I don't know how long this went on for, time itself had changed its mask in the cave, until I heard a voice, a consoler, a gentle consoler, and my own racket of anguish was penetrated.

Slowly the terrified clamps the cave walls seemed to have on my brain began to loosen, the awful weight on my heart was whispered to. I calmed, slowly breathing, until I felt a touch, a lightness on my shoulder, and I turned and peered out of my wildness at Perry Coghlan from Tumut stroking my arm with the tenderness of a girl and speaking softly, soothing as best he could in his youngest and oldest voice.

My wailing had woken him. He may well have wondered if it was safe to ever fall asleep again as each time he woke the world was a stranger place, with his enemy mate and jailer in hoarse distress, calling insensate from deep in his loins. Yes, the Boatman must have wished the whole world back to sleep, to where sleep reigned in quiet over Vern and to where I'd almost banished him before collapsing. Mustering himself into compassion for his likely executioner, and indeed signalling he wanted to live again, he reached out his unburned fingers and touched me.

I think, looking back on it all, that I had come so close, in the heightened state of what I'd lost, to death or madness. But soon I was sitting, my gob agape, slack-jawed, exhausted, a pile of fresh food about me, as Perry resumed the pained adjustments of his trunk.

XVII

EVEN THESE DAYS, I STILL SAY THE WORDS TO MYSELF TO KEEP THE demons at bay: 'How shall I be contented with the divine administration?'

The mere phrase reminds me of the scale of things, the island set amidst the voluminous banking, carping, howling and receding sea, a small solid thing amidst the ocean of emotion and the mind swelling and rearing up. 'The divine administration.' It's Epictetus. I like it, not only because it reminds me that King is small and mortal in metaphysical waters, but because it makes me laugh to think of the gods all corralled into desks in a shared building, calling and adjourning meetings, shuffling paperwork, as if the world is being run like a shire office. By holding the phrase between the thumb and forefinger of my mind, lightly like a pen as the sun goes down over the island, my submission is renewed.

At the end of three days and nights of constant writing on Wait-a-While, I coasted down from the brow of the hill on the bike and walked the ribbed sand of the beach, with epic old testament rays in the cloudy sky and red–purple groundsel shrivelling and turning into fluffy seed pom-poms all around me. At the high-tide line muttonbirds, like rags of ash, marked my progress alone in a dark coat of haunting. Dead, bedraggled, exhausted muttonbirds. Those that didn't quite make it back to their burrows after the long Aleutian flight. Some were almost coffined in sand, others protruded with a wingtip, or simply from the way they'd fallen, or the way the waves had tumbled them over and abandoned them. Some lay with their black-hooked beaks ajar, as if they'd died mid-gasp from the effort, others had wings spread almost in imitation of their flight, but wind-combed now, salt-and-pepper journey birds gone to ground.

I walked dazed from my recollections, sitting as marks on the page back at Wait-a-While, an empty longneck beside them on the table in the hut. I carried the revisited burden on the moody beach. The ocean never stopped. It never stopped here on King, turning and hissing as if full of the tiger snakes of New Year Island, and it never stopped in the bay off Iraklio where it thoroughed its way like a medical dye into every nook and cranny of my dead brother's body, left to lie in those waters where the word for 'seduce' was the very same as the word for 'destroy'.

I consoled myself with the thought that I was following Lascelles' instructions, shaking all this out of myself by writing it down, so it wouldn't kill me, and so I wouldn't have to bring it to Leonie; but nevertheless everywhere I looked the wrecked birds poked up from the sands like despondent memos. Also the beach, the coast, age old and rightly worn by the constancy, the dogged persistence of tragic tides. The whole island, sometimes so fresh and shining to behold, seemed as exhausted as the muttonbirds. And so the place wrapped around me as I walked. If it wasn't for the feelings of umbrage and desire that would rise with every alternate beat of my heart, I might have figured once and for all that that beach under Fraser's Bluff was a perfect place to die.

By the time I climbed the hill back home the idea had sprung and I went straight to the pages. I decided that rather than read them aloud or copy out again what I had already written for her, which is what I'd imagined I'd do, I would simply take them into Lascelles as the bundle they were, with the marks and corrections, the occasionally unintelligible ink-smear, the raw narrations as they occurred to me, and with nothing held back for insurance. Was this love I was feeling, or just the benefits of three nights and days of hard work? I was still unwashed, for god's sake, but quite happily so. Or was this the digger's solution, as Lascelles came to believe, a way of telling without having to speak, of getting it off the chest, a gift I could give because I didn't want it in the house, my rotting soul made material, wrapped in brown paper, tied with string, and sent out from me like an exorcised demon?

In truth, what I had in mind, and also in my heart, dare I say it, was something unconditional. Here I am, I would say, in the only version possible. Not a copy, nor a copperplate rendition, a record of events, yes, but from the midst of it, and with my heart's ear still lying close upon the saltwater grave.

A strange type of wooing it was, looking back, this courtship of lancing wounds and weeping sores. It wasn't a rose I would be sending her after all. I could never have known, though I did have an inkling, how the woman she was, born in the way she had been, in a sky-climbing storm signalling her mother's death, would forever after be looking to send the bolts of her own native lightning down into the ground. Daughter of her latitude, she would be at peace only in high drama, free only in the sanctuary of the earth's terrible power. To give her a rose or to pretend there was no blemish would be a uselessness which the western fronts would soon obliterate to grit. And so it was I gave her my boxthorned pain, the faith in my lonely grief instead.

153

XVIII

AROUND MIDNIGHT IN THE CAVE WE LISTENED TO DOGS BARKING IN the valley below, followed by a closer noise and muffled voices. It was much to our surprise and relief that Tassos himself appeared, scrambling up the side of the outcrop with two other *andartes*. Behind them came Adrasteia, wrapped in the brown head-shawl and pointing the unmistakably crisp beam of a German torch into the entrance of the cave.

The first of the two other *andartes* was Dimitris, the burly, sallow-faced giant whose music I had danced to in the villa's courtyard the night before the invasion. I recalled now that he was a doctor as well as a musician, also that his brother's son had been shot in the first reprisals. By pointing at the fire and speaking directly to Tassos, wiping sweat from his brow as he did so, Dimitris made it clear that, after the strenuous and dangerous journey he'd just undertaken, he required coffee and a restorative cigarette before he attended to the patient.

The other man was not an *andarte* at all, but a black-haired English officer dressed in Cretan garb named Spenser. His disguise was so complete that he even sported a flourishing moustache in the local style and Tassos introduced him to us proudly, explaining that Spenser had worked with *Mister John* before the war. Like Pendlebury he spoke fluent Cretan dialect and he too had an intrepid history of combing the island by foot – a skill which appeared to have been an unofficial prerequisite for pre-war archaeological investigations, tailor-made also for the circumstances of the occupation. Spenser had been evacuated from Sfakia at the end of May, and had now been dropped back into the aftermath by Britain's Special Operations Executive to set up wireless communication with Cairo. SOE agents on the island travelled under Greek codenames and Spenser was to be known as Theseus.

As soon as this Pommy Theseus stood by the fire, pulled out his pipe and opened his mouth, to assure us in a plummy tone that 'all was in hand', a deadly shiver went up my spine.

If all was so well in hand, why was my brother lying like a fucking pufferfish at the bottom of the sea?

~

Adrasteia avoided my gaze and stoked the fire, her brown hair falling out of the folds of her shawl as she leant into the smoke. The vicious-ness of the job I'd done on Perry was exposed to me by her presence. She cast not even one furtive glance in my direction and I instinctively understood the shame she felt, not for the pleasures we'd taken on the night-slope but for my missing the evacuation. She would also have been only too aware of the reprisals that were being dealt out to anyone suspected of harbouring or assisting Allied soldiers. We were in danger, all of us, the islanders burdened terribly by our presence. She and I both knew, that as far as I was concerned, it was a burden that could have been avoided.

156

We stood in the mouth of the cave, in a broken circle around the fire, as the Pom Spenser declared through the pucker of his pipe that, given Perry couldn't travel, I was henceforth required as his assistant wireless operator. This he stated with the confidence of his rank, although he was obviously suspicious enough about my moral character, and nervous enough about my state of mind – the state of mind that would burn a fellow Aussie soldier half to death – to allow Tassos, who actually had the genuine authority between the two, to assess my condition.

So before I could react to this declaration of my new role, Tassos directed me out through the cave mouth onto the outcrop, to see whether or not I'd lost my marbles.

The night had cooled. We stood without speaking at first, our attention caught by the dotted light trails the villagers were making in the valley below as they collected snails to eat. I remember they reminded me of the perforated lines on ration tickets I'd seen in Manly just after the outbreak of the war.

Then, at his beckoning, I told Tassos calmly what Perry had told me, reassuring him, and myself too, I s'pose, that my outrage against the Boatman was excessive, yes, but logical also, that I hadn't quite gone mad. Of course, a Cretan like Tassos Kavroulakis will make up his own mind about such things, and so he did. Extending his arms, he clutched me to him, his sympathies evident in the tears in his eyes, before he walked back to the fire in the cave.

When I returned Dimitris had finished his coffee from my tin cup, and after pensively smoking a Korfu Rot from Costas' red sack, he began inspecting Perry's condition by fire and torchlight. Adrasteia mopped Perry's brow with a sponge as the poor little digger was turned on his tummy and onto both sides, prodded and pushed, swabbed and stung with ointments, and stuck with herb poultices. In the doctor's deep undertone, Perry was declared to have broken ribs and severe burns, some of which had become infected. It would be best if he stayed where he was, with Adrasteia as nurse, rather than risk putting him on a mule and taking him back to a house in the village. When his condition improved, he could be moved along south through the zone, but not until then.

And so it was decided. The Boatman would be fed and nursed in the cave while I was considered safe to travel with Spenser across rough terrain towards the high ground of the Lasithi plateau.

Without sentiment or goodbyes, and feeling rather like a convict stripped of my rights, I followed the portly Spenser out of the cave and down off the overhang to where a mule was waiting for us, loaded with gear.

I looked back once to the firelight before we descended, to see Perry lying in his kit in the shadows beyond, Tassos and Dimitris standing to watch us go, the solemn defiance of their faces appearing and disappearing in the rhythm of the flames. Beside the fire, Adrasteia knelt with the makeshift coffee pot, her shawl wrapped tight again, her back to our departure. At the last moment she turned, to offer me some skerrick of dignity. By her gaze I knew she did not wonder how the young soldier she had found so enthusiastic and green could have hardened so quickly. She seemed only to be considering the possibilities of what species of hybrid monster I would now become.

With a hard swallow I stepped off the outcrop and into darkness. And with that swallow, as well as the faintest boyish blush for the sensuality she'd awoken, and an indistinguishable nod of acceptance that I would never attain her brand of sacrificial purpose, I followed Spenser down the scree of the path into the holly oaks, where we added my kit to the pale donkey's burden, and set off.

XIX

I CYCLED THROUGH THE GATE AT WAIT-A-WHILE AND HEADED FOR THE Currie post office the very next morning. I had a tail wind, the roadside pheasants browsing healthily as I followed the old telephone line through Pegarah. I found Lascelles at work beside his father: blotting, franking, sorting, stamping, the two of them visored behind the leather and cedar counter. Kenneth Lascelles was smaller and thinner than his son, with a scientific-looking beard grown without a moustache, and also a widower's non-conversational air. He was the backbone of the post office in Currie, his son John its bleeding heart and inquiring mind, its avid community glue.

Seeing me enter, my hat sparkling from the light shower I'd ridden through, the slim brown parcel brought out from beneath my coat and under my arm, Lascelles the younger hailed me at the door with a satisfaction built squarely on the privilege of information.

'Wesley,' he cried, as if we were partners in an enterprise. 'Any progress with the tooth?'

The healing of my toothache had been a collaboration between the two of us after our discussions in the hotel, but I could not acknowledge it. However, the tone of his question was all by the way of being neigh-bourly – as if there's any other, less intimate relationship to be had on such an island as this – and I couldn't quite ignore it.

'Better, thanks,' I replied, but in a voice held back, like a man who has to sing later in the evening and who's just discovered a tickle at the back of his throat. 'Could I have a word, please?'

Lascelles' grey eyes widened like the lakes after spring rains. He beckoned me with mittened fingers and a thimbled thumb to a table and two chairs where typically the islanders could address their mail, or even compose a letter while they were there. In this instance, however, Lascelles was ushering me as if into an office of consultation.

We sat down at the seats as my mind briefly strove to best judge the delicacies of my request. There was, of course, nothing at all unusual in sending correspondence of a business nature to other residents on King, but to send a personal letter, or in this case a package, to someone who at that very moment was likely to be across the road weighing nails in the co-op, was obviously a matter of some discretion. I had considered the possibilities for bullshitting, such as how I didn't want to interrupt Miss Fermoy during her duties, and how, with my tooth and all, the long ride north to her father's farm was out of the question. In the end, I had considered the first lie to be preposterous, given the culture of informality here on King, and having already ridden across the island and answered Lascelles' question as to the condition of my tooth, I had buggered up the second possibility as well. But this is where the worthy earnestness of a serious joiner such as Lascelles comes into its own, and I knew his desire to help me, and other returned soldiers like me, his sentimental loyalty to the theoretical privations of war and the difficulties of resettlement, would see me right. In short – and now that he is of course my passed-away friend I can say this – it was only to the credit of Lascelles' sympathetic nature that I had complete faith in his ability to help me send the package.

And so it went. Without drumming up any dodgy details I hinted that I was carrying material I knew to be of great interest to Leonie Fermoy. I also implied that my condition of mind – what with all I'd been through (see my po-faced hangdog expression!) – didn't allow me to just bowl in and hand her the material in person, but that given her assistance to me when I was camped on the aerodrome road in my first weeks on the island I would like to show my gratitude.

Lascelles was predictably eager to help, above and beyond the fact that I was merely asking him to exercise his postal duty of making sure an item of mail arrived at its destination. He was a little unexpectedly solicitous though, as if by us sitting at the table talking in gated tones, we were, in some way or another, working as a team once again to attend to my problems. And, as with the tooth, it would be fair to say that we were, though once again, I refused to acknowledge it. Not for an instant. This assisting of soldiers was Lascelles' passion and to take its good with its bad I kept up a painstaking politeness, with hints even of camaraderie, as he agreed to make sure that Leonie received the package with her other mail.

'It goes without saying, Wes,' Lascelles assured me with reinforced sibilance, 'that the postmaster and his son must remain the souls of discretion. And so it shall be.'

I handed over the brown paper package with a weak smile, said my thanks, and watched as Lascelles briefly assessed it in his hands. Heavier than a letter, but obviously consisting of only paper material.

I stood up, he followed, we shook hands. I tipped my hat, and made for the door. Stepping out onto the street, I couldn't help but smile more fully at how keen Lascelles himself would be to read the contents of the package I had entrusted to his care.

XX

WHEN OUR BATTALION HAD FIRST ARRIVED FOR TRAINING IN THE desert at Gaza we'd been talked down to by the British. They'd told us we were stuck out there in that merciless heat because of our fathers' and grandfathers' misbehaviour in the first war. Apparently their whoring and drinking was the reason we weren't stationed in the far more convenient surrounds of Cairo. No mention of the sacrifices our old blokes had made, or of how many, like two of my father's brothers, not to mention my mother's sixteen-year-old brother Neil, had died like pawns on the Pommy chessboard; no, just a ticking off and a warning not to get up to the same tricks. Well, nice to meet you too, we all thought. And so, after now being forced to surrender Crete, and with my brother sunk by the hallowed British navy, my immediate challenge was to work out how I could ever kowtow as assistant wireless operator to this Oxbridge Theseus! By rights, Spenser had every reason to feel a little toey in my company.

As it turned out, it was Spenser who gave me my first good belly laugh since the day the Jerry brollies rained down.

We'd travelled to the plateau by night. Spenser, who'd been up there in the days before the war, was confident he knew the way. Though he had good cause to be suspicious of me, especially given the state Perry was in when we left him, I could have reassured him. I had decided that if I was to find out the truth about the sinking of the *Imperial* then Spenser and his wireless could potentially be the way. If, for instance, we managed to establish contact with Cairo, as Spenser seemed to believe we would from a high peak called Karfi above the plateau, then perhaps some answers could be sought. Such were the conditions of tension – grief, in its pomp, is a Lord with attendant wizards, anger being always a prime mover amongst them but especially so when injustice is at the source of the tragedy – that what might appear an unlikely prospect in an ordinary circumstance seemed then like the proverbial hawser rope flung over the gunwale of a ship for the grasp of a drowning man. And it was I who was drowning, on those drystone paths of the Cretan night, drowning every step of the way with our Baby.

In truth, it was the donkey who became my confidante during those days and nights when we travelled the *kalderini*. Careful as I was to keep Spenser a few steps ahead, it was the donkey, on a firm tether behind, who gave serious and steady counsel to my mutterings.

We slept by day and around dark we'd load up the patient donkey again – the radio, the charging engine and battery (which weighed a ton) hidden in a wicker demijohn – and keep pushing in the direction of the plateau. As the moon shone above so too did the snail-gatherers' lights below. Eventually, as we were finally approaching Karfi on the third night, Spenser became voluble with the memories of times he'd spent up there before the war. On and on we climbed, in pace with the donkey's tread, and on and on Spenser went, *patousia me patousia*, as the Cretans say, puffing and sighing and rabbiting on about the incomparable garrigue we were traipsing through and the Bronze Age shards he swore our feet would be crunching down on even as we spoke. In my distress I had sworn myself to a silent kind of discipline in order to achieve my ends, I knuckled down, objected to nothing, made no sullen cracks as we travelled (except out the corner of my mouth to the mule), and I s'pose I behaved therefore like both the perfect audience and an exemplary Victorian batman.

With the paths becoming narrow and increasingly remote as we climbed, and after some doubt as to whether we had in fact stayed on track at all, it took a further night and almost the whole next day, full of hair-breadth proximity to death or torture every time we passed by a small village or even a rubbly old house tucked into a groin or tangled crook in the path, before, to Spenser's visible relief, we saw the high hulking outcrop of Karfi above us in the last hour of darkness. We were footsore, to say the least, and we could have camped right there below the high molars of grey stone, but like an excited child he wouldn't hear of it. In the lowering gloom, we picked our way across a deceptively vast and steep upland swale, open to the weather on all sides but the south. It was a gruelling penultimate leg to what had been a haul and a half.

As we made that final climb I watched the wheel of the night sky sliding slowly across the heavens above us, stars one by one falling into the distant sea. We reached the top barely an hour before dawn. On dew-wet stones, among a low prickly heath, the donkey and I watched with chagrin as the light rose. Gradually the apron of the coast to our north materialised in the distance below, also the terraced grey teeth of the morbid stone peak that encircled us. I absorbed the scale of the place, its enclosure and aspect, while Spenser, without a hint of tiredness, began to lecture me about the significance of the site.

In their end-days the Minoans had retreated from the grand palaces such as Knossos to the high mountains, in order to escape the mainland invaders. Karfi was the site of Pendlebury's greatest discovery, and Spenser had been there as well. The high ground had been a ritual site in the very last days of a great civilisation, it was literally strewn with epiphanies, and day after day the small group of archaeologists had raced each other from the village of Tzermiado up to the peak to continue the fun.

A deadly cold wind seemed to rise on the light and bite at us where we stood. Spenser didn't seem to notice, until the wind brewed into a sinister bank of muscled cloud inching monstrously across the air at eye level. The peak had been recommended for wireless communications, but it was hardly a practical campsite, and it was no place to prop. Once again we decided to pad on and brave the light, to continue through the morning.

We wound down a tiny goat track on the other side of the peak in search of digs Spenser intended for us in a cave above Tzermiado. The remarkable patchwork of greens and tans of the Lasithi plateau spread out below us and to our right. Like the coast from the Karfi peak, the interior plateau was an arresting sight, but this time I took some pleasure from what I saw. It was like a giant's football ground, ringed by grandstand mountains. At the foot and into the groins of these surrounding mountains nestled tiny white villages, and on the field itself, amongst the plateau's patchwork crops, sailed hundreds of small windmills with white rotating sails. On the far side, looming up and beyond the arena, Spenser pointed out high drifts of snow still clinging to the shaley slopes of the Dikti range.

Eventually we made it down onto the sunlit south-facing ridge where the village of Tzermiado was nestled within the enclosure of the plateau. Spenser halted and began to deliberate in eager whispers, as if to himself I might add, as to the possibility of us forgetting the cave and risking the village straightaway in an attempt to rustle up some of his old Cretan chums from the days of the dig. I sensed that even my mate the donkey was unimpressed by this when he let out a very loud and entirely cheesed-off sigh, with which I heartily concurred. It was not the first time during the previous nights and days when it seemed as if the donkey had kindly taken to speaking on my behalf.

As Spenser was weighing it all up, I suggested as politely as I could that given it was a few years since he'd last been in Tzermiado, and given that presumably quite a bit had changed since, perhaps it was best we stayed on high ground above the village and kept our noses pointed for the cave. That way, I cautioned, with the help of his local knowledge, we could make a reccy and decide how thick the Italians – who had occupied the plateau – were on the ground.

But no, all het up by his return to Karfi in the dawn, Spenser was busting to go and 'knock on the doors of my old chums'. Doggedly then, in a level voice, with my still painfully burnt hand resting for moral support against the muscled neck of the donkey, I persisted, until thankfully he saw the sense in what I was saying. We resumed our path along the ridge in silence, in search of the cave that was to become our new abode.

~

The Trapeza cave above Tzermiado, as archaeologically significant as it may have been, was, like the peak at Karfi, no great shakes as a campsite. Scrabbling down through holly oaks, I followed Spenser onto a small level area in front of a narrow diagonal cleft sprouting with parsley in the southern face of the ridge above the town. It was a good job on his behalf to find the opening: so small and also well camouflaged by the foliage.

The first thing I noticed, even while we were still in the entrance corridor, was how chilled the cave was. As we stepped even further in it was damp as well, completely miserable. Spenser explained, rather belatedly, that he and his friends had never actually felt the need to sleep in such auspicious digs, preferring to avail themselves of beds in the village where they were kept warm under goat-hair blankets, with coffee and yoghurt and plates of cherries ready for them when they woke. Pendlebury had slept in the cave once, but only once, preferring to get his romance by walking alone to various monasteries in the surrounding mountains, where he would spend the night, or several nights, only to come marching back through the windmills and the crops, renewed and refreshed for further excavations.

It made sense to me now why Spenser was so keen to make contact with the local people. Such was the prospect of the domestic comforts ahead of us. I watched by torchlight as he himself grew instantly depressed in the murk of the cave's second chamber and it must have been disheartening for him to have to face the freezing temperature, the mineral darkness, the lack of potable water (it became a regular chore for one of us over the following weeks to sneak round the edge of Tzermiado to where a mountain stream issued in a jetting staccato from a cleft), and the taut monosyllabic strine of his only companion, Private Wesley Cress of the Second AIF, unhappy, disturbed even, guilty also, and in grief. Added to this was the fact that I shared with him a scant knowledge at best of operating the only military equipment by which the two of us could put ourselves to any useful purpose.

Yet operate it we did. And in quite a collaboration. Every night, and with a degree of relief to be in the open air, we would traipse back up the ridge in the darkness to the peak at Karfi where, despite, or perhaps consistent with his boyish qualities, Spenser proved quite electronically minded after all. With our mutual tidbits of knowledge – he from the SOE training ground in Palestine, me from the lessons in the demountables at Ingleburn and also my dad's crystal set in the bellows-shed by the lake – together we managed, as Theseus and Takis (the name he insisted I adopt for the purposes of our official communications), to contact Cairo from that eerie windblown saddle on only our third night of trying.

Of course the unobstructed altitude was a great help once we'd got the gear to fire, and with the antennae hoisted towards the starlight, we were able to pass on our position and eventually to receive information as to our best course of action. Cairo seemed cheered by Theseus' descriptions of the fortress topography of Lasithi, the way the plateau was sunken within its stadium of hills; they also considered it an advantage that it was under Italian rather than German occupation.

Lasithi was also close to one or two smaller plateaux which the nobs in Cairo seemed to think were remote enough to be untroubled even by Eyetie jurisdiction. It transpired, therefore, that they wanted to drop ammo and supplies at night by parachute to one of these smaller plateaux. This, it was decided, would require Theseus and Takis to establish fast and trustworthy contact with villagers, and have bullseyes built from bonfires on the plateaux on level ground, which Cairo stressed should not be less than fifty acres in extent. Meanwhile they would direct other *Francs-tireurs*, as Spenser now took to calling any leftover dregs like myself on the island, to find their way to us to access these supplies, and we would proceed from there.

~

In those first few days near Tzermiado no one knew of our presence in the area. Or so we thought. But it will forever remain a wonder to me how the people of the Cretan mountains manage to communicate with such effectiveness and speed, as if calling with loudhailers down the throats of gorges and from peak to peak, yet all the time with no traceable sound. When we'd returned from Karfi to the Trapeza cave on our fourth night, a night in which we had already decided to begin forays into the village in search of contacts, we sat huddled near the cave entrance when we heard voices approaching from below. I prayed my mate the donkey would remain silent where it was tethered under bushes beside the clearing. As it turned out I needn't have worried, the voices continued on up the ridge beyond us, perhaps a pair of local trappers out on the hunt. But within an hour of that first scare we were visited again, and this time with no forewarning. From where we sat in silent retreat in the cave's second chamber, we heard footsteps and then sharp whispers in the entrance corridor. A match was struck, a lantern flared, its glow spread over the moss and slimy coagulated rock, and two bodies then appeared behind it.

This, as it turned out, was the Kalantzakis brothers, Antonis and Costas, from Kaminaki, a village on the far side of the plateau from Tzermiado. They greeted us, explaining that they had been expecting us for over a week, even before Spenser had met up with myself and Perry in the cave south of Iraklio. The brothers had been checking the Trapeza cave every night to see if we'd showed but on the previous few nights they'd thought better of crossing the plateau due to the presence of a visiting German deputation that had temporarily stationed itself at Agios Georgios to confer with the Italians. The Germans had now left the area and the Kalantzakis brothers were overjoyed to see us two misery-guts shivering in the cave.

From that night on we had constant visitations from the market gardeners of the plateau. The Kalantzakis brothers assured us that the orchestration of the supply drops would indeed be possible, given that their Eyetie overlords seemed only interested in chickens and girls. They took great pleasure from this assessment, but set great store by it too, and thus our plans for the first drop of supplies started in earnest.

Throughout this period I remained haunted not by one but by two images: firstly Vern's face, its features bloated and slack as I imagined them in the drowned hold of the *Imperial*; and secondly, that moment in the first madness of the brolly drop, when he had slashed the paratrooper's throat with the fannie. How, I asked myself, had I let him go off in that mad mood rather than catching him up, when I knew in my bones that only trouble would come of it? The answer wasn't forthcoming. Sadly, it escapes me even now.

~

It was on a full moon evening three nights after the Kalantzakis brothers had found us, as we boiled potatoes in our helmets on the fire in the mouth of the cave and supplemented this dinner with Lasithi bread, that I took the chance to recount for Spenser the events of the night of the evacuation. If my diplomatic tone of the last few days altered as I spoke he seemed not to notice. Without a flinch he listened to my account, to what Perry Coghlan had told me, and to my fears for the fate of my brother and my anger at how he'd been left to go down with the ship by his own navy. I had decided I needed Spenser on-side but lost control a bit in the recounting of events, suggesting that perhaps, if the Great War was any guide, dominion troops were at times considered more expendable than others. This brought nil reaction from him and I didn't harp on it. Instead I tried to convey the depth of my grief for my little brother and my subsequently urgent need to know more of what might have happened on that fateful night.

Spenser's face, lit as it was by the fire and the moonlight, betrayed very little, certainly no annoyance, if anything only a sincere and quite touching sympathy. He made it perfectly clear, however, when I'd said my piece, that my idea to make inquiries through wireless to Cairo would be of no use.

'Simply because the RN's based in Alexandria, Cress. The chaps receiving our messages in the bungalow in Cairo wouldn't know a jot about it. You see?'

This was a stymie that stupidly I hadn't considered. 'Yes, but who's to say it was the navy's decision,' I said desperately. 'To sink the ship, I mean.'

Spenser shook his head. 'Haven't you heard of Cunningham, Cress? The admiral wouldn't have a bar of it. The bloody RN's 110 percent in control, 120 percent of the time. Anything that happens concerning Cunningham's fleet is the responsibility of his admirals alone.'

'Yes, all right but there were hundreds of infantrymen on board. Whose decision was it to let some of them die? In fact, whose decision was it to *kill* them?'

I had raised my voice and Spenser's lips now pursed in distaste. 'Steady on, old boy. You're getting ahead of yourself a bit there I'd say.'

'No, I'm not!' I yelled. 'Coghlan woke up on the *Imperial* as it was hit by the *Hotspur*. He dived off without waking my brother and whoever else was down there snoring. Why else do you think he got so badly burnt in the cave back there? He didn't roll into the fire of his own fuckin' accord you know!'

After so many days alone with Spenser, I was finally boiling over. Mentioning Perry Coghlan's burns like that, as we sat by ourselves in the Trapeza cave, sounded like nothing other than a deadly threat.

In our hot helmets the water was hissing. It was time to eat. But Spenser was now looking at me very warily indeed.

~

Contrary to what might be expected, given the gravity of the situation on the island, Spenser's negotiations with Cairo over the wireless regarding times and protocol for the supply drop on the nearby Limnakaro plain were neither efficient nor brief. After he refused my request outright, I had to climb that ridge and listen three nights running to conversations about a piece that the bloke in Cairo – his codename was 'Tigermilk' – was chasing. In between the details of how he'd met her at some patisserie but snuggled up on a boat at Lake Andreotis, Theseus and Tigermilk would sometimes deign to discuss the details of the supply drop. And all in the codes tapped out by my very own fingers! This is how a beautiful and proud plateau becomes scarred by tragedy, and many times as we waited for the night of the drop I looked out from the bushes in front of the cave with my guts twisting. How dare Spenser say there was no communication possible between Cairo and Alexandria and then carry on like that with his crony! It was like something straight out of Lord Haw-Haw. I knew I couldn't put up with it.

My laughter in the end, however, was deep and rich. The supply drop was a disaster. Night after night, with a posse of Lasithi villagers – most with memories of the grand dance the archaeologists had thrown for them all at Karfi on their last night there before the war – we'd piled up the wood for the two bonfires that would mark the spot for the planes on the Katharo plain, high to the south of Lasithi. That alone was exhausting work because of the stealth required in crossing the plateau and the climb to Katharo, not to mention the inconsistency of muleteers. More than once bundles of dried oak went spiralling down steep and prickly screes.

It had been arranged for a phoney target to be built on flat ground to the west at Limnakaro. The Limnakaro bullseye would have three blazing bushfires and ours only two. That way, it was presumed by the

SOE brass, any German planes flying over would strafe the Limnakaro target and leave us to get on with it. Well, it didn't quite work out like that. After waiting for three successive nights for the plane to arrive, on the fourth night we tended our fires long after the arranged drop-off at 0200 before deciding that once again they had not showed. By 0500 we had returned none the wiser to a sooty low-beamed kitchen in Agio Georgios, on Lasithi's southeastern flank, where we began to hear the drone of planes in the distance.

We received confirmation of the mix-up from a gasping boy who wouldn't have been any more than fourteen years old, and who had quite obviously sprinted his leg of the grapevine to get to us. In torrents of dialect he informed us that the drop had mistakenly taken place at the phoney site on Limnakaro. Added to this, the three bonfire bullseyes had worked beautifully as a decoy and the empty plain at Limnakaro had indeed been strafed mercilessly all night so that no one had been able to get out there to haul in the contents of the drop. It was feared that come daybreak German planes would see the booty on the plain and descend on it. And, even worse, the nearby villages would be punished.

Spenser was suitably chastened by this news. I know because I didn't take my eyes off him. By turns he looked the blushing buffoon and then suddenly, blithely, in casual control. Truth was, it had been a good plan administered with indiscipline. There is nothing worse for morale in desperate times than a promising plan gone terribly wrong through incompetence. As the villagers wandered off through the fields towards their homes there was an uncharacteristic mope to their walk. Their shoulders were slumped, they were anxious and downcast. Like all the *andartes* I'd met so far, their appetite for doing what had to be done was insatiable, and, due in part to their relations with the archaeologists before the fighting started, they had put great faith in the British. But now, though perhaps even before now, they got a strong whiff of something less admirable. Spenser was hardly the brilliant leader they had considered Pendlebury to be, and with this ill-managed fiasco there was now a heavy air above the plateau of suspicions confirmed. Exhausted, bedraggled, with the smoke of the bonfires all over them, their spirits tired from the futility of the exercise, they departed like sad spectres from the firelight inside the pokey kitchen in Agios Georgios.

I hated the fact that I was now lumped in with diminished respect. As we crossed back towards the cave with a silent Costas Kalantzakis, I sensed that Theseus and Takis were viewed as a pair. I'd not had the chance, nor the lingo, to put that right.

~

After Costas had fulfilled his duty by seeing us back to the ridge, Spenser and I were on our own again. We entered the chill of the cave and he sat by his gear, picked the snail grit from his teeth with his jack-knife. We were a sorry pair and those tough spud farmers of the Lasithi plateau would have been better off without us. I sat there stewing, feeling terrible about everything until eventually, as Spenser readied himself for sleep, I made my decision.

I would go. My mind was not on the job of defending Crete and, as much as I admired the *andartes*, I wasn't in step with them. When Spenser had me tap out the nonsense to his mates over the wireless, I should have foreseen the supply drop would end in disaster. Instead, all I had been worried about was his refusal to let me ask questions about the *Imperial*. That is hard to admit. How one man's sorrows can lead to a hundred more.

The dejected mood of the villagers, the silence of Costas Kalantzakis in particular, had shown me my shame. Even my image of Vern had changed with the dawning of this new fiasco. I saw him alive now on the submerged ship, trying to breaststroke a way out through any porthole or passageway. His air was running out. I couldn't escape from the effect of his desperation any more than he could escape from the boat, our fates were entwined. I remained glued in my thoughts to this harrowing sight of a marine Hades.

There was nothing to be done. I had to get out of that cave, out of that fortress of mountains, to keep moving south towards the coast. The Cretans knew, courtesy of the Republican war and the years resisting the Turks and the Venetian occupation before that, they knew what it was like to lose loved ones to brutality and injustice. They understood the inevitability of human betrayal. But I didn't. Though I was quickly learning.

Spenser was soon snoring – even now I think it's somehow poignant how the plummy vowels disappear in the democracy of sleep, as does the strine – and I found myself standing over him with his polished Smith and Wesson in my hand. I watched those blubbery lips shuddering with every departing breath, the upturned tips of his Cretan-style moustache twitching like a cat's whiskers as he dreamed. And once again, as I had with Perry Coghlan, I trained a gun on an ally in the bowels of the earth.

I couldn't bear the unassailability any longer. The Imperial license to stuff up. In a fit of self-importance I convinced myself that before I walked out of that cave above Tzermiado I would do something, just a little something, on behalf of the good people there. So they wouldn't have to execute an old friend of Pendlebury themselves. I would avert the danger for them, the mishaps to come, and relieve my own shame a little by doing so. At the very least, I would declare that I was never

Takis and that the Pommy Theseus and I had never been, and would never be, a pair.

It was as I thought these mock-honourable thoughts, pretending to myself for a few brief moments that I truly cared about those villagers of the plateau, that I saw the joke that appealed to me more. Below me, Spenser's moustache continued to twitch. How dare he wear that flamboyant moustache in the name of *Kriti*, I thought. When in truth he was more concerned with a woman on Lake Andreotis than with getting the supply drop right. Like the bastards who'd left my brother to drown, Spenser didn't only deserve to die, he deserved to be humiliated first.

I thrust the revolver into my belt and walked over to the red carpet bag Spenser had carried all the way from the first cave. Taking out his shaving gear, his fannie, a map, his Korfu Rot and his scissors, I walked over to my own pile and stuffed them all inside. Except for the scissors. Gathering up my bag in readiness for departure, and also my rifle and the pig's bladder we had used for carrying water on our way up to the plateau, I walked over and placed it all in the corridor at the mouth of the cave.

In chivalrous pose then, on bended knee rather like some ironic knight, I brandished the British army scissors in the torchlight beside Spenser's plump and snoring head. With one easy snip I cut off the upturned right-hand side flourish of his moustache. I gathered my things, untethered the donkey, and set off laughing down the ridge.

~

The truth is, I felt it then, and, despite my terrible doubts at the time of writing to Leonie, I feel it now: despite my rage in the cave with Perry, it was a great thing I'd done to the Pom up at Lasithi. It was something, at last, to be proud of. The fact that it was never gonna earn me a VC is hardly any fault of mine.

The Kalantzakis brothers of the Lasithi plateau would make their way back up to the cave later that day, in readiness to assess the wrong of the day before, and my message would be clear. A man with only half his moustache is surely not to be trusted. He is either mad, or he is running with the hare and hunting with the hounds. With that one snip I had delivered my verdict, disentangled myself, and avoided the additional shame of having killed a man in his sleep. And so my laughter that morning was not only in the nature of a practical joke but, as the English themselves might say, for the rare excellence and economy of my deed. Any way I look at it now, it was the noble thing to do.

I had a clear aim in my mind now that I was finally on my own. Technically, I had a responsibility to make it back to my unit, but for the moment I just had to survive and make my way south to the coast, where I presumed I would comb the fishing villages in search of a boat. I was still prepared to believe that, with a bit of luck, I could front up in Alex, even in Cairo if necessary, and start asking questions. I would request permission, knock on doors, explore official and unofficial channels, demand an explanation. Sitting here now, on this more realistic island, I can only scoff at the layers of illusion I was under, the imaginative warp that came as part of grief's cohort. Some days I wander the beaches here and literally moan like a seabird at the way the horrors filleted my thought processes. But one thing I knew for sure was: I could not fight on in the way we had been, not under those flags and not for the principles they espoused, until I had either confirmed or scotched my suspicions of what happened to our Baby.

A full week afterwards however I was still in the arena of Lasithi, stymied in my desire to go south by local hospitality that ensued from an appreciation of my joke. Word had travelled quickly down from the cave that morning and the missing half of Theseus' moustache had aligned with local suspicions. I was making my way gingerly with the donkey, stepping down through the blood-red poppies cackling my head off, then feeling the effects when my laughter had dwindled, of keeping those bullseye-bonfires going all night, the sheer lack of sleep. And with the tiredness my healing hand began to play up, the blisters opening, and so my niggliness returned, my distress and my umbrage. I mouthed it all to my mate the mule, who by this time I had nicknamed Simmo, after the legendary donkey of Gallipoli in the first war, who had, according to my dad and his brothers, worked with a bloke called Simpson to help carry the wounded from the disastrous frontline of that other British-led fiasco. Now I reassured Simmo that we would find somewhere dry and well grassed. I would take out the archaeological mud map I'd stolen from Spenser, and plot our likely escape. I told him I would always be grateful for his solidarity but also that the bonus of my getting to Egypt to find out the truth would be that I would also be off his bloody island. The island where a clear-sighted animal like him would always feel at home but where I had lost my innocence, in more ways than one.

~

It was as we passed above a narrow lane of a small village, still hanging off the mountainside but east of Tzermiado, dressed in my Cretan bog-catchers, black shirt, goat-hair vest, AIF boots and with Spenser's Smith and Wesson hidden under my shepherd's cummerbund, that I was hailed by a short stout villager and called enthusiastically down through scrubby thyme and on through a narrow doorway. Determined as I was to press on for official explanations, my heart finished with the laughter

179

by now, I did my best to refuse but the cheery soul would have none of it. He was a middle-aged man, his hair grey, the pallor of his wide jaw a living parchment of tobacco smoking and healthy mountain air. But his delight in chancing upon me was excessive, his exaggerated happiness at the sight of me almost preposterous, and despite internal cursing I allowed myself, after tethering Simmo to a surprising gum tree beside his house wall, to be ushered inside.

He took me down a brief dim hallway, then into a small low-beamed room stuffed to the gills with women and children. With repeated references to 'Mister English' I was welcomed to a table where coffee and roasted nuts, cherries and boiled eggs had been hastily arranged. This was his extended family, none of whom spoke English, and so there was much nodding and pushing forward of various plates and a beaten coffeepot; I'd already learnt that the little amount of Iraklio dialect I had picked up from Tassos meant next to nothing on the plateau.

I was figuring I'd just stay polite and leave at an appropriate moment to find a safe place to sleep out in the hills on the southern side of the plateau. Before long, however, I was being cajoled to rise from my chair and to follow my original host, whose name was Manolis, back down the corridor and out into the street. A black-garbed woman stuffed chunks of dried bread into my bag and patted me fondly as I backed out of the house. Quite frankly, I didn't know where to look.

Manolis, still inexplicably overjoyed to be in my company, had me follow him down the narrow lane to another house. He called and banged on the worn blue door with his fist until a man answered. There was a quick spirited exchange, in which I got the distinct impression that I was the issue being discussed. The man at the door smiled at me courteously and stepped out with us into the dirt street. He was impeccably neat, with a pure black goatee trimmed to an absolute point that reminded me of Bert Regan, the president of the Colac Turf Club. He closed his door behind him and amidst more rapid discussion the three of us set off back the way Manolis and I had come.

Arriving back to the central lane of the village we turned right and continued down a drystoned slope, past doorways upon which and into which Manolis, with what seemed an alarming lack of discretion, shouted and whistled with glee for the inhabitants to come out and join the party. I saw crone-like faces peering from the dark entranceways to see what all the fuss was about and I began to feel like the lone camel I once saw paraded down the main street of Geelong. The possibility crossed my mind that I had fallen into a village of Axis sympathisers – *Gestapedes* was the local term – and that I was being marched off to some kind of public execution. Why else would they be taking such an interest?

As it turned out this little village of Marmaketo was anything but a *Gestapedes* stronghold. Eventually, with perhaps a dozen people in tow – mostly men but also women, children, and one huge Alsatian dog – Manolis led us to the village *kaphenoi*, which we entered through saloon-like doors to a fairly rousing reception. Manolis stepped to one side of me as the card players and smokers turned towards the door. With open palms upturned in my direction, he appeared to speak passionately of my bona fides and before too long I was seated at a central round table with plates of meat, potatoes, beans, bread, a bottomless glass of raki, and clusters of conversation flying about me like thrip on a hot day by the lake back home.

There was much happy laughter in the room, and not an Italian soldier to be seen anywhere. Manolis was slapped on the back and embraced, as if he was quite the hero for bringing me in. There seemed to be no fear of discovery, no reason to curtail pride and joy. I had gone from hiding out in caves, as instructed by the *andarte* networks, to being the toast of a Lasithi village. As the hours went by the festivities grew and the reason for this strange behaviour emerged bit by bit. I heard the words

'Mister English' mentioned a lot, the name 'Pendlebury' and 'Mister John' too. Initially I presumed all three of these names referred to the same person, but it wasn't until Manolis' friend with the beard like Bert Regan's explained the distinction that I could see some of the reason for all the fuss.

Back in '36 and '37, in those summer seasons Spenser had told me about on our long walk to Karfi, when he and Pendlebury and the others had first excavated on the Lasithi plateau, there had been an almost unending rapport between the visiting party and the people of the hills. This, according to the broken English of Manolis' friend, was largely to do with Pendlebury's great personality. He was given Lasithi clothes to wear and he wore them proudly, believing that the clay shards he was uncovering on the windy saddle of Karfi were part of an unbroken line connecting to the villagers he was eating and dancing with in the *kaphenois*.

This, however, had not been the case with Spenser. Whereas 'Mister John' was soon kitted out with a Venetian sword, bog-catchers and the like, Spenser refused and his relations with the Cretans were uneasy. At the time, the local people were hurt by this but they did their best to excuse his ill manners. If he would prefer to sweat all day in Irish linens and Scotch waistcoats than have his own differences absorbed into the surrounding vistas by donning the local garb, that was up to him.

So when Spenser and I turned up with the wireless set at Karfi, the people of the plateau were bemused to see that he'd donned the island *mufti*, even to the extent of the curling native moustache. When the supply drop was bungled, most people involved had let their dislike of 'Theseus' run free. And this is where I came in. Ignorant, but for once it seemed inspired, and in luck, the snipping of Theseus' moustache had made an unwitting legend of me on the plateau. The *mantinades* on the subject were already flowing in the *kaphenoi* because I had managed to perfectly express what neither a university education nor sheer bitter-ness could authentically employ – the necessary sting in the tale.

~

The hours rumbled by in the rowdy *kaphenoi* and more and more people arrived to enjoy the festive occasion. Once it was explained how Spenser had refused the local culture in the days of free choice, I found it harder to resist my role. The party went on into the night, with still no visible anxiety about Eyetie surveillance, and absolutely no acknowledgement that the whole island, including such high and remote ground as we were on, was under Axis occupation.

At a late hour I was escorted by Manolis back to his family house. I was shown into a small room, with a trough and a bed whose sheets were made from what looked to me like coarsely stitched parachute silk. The next morning I woke, disorientated, until I noticed the doleful eyes of Simmo staring in at me through the glassless window. The poor beast was nothing if not steadfast, and by his look he'd been watching over me all night.

Sometime later I was brought a potato omelette with the scent of dittany, and coffee, and told by Manolis' friend with the Bert Regan beard that I was to be taken to the village barber. (I did learn the name of this friend of Manolis' the previous evening but in the swing of the festivities had taken to calling him Bert, a name which his fellow Marmaketans, with some amusement, instantly adopted. I've wondered ever since if he will go in honour to his grave under the name of a western district racing doyen.)

At the barber's, in front of a dozen or so excitable spectators, my hair was dyed black with a foul-smelling liquid, and my throat and face, aside from my moustache, which was also dyed, were shaven clean. The barber was a tiny old bloke with inflamed drooping eyelids, but his hand was steady throughout. When he'd finished the job he bowed in what seemed an antique manner and made me a parting gift of a small ceramic jar of the dye. He handed it over with great ceremony, the jar containing a secret weapon for the months to come, and I nodded my thanks, feeling a further layer of guilt at how misplaced I intended their faith in my commitment to be.

Festivities resumed at the *kaphenoi* on that second day, and by the afternoon I felt already quite drunk again, but also increasingly uneasy. I began to falter in my politeness, to worry about the Eyeties, and to think again of Vern. He would have relished this unending rapport on the plateau but it was I who was in his place now, I who was being feted as a luminary, and, by the afternoon, I felt a familiar phoniness, like I had when he was stuck on the farm teaching himself Greek and I was off wasting the old man's time and money at school. Once again I was sure the big wide world had got the wrong man and my only possible absolution seemed to be to get to the south coast and then to Egypt to start asking questions.

The fervour of Manolis' possessive pride, the relish of the villagers for a folktale such as I had produced, broke out into dancing by nightfall. The nights of the plateau had been growing increasingly cold with the autumn and by now fires were lit in the *kaphenoi*, around which the *mantinades* continued tumbling and raucous, as the lyras were bowed. I grew glum. I had legendary shoes to fill but only Corangamite feet to fill them, and midst these unusual mountain people I felt my overwhelming ordinariness to be something more like Spenser than Pendlebury, more like myself than Vern. But no one seemed to notice my mood. My new head of black hair was praised, my health was toasted, and every few minutes a swarthy face would leer at me out of the tobacco smoke, laughing and babbling his approval of the snipping of the moustache.

It seemed a given that Manolis' life would never be the same again, and late on that second evening he began to grow maudlin in his thanks. After two days he was now inconsolably drunk, and began to cry on my shoulder with a melancholy gratitude. With the excuse of needing a leak, I extricated myself and managed to plead with Bert to guide me back to the house.

It was well past midnight. We walked soberly down the lane. Gradually the tick of the windmills in the fields beyond the village replaced the din of the *kaphenoi* subsiding behind us. At the low door of Manolis' family house I made it clear to gentle Bert that I needed to move on the following day. He tut-tutted through his shapely whiskers, not because he didn't find my desire reasonable but because he knew my departure would be resisted at all costs.

At last, after we shared a smoke from a packet of *Sigarette Nazionali* he'd produced from the folds of his mountain jacket, Bert agreed to talk to Manolis in the morning. To prepare the way for my exit. Or that was how I understood it, from his broken English. With a soft embrace, he bade me goodnight.

~

I woke late the next morning in my little room to find Manolis sitting on the end of my bed, staring at me. I knew immediately that Bert and he had spoken. I could see the worry in his eyes, the sense that his proximity to my legend was slipping away. I could also see that he wouldn't let go without a fight, though a strange and lugubrious old fight it was going to be.

I ate breakfast in the large kitchen at the end of the dark corridor. It was clear by the family's behaviour that they also had been told of my intentions. It was presumed, of course, that my keen sense of duty as a soldier was what was making me depart, which made it difficult for Manolis to hold me back. He sat opposite me at the breakfast table, tortured by a peculiar struggle between equally admirable forces: legendary hospitality on one hand and a warrior's courage on the other.

By lunchtime we were back in the *kaphenoi* and a third day of festivities had begun to brew in my honour, if a little tentatively. In the hope of preserving a sober mood I began asking about the Eyeties. Wouldn't they pounce on us at any moment? Surely such brazen celebration in the village *kaphenoi* wasn't safe? But this ploy backfired, encouraging only more rowdy laughter. The complete absence of Italian surveillance was explained away cheerfully as par for the course; they were lazy, I was told, they didn't want to be in Crete, and would most likely approve of the joke made at Theseus' expense. Bert explained over more raki that the Italians were doing their best to treat the remoteness of the plateau as a chance for a holiday. As such, a tacit agreement had been struck between the plateau and their occupiers, an agreement which involved subtle collusion to protect Lasithi from the manic streak of the Germans. Bert spoke in soft philosophical tones of this arrangement, telling me that although the villagers would take advantage of the freedom while it lasted he feared for what it may eventually lead to.

After many toasts, which I tried to accept with a valedictory grace, I made it adamantly clear that my time had come. I must leave. Rising from my chair, I did my best to make a point of publicly farewelling my principal host, but he would have none of it. He petulantly turned his back on me when I approached for a parting embrace.

Well, now I was getting plain angry. After unsuccessful remonstrations with Manolis himself, I pleaded with Bert for help. Finally, to my great relief, Manolis, who I had, after all, merely happened to bump into, sulkily agreed to guide me south out of the plateau.

Morosely then, reluctantly, in a filthy mood and without a single word, he walked me back to his house where, after I'd said my farewells to his shy but teary family, we untethered Simmo and headed across the plateau.

~

Along the maze of cart-tracks through the flat crops we went, silently, with the Dikti range looming ahead, the breeze in the rustling leaves of the trackside plane trees and the soft thwack of the windmill sails beating gently under the donkey's tread. We crossed, and crisscrossed, rows of potatoes and broad beans, just two inconspicuous farmers of the plateau walking low across the patchwork ringed by a fortress of mountains.

When we arrived on the far side, in the village of Kaminaki, where the Kalantzakis brothers were from, we passed straight through the rustic lanes, without a word, on and up a winding route into the mountains.

We climbed amongst the clonk of the goat bells for what seemed like two or three hours, rising above the plateau, with eagles soaring above us in the chill, and long views into the west, and still the towering snow-patched slopes of Mount Dikti ahead in the southeast. The sullen Manolis led the way through stony switchbacks for what seemed an interminably long time until finally he halted at a fork in the track. To the right, I could see a path slowly declining into the west. To the left, another track simply wound further up, through more stony scrub, though in truth I couldn't see far in either direction.

Standing motionless at the fork Manolis simply stared at me. His leathery face seemed no longer sad but defiant, and more than a tad derisive.

I asked him, by pointing and gesturing, which way I should go. He shrugged, and replied, in plain English: 'Free choice.'

I opened my arms wide and turned in an incredulous arc to the hills around, as if to say: 'How would I know which way to go, I'm not from here!'

He only shrugged again.

He felt, I'm sure, that I had misunderstood the reason for the festivities he had initiated on my behalf, and by his next gesture he made it clear that I had also misunderstood the whole point of life itself.

Feeling too annoyed now to attempt an embrace I thrust out my hand to shake his in farewell. He refused. His arm stayed by his side. With a look of intense dignity he stared into the distance.

Rightio then, I thought. Left with no alternative I slowly led Simmo along the track that continued uphill over the mountains.

But after only a few steps I heard Manolis shout. I turned around.

He stood, this enigmatic spud farmer of Lasithi, brandishing a lemon in one hand and with his other pointing above us at the sun. He shook the lemon violently in front of his face and thrust his pointing finger repeatedly into the sky. He said a word, in his own language, one word, over and over again, as he shook the lemon and prodded his finger into blue air.

He was telling me something, but I was none the wiser. And so he concluded finally that I was a dead loss. He turned in disgust and walked away.

XXI

IN THE DAYS AFTER I'D LEFT THE PACKAGE WITH LASCELLES I HAD NO peace. The straits were pitched in the furies of late autumn, warning only of a wintry future, coming headlong at my hut. When the easterly blows, in this ever westerly realm, it seems indeed to be against nature. It is like being caught in a backlash where the routine of dominant forces is finally overcome. Added to this, just as the westerly invariably has a degree of southerly in it, thereby mustering the icy objectivity of Antarctica, so too the easterly often holds a glancing wedge of the north, the fuming streak of the mainland, which rather than the clean truth of the south, seems to usher in a man-made retribution, as if every scuffing whitecap contains a wicked human curse.

I battened down, wrote not another word, and worried myself sick at how my package would be received.

Then, after four days in the brunt of the weather on Wait-a-While, days in which not even a rodent let alone a wallaby was seen, the backlashing petered out and in some kind of missed meteorological stitch I went for a ride.

My limbs were stiff but it cleared my head to roll downhill to Naracoopa and inspect the damage. I pedalled south through the storm-muddied tunnel of tea-tree beyond the jetty until I popped out onto the Tuddenhams' bone-strewn pastures running along to the reefs of the shore.

For a while I stood amongst scurrying ground birds, lichened boulders and terraced cowpats, observing the washed-up feeling you get after such a storm. It occurred to me then how the weather on this island could wear anything away, flesh and muscle, joy and sadness, a caustic idealism such as mine, or even a commitment to die. For what would be the point of that? On the coasty paddocks the new light picked up the blond glare of bones. It would happen soon enough. Right then it seemed big-headed, vainglorious, among other things, to bring it on any quicker. So any terrible thoughts I'd had during those wrecking days from the east I now dismissed as inconsequential.

I made my way back through the tea-tree and wheeled the bike out onto the long jetty for a peek. Not a soul around. I scouted out for an hour or two along the beach north of there, wandering parallel to the narrow road and right past where I now sit, and then, pushing the bike back up the long haul to Wait-a-While, noticed my gate had been closed with one less loop of the chain. Pushing through, I warily rounded the tank stand south of the house to find not a visitor but a box waiting for me under the bullnose at my front door.

I stepped inside, fired up the stove, put the kettle on. Didn't wait for it to boil though. I sat down at the table and inspected the wooden box. Printed on its flat lid, in faded lettering, were the words:

BINNEY BROS. STATIONERS

MURRAY STREET COLAC

For a start, a shiver went up my spine. The Binneys had run the newsagency in Colac since long before I was born.

I knew now where the box had come from. She was half Ondit, half whaleship. The Ondit half was the box. The whaleship half lay waiting under the lid.

Gently prising it off, I found inside the parcel I had sent through Lascelles, and beside that a small object wrapped in white muslin.

Lifting out my pages I could see they had been resting in the box, along with the muslin-wrapped object, on a bed of carefully arranged green tissue paper.

Holding the pages again in my hands it was immediately obvious that, at the very least, they had been looked at, and then loosely repackaged.

I placed them aside on the table, thinking the worst. Then, lifting out the object in the muslin – it was heavy in the hand – I folded back the cloth to find a cut-glass bottle of ink. At the bottom of the box lay a note.

Her handwriting is backhanded, as if each word is walking into a gale.

Dear Wesley,

When I was little at Yellow Rock my Pop showd me how to do this. He made his own from cuddlefish, for the scrimshore you see. So, happy memories for me, catching them at nite with the squidding lite, preparing the ink saks in the morning. Im glad to have a reasan to make some more.

I read what you sent me but wood hate for anything to happen to the pages here at Tucks.

Leonie

I sat stunned, bottle in one hand, her note in the other. Until the over-filled kettle started splurging hot water all over the top of the stove.

~

Just before midnight I thoroughly cleaned my old fountain pen and sat down to write. Such a churn of contrary emotions were now moving through me: honour, dishonour, anger, wisdom, belief in some possibility of warmth and dignity, and a total lack of regard. I pressed on regardless, committed now to bringing my shadows out into the world rather than letting them fester into dark and dampness.

With the first scratch of my nib on the paper I was propelled both forward and back. I suffered all over again, but this time wondering in dark brown *cuddlefish* ink whether or not every route we take, left or right, east or west, through bitter citrus or healing eucalyptus, will always, eventually, lead us to where we are ultimately destined to be.

XXII

I HAD NO BETTER FRIEND IN THOSE DAYS THAN SIMMO THE DONKEY. He'd travelled with me from back at the smoky cave with Perry Coghlan, through the hot days and cold nights with Spenser, hauling the wireless gear night after night up the steep climb to Karfi, and now beyond on a track of free choice, which I hoped would take us towards the south and the sea of caiques, but which looked likely to take us down a dead end to some macabre goat-fold full of like-minded corpses.

And I ask you this, how *do* human beings generally behave to such dear friends and companions as the donkey was to me? It was he, of all creatures, that had done me no wrong; he was at times niggly, at times blunt, but that only saw us well in harmony with each other, and it had even crossed my mind as I noticed him quietly biding his time in the narrow yard back at Marmaketo, patiently waiting and watching as my exalted status in the town turned sour, that he quite possibly was some higher, more loyal, incarnation of life. But a donkey is a donkey after all, especially to an Australian, who has little experience of them, and only knows of their status in life's pecking order by how they compare to a horse. Yet I figured now that an inverse of that pecking order would be just the sort of irony the world would dish up. Yes, a donkey as confidant, as priest and loyal sage, its only flaw a stubbornness born from being so tragically misunderstood by slow-witted humans, who thought of themselves as its masters.

But three days and nights out from that fork in the road at Marmaketo, days and nights in which I had wound southwards but up onto increasingly steep and treeless terrain, where the temperature seemed to have halved and all the sustenance of plants had gone from the world, I was faced with yet another moment of difficult choosing, though this time the choice was not exactly free.

During those slow-going three days and nights I had faltered, doubted, taken a promising looking turn-off by an abandoned wayside monastery, doubted again, turned back, taken another wrong turn, and found once more the route I had chosen back at the fork. I'd been forewarned at Marmaketo that the way south could be difficult but, despite the view from the plateau of the towering cold grey slopes ahead, I had no way of knowing exactly what that meant. Eventually I had climbed upon Simmo's back to ride higher and higher into the cold landscape of schist and shale.

Now, as the donkey plodded on up the steep rubbly gradient, the mad zone of the Marmaketo *kaphenoi* receded like a hospitable lowland behind me. We climbed even higher towards the chill crystal of an azure sky, so high in fact that I became dizzy on my perch, in part no doubt from worry and also my meagre provisions. With Bert's words of warning about the difficulties of the mountains resounding in my ears, and still with insistent mental flashes of Vern tearing away from the dead German in the bloodstained oleanders beside Tassos' villa, I had to climb down off Simmo's back to walk on solid ground.

What about this island? I thought, with my feet slipping about on the shaley ground as we climbed on. Full of golden oil and fragrant airs one minute, human warmth and generosity the next, only to become as inscrutable, complicated and eerie as the moon. One day I'm surrounded by an invaded people chiacking in a well-stocked café, the next I'm struggling alone up a purgatorial scarp, where nothing nutritious seemed to have survived the great earthquake of 600 AD Spenser had told me about. My brain clanged against its casing. I expected to sniff the burning wings of Icarus at any moment, as nut by nut and cherry by orange I chewed through all my panniered food.

So it was that on the fourth consecutive day of directionless looping and climbing I once again backtracked from a turn I'd taken, reorienting myself and climbing again towards the southern sky, but still unsure of the route I was on. Hours later, Simmo and I stumbled into the rocky duct of what appeared to be a remote windmill site.

A wind of ice had been whistling about us in the previous hour of our ascent. I was worn out. I ducked into this roofless ruin and pulled a reluctant Simmo on his tether deep between the loosely masoned walls of the shelter, to save him also from that bastard of a wind. The gap of the stone wedgecut was barely fifteen feet wide but substantial enough to get us out of the worst of it. It had been haphazardly floored with timber planking many years ago and was now partially filled in by the large stone boulders of the collapsed windmill. Perhaps in some height of summer it was once inhabited, by a shepherd or some visionary klepht taking refuge from an encroaching world. It seemed barely possible in its present condition. I looked out from an uneven seat on the pile of rocks onto a remorseless hill-face over a canyon of air, where more white rock and funereal shale fell in streaks from the sky.

Simmo stood dead still in this closet, arse to the opening, eyes staring straight back into me as if he already knew what was coming. I understood why he didn't want to shift his feet amongst the awkward angles of the rock clutter and old flooring, but nevertheless his stillness and stare were unnerving. As if all we had between us was a truth as bare as the mountain.

So I got up and tugged him so that he stood side to side across the open entrance, rather than facing me. And there he stood, my buttress to a world closing in, the knowledge in his eyes having already planted the seed of his own demise in my head.

After extensive rummaging and double-checking of my kit on the way up in the wind, I had verified that I was not only low on tucker, I was out. One last sliver of cooked marrow remained, a morsel the size of two thumbnails, and with one eager slurp it was gone. With that swallow my plight sunk heavily upon me. I had barely eaten anything since the middle of the previous day, I'd rushed out of the plateau in a frustrated panic, refusing the dogged hospitalities, unprepared, with late autumn closing in towards winter. I had climbed a barren mountain with no exact knowledge of where I was going, and now from my seat in the wedgecut of the windmill I realised that, amongst his other criticisms of me, Manolis must have thought I had a death wish leaving the way I did. I huddled in on what felt like the edge of falling, with no food, no water, no mother or brother, and with more mountain still rising above.

Sometime in the next hour or so my body began to shake, my teeth to rattle. Our Baby may well have been at the bottom of the sea and I high on an alpine moonscape but as those minutes and hours went by our fates began to amount to pretty much the same thing in my mind. To be honest, I was terrified. There were no sharks to gouge me but an enormous black vulture was circling in silence over my head, as if, like Simmo, it knew what was coming next. I knew vultures preyed only on the dead and so I became further spooked by its presence. It was reading my mind.

Shaken, I prised out some worn and tired planks of the old mill structure and was able to make a fire to keep warm. And slowly, ever so slowly now, with an ache and gnaw in my guts, the night crept like the devil's glove over the white hand of the world.

~

I lay awkwardly all night long, like something strewn upon the rocks, the cold whacking me each time I woke, ruining any relief from the nightmares. By the time the sun eventually rose I had a plan of action fixed in my mind. Sitting here now it seems half crazy but back then it could not be avoided: I could not continue without food.

There before me stood a carcass of meat. Occasionally it would blink or protrude its teeth, they were its only movements. It was the only living thing, apart from the vulture, among the cold boulders on that Mediterranean moon.

As a weakling sun inched higher above the jut of the windmill, I hoisted up my body, took out Spenser's revolver, and shot Simmo.

I had aimed for the plate of hard skull bone just above his eyes but at the last minute he turned away, the bullet smashing into the base of his ear.

I heard his awful cry as he buckled forward amongst the awkward rocks, his foreleg making a sharp crack as it snapped when he fell. In high glare I watched him shudder and shudder again. Another bullet. Not stone dead, but then, soon enough.

My own shaking ceased, my soul was stunned. On that precipice of a morning I was the beast, as the donkey's old muscles stiffened and a rectangular lake of dark blood pooled in a gap of limestone cubes at my feet.

~

We had a thing for butchers back in Colac, a thing for steak like butter, and how it got that way. There was the grass, of course, the lake air and breeding, but there was the craft, to be admired, of butchery. George 'Rowdy' Lee was the pick, a quiet bloke, with his well-dressed carcasses hanging expertly in Murray Street. No amount of small-town gossip or bluster or big-noting could ever dissuade my father that Rowdy Lee wasn't a kind of genius. I remember him as pigeon-chested, small, with a silent confidence. Brief in conversation, occasionally he'd toss us kids cigarette cards, and if you caught him on the right morning you'd be treated from behind the counter-wire to an exhibition of flamboyance with the blade.

I was laughing, laughing black as the first war whores of Cairo, hacking into Simmo with Spenser's fannie. I was thinking of Rowdy Lee, his Otway sawdust and shining plate glass, back on that other earth I had lost, as he honed his steels and looked out the window across Murray Street onto the war memorial. By contrast, I split the hide artlessly, gouging through corded sinew into the aged and marbled meat.

As I hacked away I could feel those eyes upon me. Black eyes, under hooded lids: expert, fierce and eternal.

When my belly was full – the roasted meat tasted in the end like a hessian sack, so coarse and hard to tear apart, I'm sure the vulture would have made a better job of it – I carved out a dozen or so chunks from the carcass, mostly by gouging at the hindquarters with the fannie, wrapped them singly in torn cloth from my spare Cretan shirt and stowed them away in my kit for the journey. I hear the ripping sound now as I tear the flesh away from the old hide. It's almost identical to the tearing of the shirt. And I sit, to all intents and purposes ready to continue the climb, but fixed to the spot by a self-disdain deeply nurtured by exhaustion, isolation, redoubled grief, and the parched freeze of the air on speech-less heights.

I sat by the fire unable to escape the eyes of the circling vulture or the slain donkey. Among the blood and stones, it came clear to me, with the philosophical energy afforded by the meal. The beast lying exposed across the angles of the boulders, cratered like the bombed groves around Iraklio, had fulfilled its duty and been repaid with a misfired shot and amateur butchery.

So it was, so I felt and do; and in that high ruin I attained a thorough complicity with the nature of the world, my own cold shale of treachery finally shedding a few drops of salt moisture down my cheeks, not for Vern this time, not even for Simmo who had carried me high to the realisation, but to what both of those deaths now symbolised: a random world without a god.

~

The turn of the mountain path, then its switchback into the opening of a valley and the downward pass when I came upon it barely an hour later, represented nothing to me other than my own shithouse lack of faith. So my one true and undivided mate had been butchered needlessly, by a weak man panicking at the top of a farm ladder, a man who'd lost his brother but who could have pushed himself further, pushed himself higher up the path and seen what now his eyes could see: across two small brown spines of land, a white village, waiting in its high fold at the end of a narrow vale.

Slowly, as I walked the three hours down the path through the easy ground, I threw each wrapped piece of Simmo's flesh away from me, watching them thud or stick in the dried streambed to my right, or even roll to the butt of some stunted tamarisk or bush of thyme, plants that began to appear more profusely as I continued. I could not stomach that guilty meat if I didn't need to. Now, in what was already a mental pile-up, I had the further image of the cratered beast – loyal mate – lying akimbo over the windmill's rocky cubes, to add to all the rest.

I went along the valley and down, through an apple orchard on the slopes above the village, where I was noticed but not harassed by farmers painting the trunks of their trees. Still disguised in Cretan garb, my hair dyed and cut, I walked straight into the heart of the village, and managed to eat two apples from a tree on the way. I was no longer hungry, not even thirsty, but I did want to fill my water flasks before I headed out of the small tumble of lanes and on over what I hoped was only a two or three day distance to the coast.

After Marmaketo I was wary of being propped up again in the village *kaphenoi* like a trophy, but nevertheless I needed to know the whereabouts of water: a cistern, a well, or a spring. Eventually I was taken in hand by a widow who would brook no argument. As she ushered me like a chicken through her doorway, I thought that I might hit her – with one smart backhand bloody her tawny nose – to reject her hospitality, but knowing the Cretans as I was beginning to, I thought better of it. Just as I had been feted so fervently in Marmaketo, I could just as easily be shot as some fifth columnist in this town on the southern side of the range.

Inside her dwelling – low beamed, dim, smelling of dittany and the dirt floors, with some vast and dark-timbered loom taking pride of place in the one main room – I found to my shock a Kiwi soldier, a big Maori bloke, waist deep in a tin tub, his kit sitting neatly by the wall in the corner, on top of which a lucky-looking cat lay sleeping.

We were both caught by surprise but said g'day. And then the Maori simply proceeded with his washing, asking me questions from the tub, as if it was all in a day's work.

I told him nothing of what I'd been through, only that I'd come over the mountains through Lasithi and was on my way to Cairo to rejoin my unit. When the toothless widow had left us alone again, after bringing coffee and hard biscuits to the table, the Maori told me what the battle around Chania had been like and how, after sticking it to the Germans in one last ditch charge, he'd struck out with a mate from the evacuation at Sfakia where blokes were fighting each other to get on the boats. He and his mate had walked away in disgust to the east, figuring they could do better. They'd ended up being sheltered in a monastery at a place called Preveli, where they'd waited for many weeks for a boat until his mate got restless and convinced him to take up another offer from a Cretan who promised he could get them on a caique from a place named Tres Ekklesies. They'd left the monastery, but one evening while getting water from an apparently safe well as they travelled towards Tres Ekklesies, his mate had been captured by Germans. They'd been betrayed. He told me from the tub that he'd been on his own ever since.

Then he said in a whisper, in his strong Kiwi accent and with a flashing smile: 'You've got to be careful, old mate, even with the locals, yeah. There's some turned bad, some workin' for Jerry. The old girl here told me it's the Turk in 'em you see.'

He soaped his big body happily and said he'd been living with all the comforts in the little house for over a month. He was in no hurry to leave, he said, not with winter coming on.

In the state I was in the Maori's good cheer was enough to turn my stomach. The Maoris were bloody natural fighters, make no mistake, but I could take no solace from the meeting. Swallowing hard, I asked where I could fill my water flasks and he gave me directions, saying he'd also leave the water in the tub for me to get in next. I nodded, as if this was how things would run, then quickly polished off the coffee and scrammed before the widow re-entered the room. I heard the big Maori calling from the tub as I went through the door but I wasn't about to answer. I'd leave him to his soap and water and his cat-scented kit. I'd had enough of the widow's hovel, even before I'd set foot in it.

With pockets full of biscuits I followed the directions to the well, wary after the encounter.

At the well I washed my face and neck, alone but for a curious and bell-less goat who repeatedly butted my gear as if there was something inside he wanted. Perhaps it was the smell of native brethren he was trying to get at, the smell of my panic, the residue of a coward's donkey meat. Whatever it was, he was persistent.

I headed south out of the village then, along a reasonable *kalderini*, keeping the sun ahead of me. By late in the day I'd passed the outskirts of two smaller villages, in one of which I managed to order some bread in an empty *kaphenoi*. As I sat outside, chewing the meal on the deserted lane, I had a sense of mountains turning into hinterland, of life beginning perhaps to be influenced by the prospect of the sea. I'd come down off the ranges a little way and, although you couldn't see the water from where I sat, the world now seemed to exist somehow in relation to it. Or at least that's what I fancied as I sat eating the bread.

The uneventful hours of wandering after this lunch I can hardly recall but what happened afterwards, in the monastery of Agio Dormiton, I will never forget.

Before nightfall, waylaid finally by weary legs and the stinging cold, I sat with brow in hand by a path beside a flat and uncultivated field, with a white building at its southernmost end. I raised my head to sniff for salt in the air but felt only the windless chill of diminishing returns. The well-fed hopes of earlier in the day were stripped away by the lowering light.

Gradually, with a slow ghostly sibilance, it began to snow.

More from weariness than anything else I stayed right where I was, watching the field turn slowly white. I once saw snow falling on the hills above Lorne when I was a child but that was more like sleet really, the pale grey of heron feathers. This was pure and falling white like it had during our shemozzle at Vevi. Twisting round to look back up at the way I'd come off the highest peaks of the massif I saw the sky above me had turned to a shifting, purplish mass. And now a wind scoured down off the slopes.

I set my eyes back on the field. Gradually the fall of the snow became mesmeric, the way each flake fell independent but connected to those around it. The brief wind died off and the rhythm of a visual puzzle set in, each white piece falling seemingly at the same speed but landing before or after its neighbour. My limbs grew heavy and my mind drowsy. Then a hare shot across my vision, its long body scampering low over the bleached flat of the clearing, its ears standing on high alert between the falling flakes. I watched it go, my soul suddenly alert to some wilder dignity, until it appeared to vanish into the building at the field's far end.

Unthinking now, and sodden too, I gathered up my things and set off after it.

From the path to where the hare disappeared would only have been the depth of perhaps two footy fields but that simple journey seemed to take forever. I was disoriented in the whiteness and, unused to such conditions, with the soles of my boots now as smooth as kelp, I began slipping about. I crossed the field as if on eggshells, as they say. Still I stumbled on, squinting through flurries towards the building at the far end, which now seemed to have vanished as if into the sky.

After I don't know how long of ginger-stepping through the field I reached the other end but still for the life of me could not make out the building. I peered about, afraid, as the darkness began to come on in blurry consort with the snow. Then, as the white flakes seemed to dwindle off and stars emerged in the sky above, I heard the tolling of a bell.

In shock and relief, I listened intently. The bell rang out again. Not fifty yards ahead of me. Was it being rung by the hare?

I stepped forward until, unannounced, the ground changed under my feet. I'd come off the field onto what I later discovered was the courtyard of the Monastery of Agio Dormiton. And with the lack of give in the flagstones, and the fresh snow on top, I immediately went arse over tit, arms outspread across the surface. The bell stopped. I lay there stunned amidst the lingering peal, drenched to the bone.

XXIII

MY WRITINGS TO LEONIE MAY WELL HAVE BEEN FILLED WITH THE darkness of my world but her reply, despite its implication that something might go awry with the pages on her father's farm, had focused only on her own 'happy memories' with regard to the ink. She was being gentle with me, I think I understood that. But when I encountered Uncle True not long after this – we were both making our way into Currie for supplies, he coming at a shambolic angle around the racetrack from the northwest, me pedalling out of the east to merge at his side along the town road – and he said if I needed a bob then he needed a hand for a day or two's gurrying, I had no need of money but even so I couldn't resist. Yeah *gurrying*, he said again, sieving the local word through his own inherited whaler's burr. I had not the faintest idea what the word meant or what I was in for, only that I needed to take the risk.

When I arrived the following day he was in the grass yard behind the house, the onshore was uncharacteristically light for the west coast, and even lighter behind the protection of the house. I remember sighting the lenticular as I arrived: a single reef of jagged white cloud, seemingly fixed in place with guy-ropes high above our heads.

Uncle True had three timber barrows tumbled off to one side of the clearing with half a dozen or so saucers of methylated spirits sitting at various angles on top of them. These saucers, along with dry sheaves of gum branches laid out on the clover all around the yard, were to keep the blasted flies away from the big pile of two or three hundred muttonbirds which sat in an unruly heap right in the middle. Alongside the birds were three forty-four gallon drums, empty, waiting patiently, as I would find out, for the gurry. Next to the barrels was a wooden workbench, with the scratch and wear of the ages, and also with Uncle True's tobacco tin and bottle of rum and cloves on top.

When he noticed me pedal in he was quick to smile. Then he began briefly to hop about and look busy. Incapable of small talk, he took me straightaway through the process in which I was required to handle, squeeze, and twist each bird in the pile over an empty barrel until every last drip of oil had trickled out of their guts. Taking up a dead bird in his hands, he demonstrated this and a thick grey-brown syrup oozed out into the barrel under True's experienced squeeze and twist. 'Then,' he said, in the faint American accent leftover from his father, 'you'll hand 'em to me and I'll scald 'em and pluck 'em. Should take us all day, even with Leonie. She'll be here mid-mornin'.'

Uncle True then promptly went over to his bench, flicked his tobacco tin open with a thumbnail and began to roll himself a smoke. He offered the tin to me, took a slug on the neck of his rum and cloves, and started to yack about the wherewithal and pros and cons of this muttonbird consignment.

I was content enough to listen, knowing now that my punt had indeed paid off, that Leonie was prepared to show knowing full well I'd be there. I noticed again, as I had on the day I'd bumped into him pumping worms on the beach at Yellow Rock, that despite the fact he was a pretty ugly bugger Uncle True and Leonie were nevertheless alike, in colouring certainly, with those driftwood cheekbones that made a habit of catching the light of the strait. His hair was ash-white with the years of salt, and his Fermoy-blue eyes had turned the same cloudy, coppery green they'd been that day when he was sandworming on the beach, though I now noticed how the whites around the irises were stained almost the colour of the gurry, from his hard living no doubt, and, as Lascelles might reflect, from god knows what other incidents lingering in his body.

As it turned out, having Leonie on the way and myself already there, Uncle True was in no hurry to get on with what looked to me like a large amount of very dirty work, preferring instead to yarn and question, and to complain about a bloke called Vince Moynihan, who was to pick up the processed birds in his Cessna the next morning. I found his procrastinations odd, but in a world gone wrong Uncle True's way of living made as much, if not more sense to me than any other. He seemed to live by the belief that there was no point rushing straight into the maw of human work, and even though he didn't technically own the family house and paddocks, his brother Nat was quite content for him to camp there, as he had for the fifteen years since their father, Old Nat, the 'Pop' of Leonie's letter, had died. Though they had hardly spoken about it, the brothers had somehow come to this arrangement, and having no rent, few overheads, and even less ambition, Uncle True was free to continue his interrogations of tobacco and rum and cloves for as long as his body, and in this case my patience, held out. Occasionally a business deal like this one would come his way, usually over the bar in the hotel, and Vince Moynihan was set to fly the muttonbirds illegally back to Moorabbin on the mainland where they'd be tinned as 'squab in aspic' and exported to the Yanks. But True's chat now was more in keeping with the majority of his days, where he'd gather his food off the beaches and, by the look of the material I saw later that day inside the house, hole up in the west coast weather reading adventure stories and books on spies and espionage.

'I've been wonderin',' True said eventually, having exhausted his assassinations of Vince Moynihan, 'whether or not you ain't signin' on for a settler block because there's something you're not right about. I mean, quite apart from not acceptin' charity and that. More so somethin' . . . that you ain't happy with.'

I said nothing. Given our first meeting, I shouldn't have been surprised by his frankness, but I was.

Uncle True puffed at his smoke and leaned a bony hip into the bench. 'Like I know what I'm talking about, when it comes to these things, being ya champion bludger and that. Anyone'll tell. Never bought my land, never work, the yard and shed here full of the sea's charities. Truthfully though, only thing I hand over coin for is the rum. And sugar for my tea, and this and that. Cartridges for me guns. Well, a man's gotta eat.

'Anyway, as I told ya before it's one thing to go mendin' your own snares but it's a gift to know how to receive, ya know that? There's always things lurkin'. And when you don't know the history of a thing, of a fella, well, he's a stranger, ain't he, and somehow seems to lurk all the more. Like a shark under the boat.'

He was looking beyond me now, out over the yard to the sky above the sea. But then he turned and bored his gaze right into me.

'Take my brother upstanding, my brother Nat. Irons his money. Never leant on anyone since the day Tuck White gave him a leg-up with the cattle. But he's my brother, see, and so I know why. It ain't coz he's any more decent than me or any other bludger. Well, perhaps he was born a touch narrowed in our ol' Patsy's womb but he ain't that naturally obsessed with his cattle, that's not the meat of it. There's a reason, a thing behind. If you think you got holes, and you don't mend 'em, you won't hold out your glass to be filled.'

Despite what I'd been writing to Leonie I wasn't, you might say, used to such conversations at that time, and I looked off into the sky myself now, uncomfortable. Confronted by the truth in what he'd brought up out of the blue, I was equally uneasy about the deeper level of his talk.

'Well, no one's perfect,' I ventured.

'Perfection's got nothin' at all to do with it,' he said, quickly. 'I'm talking about degrees of rust, there's no clean tin round 'ere.'

I looked around the yard, following the sweep of his arm. He was right, of course, every surface you looked at: shed, troughs, barrels, bikes, ploughshares, metal craypots and other traps and snares, were in varying stages of being chewed by salt.

'For instance,' he went on, 'you'd think no one on this island is as right as my niece but still it's all wrong, you see.'

'How do you mean?'

'Well I'm as lonely as the next codger,' said Uncle True, 'but she's not, she's . . .'

He stopped, readjusted his boot where he leant it on a bent metal crate beside the bench, took a sip of his rum, another puff on his smoke.

'Well, seein' ya want to know, my brother was plain knocked out when she was born. She came straight on, like a child of the island, right out of the barrel of a filthy storm. But he wasn't knocked out by her, not by the gift of her, but by him losin' his Alma in the birthing. Leonie's mammy. It was a shock to us all. But do you think he just went away and wept on the rocks, untangled his lines, pulled himself together, and loved the girl double after that, once the storm died out and the shock went east? Nah, he did nothin' of the kind. He was as sock-headed, as selfish and tight-knotted a bastard of a man as could ever be and that was the house she grew in over there at Tuck White's. Rose Robinson fed her, pedalled through the after-blow to the horror and joy of it on one of Doc Ray's bicycles, and that set the line. By the time the girl was three and properly had her legs she'd run off twice, maybe three times a week from Nat, off over the heath and sedge, through the boxthorn on the Haines Road, never mind the sleet in winter or the summer snakes, with that beatin' heart of hers set for Brian and Rose's. Of course, she had a child's idea of just how close or distant a love like theirs could be, and that's a natural enough fact I s'pose.

'He lost her over and over. Glyn Shakespeare down in the swales on the next farm south'd find her steppin' through the lambs in his paddocks and bring her back to a whippin' from Nat, but the pain of the belt never cured it. She kept going, so in the end, when she was gettin' on for school age, he locked her up.

'Brian and Rose went to Bob Balme, the cop, but he was new, a timid bloke too, reluctant. I went in with my fists and got bloodied up by my own brother and right in front of the girl. None of that did any good at all actually and the upshot, I'm sorry to say, was that we left her with him. Now then, he never punished her beyond the belt for her runnings-off but they were that frequent anyway and he never loved her outright either. Though she might disagree.

'Anyways, by the time the first war finally blew itself out it's like she'd fought one herself. She was about eight and pretty much wild on the island. He couldn't hold her in the house and so let her go. Sometimes she'd make it barefoot to school in Yambacoona, which she liked, sometimes she crossed the Sea Elephant to Brian and Rose, sometimes over here to me and we'd have a fine ol' time as a rule, she got into all my books on the shelves, but there was no schedule to it. Sometimes she wouldn't show for weeks. Except no matter where she'd been by day, every night she'd always make it back to sleep at Nat's.

'And that was all well and good, and in the end we surrendered to it, like somethin' in the sea, ya know, something bigger than us and brutal we didn't see coming, something steep from five or six thousand mile off that felt a helluva lot more powerful, somethin' strong holdin' us in place, the ocean powers we learnt how to live with, even to enjoy: the sight of her on the roads, coming along so small but knowledge-able under the big paperbarks, her strength and boy's trousers and face deadset, and her drop-ins for a chat or to go birdin'.

'Until she started spendin' time hangin' round on the junction just west of Shakespeare's farm. This bloke, Rickie Keith he was known as, on account of I dunno why, had propped in an old Hickmott wagon he'd converted on a tiny piece of shit land given to him as a settler block when he'd got back from the war. He's long gone now, but he was well enough liked, Rickie. Soft spoken, easy to smile. Always had a patch of spuds and beet and whatnot he used to spend time in next to his wagon. He took a liking to Leonie as she'd come by, and she to him, and before long she was spendin' time under the awning he'd rigged up, and in the wagon with him, playing cards she always said, and listening to his stories of the war, and eating pancakes. Nat, not surprisingly, had warned her off the bloke, told her he could be dangerous, having washed up from the Somme or wherever he'd been, but as usual she took no heed, probably reasonin' he couldn't be any more dangerous than her old man himself, all his grim beltings.

'Till one night a sou'westerly came in almost as bad as the one she'd first breathed in, I remember the colour of it to this day, the eerie green of cold coming high above the purple through the big windows from inside the house. Leonie was nine years old at the time and she got stuck in the wagon with Rickie Keith and never made it home.

'Well, come dawn, Nat was straight over there in the sholtie and cart with his carbine and callin' her out and Rickie Keith too. When no one came he fired shots into the air and then through the wheels of the wagon until the door Rickie Keith had rigged up finally opened. Nat ordered Leonie up onto the box of the cart and bailed the poor digger up against the wagon like a bushranger with the carbine. Then he told the girl to take the sholtie to fetch Bob Balme, which she did on the storm-swiped roads, purely terrified as she was by the shots he'd fired. When Balme came back on Nat's own cart – with Leonie still at the helm I might add, yes, a nine-year-old girl clickin' the sholtie for the walloper to the scene of a crime – Nat claimed that the friendly soldier had molested his daughter, had kidnapped her in his wagon, and that if it wasn't for him taking matters into his own hands at dawn with the carbine, she'd still be in there, his only soul on the earth and lucky to be alive.

'Bob Balme had no choice but to investigate and so it went, for months in fact, the big news, with Leonie having to answer questions she didn't even know the meaning of, and Rickie Keith whittled away by Nat's demands of that pliant copper Bob Balme until, with it all over the Tassie papers and even *The Argus*, as a curious tale from the backward islands no doubt, the poor digger just packed up his kitbag one day and left on the cargo tramp. An innocent verdict was given but it was too late. He'd come back from one war only to find another waged against him. He'd been given no help from the Settlement Board: no fences, no housing, had not much of an idea about farming, and now this. But, in truth, it had nothing to do with Rickie Keith. It was Nat's war. Still is. And if you don't believe me, you can head up past that junction next to Shakespeare's and 'ave a look at Rickie Keith's wagon, coz it's still standing there by the join of the roads. Or what's left of it.'

He went on. 'After that she was different for a time. I reckoned she'd found a friend in kind ol' Rickie Keith, a friend from elsewhere, which was a big part of it. Unlike every other bugger on King he knew nothin' of Alma dyin' to bring her into the world or her father's trouble with that or what she'd had to put up with. I imagine it was all cards and pancakes as she said, just somethin' nice in that wagon, and I've asked her and she says it was not much more. Anyways, I reckon she took it all to mean, even as a kid, that she was destined to be friendless on the earth. Cursed. I dunno to be honest but for a time the people already here, those of us *from* here, who remembered her beautiful mammy Alma from Victoria and the storm and knew all about Nat and her and that, well, for a time we didn't count for nothin'. She just shut up shop on the lot of us, even me. Got herself one of Doc Ray's bikes and you'd only ever see the back of her, takin' off to some place or another, up high onto the gusty capes, up onto the Wickham uplands and the like . . .

'But then one day, I dunno, maybe a year and a half since Rickie Keith packed up and left, she showed round here wanting to know about the scrimshaw, of all things. Was almost like meetin' a stranger. She'd grown up a bit and she didn't come in sniffin' but speakin' whole sentences and knowin' what she was about.

'I was just glad to see her, couldn't help her enough, showed her all the pieces of our pa's in this house – of course she'd seen all the stuff Nat had on the walls back at Tuck's – but what she wanted was the knowhow. Well, I couldn't help her with that coz I never learnt from Old Nat. He taught the eldest and no one else. So Leonie's dad got it all but wasn't much interested, gettin' madly into Tuck White's cattle and that when he was young.

'Anyways, what I could show her was how to get the ink, coz that was one of my chores when we was young. So I give her the rundown on that, it was all I could do, and we went around for a few days then catchin' cuttlefish by lantern at night in the coves, and fixing up what had been lost between us. I showed her back here in the yard, on this here bench if the truth be known, how to cut out the sac and dry it to dust and the like and add water and I told her she was a clean slate to me, I didn't care to think about the past and that she was as at home in the old Fermoy house where she'd been born, as anywhere in the world.

'She took it all on board and went off her own way but she'd stop by at least from time to time after that. Showed me the ink she made and told me too just why she was makin' it for Nat, thinkin', god bless her darlin' heart, that it would cure him to set his hand to the ol' art rather than workin' with bulls his whole life.

'You see, young fella, she's stayed with him, that's what you gotta know. She stayed with him right through, you see. Right through it all. Just out of worry and love. She spent bloody months waitin' for the right weathers and gettin' enough ink at night so he'd be right as rain and accordin' to her he actually did turn his hand back to it for a while, on a rib of our pa's, but ended up throwin' the results into the lily lagoon by the gate on Tuck's there. Stormin' around afterwards, she said, worse than ever for weeks.

'But she's stayed there all right, every night she's back there. It's damn unnatural the amount of love that girl's got for a father like that but, yes, she's stayed . . . right through . . . she's nursin' animals and wandering down to talk to the swans on the Sea Elephant, but she ain't got closer to anyone than she is to me and the Robinsons this whole time.

'So,' and now Uncle True squinted straight at me as he spoke, 'you'd be best to get a lookout or somethin', or watch yourself is all I'll say, coz my bet is that where my brother's concerned you'd be walkin' pretty close to a boxthorn right now. You wouldn't want to end up the way of Rickie Keith . . .'

The day of work hadn't even begun but there were so many sparks flying in my head now and I didn't know where to look.

'But, True, she's not nine years old anymore,' I said.

'No,' he said pensively, running his fingers through his stubble. 'No, in many ways she's not.'

'But . . . do you mind if I ask, does he still hit her, do ya reckon?'

The old beachcomber stared at me again, this time without speaking. It was a look unmistakeable for the guilt that he felt. He'd never been capable of doing anything much about the situation. Except by being a friend to her, no, a proper uncle, and to offer a gumbo and a good ear whenever she felt the need to come by his way. But right then he ceased to be able to put his feelings into words.

With the silence came the beginning of work. And it was then, by way of a lighter conversation bearing at least some resemblance to the eternal small talk of the weather, that I mentioned how that morning I'd found muttonbird feathers in my pocket. As I gingerly wrung the oil out of each sad and sooty bird, Uncle Truc told me how the birds moult before they take off in the autumn and that the feathers get into everything. 'You wait,' he said in earnest, 'from this one day of workin' 'em you'll be pulling 'em outta the hair in your armpits for months.'

We set about it. Being inexperienced it would take me an inordinate amount of time – a good ten minutes – to be sure I'd properly gurried each bird and, given the size of True's pile beside me, of cast-off hook-beaks and tiny heads, legs and wings flung and flopped into light-catching angles, eyes blank as charcoal but still facing you, I knew that I was terribly slow. But not once did Uncle True even look sideways at what I was doing. He stood at his bench ripping the feathers away from the birds in clumps, chopping the heads and wings and feet with his hatchet, and placing the prepared bodies in a hessian sack with a stencil of a red poll on it that he had hanging from the bench beside him. When my gurrying was extra slow he'd patiently wait for the next bird, happy now in the release of the activity to yarn away about things that had occurred to him concerning people and life, certain notions he had, in which occasionally I'd catch more glimpses of his disapproval for the way his brother Nat conducted his farm and affairs. In the midst of his reflections he would often get a slug of rum in before I handed him the gurried bird and, of course, at all times he had a roll-your-own hanging from the corner of his mouth.

To my surprise Leonie showed up right on time, pedalling around the back shed from the northern end of the yard, to a generous 'Hooray' from her Uncle True. She pedalled right up to us, leaned the bike against the narrow end of the plucking bench and reminded her uncle that he'd forgotten the scalding.

Anyone else on the island would have pointed this out as an example of why True Fermoy was a hopeless case. A dipso worth a laugh at the pub but nothin' more. He'd even mentioned the scalding of the birds when he was explaining the process to me, and then the two of us, caught up as we had been with Leonie and Rickie Keith and the Fermoy sorrows, had completely forgotten it.

Slapping his weathered forehead with the flat palm of his hand, he grinned at his niece like a ham actor. He shook his head, as if he cared more about the scalding than anything else on the whole island. 'Well it's lucky your friend Wesley here's as green as the grass. And as slow. Not much wasted, we've only done ten birds.'

It was as if he could have lectured us then on the merits of starting work late, as we had, due to his rhythms with the rum and cloves. Fact was, if we had've started on time he'd likely as not have remembered the scalding, but that wouldn't be the point, as he saw it. If you take your time, like a leatherback, I imagined him saying, you'd be the last in the race to make mistakes. And here we go lassie Leonie, and Wesley the War Hero, this mornin's the proof of it. We've been conductin' important business that required our full attention. Anyway, let's get the fire goin' and conjure up the water.

Between the plucking bench and the salt-eaten red shed behind us was a setting of driftwood and rubbish waiting to be lit. Beside it sat another drum but this time sawn raggedly in half, and blackened by past fires. Leonie crossed the grass and disappeared into the shed before re-appearing in a leather apron even heavier than her one at the co-op, the kind which I'd seen fellows wearing in the abattoir. She still hadn't said hello to me yet.

She bent down and struck a match into the rubbish and wood, which caught immediately. She then walked over to where True's saucers of metho sat on the barrows, picked one of them up and tossed the contents onto the pile. Flames immediately surged, grasping the strait wood hungrily.

The fire was soon all ablaze and, as she stood waiting for it to shift itself down enough for her to put the half-drum on top, Uncle True ran a thick brown hose from a tank by the backdoor of the house, ready to fill it with water when the moment came. I watched these two Fermoys at work from my spot at the gurry barrel, but suddenly from a great distance. They may have had their troubles but they were at home there at Yellow Rock. It was I who felt like the stranger on the earth. 'As green as the grass,' True had described me as in jest to his niece. 'As dark as a cave,' was how I put it to myself as I stood there by the blackened barrel.

But then she turned her face, all lit like a lamp from the fire, bringing me back into the picture. And all the scribbling I'd done in those last few days, page after page of it, seemed instantly to have been worthwhile. Was it the nature of the work itself, the act of recollecting or the ingredients remembered, or simply her acknowledgement that I existed on this average island working day? Either way, my voice replied to her hello with a transparent eagerness, as if I'd unclipped my battle gear and stood in the heart's mufti before her, saying, 'Yair hi, hello, g'day!'

By lunchtime I had learned that to gurry a bird in ninety seconds flat was acceptable, given their internal structure and the slow drip of the oil and the way this varied slightly from one to the next. I stood and watched as Leonie took this full allotted time over the barrel to last out the drips, before handing the bird to me to scald in the drum of boiling water. I would hold each bird by a wrinkled claw and submerge it twice, once to loosen the nibs and the next to make sure before laying it on the ground beside me. When I had a pile of twenty or so I'd carry them quickly to True's bench, in between Leonie handing me more birds and making sure I didn't burn myself. Uncle True would then cut off the legs and wings and head, in four always slightly tentative movements, and then he'd pluck the bodies. We'd work like this for half an hour or perhaps forty minutes, shooing away the flies, glancing westward above the roofline of the house to see where that reef of cloud held in by ropes had gone, and then Uncle True would call for a rest to smoke, and in that five or so minutes break Leonie or I would stoke the fire with more wood from the tumble – you wouldn't call it a stack – that True had over near the red shed, and make gentle conversation. In this manner lunch arrived with perhaps a third of the original pile completed.

We stayed outside to eat but moved to the chairs and table True had positioned at the Wickham end of the house, where his mother's correas still stood in a wind-sculpted hedging around an area of about ten or twelve square yards of thick lush kikuyu. From the bottles and butts all around it was obvious that this was a place Uncle True liked to sit.

Leonie had removed her abattoir apron and wore a thick woollen dress with a sleeveless vest over the top in a brown and yellow argyle pattern. I had come unprepared but wished I'd left my coat on as I worked, for I was filthy with oil and grease and grit and ash, and of course feathers also. Uncle True had worn a knee-length coat for the plucking and he kept it on, filthy as it was, during lunch. So Leonie looked not only beautiful to me now, but heroic and shining as well.

In the afternoon we worked like Trojans, with True filling Leonie in on the Vince Moynihan arrangement and how the rush of it all was not to his taste but that it was the nature of contraband to require last-minute arrangements. Leonie didn't say much as her uncle talked but when she did it was only to agree with him, or to ask if he needed a rest.

By 4 pm the unnerving stillness of the day had finally begun to shift, with a constant range of cloud moving across, untethered and scudding from the open west. As if in tune with this, Uncle True's mood also began to change, as his cursing at Moynihan's expectations increased, not to mention his curses at the 'bloody yowlers', as he called the birds, until finally at around four-thirty, with a third of the pile still to go, he announced he was done for the day. Already feeling some kind of investment in the process, what with the talk we'd had in the morning, the burns on my hands from the fire and the water, the gurry all over my clothes and skin, I felt like protesting that it would be good to finish the pile, but Leonie got in first: 'No need for you to keep going, Uncle True. Wesley and I can knock the rest off and you can go inside and put the dinner on.'

'Dinner be damned, girl,' Uncle True replied.

'Yes, well, have your sherbet, of course. But if we keep going we'll need to be fed. That way the whole thing with Vince Moynihan won't hit a snag. We don't want him flying over tomorrow and being disappointed. And I'm sure Wes here wants his money.'

Uncle True raised his eyebrows, pursed his whole face up in pained consideration. 'Whatever you say, girl. We can't stiff the war hero, I suppose.'

'Good. We'll be in when we've finished for stew.'

Uncle True snorted and rolled his eyes in a delinquent fashion. He walked off in the direction of the house.

~

An hour after the stars had appeared in the black pouches of the sky between clouds, we still had fifty or so birds to go. It was all harder in the dark, of course, colder too, we were both covered in gurry and I wasn't as good at the plucking as Leonie's Uncle True.

Tentatively we'd begun to talk, even before the sun went down. She told me a little about her father and True and I asked her not about the ink but about the scrimshaw.

'They don't have much in common, my father and my Uncle True, but they do have this: anything to do with their own father, what he did, his life, and what he made, is of interest to them. They don't appreciate anything better.'

'So what made True the way he is?' I asked, mid-grimace, as I plucked a smaller bird without light.

She glanced at me quickly from over the gurry barrel. Even in the dark I could see her flashing scorn for my question. As if it was laughable that a bird at sea like me, and with such heavy wings, should behave like some wetback suitor inquiring about the more obvious members of her family.

After a squidging twist of the yowler in her hands, she said: 'There are things I'd do for Uncle True I'd do for no one else. This, for instance. I don't believe in killing birds in such quantities. And I've not much interest in breaking the law either, not like some on this island.'

I blushed in the darkness, dressed down, thinking about that episode with the digger in the wagon, Rickie Keith. What I'd asked had come out stilted and wrong. Even on moonless nights we cast a shadow.

When the last bird was done we cleaned ourselves up as best we could, to sit down at the long old log-table in the house at Yellow Rock for what Uncle True declared to be, with a short-lived humour thoroughly inflected with the day's rum and cloves, 'squab in aspic stew'. The big room was surprisingly neat, the wooden floor swept, the timbers polished with wax from the wild bee-combs and gleaming, books and magazines stacked neatly on the shelves, the glass of the sideboard tea-polished too, the top of it dusted buff. I wouldn't have doubted that behind the wide brown curtains the big windows facing twelve thousand miles of unbroken water were washed against the dark night as well, such was the fastidious gleam of the interior. The only exception to all this cleanliness were the spiderwebs left on the walls and in the corners of the ceiling. They were extravagant, hairy, colonising things, and easily swept away. Uncle True obviously had a soft spot for spiders.

Leonie explained later how it was with this houseproudness of Uncle True. A mixture of devotion and fear saw him keep the inside of the home as respectable as a shrine. Like his brother, he respected anything his father had made and also felt his mother Patsy's constant watching of her kitchen from beyond the grave. But also, given he paid no rent, he had to guard against the potential coming day when Nat would turn up unannounced from the east and manhandle him out of the place because of its disgusting condition. Uncle True might be a hopeless case according to some, but they would never say that about his parents' house. It was the one discipline he required of himself in life and he attended to it as if everything depended upon it. Which, given the lack of alternative snug accommodation on the island, and the punitive winters, it may well have.

The stew was predictably salty, the potatoes nutty but overcooked and at the head of the table Uncle True was quite spent. He sat, flagging then luffing like a sail in his chair, his big left hand fixed around his crystal glass, with his eyes closed most of the time. Leonie and I talked amongst ourselves, almost as if he wasn't there, of life on Wait-a-While, and for a good hour or so of her father's Brangus cattle, which Leonie confessed for the first time to hating, because of the way they were enemies of the island trees and groundcovers, and for the way they stiffened the ground with teeth and hoof. As it turns out this passionate confession was not just a first to me but to anyone, including True and the Robinsons, and given what she's come to create in the garden around us here at Naracoopa that's a fond memory to me. Obviously enough, the day we'd had, of sharing the gurrying of Uncle True's yowlers, had brought the right stuff out of the inside of us all, not just the birds.

Eventually, with the stew polished off and Uncle True well and truly nodded off at the head of the table, it was clear the long day and night had reached a natural conclusion. I still had to ride home across the dark roads of the island, with only the bicycle's wonky carbide lamp and my thankfully ungurried overcoat for protection. But there was no question of my lingering or of her coming my way. She said she'd prop with her uncle until the morning and so it was. She waved me off, smiling a trifle fondly I imagined, at the back door of the house at Yellow Rock.

I rode home, as if in pursuit of the beam of milky blue light from the whistling bicycle lamp, dodging wallabies down the unmade avenues of the windy farms and then along the owl-studded tracks of the east. As I pedalled, I reflected how Leonie's history may have made it hard for her to broach the contents of my pages. It would have been easy, I had thought in those previous days, for her to have come around and for us to have gone fishing at the Naracoopa jetty. Easy then for me to open up more, in the unhurried gentleness that jetty fishing can bring. But she had never come, we never fished, and thanks to Uncle True I now knew more about her reasons. Having gone so far as to get me up on the floor – using the strangest methods of course: dry kindling, family histories, a black eye – she now deferred in the dance. I was to lead from here on in. Well, at least till the end of that tune and the beginning of another.

~

It was around this time that Lascelles found something in one of the new books he was having sent in advance for his planned Memorial Reading Room that brought him out to Wait-a-While on his old man's Velocette. These were the keen years after the war of course, when a lot of writing was taking place. I might have disappeared from the mainland, tangled myself in Bass Strait knots, but a lot of other chaps were doing precisely the opposite: blowing their trumpets in a national brass band of victory, recovery and justification. The journos and hired hacks were actually to blame, they were typing up the heroes at a furious rate, the acts of endurance and derring-do, the superhuman survival stories, and all with a great moral certainty. They put it all down in such a dignified way, as if immune to the ugly damage in the heart, and theirs was the complete opposite of my renditions, where loss and bitterness drove the pen, drove page after page of Leonie's cuttle-ink across the prickly hummocks of my catharsis. I do consider myself fortunate here at Naracoopa, in these days of my re-writing, not to have only weeping wounds for posterity, but rather to have had the chance to heave the timber and mark the spot, and then watch it all burn. Hate without love is universally recognised as evil, but equally love without a lineage of hate, or at least of bitterness and regret, is a flimsy thing indeed. A boat without ballast. Thus I believe the life we have built here will survive the squalls and vicissitudes of this our blue paddock.

Despite his interest in me and my condition Lascelles had never before had the gumption or gall to visit my hut. But now he was like a man possessed, and terribly excited. What he had to show me was all in a freshly published book, by a bloke I'd never heard of, a journalist by the name of Noonan. Apparently this bloke's brother had served with the 2/7th in the Med, and once Noonan's book was put in front of me on the macrocarpa slab at Wait-a-While, the reason for Lascelles' visit, and his excitement, became clear.

I read the passage, which Lascelles had already underlined, and leant back on my chair. 'So?' I said.

Lascelles was standing eagerly on the other side of the table. 'What do you mean "so"?' he said. 'It's you isn't it, Wes?'

'Not exactly.'

'Not exactly? How many Wes Cresses were there on Crete?'

'I don't know this Noonan bloke from a bar of soap. But the stuff he's described here is rot. What do they call it in your Literary & Debating society in Currie? *Fiction.*'

'What, so it didn't happen?'

'Not like that.'

'But the bloke he's describing, it's gotta be you. How about this bit:

Though he was from western Victoria, Cress seemed to have prior knowledge of war, and of what was required in working with the Cretan andartes, that the rest of the men didn't. He was fearless for a start, with a pretty black sense of humour, two qualities which the locals loved in him. Once, when my brother Bob was waiting in a cave with a small group of Bandouvas' followers to ambush a convoy of Krauts near the road between Iraklio and Retimo, Cress took matters into his own hands. The news had come down the line that the jeeps were approaching but that there were Anzac POWs on board. Hearing this Cress set off for the open road with Mausers blazing, as if bullet proof. We presume he shot the tyres first but then he stuck those jeeps up all on his own. By the time the rest of the boys arrived, including the andartes and a Pom under an SOE codename, the diggers on the jeeps had darted off to freedom. Nobody had seen anything like it and no one could quite work out how it was achieved. Bob used to say Wes Cress was the wild colonial boy himself but amongst the boys in the POW camps at that time he gradually became known as the King of Crete.'

What I wanted to tell Lascelles was that although, yes, the fella who held up the jeep was me, the story would mean nothing at all unless you knew its undersong, what had happened beforehand, the terrible events and betrayals, the morbid emptiness that eventually saw me capable of such cavalier and so-called heroic behaviour. I wanted to tell him right there and then about the shock, about Vern, about Perry and even Simmo, I wanted to tell him about my anger, about how nothing mattered anymore, about how your own country can betray you, your own king's navy, and how you can betray the whole show too, when all bets are off and all things become possible.

But I didn't say that. I didn't say any of that. I fell silent right there at the table and I stayed that way for far far too long.

Three

Death of the Virgin

XXIV

THE BELL WAS SILENT NOW BUT THROUGH A TANGLE OF FOLIAGE I SAW a gentle golden light. With a click the light went suddenly out. There was shuffling, footsteps crackling through fallen sticks, and finally the sound of liquid hitting against the ground. Someone was pissing.

The sound was heavy and went on and on, surely for longer than any man could possibly need to empty his bladder. It stopped abruptly and I heard the shuffling footsteps again. A door opened with a rasp, the golden light reappeared, and then with another rasp the door was shut, the light went out, and I was alone in the darkness and cold.

I moved forward, carefully over the slippery stones. I skirted the shape of a large tree and under my feet heard the crackling I'd heard under the pissing man. Eventually I came under a shelter of sorts where the paving had not been snowed on and where I could proceed more easily. Steering as faithfully as I could towards the light I smelt food being cooked. The rich, slightly musty smell of tomatoes, marrows, and dittany.

Cold stone walls with a coarse gnarl of vine climbing upon them. I crept sideways, a crab in a cleft, feeling the structure of an open corridor. I seemed to leave my body and saw myself as if from somewhere back high up on the massif. Had I imagined everything? Was this whole predicament a dream I wouldn't have to explain to Dad after all, when I woke up in my bed on the lake? Or was I still perhaps in the upstairs room of Aunty May's pub in Manly, where it could all be washed out in the surf? What about the unhooking of the war's barbed wire from her Charlies on the night-slope? Was that too some kind of ruse?

Slowly my fingers found their way along the wall and onto the cold jamb of a door. I heard movement on the other side. I waited. Nothing. With palms flat I frisked the wood, found a handle, turned it, hearing the click I'd heard before from out in the snow. Then, startlingly, I was exposed, staring into the light.

~

I stood at the top of three broad stone steps, with a long heavy table set down below me, a massive hulk of oven with an enormous dented copper flue. I was frozen, my boots heavy and damp, my hair a wet nest of running dye and melted flakes. A wiry hand with long fingers beckoned me from below, at the same time gesturing to shut the door.

I did as I was told, instinctively replacing a black fabric sausage over the draught. Enclosed now, at the top of the three broad steps, I peered down into a large kitchen where a monk leaned over a table sparsely arranged with bowls of food. He wore a long charcoal soutane and the square Orthodox hat. He looked at me as if I was no surprise at all.

Waving me down from the steps, he said, in perfect English: 'You must be cold and hungry.'

Unnerved, I managed nothing in reply.

'Leave your bag, come down the steps to the fire. I have some clothing.'

I did as he said. As I hefted off my filthy kit, he shuffled off through a door at the far end of the cavernous room, beyond a giant cope and hearth. I noticed a large red dish on the stovetop, with steam pouring off it. In the bowls on the table were cooked marrows and sauce.

Soon the monk returned, a smile playing on his lips. He handed me a bundle of garments. 'You may dress in the corner,' he said, 'but first you must bathe.'

From an ancient-looking recess in the wall between the stove and the door he dragged a large tin tub and placed it on the floor near the end of the large table. He began to fill it with hot water from three cast-iron kettles on the enormous hearth. After emptying each kettle, he walked to a far corner of the room where, under long ladles and spatulas hanging from a horizontal beam, he pushed an iron tap to one side and filled the kettle in his hand with silver water.

When there was enough water in the tub for me to wash I took the hard soap from the monk and stepped up to the tub.

Neither of us said a word. Soon the water in the tub was dotted with dead fleas and, once I was washed, I dressed in the clothes he gave me: a pair of boofy pantaloons, a blue shirt, and a rough goat-hair jacket edged with black. Long green socks reaching up my calves to the bottom of the pants completed the costume. All I needed was for my moustache to grow and I would have passed as a freedom fighter from the days of the church made of milk. I felt warm, grateful, but quite ridiculous all the same.

Removing the tub and gesturing for me to sit at a chair in the middle of the long table, the monk resumed his position: crouching forward, his weight balanced on long splayed fingers at the other end of the table.

He offered his name: 'Andreas.'

I introduced myself as well. 'Private Wesley Cress,' I said. 'Second AIF.'

His narrow shoulders hunched, his fair features and concave face pointed slightly to one side, he now looked disgusted by something. I wondered if I'd been mistaken to offer my details. But he turned his face to meet me and smiled, saying, 'You are lucky, Private Cress. Winter has arrived. Yes, a lucky man. You should eat.'

The meal was nourishing and when I'd finished one bowl of stewed marrow he pushed another across the table. There was so much of it, it was as if he knew I was coming. But he told me he was alone in the monastery and had been since just before the war. 'There are many monasteries on *Kriti*,' he said, 'some are now empty. But I grow my food and I wait and see.'

'Your English is good,' I said, by way of a question.

He looked again to one side, as if down some far isthmus inside himself, and replied cryptically. 'I learnt this from old friends, a long time ago.'

As we talked it became apparent that, despite his isolation, he was well abreast of the progress of the war. It was in fact from Andreas on that first night at Agio Dormiton that I first heard something of the German perspective of their pyrrhic victory on Crete. How Hitler had been dragged into Greece by Mussolini's one-upmanship. Andreas was also the first to inform me about matters I have heard a lot about since. A battle was raging around Rostow in the Crimea that would set the stage for more terrible human slaughter in the months to come.

Eventually, when I had eaten and also finished the thick coffee he served after the meal, the monk damped the stove and led me back up the three stone steps and out of the kitchen, across the cold exposure of the open corridor surrounding the courtyard, and into a warm stone cell where a small iron brazier was burning. A narrow bed sat in the corner.

'I keep this room alive in the winter,' he told me. 'The *magali* is always alight. Just in case.'

Placing a beaten copper mug of water on the sill above the bed he crossed himself lightly, said goodnight, and left the room.

~

The next morning I woke to a fierce yet cold sunlight, as if someone had tampered with the thermostat of the earth. The *magali* was all but out, the walls were icy white. Looking outside through the window where the copper mug sat, I saw the snow fixed to its spot over the courtyard and also over the field beyond, as if, as I say, by the force of an inverted sun.

Draining the mug of water I slumped back onto the bed, disoriented but nevertheless relieved at the comfort of my situation. I promptly fell asleep again and didn't wake until well into the morning.

When eventually I did rise and dress (in what seemed an even more ridiculous get-up in the light of day) I heard the homely clucking of hens and saw that the snow had begun to melt from the courtyard and field.

Soon I was venturing out to find Andreas. From my rough introduction in the darkness of the previous night I had imagined a very different monastery to the one I now found myself in. The corridor I had thought was open to the snow was actually behind a half-wall at hip height, which was entered through an arched opening opposite a large and thriving plane tree which, although almost bare of its summer leaves, dominated the courtyard. I could see now that it was the combination of fresh snow and the enormous fallen leaves of this tree that had made the crackling sounds underfoot the night before.

A single wooden chair sat alone on smooth stones at the courtyard's far end, before an uneven white wall of stone. Beside the chair a narrow series of stone steps, bowed by centuries of treading feet, led up to a higher level, which in turn gave on to another set of steps leading to a higher level again.

I walked up the first set of steps towards the early winter sun where it shone invitingly against the higher half of the kitchen's outside wall. At the top of this first flight of stairs I saw the monk, kneeling among the plants of a terrace garden set on the kitchen's rooftop.

Hearing my approach, he got up slowly from his knees and made a brief solemn bow of his head. He said, 'You must be hungry,' just as he had the night before, and then turned to peer off into the tangle of dead plants beyond. With that one look-away he seemed to be assessing each and every effect of the first onset of winter on his kitchen garden, and also every possible culinary solution to the fact that I was a hungry soldier desiring food. I nodded, as humbly and gratefully as I could, and he told me to follow him to the kitchen.

Again I sat at the long table, which was now covered with a waxed cloth patterned with colourful geometrical shapes. Andreas fanned the stove, stooping and blowing loudly into the mouth of the fire, before cooking me an omelette without any talk.

As I began to eat, the monk resumed his stance of the previous night, which I recalled now like a forgotten dream. His shoulders crouched forward, he bore his wiry frame on those long fingers splayed downwards into the coloured shapes of the table. With his face set askance from mine, he narrowed his eyes into an expression quite peculiar in its blending of wise reflection and immense distaste.

Was my unannounced visit keeping him from something? I wondered. Well, yes, obviously from the upkeep of his winter garden; but was there something else in his mood, something other than the preoccupied air of a religious man presumably devoted to the habits of his solitary life?

As I chewed the omelette I watched him clean the pan and heavy iron of his stovetop with oil and paper. I wondered if it was the haphazardness of my turning up, astray in the middle of the night, and my unannounced entrance from the war into an existence more orderly than the military life itself, that was the cause of the conflicted atmosphere of the monk. It was a feeling I had, a hunch our mother would have said was just *in my waters*, and yet later I realised that quite the opposite was true. My arrival in that first snow of the winter had in fact been a sign of predestination for Andreas, and as such a confirmation of his duty, in both its happy and burdensome aspects.

When the omelette was finished he raised his fingers from the table and announced rather formally that he wanted to speak with me out in the sunlight.

'And I will make us *kafe*,' he said.

A few moments later we were back up in the rooftop garden, where a bitter breeze had picked up, blowing down off the massif. From a garden box near the open trellis wall he took a brown shawl and wrapped himself in it. He handed me a grey English-style car-coat from the same box.

We sat down on a low stone bench amongst the bareness of his staked winter stocks.

'You must speak. You must tell me your trouble,' Andreas said.

At my desk here, at the other end of the world, the eye of the needle widens for a moment and I see it clear. In a war of destruction, of hollowing loss and repetitive suffering, a solitary monk and a soldier gone AWOL sit together on a cold garden bench. The garden is full of the previous summer's dying plants. With a shiver the soldier wraps himself tight in an English car-coat, against the cold north wind coming off the raw mountains he has traversed. The monk wears a black hat, and a brown shawl folded in against the wind around his long grey beard. The soldier is lost, and in his mind he hears the words of a Cretan girl saying: 'You are so far from home'. He carries injustice in his heart. Injustice and shame. He carries these things heavily. The monk is still, not with repose but like a child's toy-top spun so fast it appears not to move at all. His back is straight as a sword, his pale concave face peering into the soldier's, waiting with an active acceptance that deep pain and harrowing sorrow is humanity's inevitable and shared burden.

You must speak. You must speak, because you are here.

~

I began. Perhaps naively I stated straight out that I had been assisting the *andartes* above Tzermiado as a wireless operator. But things had not worked out and I had struck out on my own. I had crossed the mountains, not knowing the tracks, and ended in such distress and hunger that I slaughtered my donkey for food.

I said this in a tone of sincere confession. Instead of sympathising, however, he asked me whether or not I was AWOL. I said that I s'posed so and then, to my surprise, he said that, given I've been with the *andartes* on Lasithi, I should have heard of his friend, the Englishman Pendlebury. He told me that before the war the archaeologist had stayed with him in the monastery on a number of occasions. He had slept in the same bed as I had the previous night.

The monk smiled at the memory. Then, as if we had this friend in common, I found myself elaborating on the stuff-up with the supply drops and how embarrassing it had been for me to have teamed up with Spenser.

~

We sat often in that rooftop garden during the first few days. I felt free to talk, partly I think due to the reverence I'd been taught to hold for priests back home, but also because of Andreas' extreme attentiveness. Led along by the quality of his listening, the sincerity of a monk's attention, I spoke of the mess that had ensued from that last night of the battle. I told him what I had done to Perry Coghlan in the cave, also about snipping Spenser's moustache, the humour of which did not seem to impress him overly much.

After a few days of such talking, of resting, sleeping and eating, and bringing Andreas well up to date with my war, and even some of my life before it, I began to outline for him the outlandish plans I had for fronting up at Alexandria. I would travel alone, I said, it would be easier to smuggle onto a caique that way, and I would not fall again into the trap of bonding with anyone, villagers or Allies. I would sidestep the official progress of the war and front the brass with a brand of courage based on the facts, and with nothing to lose.

Andreas said little in the course of these descriptions, other than to nod and encourage me to keep telling him how I felt.

At night, alone in my little cell, I would dream vividly, including dreams of further conversations in the rooftop garden. On one occasion, as I was describing our Baby dancing on the bombed-out rafters of Iraklio, I looked up to find that my listener was no longer the monk but the hare which had first led me into Agio Dormiton. I woke from this image with a raging thirst, and on another separate occasion I dreamt of the same hare, a dream in which we compared the birds around the lake at home with the vultures of the massif where I had shot Simmo. I recounted memories to the animal, the taste of plovers and yabbies, the flash of bronzewings and the scuttle of landrails, and how Vern would swim even as an eight year old right across to Vaughan Island, just to count the pelicans' nests. The hare listened and, as it did, I saw Simmo magically reassembled and healthy, making his way back down the shaley track towards Lasithi. I woke thirstily from this dream too, and drank from the copper mug on the sill above the bed before sliding back into a sleep that felt like the proverbial seventh heaven.

~

During the cold mornings at Agio Dormiton I would often remain wrapped up under the big plane tree in the courtyard, resting my blistered feet, allowing my burnt hand to finally mend once and for all, as Andreas shuffled from kitchen to chapel, from duty to routine among the terraces and deep in the bowels of the buildings above and beyond. For the first time in months I felt safe in the austerity of his care, and my urgency to press on subsided. In time, I took to fixing my own breakfasts on the giant hearth, from where I would hear his chanting muffled by the walls, or I'd hear knocking sounds, or footsteps, as he went about the daily regime. Typically it wasn't until mid-morning that I ever saw him, and often only briefly as he came back across the courtyard from praying before the icons in the chapel, or went out across the field towards a village in search of food or information. As the weather grew colder it wasn't long before we abandoned our afternoons on the rooftop garden and would sit, for long hours and into the evenings, in the warmth of the ancient kitchen, where he gave me his attention while tending to various stews and brews cooking on the stove.

It was during one of these afternoons at the table in front of the hearth that Andreas first showed his hand. I was explaining to him the devastation our mother's death had brought upon our father, how she had been so tender and strong, so spirited and forthright, and funny too, the captain of our team, so to speak, with Dad her labouring muscle and doting deputy. I declared outright to Andreas that I refused to return to Dad in my slouch hat with some bodgy 'missing in action' story about Vern. I'd demand answers from the RN, I told him, even if I had to go as far as buttonholing Admiral Cunningham over his gin and tonic in the Shepheard's Hotel.

The monk listened in his customary fashion before bringing a sudden halt to my frustrated outburst. Waving the beaten metal of the spoon in his hand he declared straight-out that I was a fool.

'Are you unwell, Wesley Cress?' he asked, with disdain in his eyes. 'Are you insane?'

'Nah, definitely not,' I fired back. 'It's a navy that considers it necessary to torpedo their own when –'

'Stop it!' Andreas shouted, his face suddenly explosive with anger. 'You cannot be so stupid, not here at Agio Dormiton!'

He turned his back on me and stirred the steaming pots. The ferocity of his voice still echoed amidst the stone walls of the monastery, but he said nothing more, so that I began, as if by force of gravity, to slowly comprehend the impossibility of what I had intended to do.

It became clear to me that, after the reprieve I was afforded by Spenser, when he had discovered the mess I had made of Perry Coghlan in the cave, and after my snipping of his moustache and going AWOL, I would most certainly be court-martialled the moment I got off a boat. Wireless contact from Cairo to Crete with an indignant Spenser would ensure, for instance, that my savaging of Coghlan would be brought back to the table. Any chance at redemption through assisting with the wireless at Karfi was now gone. The practical necessities that had made Spenser turn a blind eye to my guilt would no doubt be reviewed.

So it became evident to me that I would be done for on three counts: one, for nearly killing Wireless Operator Coghlan; two, for gross and physical insubordination against an English officer; and three, for going AWOL. And no amount of extenuating circumstances would get me off the hook. My humiliation of their phoney Theseus would see to that.

At the hearth, Andreas ceased stirring his pots, but did not turn to face me yet. The stone room fell silent, until the blinkers of grief fell away there at the long wooden table. I raised my eyes to the heavy rafters of the ceiling and began to sob like a boy.

Now Andreas turned to face me. From deep in the folds of his soutane he produced a handkerchief and handed it across the table. He then placed two stained cups on the coloured squares of the waxed cloth, and pouring thick black coffee for us both, he sat down opposite, saying: 'Wesley Cress. It is time for me to tell you about John Pendlebury.'

~

'When he first came here, by chance on one of his many long walks across the island, I cooked him a chicken. We talked. He had good Greek, even our dialects. He was curious about the customs of *Kriti* and asked me questions, some of which I could not answer, but it made us both happy when I could. We grew to like each other very much. From time to time, increasingly so as the war approached, he would appear unannounced from across the field or come striding up the steep slopes from the coast, *katsouna* in his hand, to resume our conversations.

We talked of the likeliness of the war reaching *Kriti*, of the possible outcomes when it did so, but also we spoke of his passion: Minoan archaeology. He would sleep in the bed which you use now and in that small copper mug on the sill he would leave his glass eye every evening, as if it was a vanity of the day which would only retard his dreams at night. In the mornings, like you he would meditate and rest, he would light candles in the chapel of the Dormiton, reflect on the icon of the death of the virgin, and by lunchtime we would sit amongst the plants on the roof and speak. He would stare up onto the mountains, thinking as always about the distant past but increasingly, particularly after Mussolini's army came over the Albanian border, assessing the possible horizons of tomorrow, next week, the future.

'Like you, Pendlebury also was suspicious of the British. His own people. But, not only that, he hated the Cretans as well. Yes! My people. Perhaps he had no time for the current humanity at all. But what he enjoyed, perhaps the only thing he loved, was the spirit of freedom in life itself. The spirit, beyond ambition or army, or right purpose or custom. He loved to be free to approach the spirit of truth. Everything else, everybody else, was, in some part of his being I suspect, merely an obstacle to this.

'Here at Agio Dormiton we are sheltered in prayer, but we are also terribly exposed by sacredness. We have built a sanctuary amongst the wilfulness of the world in order to approach the truth of the icon, the virgin and her death, a thing both difficult and hard to accept, but also real and beautiful. John enjoyed coming here for that reason, also for the food, but such a sanctuary of stillness and exposure could only hold him for a short time. He was a physical creature, born to move, to scale heights and outsprint danger. And, though he may not have put it in these words himself, I would suggest that his idea was to treat the whole earth as a monastery such as this. All behaviour to the contrary, as exhibited by the Germans, his fellow British, the Cretans, indeed by every race on the face of the earth, was in conflict with this spirit. And nothing, no act of sabotage or defilement, could surprise him. He would become disgusted of course, enraged, and then he would walk the coasts, the plateaux, pursuing his vision on the ridges and down through the throats of the gorges, always drawing nearer to the horizons of freedom.'

Andreas fell silent, coolly pursing his lips. Was he sizing me up, as if still debating whether I was of sufficient quality to hear what he had to say? He took up his cup, sipped, returned the *kafe* to the table, peering at me as if from deep under his eyelids. Then he smiled, either from the pleasure of the *kafe* or the tale to be told. He went on.

'We had an understanding, he and I, an understanding that there could only be one allegiance, whether in a time of war or between wars. This allegiance was not to an idea but to the spirit, and through the self, to God. For John this revelation came in a shard he had found, in the stronghold at Karfi, not long after the Royalists had bombed *Kriti* for supporting Venizelos. You see, Wesley, like you we have been attacked by those who others think of as our own. But they are not our own!

'The shard Pendlebury found was just a small thing, a sliver of stone from a dream of the past, and although he found it high on that peak, a long way from the coast, it showed a dolphin in the sea. As it leapt between the waves, the dolphin carried a man on its back, but that was not all it carried. Clinging to the back of the man on the dolphin was a small child. For Pendlebury the shard became the key to the universe. In the garden here he would hold it in his hands and I would see in his eyes – even I suspected, in the one made of glass – that it had entered his soul. As only the truth can do.

'A dolphin carries a man carrying a child. The chain of relation. The complete story, but without the mother, just as we are here at Agio

Dormiton, where the virgin has died. But are we without her here? In the shard the journey of life is caught in midstream, bound in the salt sea of our mother blood, the earth is our womb and daily we dwell within it and live with the threat of our own expulsion, from time and from all possible love. For John, the eternal icon, the relationship at the heart of our human nature, was a dolphin carrying a man carrying a child.

'For you though, Wesley, the rider of the dolphin has temporarily forsaken the child, he has shrugged him off, he has left him to drown in the sea. His very own child. Returned to the mother. You have been travelling across *Kriti* not with the key to the universe but with the key to the underworld. And you have suffered greatly for this contortion of nature.'

~

That night, when I went to my cell, the first thing that caught my eye was the small copper mug on the sill above the bed. I imagined the archaeologist, after a day of conversations with the monk, removing the silica eye and setting it aside in the copper mug. I saw him lying down to read one-eyed by candlelight, some periodical from the British School in Athens perhaps, until he was finally ready for sleep. And there, in the months and years leading up to the suicidal descent of the blond young men of the *Fallschirmjaeger* onto the island, he would dream through the night.

As I dampened the coals in the *magali* and lay down myself to sleep I felt my course had been altered. Yet again. I drifted off like Pendlebury in that plain timber cot between stone walls, knowing well why the shard of the dolphin carrying the man carrying the child was so important to him. Simply put, neither the dolphin nor the man was struggling with its burden. The child that they carried felt safe and free. At any moment any one of the three could be torn asunder and thrown apart, by a rogue wave, or the insatiable demands of human tragedy. But in the heart's eye of the man who had scrabbled and scraped into the grey schist of Karfi to uncover the shard, none of that need ever have happened. As a piece of pottery, a scrap of hope and truth, it had endured. As an idea, it still persisted. And now, perhaps because Andreas himself had seen the shard and because I now lay in the archaeologist's bed, it became a fresh and living thing to me, a shard not only of ancient times or of yesterday but an aspiration for today and tomorrow.

Drifting off into a dreamless sleep, I felt in need of no other image. No nightmare could touch me. For once the waking hours of life had given due recognition to the deeper desires of my being.

~

The next day after lunch Andreas resumed the account of his friendship with the archaeologist, but this time taking a surprising slant.

Once again sitting over two coffee cups on the table, he began to tell how in the days before the war he had shared the duties and rituals of monastic life at Agio Dormiton with two other monks, Kiefer and Dimitrios. As rumours increased of the war's approach, as Pendlebury and others brought news of the invincible march of the Nazis through Europe, the three monks found themselves divided in their response. Kiefer was of German extraction. He had made a pilgrimage as a young man to Greece, and ultimately to Crete, where he had been compelled to take vows as an Orthodox monk. Dimitrios, on the other hand, was a native Cretan, from Galatas, in the north of the island, near Chania.

According to Andreas, as the likelihood of conflict grew greater through '38 and '39, the German monk Kiefer began to struggle with his allegiances. And when finally the staunch neutrality of Greece's fascist government was overcome by the Italian and then the German invasion, the blood in the German's veins had proved stronger than the prayers in his heart. Dimitrios and Kiefer began to bicker and then to argue vehemently until finally one morning the two of them clashed in the chapel, right at the foot of the virgin's icon. They came to blows. Blood was spilt on the sacred floor.

Within days of this catastrophe they had departed for their respective homelands: Dimitrios to his family in Galatas, and Kiefer to join up with the German units as they pushed south towards Athens on the mainland.

Andreas was left alone at Agio Dormiton. On Pendlebury's first visit after the departure of the two monks, on a field trip to the south coast for the purpose of arranging efficient networks against the coming invasion, Andreas and he discussed their decision to leave, and also that of Andreas to stay behind alone. By this stage the archaeologist had been fitted out in a British captain's uniform and issued with an army car, but he preferred to walk when he could and also to maintain one or two Cretan flourishes in his uniform, such as the Turkish sword-stick he wore slung from his bandolier. Every inch of him was ready to fight but as Andreas put it, 'not for the British against the Germans, or even for the Cretans against the invaders, but so that the child would continue its journey on the back of the man who rode the dolphin.'

Both Andreas and John Pendlebury had agreed that the other two monks' transition from meditation to war amounted to an eviction of the possibility of truth in their lives. It was clear that only Andreas had remained steadfast in his vocation, only he had laid sufficiently deep roots in the ground of his spiritual life not to be swept away by the war as if by rain gushing down the Arvi gorge.

'But Pendlebury too was a fighter, no?' I challenged Andreas. 'Surely he would have seen the logic in Kiefer and Dimitrios wanting to join in the war.'

Andreas was unimpressed by this remark. 'John Pendlebury was unhappy,' he replied. 'Unhappy that the monks he had admired in more meaningful days here at Agio Dormiton could suddenly change direction. He viewed their monastic pleasures then as mere stylisations. The blood spilt before the icon represented to him an unnatural rifting caused by an evil wind. The dolphin was knocked off balance and the man and child were thrown into turbulence. It was the severance of the connection. Something akin to the Mycenaean invasion. And, in my own way, I agreed with him. The dolphin has a predestined leap, from which comes its natural grace. It is the fragility and uncertainty of man which requires assistance through meditation, it is we who need to be supported and shown the way to such grace, so that in turn the child of man is not cast into the sea before it has even learnt to swim.

'Ultimately John believed that the Fuhrer had mistaken himself for the dolphin. The way he parades across Europe in the guise of a predestined leap. But he also believed that this uniformed dolphin will be gored and the whole Nazi enterprise will sink. Yet all men have been caught up in this epic misapprehension. The British are caught up, all its dominions, the Greeks and Cretans. Your Australian army and your brother are included, Wesley. For the vain presumption is doomed to fail and when the war that has ridden on its back then ends, even the Allies will have nothing to hold on to. They too, slowly but surely, will also sink. Unless they learn the truth of the shard.'

~

Later that day, wrapped up in a coarse blanket under the plane tree in the courtyard, my mind grew troubled and filled with angry illogicalities, butting like persistent goats up against me, as I thought of Andreas' words. It seemed clear that as a solitary monk Andreas lived a devotional life, as much in the mind as on the earth, but how could John Pendlebury, the man who Tassos had described as a *pallikari*, a great warrior, the man who had combed the island, revolver in hand, sword across his chest, harnessing the villagers' fire to fight into a systematic force, how could he have reconciled such a transcendent attitude to the war, if that's what it was?

As I sat under the tree, feeling confused and unsure, looking out over the flat field through which I'd arrived in the footsteps of the hare, I once again imagined Vern in my place. Vern, who was known to shoot the odd hare from the saddle of his mare between dashing off poems in the days when he was alone on the farm. He undoubtedly would have held a better conversation with this monk than I.

Eventually I closed my eyes and saw him again, this time not struggling to find his way out through the RN hatches but as a blurry figure on a fading gypsum shard. Yet he was not the innocent on the shard, not the child on the back of the man riding the dolphin, he was the rider himself. In a wince, I closed my eyes more tightly and saw that there was still a child on the shard. A child being flung. His hands were outstretched in desperation, his face alarmed and forsaken, as he fell helplessly off the man and the dolphin, slewn awkwardly through the air.

The child was me.

So the days passed in winter gloom and a series of severe windstorms which scoured down off the mountains and whistled up the big monastery chimney. The summer courtyard was now bare, the leafless plane tree opening up a grey sky etched with the pale brown tracework of its branches. My question was when, and if, and now for what purpose, I would press on to find a caique to take me to Alex or Cairo. Would I actually, as I had pretended to the good people of Marmaketo and to the Maori in the village tub, just rejoin my unit, now that Andreas had convinced me that buttonholing top brass with my questions about the *Imperial* would be a futile task?

And yet still my desire for answers burned, as well as an almost gravitational reluctance to resume the war, a shithouse bitterness of feeling that seemed somehow embedded within me by the facts, even though in all likelihood there would be no official documentation of Vern's death issued by HQ. I'm sure that, as far as the paperwork was concerned, he could have been as alive or as dead as I was. But I knew otherwise, and so, it seemed to me, did the sad whispery weather falling through the plane tree onto the flagstones of the courtyard at Agio Dormiton.

Back in Iraklio Tassos had described how, in the days immediately preceding our arrival, Pendlebury had been working in a frenzy, venturing far and wide in a race against time to solidify the *andarte* networks. This was when he had taken to leaving his glass eye on the desk of his shambolic office, to let visitors know when he was away and could not be contacted. Instead he wore a black patch over the empty socket and, with the motley of military and local garb he was wearing, he cut a curious figure as he went about the valleys and plateaux marshalling the native networks.

One afternoon in the kitchen, Andreas furthered Tassos' rendition by describing how Pendlebury had visited Agio Dormiton on one last occasion during the days of the black patch.

'He missed his wife and children, though not like a Cretan. They were a guilt that he lived with, I believe. A former life, which he had outgrown. But I understood this, not only because I lived alone here at

Agio Dormiton but because I myself had been where not many Cretans had before me. When I was young my family had sent me to London in the days when Venizelos and the Royalists were bickering over our country's entry into the First World War. From there I travelled extensively: along the coast of France and down the Italian peninsula, all as a Greek neutral you see, and I developed, in the midst of that other war, an affection for the discoveries of solitude. The train of thoughts you have when you travel alone. The pathways in the spirit you can pursue. Without the restraints of gossip or custom. Increasingly as I travelled this new condition deepened in equal measure with the deprivations that I saw, but I began to feel that it was not so much a discovery I was making as a reacquaintance I was experiencing. A reunion with a source, the familiar light of a known horizon. And gradually, in fact on an empty train one rainy afternoon between Oxford and London, I grew homesick for that horizon. Homesick for god.

'When I discussed this journey with John he expressed similar feelings himself, indeed I believe they were feelings which united us. He spoke of thoughts he had on the long miles walking the massifs. His deepest peace, he said, was to be found in a pass gemmed with poppies, the scent of citrus in his nostrils, in solitary meditation on the meaning of the shard. The meaning he had dug for. The meaning he had had to journey so far from his home to find.'

To my surprise, as I listened to this talk of redemption and solitude, I began to be seduced into thinking that perhaps I too was destined for a life which afforded me such insights. But, as if sensing my thoughts, Andreas began to talk then with great emphasis of the distance I had travelled. Not the distance over the plateaux and mountains from Iraklio but the further distance from the south of the world, from Australia. From my family. Which, as he said, was quite obviously a considerable ingredient of my distress.

And so, by way of conducting confession almost, or as if he was some torturer bent on teasing out the truth, he had me describe the life we had on the lakes, the farming and the society, the drystoning and the birds, the fishing, the droughts and the floods. I found myself talking proudly of the country, the things my family had built there, and, just as I had on another faraway night when Adrasteia and I talked in the courtyard of her uncle's villa in Iraklio, I told him enthusiastically about the craters of Red Rock, even laughing about the early years when first I, then Vern, were made to pick the scoria out of the paddocks when we were too young for other jobs.

As I recounted it all to the monk, the use we made of the old rocks for fencing, the trips to Colac on the horse and jinker, I had the realisation that what I was describing was a way of life, rather than a way of thought such as he had described, and I saw, for the first time I believe, how we'd in fact lived like animals on the lake after our mum had died. We had land, it was good rich land, and in that both ourselves and our sheep were privileged, but in no other way. The closeness we were allowed as kids to the old family stories and songs, to the bandicoot and the blue-tongue, was countered now by the way our lives were presented back to us. The identities we had foisted on us in the aftermath of our mother's death. Shrill identities. 'Upstanding. Hardworking. Australian.' As opposed to 'Amoral. Deep feeling. Stateless.' Under the close watch of the monk of Agio Dormiton, the full sadness of this situation dawned on me greatly.

'And your religion?' Andreas asked, as if he once again was reading my mind. 'What were your teachings, your rituals, your customary way of approaching the divine?'

I scoffed loudly then, in full larrikin volume. I remember looking about at the monastery kitchen, the centuries of cooking smoke on its walls, the solidity and the grime, and then at the man in front of me who was peering into my eyes with an intensity almost vicious in the extent of its feeling. And all that came to mind at that moment was sheep. Poor dumb sheep. The sheep I saw through my bedroom window every morning as a child. The sheep I sheared, knackered, dipped, shot, boiled. St Brendan's was only a mile down the road and before Mum had gone we'd been regulars at mass, but not after that. And despite the fact we had pigs as well, horses and hens too, and geese and always dairy cows in the way of mixed farms like ours, all I could see in answer to Andreas' question about religion was sheep. Speechless sheep, thoughtless even, on the slopes of our paddocks. The lambs of God. The soldiers of war.

I looked for solace now in the eyes of the monk on the other side of the big table. But he simply stared, said nothing, until I found myself speaking further, filling the silence, delving deep into the gathering darkness.

Time after time, I said, it was my father in his own grief who had let me down, and year after year he'd got it arseabout by sending me away and keeping Vern close. He never knew the sacrifices I'd have made for it to be otherwise. To be a young farmer full of nous and nods and grunts of dry surmise. I never got the chance to work the farm. Only to fight a war, supposedly *for* the farm. But it was a war I'd already lost in my own heart, and once you lose your heart like that can you ever find it again?

~

Later on that night, in my cot in the monk's cell, I held the copper mug in my hands and sipped at the water Andreas had poured for me. The bed was firm and clean, the *magali* had warmed the room, but I lay thinking how all around us on the island the terror continued. Women and children were being lined up and shot, even as I lay there. To the south, across the sea to North Africa, to the east across to Smyrna and pushing out towards Russia, and back up the other way into the battlefields of Europe, the landscape was damp with human blood.

A wave of guilt like dysentery washed through me for my relatively safe situation. But that's all it was, a wave. It came, I felt it, and then it passed. I placed the mug up on the rough white sill, stoked up the *magali* for the night, and blew out the candle.

I was done. Having described it to the monk I was done with what I was, who I had been. Done with sheep, with war, with other people's company. I had at least matured enough to understand the solitude which Andreas had spoken of and I planned to seek it out further. It seemed the only logical response to the world. I was sure in my heart Vern would have felt the same.

From the courtyard outside my cell I heard the sound of the monk taking his nightly piss against the base of the plane tree. Once again the stream of liquid battering the trunk seemed to go on and on. When it finally finished I turned to the wall and sank away gratefully into what seemed like a premonition of death: a black void.

XXV

T HE RACE DAYS HERE ON KING HAVE ALWAYS BEEN SINGULAR AFFAIRS, but very proud for that, and relished, among other things, for the true unlikeliness of them ever taking place. The runners are made up of mainland cast-offs and Tasmanian hand-me-downs, horses earmarked for the pasture or pure dotage who've been resuscitated to compete by the keen intent of new island owners and, of course, by the tasty grass. Like the islanders themselves these horses are more often than not rugged up through three or four seasons in heavy quilted wools but unlike their owners they are never fully exposed to the everpressing insinuations of the Bass Strait winds. Racing is a festival here, an orna- ment, and such nags that are lucky enough to avoid the abattoirs, are given every cosset in preparation for the race. They're given snug hard- wood stables fit for the Christ child himself, or, if outside, they stand in the leeside of Dutch barns, and on the best chomp as well, even at the expense of cattle and sheep whose only benefit to the farmer as race season approaches is mere money. The island racehorses, on the other hand, can bring their owners the genuine prerogatives of true one-upmanship and pride. And all with a tone of mirth, due to the absurdity of the races taking place on an island ideally suited to creatures who abide in burrows.

The Fermoys had never raced a horse, partly due to the frivolity of the enterprise but mainly because horses weren't Nat's thing, but I had been asked by Brian Robinson to go to the cup with himself and Rose and figured there was some kind of chance, given the co-op's involvement with running the meet, that Leonie would be there regardless. Although we'd had our day over the gurrying at Uncle True's, I'd still not seen her at Wait-a-While since she left the box of ink at the door that first visit. Every now and again I'd arrive home to find another such delivery, of ink and my most recently sent pages, all repackaged and waiting for me under the bullnose. I knew from this that she must have been watching my movements but nevertheless I hadn't been game enough – given what I'd written and given the added complication of what True had told me about the trouble with Rickie Keith – to front up at the co-op on one of her days there, let alone to head up north to seek her out. I'd come to rely, therefore, on my writing as a form of communication. Which still felt decidedly risky. When it came to the issue of actually seeing her I could only hope for pure happenstance, and, despite the smallness of King and how omnipresent she seemed upon it, that was not a foolproof solution. Good friends, even family, could go years on their circulations of the island without ever bumping into each other. And of course, if she knew when to drop off the packages without bumping into me then I felt as if she knew where I was the rest of the time as well. I reasoned though that she'd never pick me to attend a big social occasion and, as a consequence, I figured race day was the go.

The morning of the meet, however, as if in anticipation of an event which I wasn't sure my nerves could handle – not my shell-shocked nerves, which were being both stirred up and greatly helped by the writing, but my purely romantic nerves – (a man confesses to dubious things by post and then sallies off to the races to woo the girl who knows it all? From a certain distance one would have to say to that, and with clear derision: *you've got Buckley's*) – I found upon waking that my eyes were stuck together as if by the heavy sea-mist that hung in the air; and that I could barely prise them open as the day demanded I awake.

I've learnt since that some mornings are just like that here: the mist rises from the strait to meet the lenticular hovering like a halo above the swatch of land. The result is a sticky density in the air that I liken to nothing other than the density of a dream. You can see the motion of the mist like a sculpted thing, the light too, streaming past as you cut the wood, or pouring down the gullies with the mobility of solid water itself. But now, on the morning all my previous days on the island had been decidedly leading to – even the days before my arrival, even the months and years – the salt mist had jammed my lids in a bout of littoral conjunctivitis. I'd been blinded – well almost, I could just peer through my sticky lashes at the room – occluded anyway by the conditions of the tiny spot that is the island in the wide engulfing of blue-green fate and power.

The body is a contrarian no doubt, and, as Lascelles had already pointed out to me that day in the pub, sometimes the body is your only voice. I'd gone so far as to admit to myself that yes I was prepared to accept Brian Robinson's invite to the meet, but not so far as to prepare myself for the deeper course I was now set upon: to face up to love.

I lay back and stopped trying. Pulled the blankets up around the stubble on my chin. Relaxing my eyes, I went where my body demanded my spirit should go.

I had loved only once before, in puberty, or at least not long after. She was from a farm at Balintore, on the edge of Lake Colac, not even ten miles from our place on the shore of Corangamite. One summer, in the wake of Mum's death, our fathers had a bit to do with each other, I still don't know why looking back, although her father, Ray Murtagh, was known for his innovations and was probably helping the old man out by clueing him up on the science of the place, the chemistries of the dirt and what could be done with the gaps between the cooled volcanic lava or somesuch. That neighbourly gesture, or collaboration, or tutelage or whatever it was, didn't last long, just that one summer in the middle of the Great Depression, but long enough to shape the man I was to become.

So we were there one day, on the fresh lakeshore at Balintore, catching tench with her brothers from their jetty out front of their pile, and all was normal or thereabouts, when I was sent back up to the house with a full bucket of fish, to empty them in the trough and bring it back empty and ready to fill again. I was also to ask for passionfruit, which grew on their trellis, off their enclosed back courtyard and which could tide us over for the rest of the afternoon.

I remember I emptied the fish into the trough, smelt the gunpowdery whiff of the darkened smithing shed nearby, but what I really can't forget is when I came around the brighter side of the back of the house to get the passionfruit.

She was down on her haunches amongst the quartz pebbles of the courtyard, her brown hair was wet and combed, she seemed freshly showered and was idling there on her own, as if in some wistful, reflective moment. Her skin was browned almost to the colour of her hair by the summer, her head was set at a languid or recollective angle, and as I unwittingly rounded the house side with the empty bucket, the sight of her changed the whole set-up of my world.

One glance, the aromas around, her freshness and the unexpected privacy of the moment, along with the disinterested kindness she had shown me in previous encounters, and reality itself out there at Balintore seemed to gulp and then glide onwards into the serenest thing. The everyday lakeshore world was transported into full feeling right before my very eyes.

What I can't remember now is whether I too leant down amongst those white courtyard pebbles, or whether we spoke right then, or whether I just made my explanations and went straight to the passion-fruit vines. To be honest I expect we must have spoken and that I too must have leant down and toyed with the pebbles, but it is the pure charge of my feelings at the first sight of her which overwhelms and dominates me. All else, really, is a consequence of that.

Her name was Sarah Murtagh, she was a year younger than I, and I lay adrift under the blankets at Wait-a-While, reflecting on what had happened.

The rest of the afternoon fishing was marked by the distance I felt from her brothers and Vern as we continued dangling our handlines from the jetty. We hauled in the redfin and tench and I barely cared; back at home later that night I couldn't sleep for the delicious thought of her there amongst the pebbles of the courtyard. My body had already burst from its cocoon some months before but now it was some other part of me altogether that had finally reached its potential. And that night I was ecstatic with my secret. Not because it *was* secret – it felt in a way as if the whole world knew or, better put, as if this new full brimming feeling was synonymous, indivisible from the world and everything else in it – but because I had been transformed, in that miraculous event that turns ugly pupae into sacred moths, gawky tadpoles into perfected frogs and slow-moving caterpillars into the full fluttering through the air of beautiful butterflies.

But I had to roll over, there in the bed at Wait-a-While, and squeeze those sticky eyes shut in a grimace at the thought of what happened next.

As the days of the summer went by, and we made further trips in our Dodge to Balintore, my feelings only grew. We would stay for cook-ups in the dusk on the lawn below the Murtagh's covered front verandah and I confided in no-one. Well, Vern was too young and the others were her brothers, and besides, it was only to her that I had anything to say, only with her that the difficulty of words could be superseded. And one night, during one of those cook-ups on the lawn below the Murtaghs' front verandah in which our dad was getting on famously with the Murtaghs and their friends with beers in hand by the fire, I managed to conjure a situation – or did she manage to? – where we ended up together, and alone, in that gloomy smithing shed with the enormous stitched bellows and the sharp smell of cordite.

She had a dress with no sleeves and the dark skin of her limbs almost disappeared into the darkness of the shed. I don't know how we began but we nuzzled like horses, my face in her hair, and the smell of it now overpowering the ammo, and then our lips were touching and our young teeth clicking against each other as we kissed. We knew it couldn't last for long, they would wonder where we were, but I remember she was alternatively solemn and amused with what was happening and, as we emerged from the shed into the sound of cicadas, my feet hardly touched the ground. She was new, minted, and I was buzzing like a bee.

Sorry to say, that was the only time we kissed, as whatever charitable instinct or pastoral inventiveness had brought our fathers together now seemed abruptly to scotch itself. The freshwater of Balintore and Lake Colac became another country again, suddenly the most unlikely destination for a family outing, and I was left to contemplate my options. I could ride over there and hover around the jetty in the guise of fishing and hope she'd see me, but it was more than likely her brothers would sight me first. But maybe they'd send me back to the house again,

I thought, as the bucket filled and they grew hungry. I could take Vern along too, as a further decoy. At that stage, prior to his own emergence in puberty and before the negation of my own, he'd do anything I asked. But then of course I'd be responsible for him, we could hardly afford any more trauma after Mum, and I wouldn't be able to slip away. No, I'd be better on my own.

What I really couldn't face, however, was sticking out like a sore thumb. Why would I all of a sudden be looking for tench and redfin on their jetty when I'd already bragged that summer about the fish to be had in my other favourite spots on the lake? I would stand out all right, in the full exposure and freshness of my innermost feelings.

Compounding these difficulties though was the fact that I'd been making blues on the farm. I was my father's son after all, set to head to boarding school that year but feeling also as if there was still time to show my father how big a mistake that was by showing him my suitability for the *real* tasks in life. Not books, not pushing a pen around some Lands Department office, not even as a gumbooted vet who'd make his rounds like some Inspector of Beasts. I wanted to fence, drench, dip, plough, slaughter, drove to market day, and understand the innards of all the newfangled machinery that was coming on. And now love, this dam-burst in my heart, this catching of my breath and gliding in my mind, was getting in the way. I put the tractor fuel in the Dodge for a start and was made to suck it back out through Mum's flower hose. I turned the wrong way with the hardwood girder for the hayshed we were building and nearly beheaded Vern, and then, one night after haymaking, a storm had come in thick and sudden from out over Pirron Yallock. I was told to tarp the bales on the tray of the trap. We climbed up on top to get home quick but I'd tied it slack and the ropes got caught in the wheels and soon the whole show began to slip with the momentum toward the horses. My reflexes have always been quick but Dad got dragged forward and sent tumbling from his perch and was trampled. He was cut up amidst all the rain and the lightning and broke his collarbone, and all because I hadn't tied the tarp properly. Since Mum had died he wouldn't sleep in their bed and over the next few weeks his reluctant and cranky convalescence in our two-room sleep-out above the pines was confirmation enough that I was well destined for St Pats, Ballarat.

I went to bed those nights in a welter of confusion, traumatised by events. Our mum had died, leaving Dad alone and Vern with a kind of immortal glow from having spent the last months of her illness sleeping in her bed with her, and now this. I began to flounder in my feelings and to form the notion that the richness of a life of love and beauty was a direct antagonist of the productive life we required on the farm. Because only I knew what was in my head when that girder had swung and nearly sent my little brother off to heaven to be with Mum. All my judgement, and what I considered my natural skill around the place, was now being frayed by the endless pros and cons of a bogus fishing trip to the Murtaghs' jetty at Balintore. The delicacy of emotion that had been born as I came around their house side to the pebbled courtyard and saw her, was now convoluting, twisting in her absence. So I lay awake in the sleep-out, listening to Vern's smooth breathing beside me, the 'mopoke' of the owl in the pines, and eventually made what I saw at the time as my fair dinkum manly decision.

As I see it now, with the benefit of what I've been through and all that has been shown to me of the unjust gulfs between outer and inner worlds, worlds of pretence and substance, I clamped down on love and wrung my heart dry, like a rag from the laundry cupboard that has done the job and now the job is over. I tossed it into the corner and every-thing that went with it. I made my investment, right there as an earnest and sincere young boy-man in the sleep-out, I made my investment in doing 'the right thing'.

I would not chase down and quench the sweet fire that made me toss and turn with anticipated joy and kiss the pillow endlessly. I would not water the flower, I would disregard it like a worn piston-housing, like a dank splotch of wool or a stillborn collie, because that way we could get on with it, make a go of things around the lake, and not be distracted forever and a day by the click of kissing teeth in a strange smithing shed.

And so it was I made no more mistakes that summer, none indeed of that nature forever after for the only mistake worth not making had already been made. Instead then of riding out in search of Sarah and love in the guise of tench, I knuckled down.

It occurred to me behind those gunky eyes on the morning of the race day at Wait-a-While, that perhaps I had bequeathed all that to Vern. Not Sarah Murtagh herself but, yes, I left for boarding school, I took what was in fact his rightful place among the scholarly books, but more than that, I left a place behind for him. An untrodden space for a heart of beautiful things. And what I had to do with girls and women from that day on was sociable, fun, wisecracking, but nothing more, so that no wagon with me at the ropes would end up as a death trap on the slopes of love's volcano ever again.

With a heavy heart at the thought of all this, I forced my eyes unstuck from the consequences of Sarah Murtagh. I got out of bed, washed my face at the sink. My eyes remained swollen but eventually the gunk across the lids and lashes was washed away. Before we went to the track, Brian was coming by mid-morning for a beer and they weren't even on the ice.

~

By the time he showed up around eleven I was still in no mood for drinking and I told him so. 'No reason for you not to open one though,' I said, and, laughing at the sight of my swollen eyes, he agreed and told me I looked like a sunburnt blowfly.

We sat at the table and, with a glass in hand, he admired my hut. He was all excited with the mood of the race day but was taking a kind of civic pause to admire the work of a man who he'd helped up onto his feet. He hadn't been on the land since he'd sold it to me. We spoke of the expense of the Aga stove I'd had brought over on the boat, how it was worth every cent, just for the canny way you could control the heat in different parts of the thing with the effectiveness of the dampers and screw-vents. He shook his head in wonder, with the humble unknowing of a man for whom all meals were cooked by his wife. I could tell he was glad for me and felt in some way a sponsor of my domestic happiness. I didn't want to wreck the cheery note so played along, singing the praises of not only the hut but the block as well. But when he nodded towards the ink bottle, pen and paper, over on the small table with the volume of Epictetus under the northern window, and said, 'Young Lascelles mentioned you'd been writin'', a tremor went through my veins.

I pretended to ignore the remark at first, got up from my chair and suggested we go. I'd planned to boil an egg for Brian and serve it with some of the abalone I'd picked up the previous day because I knew he'd like such a feed on race day, but now I changed tack.

'Hold on a minnie, Wes,' he said, with broad amusement. 'Let me finish my beer. There's still plenty of time.'

Brian Robinson was, in fact, so at home in his skin, and also within the second skin of his island, he was irrepressible. I miss him, even now. It was his customary manner that, in the most jocular of ways, he'd make it clear there was no way he'd do what he didn't want to do. An enviable trait. And so, not knowing where to look now, and with sudden urgency in my blood, I turned back to the stove to boil that egg.

Brian rattled on about this and that from his pew at the table but I could sense him peering at the back of my head, trying to work out what had got into me all of a sudden. But I knew he wouldn't fathom too hard. There would come a point, perhaps only a turn or two down the track of his thoughts, where he'd surrender all speculations to the idea that my oddness of behaviour, and increasingly the abruptness of men in general, was all to do with the war. Which of course, in my case, that race day morning in the hut on Wait-a-While, was perfectly true.

As the water was simmering so was my blood, at the thought of bloody Lascelles, with the sly discretion of a nosey postmaster, steaming open my packages and reading my accounts before re-sealing and delivering them to Leonie. It was his vocation to understand the hearts and minds of soldiers, so he could work tirelessly on their behalf to make sure everything was done and everything was available for them to enjoy a normal Australian life on their return. He would leave no stone unturned, no package unopened . . .

And of course at his lookout in the PO he'd see all the to's and fro's. The way a letter is copperplated or enveloped, the nervous way it is posted, the promptness and tone of the reply. I was now convinced he'd seen me coming, that's for sure.

I could have written all the stuff that came after, my wild colonial heroisms when I finally saw beyond the search for justice and reason of those months immediately after I missed the boats. But I wasn't writing for him, was I? I was writing *because* of him.

At the thought of my tales of darkness, my sins, being broadcast all over the island, I could stand it no more. Turning my back on the egg and the bubbling water on the Aga, I held my palm out to silence Brian

Robinson's genial prattle, and said: 'What exactly did John Lascelles say to you about my writing?'

Brian was shocked of course, at being so pompously silenced, but then he grew po-faced at the request.

'Ah, nothin' too much. Just that you'd been sendin' packages to Leonie Fermoy.'

'*Yair?*'

'Well yair, but only because we were talkin' about Leonie and agreeing what a good sort she was. Given what she's put up with.'

'But how come you were talking about me? What have I got to do with what she's bloody well put up with?'

A cloud scudding west passed over Brian's face. Just as quickly it was gone but he said: 'Hang on a minute there, Wes. Bugger all was said about you, if you want to know.'

'Yair, well *what?*'

'Look fella, it's not a crime to be keen on a lass. She's not married or anythin'.'

Poor old Brian Robinson, with this remark he really blew the lid off my fury.

'Look here, mate! I don't have any worries about *that*,' I shouted.

Brian's mouth fell open at my volume and force. He couldn't have known what that morning's memory of the day years ago at Balintore had to do with the pitch of it. But I left him in no doubt anyway that he'd got his surmising wrong.

'What I want to know,' I went on, 'is what that fucker Lascelles said about my writing.'

Brian took a well-earned sip of his beer. 'Well, as I say, bugger all. Only that Leonie's been happy to receive the packages when he delivers them. And that she'd said they contained your "lovely writin".'

'That was all.'

'Too right that was all. Lascelles himself said nothin' about it, only what Leonie had reckoned to him. Which, I might say, he seemed happy about, on your behalf.'

Turning back to the stove, I spooned out the egg. I'd burnt the toast so scraped the charcoal off into the sink, smeared it with butter, my mind still racing, then scalded the abalone with the water from the stovetop and presented it all to Brian on a cracked hospital plate.

'By jingo! Magnificent, Wesley. You eatin'?'

I managed a thin smile. 'Maybe some toast and ab,' I said, before turning away again.

~

We growled out of Wait-a-While in the Robinsons' new truck, Brian marvelling continuously at how green everything was for the middle of summer. 'Green as Lasithi,' I heard myself saying, and as we crested the remainder of the hill I was suddenly describing the plateau where I lived in a cave with a certain Pommy officer with the codename Theseus, as if it had no qualms attached, no tragic aspect, just goodhearted peasants who knew how to best use the pastoral advantages of their altitude.

Brian betrayed no surprise that I'd mentioned a moment from the war. His only comment was that he never knew Crete was an island of snow-capped mountains and green summer plateaus. Needless to say I didn't go on to tell him it was also the original home of labyrinthine complications. 'Yair, not many people here know about snow in the Med,' was all I said in reply, wondering now at how the other island had snuck into my conversation at all.

More pheasants than usual seemed to line the road as we bumped along, almost as if with their flourishing magenta and mustard markings they'd come out specially for race day. The air was fresh now and the sky woollen with cloud but the cabin of the truck was warm and smelt of molasses. Brian manhandled the long stick of the gearbox and asked no more questions. By the time we were veering south he was well and truly anticipating the meet.

'Horses aren't really my go, but it's good for everyone, isn't it, to kick off the year. A celebration of our own, around Christmas and that. Plus, it's a lot more exciting than the euchre tournament.'

We swung north then in a surprising loop, as if Brian was that content he just wanted to take in the scenery. Soon we were round the corner near my old haunt by the ten sheoaks. I hadn't passed that way for a while and looked across Brian out the driver's side window.

'Yair. That's where you first propped, weren't it?' Brian said. 'When you showed up.'

'That's right.'

Back on the Main Road to the track the festive pheasants had thinned out but the racegoers were thick on the ground. People were on foot, on bikes and horses, carts and tractors and cars; we even saw a motorbike and sidecar going by with the rest of the crowd streaming out of Currie. The pub had put on a Cup Day breakfast and no doubt they were all half-shickered already as they bumbled along. No sign of Leonie amongst them though. Not that I expected there to be. She'd told me at Uncle True's, amongst other things, that she never ate breakfast.

We parked the truck trackside, paid the entrance fee to John Lascelles' father who was collecting the gate, received our programs, and strode into the affair.

I was shy, and Brian knew it. I'd avoided all crowds since I'd arrived and straightaway was raising a few weather-flecked eyebrows with my blue suit, red tie, buttoned collar. They'd all been abreast of my movements, of course, and in their minds' eyes at least, as they lay down at night, I'd become a fixture. From north at Wickham down to Stokes Point in the south their minds could reach out and touch each farm or house, each person on it. No one could escape, not even me. The crabby hermit soldier, or the seventh star of the Pleiades, rarely seen yet helping to define the other six.

The words came to me, as I reeled from the conviviality of the knocked-up Turf Club crowd. They came amidst my flinching and prickling, and as the sweat poured into my shoes:

I will love you with the power of two men, one for who you are, the other for what you'll become.

It was most untimely. Perhaps it was all the writing I'd been doing but, either way, as Brian and I met up with Rose Robinson, who'd come to the pavilion house before with her sister Annie to lay out the sponges and the flowers and vases, and as I was introduced to Annie, a small fat woman with an earnest Presbyterian manner, and also to Ray Sykes of the race committee, I was almost blinded by the phrase.

I squeezed hands with Annie and Sykes and then blurted rather brusquely, given the ladies present and the concentrated formalities of the Cup Day pavilion in this the endless ephemerality of Bass Strait, that I was 'busting for a piddle'. I shot off without waiting for reactions, nor for the inevitable humour of Brian's admonishment. I scooted away, taut and upright in my suit, my head swimming as if from a close-run thing, before the first race had even begun.

I ended up, just for the distance I needed to put between the privacy of the phrase and the public occasion, way out beyond the saddling paddock and the other clearings, down behind the turn into the home straight and the clumps of trees which huddled right up to the rail as if for a better view. I pissed in the shadows and when I finished something inside me began to resemble unity. I was excited, even gasping a little. The power of two men, two hearts of love, came rushing into me. One born a loyal plodder, the other, the younger one, exaltedly riding out on the sheer green slopes of his home volcano.

Then, as I emerged from the darkness of the paperbark stand, out into the brightness of the event, the truth and power of the phrase dissolved into a million or more infinitesimal granules coursing through my bloodstream. I shuddered and shivered. I looked back at the gleaming green of the scythed and well-tamped track and a banjo began to play from the podium somewhere between the pavilion and the finishing post. I had no armour. I felt too intense for a day of sociability such as this, too bound up in a new becoming, and had to remind myself, ironically enough, of my purpose in being there at all.

I had to re-emerge all over again. For the first time ever, I am sad to say, and in a great show of sanity on my behalf, I reflected how all those small figures around the pavilion, those people of the island growing larger as I moved towards them, how all of them would at one stage, if not already, be struck down by a tragic beauty such as this. And I thought too, once again for the first time as I rounded the stabling paddock where the cloudy summer light was beginning to bronze on the flanks and rumps and sieve itself through the manes that would soon bolt along in the maiden handicap, how such an awakening was not exclusive to the tragedy of war. And, so it followed, it was not exclusive to me.

These are the reflections that a rewriting of the material allows. The luck that those self-obsessive pages, the words that poured like roaring forties rain and likewise knotted in personal tempest, thankfully burnt in the sympathy of flames. So that now I can see myself quite clearly on the early edge of that race day, emerging in my suit from the paperbarks, reapproaching the track and allowing the stately foreignness of a banjo's pluck, as it played the 'Londonderry Air' on the bandstand by the rails of the straight, to gather me in.

As it turned out the sad tune was just a loosener, for it wound up as I came walking over and then recommenced as I drew into the circle, this time with the help of accordion and tuba. A jaunty 'When The Saints Go Marching In' went this way and that on the late morning breezes.

The bookmakers had set up in a row under awnings beside the small bandstand. I searched the crowd for Leonie or the Robinsons until my name was called from the naturally tiered seats on the old clubhouse hill and Brian was beckoning me over.

On that slight elevation then I sat down beside my friend, his wife and sister-in-law, surveying the view and admitting that, yes, I felt better for the stroll. On the green of the track near the finishing post a swan was rummaging amongst the grass blades. Along with the band, the sound of the crowd was rising. Brian had warned me that Cup Day was always a boozy affair and everyone seemed to have a glass or bottle or flask in hand. That was natural. The humour on the faces seemed natural too, even if, due to the higher stakes and the rumours of the powers of certain Victorian horses, there was also an added layer of studied connoisseurship in the air. Brian nudged me, stubbing his solid index finger into the program. Bonny Cologne was the horse he was bringing to my attention and, as he began to list his reasons, I caught Lascelles out of the corner of my eye, dressed not just in his usual slouch hat but in full infantry uniform, talking happily to a cluster of punters making their way around the band to the bookmakers. In his hand was a black half-bucket and, as the cheery punters threw in some coins and a note, I screwed up my face with distaste.

'What? You know better do you, Wes?'

I had to laugh at the mix-up. A clearing laugh. Brian had taken my sneer at Lascelles to be my opinion of his Bonny Cologne. I played along, suggesting I couldn't judge before seeing the horseflesh itself and that nor could he.

'Yair, but it's a bit of fun and it's over from Cranbourne,' he said. 'Didn't mind the boat, they say. Placid as a lamb she is but swift as, well, a swift. Been stabled here too, near the track. That's gotta help.'

'Not necessarily,' I replied.

'No?'

'No, well some mares like to be floated to a race. Gives them a sense of occasion.'

'Did ya hear that, Annie,' said Rose Robinson. 'Have a listen to Wesley.'

'Aw barley!' hooted Brian. 'Wes here knows bugger all about it. I've had the tip from Sykes, he's the one who brought her over. That'll do me.'

'Yair, but he's involved, Brian,' I said, playing the worldly main-lander. 'He's spent money and wants it to win. Hardly in a position to be handing out advice I wouldn't reckon.'

Brian's eyes began to sparkle at my conversation. But then a mottled hand was thrust between us, a shadow loomed in, and I was being intro-duced to Clem O'Connor, Syke's offsider on the committee.

'Yes, meet Wes Cress, Clem. He's bought my land above Naracoopa. Wait-a-While.'

Clem O'Connor shook my hand. 'Clementine, glad to meet you, Wes. Where did you serve?'

He was a tall man and, standing right in front of us, was blocking the view out onto the course. I peered up at him and decided to do no more than simply repeat my name, 'Wesley Cress.' My voice was dead, in order that his big looming shadow would move, and let the rest of the island back in. Without missing a beat he returned his focus to Brian.

They discussed details of the day, the breaking cloud, the turn-out, and O'Connor agreed with what I'd said about Bonny Cologne. Though Brian was sensitive enough not to draw me into it.

Soon the horses began appearing for the first race, making their way back up the straight towards the clump of paperbarks on the turn. The day was shining, the cumulus in the sky finally beginning to fleece apart as things were about to get underway.

There was no way we could miss each other, if she was there. I volunteered to do the honours with the bookie, took the Robinsons' money and stepped down from the portable seats on the hill into the milling throng of bodies and keen voices on the flat trackside.

Faces both familiar and unfamiliar touched the brims of hats and ladies smiled as I made my way to the fat man with red mutton-chops, a bookie's bag and the pensive conga line in front of him. DAWSON. I took my place in the queue, the Robinsons' money resting quietly between the printed pages of my programme. I had a look around.

All the men were brilliantined and in suits, though some I noticed had muddy boots below. It seemed odd that everyone on this salty crumb in the ocean was so suddenly togged up, comical even, a fact that didn't escape the racegoers themselves. Like children playing dress-ups they were relishing not only the event but its ludicrous formality.

There was a small green tent with a white roof between the hill and where I stood in Dawson's queue. It occurred to me, from the things people were bringing out of it: sandwiches, ginger beer, pies, lamingtons, bowls of peanuts, apples and pears, that it was the race-day annexe of the co-op where Leonie worked. I watched closely as people lifted the flap, going in and out. I imagined she was in there, serving. Which would explain why I hadn't spied her so far. That was why the whole track, despite the happiness and the relish in the air, the colour of the bunting and the wind-rippled laurels of banksias and roses, lilies and gum flowers around the finishing post, had been a puzzle to me. A gauntlet, yes, with the gaze of humble multitudes on Wesley Cress, the spindrift who resents civic charity and wraps himself away like the war's own enigma, a gauntlet to be run, but a puzzle to be solved just the same.

But now I thought I had it, she was in the co-op tent, working. And so, while the others in the queue talked of who had come and who was still to arrive or they spoke of serious bets they hardly ever got the chance to make – wagers that had displaced for a day the usual ones on the milk or the catch or the laying chooks, or even the private augural bets they made with themselves in pastured solitude, on the flight of gannets or sea eagles – and while they narrowed their own brows amongst this chat to focus like birds themselves on the form in print on the programme in the queue, the words came like a pigeon with a message, from over the sea of occasion, back into my mind.

I will love you with the power of two men, one for who you are, the other for what you'll become.

As it was, I was happy to stand in that stalling queue, for once relaxed in my own shoes amongst other people. I didn't wonder that something was supplanting the war in me, a love coming like a laurel wreath to bury the screaming death throes of the black Stukas. But I did reflect, as always, on the progress of Vern. Adrift in those waters still, his soul most typically was flat and dark with the water wings of a ray, but right there in the hopeful moment it became more a skate-shaped pocket of light, a glow from the inside, currenting through buckling depths and each time a fish, or thought or idea, or a tear, passed through that pocket of light it could be seen. Glimpsed. Travelling through my brother's soul.

The phrase had come, as if lit by that pocket of briny light, as I stood in my suit in the formal dryness of the queue. Until, like some unwitting yet genial blot, Lascelles was helloing me from the grass near the band-stand, and coming over, to once again block the view.

'Wesley, hello, it's terrific to see you here.' He emphasised the *you*, that was fair enough, I suppose. I thrust out my hand for him to shake.

He launched straight into it, the reason for the black half-bucket in his other hand, and, as if he had just shot a brace of plump chestnut teal, announced what it had to do with me.

'We're raising money, Wes, for an island memorial.'

Something in my face must have fallen. There was also progress in the bookie's queue.

'Look, before you turn away, let me explain my notion.'

'Nice uniform,' I said, caustically. 'You a tram conductor?'

'Look, Wes . . .'

I just stared at him. Cold and cruel. Lascelles should've known better if he'd read my packages.

Yet it seemed Brian Robinson was right after all. He hadn't read them.

'Leonie mentioned to me how you've been writing down some recollections of the war,' he began. 'And well, I know myself how many packages there's been. I don't know what you've been putting down on paper, and I don't presume to know anything about what you've been through, other than that it's given you a sore tooth . . .'

He smiled, as if he'd surprised even himself with the joke. 'But anyway, I have an idea that what you've been up to could be in step with my notion of a memorial with a difference. And, more to the point, with a practical purpose.'

'Is that right?' I said, with a merciful tad of drollery, relieved to confirm that he hadn't been reading the packages. Even so, I was a little preoccupied with the fact that Leonie had mentioned anything at all to him about the contents of what I'd sent. Perhaps, I was thinking, she'd done it to get him off my back. It hadn't worked.

'Rather than raising funds to erect a plinth with a plaque, I thought we should construct a small library and reading room instead.'

He looked at me, his eager eyes, the buttons of his perfect uniform shining gently in the pewter sun.

It seemed a nonsensical idea.

'For solace and reflection in writing and reading,' he explained. 'A quiet place to help improve the recovering world.'

You had to hand it to him. 'Improve the recovering world.' Was I hearing right? He needed his head read, by some well-trained professional given that his friend Dr Freud had cleverly died in the very month the war began. Well, if nothing else, that at least remained a mark of the good doctor's intelligence!

Just as I was about to sarcastically suggest, prompted by the atmosphere in which we stood, that a government ration of horse anaesthetic might work just as well in terms of solace and improvement as a library and reading room, I came face to face with the open bag of Dawson the mutton-chopped bookie, who I might add was years later jailed in Melbourne for medium-scale extortion. It was my turn to place a bet.

I slipped the Robinsons' pound note out from the pages of my programme and rooted round in my own pocket for some coin. There was a moment, as I looked down at the shillings and guineas in my palm and then back up at Lascelles, when I wondered if he expected me to toss something into his black half-bucket. I frowned, simply at the complexity of that, and then with a simple nod down at the list of maiden handicap horses in my programme, excused myself from further discussion. Lascelles looked disappointed, even a smidgen annoyed, but what was I to do? I had someone else's pound note in my claw, their tips were marked in pencil on the page, and burly Dawson was breathing down my neck to get on with it. The race wasn't far off starting. Soon the starter's gun would rap the air. Lascelles would have to bloody well wait.

Of course, the timing was convenient and I was able to fold a hint of farewell into my nod towards the programme in my hand. I turned to face Dawson as Lascelles walked away in his halting gait. I held out the Robinson pound to the bookie. 'Bonny Cologne,' I said, with some relish for the task. 'On the nose.'

~

After the bet I lingered near the co-op tent, from which the steady stream of pies and fruit, cream horns, double-decker lamingtons and sponges on paper plates still emerged. Looking across the track, the jockeys' silks were beginning to organise themselves in a ragged line at the three-furlong mark. I breathed deeply through my nose and turned.

As yet another group of people emerged from the tent flap with an urgency for the race, I peered into the gap towards the industry within. I saw a trestle-table piled with produce, a man and a woman choosing cakes, another man and woman leaning over and serving behind the trestle. I only had a moment, just the time it took for the group to emerge and the flap to swing back down, but there was no Leonie. It was only a little tent and despite the gauzy green-tinged light inside the canvas walls, the air, and the situation, was clear in that one respect. There was no Leonie.

I made my way back towards the hill. Suddenly with the race about to start, everything seemed urgent. *I will love you with the power of two* . . . After so long in coming the words seemed already native to me now, like muttonbirds from the Aleutians, as if I was their burrow. I hurried up the slope of the hill, loosening my tie, convincing myself it was still early in the day, wondering if she'd been held up by duties to her father, wondering also then, though not for the first time, but unexpectedly as I approached the Robinsons in their seats, their field glasses trained on the silks in the distance, whether Nat would really have given her that black eye; and as I turned to sit down beside Brian, nodding that, yes, I'd made it to Dawson in time, the full quid being officially on Bonny Cologne, and saying that no, I myself had abstained this time, commenting that I wanted to see the tread of the track before I took the plunge, the rifle shot went off in the distance. For a moment I saw nothing but the blue smoke of spent mortars drifting through the air above the slope beside Tassos' courtyard. I was oblivious to the rhythm of the race, instead trying to negotiate through the labyrinthine scenes; a phrase like a muttonbird somewhere within me shivering, without a mate, my own memorial perhaps, the only one I could capably build.

By the time Bonny Cologne had come in third I was drawn by local crescendos back through the ledgers of memory and hope, with my astute approach to the turf being acclaimed on all sides. Half in jest of course, though Rose Robinson was adamant. She said from now on she would pick my brain. God help her with what she found, I thought, and by the farcical humour of that joined my hosts with a smile on my lips. Closely followed by a cigarette, to calm my nerves.

The next race was worth a few quid and, during the wait, expected cloud, arranged in serried clumps from out west, began to canopy the meet. Now the light took on a shining silver and, as I munched on one of Annie's scones, I watched Lascelles continue to solicit the punters. 'A library and reading room,' he explained time and again, waving his bucket around, enthusing, convincing, 'a place for reflection', sweating as a slight humidity came onto the track with the cloud. There were a couple of other blokes in remnants of their uniforms too, no doubt SS taking up the chance, and I watched Lascelles approach these two as they stood talking by the bandstand – one of them seemed friendly with the banjo player. The pair of settlers seemed to give Lascelles a fair enough hearing and one even threw a coin into the black half-bucket. Grateful as they no doubt were to have been given their sedgy blocks amongst these farms in the middle of the sea. What had they seen? I wondered. What do they see now, through the veils of charity? A missus and kids? Or perhaps just the next race, a punt and a beer, a smoke and the recognition, which has never ceased to visit me, of the helplessness of men. Ordinary men. As opposed to commanders and captains, generals and kings. As opposed to Tiny Freyberg or Peter Pan. Or John Pendlebury, whose last words as he faced the German firing squad, according to Uncle Tassos, were 'Fuck You!' Once again I smiled blackly and through the brighter happenstance of misinterpretation was engaged by Rose in a discussion of the merits of Running to Paradise, the favourite of the next race.

~

Once again Brian did his money in the WT Jaynes Handicap, and once again, having still abstained from making a tip, I looked like a know-all. But, of course, I knew nothing of what mattered to me, and given the third race was coming up, the maiden trot, I was beginning to amass dark clouds inside. Out of pure frustration, I blatantly declared my hand for the trot, stating firmly that Bonny Cologne, who had missed out on the gallop, would square the ledger. No risk, I told them, out of the sheer depressed sense of love having no future.

Truth was, I didn't give a fig who won, and was starting to care even less about the kind Robinsons' money. The fact that I'd turned about in my assessment of Bonny Cologne interested Brian, who said that he'd known it to happen before, a fancied galloper turning out better on the trot, like a footballer who arrives with big wraps as a full forward and ends up club champion as the very opposite in craft and mentality, a full back. So, strangely enough, my tip had an air about it of the unforeseen and the 'just maybe', which can of course be deadly. And thus it was that, by the time I was descending the hill again to find my way through the strains of 'Wild Colonial Boy', the Robinsons and I were finally in concert and I had pledged a whole pound of my own to sit on top of theirs on Bonny Cologne and, as I found out when I stepped up to Dawson, at better odds than in the gallop.

It was as I stepped away from Dawson with the single betting ticket in my hand that I saw her. Or, rightly put, I saw her Uncle True, obscuring his niece with a ragged brown suit, a trilby perched like a tern on his head, a smoke hanging like a stalk of grass from his lips, a shadowy bottle of Boag's in his hand, until suddenly she sidled round him. At the sight of her, rather than feeling finally pleased or even relieved, I quaked, not with romance but with the instantaneous worry of what she would make of me, as I was suddenly thrust from that race day slope back into my shame and the terrible consequences that had finally occurred on the high terrace of Agio Dormiton. All of which she now knew about from the last package I'd sent.

XXVI

As the winter passed its difficult peak and the year of '41 was left behind for '42 it was clear to me that I couldn't stay at Agio Dormiton forever. Andreas had pickled and salted and dried his foods over the warmer months but, even so, I noticed our meals growing smaller at night: fewer seeds and grains, one marrow instead of two, less bread, even the olives were less plentiful as he rationed them to carry us over into spring. I began to feel like a burden to the monk, who, despite the ferociously cold winter, maintained his consistent routines of early rising, praying, cooking, cleaning, bell ringing, and talking with me. We had spoken of so much since I'd arrived, his company was both a university, a seminary, and a kind of nuthouse for me, and I began to wonder how he was benefitting from it at all. Would he have preferred complete solitude, to be alone with his labyrinth, even in the eye of winter, I wondered. Perhaps, but I knew it was somehow irrational to journey on in this weather, and anyway, where would I go and what would I do? There seemed not one path open to me that I could take, except of course to stay hidden. And so I resigned myself to stick it out and eat less until the time, or a new resolution, came.

It was not long after this that I began to feel as if I existed truly for nothing in this life. The kind of feeling for which the Australian lingo, as it's spoken every day, has no expression. There was nothing humorous about it, nothing jaunty or dry. I could not be a soldier, I was not a monk, I was in a foreign land, and a foreign land under siege, with a man whose intensity was as trying to me as no doubt my presence in his monastery was at times to him. It was winter, I could not be useful, the only book I had was a Zane Grey western that took no exhausting whatsoever, my feet were healed, I was physically fit but felt like a ghost of the former man I was. Gradually too, even my dreams of Vern began to fade, or should I say, to be replaced by dreams of a composite of Pendlebury and Vern, a kind of Oxbridge savant with an Australian accent, who would ride the dormant volcanoes of Corangamite in search of Minoan shards. This figure was like a brilliant shimmer on the edge of the lakes, part Arthurian, part boundary rider, and I would be sent out to fetch him back for the old man but never get close. Pendlebury/Vern would gallop away from me in full declamation, thundering down the steep green craters of my childhood and up again to the treeless rims on the other side. I would *cooee* across the chasms but to no avail, my voice swept aside by the lake winds, just as I felt my identity was being erased by the cruel elements of my war.

Andreas had never shown me through the other rooms of Agio Dormiton, the warren of corridors and cells he would emerge from into the kitchen each lunchtime, nor the clerestoried rooms on the three terraces above the cell where I slept. But one morning, waking to that lost feeling of chagrin and uselessness that held me increasingly in its grip, I found myself stepping up to the terrace garden on the kitchen rooftop and then further beyond, up the next flight of stairs.

I came to a stone terrace on that next level, rectangular and loosely paved, with a small white room at its southern end and a small bare winter tree by the wall on the other. Under the tree was a stone bench and a mossy-looking birdbath, the kind you'd see in the gardens of the bigger western district piles back near home. Beside the birdbath was a neat pile of leaves.

I imagined monks sitting here in less conflicted times, Kiefer and Dimitrios perhaps, or any number of monks going all the way back to Byzantine days, resting or praying, enjoying the views over the wall to the mountains after an hour in the garden. Peace had reigned here once but now it seemed a peace abandoned. And it was me on that second terrace, not a monk. I had done no gardening, no praying. I was a worn-back soldier and yet I'd not even done any fighting for the last few months. I felt as if this tranquil and level terrace should rise up in disgust at my presence, rather than remaining flat and cold and calm.

I walked across the paving to where the low room stood alone at the southern end and peered inside through a small window by a heavy black door. What light there was in the cold February air had found its way through the higher windows and was switching on and off as clouds sailed past the sun. There was a low divan I could see, like in my room, but also a bookcase and a chair. I turned the door handle and went inside.

The room smelt ever so mildly of paint, and also stale cigarette smoke. I stood in the doorway then walked over and sat on the edge of the chair. I inspected the books on the low shelves – all the titles in Greek of course, and illegible to me, except for two books on the bottom shelf in German, which, although I did not speak or read, was almost as familiar to my eyes as the Greek, it being the language of the occupation. I presumed from those two German books that this room had once been the monk Kiefer's.

It occurred to me that perhaps a change of rooms might pep me up and I wondered if Andreas would allow it. Well, I couldn't see why not,

Kiefer would not be returning any time soon, or if he did it would not be in the name of peaceful devotion to the virgin.

Rising from the chair by the bookshelf, I walked over the cold white floor to test the monk's bed. Lying back, I found it softer than the one in my own room, softer and lumpier too, like a mattress from home.

I sank into it and closed my eyes. Saw immediately a pattern of Messerschmitts. The black and white swastikas.

Opening my eyes again, cotton-wool clouds were moving through the clerestory window under the ceiling. I watched as the clouds were severed at each joist and frame. The weather's procession sectioned up like the companies of a battalion.

Before long heavier cloud moved in, the sky became a deep and uniform grey as the morning darkened. I began to feel unwell again. Horribly alone. There was only a thin embroidered cover on the divan but I got in under it. Before long, my head began to spin, my body began to shake, as the rain began to fall outside.

When Andreas found me in the late afternoon I was still in the grip of it. Still with eyes shut and curled like a slater into a black ball under the blue embroidered cover. On the shore of things I was distracted by a flicker of phosphor. An unbunching ligament of light which moved towards a glowing hare until it ran up under my eyelids and out of view.

And then he was holding my hand and talking, in a deep husky baritone. I was being towed back in.

~

The monk pulls the chair up beside the bed. I feel his touch. He is holding my hand. Squeezing it from time to time. My eyes see but in reality I am still a long way out.

He brings a glass of water to my lips. I drink by rote. I speak too, though not normally: one weird phrase, which seems to use my tongue for its own purposes:

I grieve like cockatoos.

Some time later we were standing up in the white room, but still I was falling. Through a murk of blue now. My neck was outstretched. Across the cold space where things used to be. Before unity broke apart into the rough fragments that became its creatures.

We left the room. He led me down the two flights of steps and back onto the plane tree courtyard.

Then he said: 'I have a task for you.'

~

We stepped across damp flagstones and into the kitchen, down the three steps and through a door in the far wall beyond the hearth, into rooms I'd never seen: an unlit warren of musty corridors and cells with their doors flung open, each with a divan, a small table, an icon of the assumption of the virgin on its white wall.

The narrow corridor curled to the right until it wound back to the left before abruptly ending at a tiny timber door. Andreas fished a skeleton key from within the folds of his soutane. He opened the door to reveal an even narrower winding stair.

'Come,' he said.

Like another species of human entirely I followed him up the small slab steps.

We arrived at the spiral's end: a trapdoor above our heads in the ceiling. Andreas hauled himself up through the hole then, with mittened fingers, beckoned me to follow.

We stood in a belfry. A clear space sprung with a brown wooden floor. Its walls were painted orange, quite startling after the previous gloom. In a dormer of cut stone facing north to the melting mountains I saw a bell with a black rope trailing down from it. At the bottom of the rope was a stone, what looked like an ordinary sea stone, tied both as a grip and a weight.

I began to feel my feet on the beams of the floor, began to understand again that I had limbs. So that when Andreas motioned for me to step forward and ring the bell, I did so.

Gripping the cold stone at the end of the rope, I pulled. I felt the knock before I registered the sound. A dull thud, then the peal.

The sound sliced like silver through the earth and, by the second ring, my induction back into the land of the living had begun. It was as if I had come back to the surface, like Pendlebury's shard, after thousands of years of burial and exile.

Through the dormer above our heads I watched oscillating iron swinging in the retreating light of the island dusk. The tones rang out, thousands of granules of sound fitting together to make an impression on the air.

I listened and then gripped the sea stone with both hands again and pulled, the bell was struck and rang, this time with a deepening round, a ship sounding its horn in a fog. I had seen things that only courage and cowardice can see, and so, after a moment's pause, I rang the bell once more, as if to say that I had mourned and wept my way, and travelled to the source of things, first by walking and then, as monks always do, by remaining still to the point of vanishing, and that somehow I was keen to re-emerge and accomplish a safe harbour.

Andreas was studying me, assessing my progress and no doubt considering the task he would confront me with next. The bell had jolted me clear, and along with the relief I felt, my respect for my host, the concave-faced Andreas of Agio Dormiton, instantaneously deepened. He was a master I had never known existed or needed to exist.

~

Dinner after the day I'd had came as an after-glowing ordinariness: no void, no bell, just a single stewed marrow, thin olives, and a scrap of bread with oil in the kitchen. As I ate Andreas stood, not in his usual pensive position but instead busying himself with damping the fire in the stove and with polishing the monastery knives and ladles. When I asked him if he was going to eat he came immediately over to the table and took a single olive, but that was all. Then, when I'd guiltily finished what food there was in my bowl, he said: 'It has been a day of new horizons. You have finally become useful at Agio Dormiton. You have rung the bell that welcomes in the darkness. Perhaps you know now that there is no light without it. The night must cover the earth. We sleep to dream, Wesley, we must be disciplined to achieve peace.'

I looked at him, no doubt adoringly. But the monk frowned, hung another polished ladle on its rack in the corner.

'Each day we see only so far and no further,' he said. 'We continue in the hope that each new day, with the help of the darkness in between, we will see a little more.'

'Like digging for shards,' I said.

'Each day at Agio Dormiton is a fresh toiling, a new layer of discovery.'

I beamed at him from the table. I couldn't help it. I felt I had personal proof of what he was describing. I felt somehow ordained, ridiculously renewed.

'So now, if you come with me . . .'

He picked up a smoke-stained lantern from the bench under the knives and ladles, lit the taper with a match, and walked up the kitchen steps and out into the night.

~

The room on the highest terrace was beautifully warm after the cold outside. As opposed to the clean austerity of my own cell, and the one on the second terrace, it also looked very much in use. In the far left-hand corner as I stood at the door was a lit *magali* with a half-empty basket of chopped fuel beside it. In the opposite corner to the *magali* was an unmade bed, its black and grey blankets rumpled. On the long wall beside the *magali* was a bookcase stuffed with loose sheaves of paper and many books, and beside it, on a long trestle table running to the room's far corner was, to my great surprise, a wireless set not unlike the one which Simmo had carried for myself and Spenser up to the Lasithi plateau. Beside the wireless, and the table strewn with more papers and books, under a curtained window on the southern wall, was an armchair of orange leather and another smaller bookcase, this one with only two shelves, one of which was taken up with devotional objects: icons of the Dormiton, brass incense dispensers, and the like.

Andreas bent down on his haunches by the *magali*, reached into the basket of wood and stoked the fire. 'Please sit down,' he said coolly, motioning with long fingers towards the armchair on the southern wall.

I did his bidding and, once he was satisfied with the state of the *magali*, he came and sat on a wooden chair in front of the wireless. Raising his knuckles gently to his lips, he peered at me in his customary way, as if trying to gauge my response to the room.

I could not hold his gaze. In the bookshelf behind him I noticed that, as with the room on the second terrace, some of the books titles were in German. And in the smaller shelf to my left I saw a handful of books in Greek but also in German, Italian, and English.

'Before the war this was our modest library,' Andreas explained. 'But after the invasion of Greece, myself and Kiefer divided those books of a theological nature and stored them in a cell beyond the kitchen. This room we kept aside for more immediate affairs.'

I nodded.

'Then, at about that time, we were fortunate to come by this wireless set.'

He gestured to where the switches and dial of the wireless sat somehow complicit on the trestle table.

'At which point,' he continued, 'we were able to give this room over entirely to monitoring the war.'

'I see.'

'This being the highest terrace of Agio Dormiton it is practical for receiving signals. Dimitrios was convinced to exchange cells with Kiefer, who had previously slept on the second terrace. Brother Kiefer then slept on the bed in here and, since his departure, I have taken to doing the same.'

'And so . . . you listen to the wireless here?'

Andreas smiled benevolently. 'I do.'

He turned in his chair and flicked the metal switch of the receiver and began moving the dial. He hadn't moved it far at all before a German voice was transmitted into the room.

'Radio Bremen,' Andreas announced over his shoulder. 'Very informative. Do you have any Deutsch at all, Wesley?'

'I do not,' I replied.

'Yes, well my own is not so good, though Kiefer was instructing me before he left.'

The monk bent forward, his neck leaning towards the radio, his knuckles folded on the table in front of it, listening intently to the voice. I sat in the armchair, beginning to feel unsettled again.

Absorbed in the broadcast, the monk remained with his back to me, focused on the voice coming through the crackle of the set. I was left sitting there, and became suddenly confused. By appearances it would have been easy to construe the room I was in as the lair of a fifth columnist.

To steady myself, I reminded myself that Andreas was a monastic scholar. The room, the German books, the wireless, were all part of his search, his vocation. How, for instance, could a friend of Pendlebury's possibly be a fifth columnist? It was absurd. I was exhausted by the day's events, I should calm down and avoid any more psychological traps. Hadn't I already undone the brainwashings, hadn't Andreas shown me a truth beyond the oppositions of war, beyond an earth carved into regiments, beyond manipulative notions like *the free world*? The world could only be free if we stayed conscious of the virgin's death, faithful to the dolphin and his riders. It was impossible that a monk who had spent years in meditation on the death of the Madonna could be at work on behalf of Hitler.

And yet I squirmed a little where I sat in my chair.

Andreas remained hunched, the scratchy German voice ratcheting on from the wireless barely inches away from his nose. The *magali* burned. As the room grew stifling, my mind began to feel airless too, crowding with doubts. Could this religious persona be deadly? Was it the perfect disguise for the imperfections of a man? Did he plan to enlist me now, in his other work, his real work? Did his peculiar pent-up moods, his ruthless intellect, his *cleverness*, all fit with that picture?

Hoping like hell that I was wrong, I leant back in the chair and tried to calm down.

Nevertheless I found myself compiling a quick inventory of the information I'd given to Andreas since my arrival at Agio Dormiton. Manolis and the people of Marmaketo, who had celebrated my mythic status and crowned me with laurels, what if they were now somehow in jeopardy and vulnerable to German reprisals? What about Tassos and Adrasteia? What if their roles as *andartes* had already been communicated, their villa already been sacked, the two of them stood against the courtyard wall where Mug had plucked the chickens, and shot? Had the children of the villages around Mount Juktas been killed, the women raped and garrotted, because of my loose mouth? And, of course, there was the issue of Theseus and the wireless up at Karfi. As much as I despised the Pom I had chosen not to shoot him because I didn't want to be responsible for his death. And what of all the villagers of Lasithi who were helping out with the supply drops?

My guts began to churn.

I remained stuck in the chair. With the German voice rasping through the static, my head began to spin like it had earlier in the day. I was sweating. Now I doubted if I could trust any thought, any notion, as my own. Only a few hours earlier I had rung the twilight bell, felt cleansed as never before, but was all that just bulldust? Despite the light in the room, was it still dark after all? Was I still falling? Well, *was I*?

Eventually Andreas turned back to me from the radio, his normally pale face flushed, and he furiously rubbed his eyes. I found myself scanning for a weapon somewhere in the folds of his soutane. I mentally checked for my own revolver and realised it was back by the bed in my room.

'In 1935 we had to bomb *Kriti*,' he said, 'to make people realise the world must move on. Yes, when I say "we" I mean my family, the king, and Metaxas, his government. We were all of a similar mind. But our action back then was just a handful of stones on the roof of a shepherd's hut. It has taken the Bavarians to do it properly.'

He smiled, and now, in the yellow light of that sinister room, with his blue eyes peering and the jut of his forehead and chin, he even looked like one of the Bavarians of which he spoke.

'It is for momentum, Wesley,' he said. 'The war. This whole war. A predestined leap. It's natural, don't you think?'

With the benefit of time, which the weather passing over this island and on through Bass Strait proves is inseparable from space, I see it now from above. A monk is visited on the first night of snow by a lone soldier, a soldier at odds with his own army, a soldier with a weight like bluestone in his heart and with anger roaring like a bushfire in his mind. The monk hears him coming through the snow, waits for the heavy door of his kitchen to open. He knows there will always be those self-divided men, sheared away from their countrymen by the painful truth of experience. The monk, of all people, understands that. He sees it coming.

～

I could not speak to confirm or deny my suspicions. Instead I imagined a time before my arrival, when the monk I had never met, Kiefer, had convinced Andreas that the grand, ambitious sweep of the Third Reich, its historical high-mindedness, was a natural fit, particularly for an intelligent monk such as himself. More natural in fact than the compassion of the martyrs.

Andreas continued now to speak in abstractions, bloodless words he pushed this way and that. Words about Metaxas and the Greek fascists, the pre-war complexities I would never understand but which to him were an entrée, an underlay, the prelude to the battle we'd lost. It became clear he'd decided the time was right to come clean. I would be his recruit. The battle had been won and not lost after all. I'd already learnt on Crete that any object can be made useful, any implement or kitchen tool, and anyone who wields it has something to offer the battle. Women can cook and nurse, seduce, and fight; children can run messages over the crags, and fight; and priests can sidle up to snagged paratroopers with foreign swords, and kill. Or alternatively, and every bit as ruthlessly, a monk could conscript a farmer-soldier's soul.

What followed was a shocking few minutes of fervent phrases, unintelligible Greek names, and poisonous jargon interspersed with jagged smatterings of German. The monk then looked at his watch and turned back to the wireless, saying: 'But you will understand this better than I.'

He began to fiddle again with the dial until, in a crystal clear tuning, came plummy tones I recognised, the voice of Lord Haw-Haw . . .

'*This is Germany calling . . . This is Germany calling . . .*'

Haw-Haw had given us a good laugh over the raki in Iraklio and, contrary to his intentions, he'd even helped keep up our morale. Such was the bulldust he spouted. His phrase about Hitler having a bullet for every leaf on Crete and a bomb for every olive may have niggled at those in a weakened frame of mind after the hiding we'd copped on the mainland, but the slurring voice had pretty much always sounded half shickered to me, and never more so than now, as he whined on in his nasally plum through the wireless set in the high room of the third terrace at Agio Dormiton.

To my horror, I found that Andreas was taking Haw-Haw quite seriously. It was as if he intended somehow for the broadcast to wheedle me out, to confirm what he had decided from day one was my own ambivalent, if not treasonous, state of mind. As Haw-Haw bleated his

'Views On The News' – I'll always remember the phrase that Downing Street was like a porter's lodge to the House of Rothschild – Andreas turned to look at me with happy eyes.

I finally realised then how things would turn if I didn't take great care to play my cards right. I had a lightning decision to make. So, taking a leaf out of the book of this man who I suddenly suspected of being not only a German sympathiser but perhaps even a German national in disguise – he was paler than most Cretans after all, with the sandy-coloured hair of his youth still showing in places on his head and through his beard, and that concave, almost Nordic-looking face – I corkscrewed inside and showed no sign of incredulity at what he was expecting me to believe. In truth, I sensed my moment of death or survival had arrived and I'm happy to say I recognised it in a flash and reacted with a nimbleness borne of pure fear that a pistol would be produced from within his monk's costume and I would die yet another pointless death and be left out for the vultures to eat in the field beside the monastery. Like Simmo, I would be brutally devoured. Like Vern, I would be truly *missing in action*, never to be heard of again.

The problem was that the ability to pose and pretend has never been my strong suit. Once again it was Vern who would have made a more credible fist of things but I had no choice other than to try. As Haw-Haw carried on and on – something now about the despicable methods the British were using to fight the war and how one day their government would be held to account – I feigned sincere interest. Andreas inspected my reactions with the insatiable focus of a sheep dog. My performance was rough as guts, its saving grace being that it was crudely understated – it could hardly be otherwise – but as the minutes went by I was relieved to find it having the desired effect. Andreas seemed to interpret the lack of outright protest as a vindication of his strategy. I'm sure he felt, as I remained largely deadpan in my chair, that he had buttonholed me correctly as a ready-made fifth columnist he could put to great use.

Soon the wireless reception wavered as pulses of interference crossed the signal. Eventually Andreas leant forward and switched off the set.

He turned to me then to begin his own pitch.

I listened patiently to how the Third Reich offered the first historical opportunity for the human spirit to seize its potential, how for too long we had been drugged by the menial trading of merchandise rather than rising to a destiny superior to the survival techniques of mere animals and Jewry. I swallowed, nodded, and agreed.

'The true Cretan does not yet realise,' Andreas told me, 'how he, as the descendant of Minoans, is far nobler, more efficient, and with purer blood than the cross-bred British. The Cretan has the purest blood in the whole of Europe, even purer perhaps than the German himself.

'But the English,' Andreas went on, 'come south like lords and ladies. John Pendlebury could have told you. The way the British School in Athens, Evans and all that lot, behaved. How they treated the Cretans as their galley slaves. Yet he was out and away, at every opportunity, into the mountains. Trying to shake them out of his hair. A little like yourself, Wesley. Haven't the scales fallen from your eyes as well?'

I nodded slowly, solemnly knitting my brow. 'Well, perhaps there's some sense in what Haw-Haw has to say,' I ventured. 'I've never forgotten the warnings he broadcast into Iraklio before the brolly drop, that for us Allies Crete would be an island of doomed men and sunken ships.'

Miraculously Andreas took what felt like my ham-fisted bait. An errant sage suddenly stupefied by politics, he almost shouted his agreement.

'And isn't that precisely what it has become! For you in particular, Private Cress! Doomed men and sunken ships indeed.'

I nodded again, masking my horror with a sad face.

~

I learnt quickly on that evening. My anguish, which I'd presumed healed only a few hours earlier with the bell-rope in my hands, was as deep as the Mariana trench. Andreas couldn't touch it, Lord Haw-Haw couldn't touch it. It was not something I'd worn like a caul from birth, not a festering maniac fury as I imagined Hitler's to be. It was more a shame at being alive. When others, one in particular, was dead.

As I lay down in my bed that night, not to sleep but just to stare into the darkness, I realised that the condition I was in was now beyond the war. I was cut adrift, from the spirit of my mother and her gifted son in death, beyond region or redemption or progress. I felt truly alone and I know now, from the high sky of hindsight, that that's what my freefall through darkness earlier in the day had been a presentiment of.

How could I explain all this to Lascelles when he came out to visit me here with all his good intentions? The reasons for my coming to believe that no Australian worth his salt should walk away from a known enemy he could easily kill. Spenser's revolver was under my pillow, all I had to do was climb back up the terraces and pump one into him as he slept. Technically it was my duty as Private Wesley Cress of the 2/4th Australian Infantry Battalion. But my time on Crete had already put paid both to technicalities and duty.

No, I would not kill Andreas because of duty or rules and regs. I would kill him because he'd shat on my soul. He'd played the holy man to my distress, teased me out, his blasphemies knew no bounds, against God, against God's mother, against nature, against history, and against me. Like the Devil himself he had colonised wisdom on behalf of his war, used it as his weapon, and as a result – this perhaps is something Lascelles did come to understand about me – like an Australian convict from the days of the old Enlightenment, I would never trust such wisdom again.

~

Deep in the night, surrounded by the iced hush of the slopes of Agio Dormiton, I sat propped up in the bed cradling Pendlebury's copper mug. I had listened for Andreas' nightly piss against the plane tree and finally it had come, its steady force more that of a bull's than a man. I heard him stomp across the flagstones and push open the door of the chapel. That was unusual. He would hardly be paying his respects to the virgin at this time of night.

Or would he? A pissing bull amongst the icons, his dick in his hand as he lit a candle for the loss of my innocence.

After an hour or so he came out again, stomped back over the stones and climbed the steps towards his room.

~

I packed my kit, went outside and across the courtyard into the kitchen and stole some dried bread, two marrows and some olives. There would be no one at Agio Dormiton to eat it anyway. I put the Smith and Wesson in the pocket of the car-coat and dampened the glowing *magali*. And then I waited, drinking clear winter water before I made my move.

Some time later I lit the taper of the storm lantern and climbed the terraces. At the top I looked for my bearings, memorising exactly where the door would be in the dark. I snuffed the lantern, set it down on the ground, and walked slowly towards the room.

The door made a loud click as I opened it and I heard Andreas' body shift in the divan. I froze. Waited, with the door ajar.

There was no more movement. I stepped in and turned to the left. Stood there, listening to his breathing. It sounded smooth, restful. Unexpectedly, I changed my mind. I would not shoot him in the dark, asleep. As if he was nothing, something thrown out, someone who'd never thought or lived.

I wanted him to know.

Heading back out through the door onto the cold night terrace, I stood shaking in the night air. The contrast was sharp, between the round warmth from the *magali* in the room and the thin chill of the island night.

I found the lantern where I'd left it, lit the taper with a match and walked in a moving spangle of soot-streaked light through the darkness of the terrace and back into the room.

Quickly I registered the outlines: the bookshelves, the wireless, the paper piles and sheaves, the two chairs. Then I turned to find him staring at me.

His head was flat back on the pillow, as if something was pinning him down. His eyes horrified. He knew all right. He had seen Spenser's pistol in my hand.

I fired shots. I dunno how many, but I emptied the bullets into him. At the first blast his body sprung up where it lay. The next split him in the throat and blood began to jet as if from a broken mains. The last shots were because I wanted it to end. I'd seen too much, done too much already. When the final shot rang out he was still. The blood was still running brightly but it was over.

I stood there grinding my jaw against what destiny had demanded. I don't know for how long.

Next thing I remember, I was sitting in the orange chair with a sense that the storm lantern was no longer needed. Through the patterns of the curtains on the window of the southern wall light had begun to seep into the room.

Dawn arrived, like another whack. It appalled me. The way things just continued.

I left the room quickly, knowing I'd have to get as far away in as short a time as I could.

As I stepped off that highest of the three terraces to descend the stairs and gather up my kit, I glanced across the damp stone of the high railings to my left. To my surprise, over the treeline of the slopes below, I saw the horizon of the sea. It had been there all along but Andreas had never dared, or bothered, to show me.

XXVII

S HE LOOKED HAPPY, UNCONCERNED WITH HER UNCLE'S OBVIOUSLY riotous and ramshackled state, quite used to it no doubt. They ambled along on the patchy lawn, Uncle True in full verbal swing, and her a blonde sliver of graceful attendance next to him. Immediately with this apparition (not to put too fine a point on it, but an *apparition* she was, given I'd jettisoned all hope, like a cormorant throwing his tucker out of his gullet before flying away from danger) the admissions I'd made in the pages quickly became entangled with what felt now like a distant memory of a phrase:

I will love you with the power . . .

The phrase may well have been painted on a tin sign perforated by the shots I'd fired. My mind, any music in it, grew slipshod. As she took her Uncle True's arm and they stopped to listen to the band it occurred to me that she already had her world of broken men, a pair of brothers no less, and somehow like Vern and I, two halves of a sorry whole.

So despite the deliverance of her, and the look of her: in a green dress, a crimson hat with a sparkling clip, her sea-foam tendrils falling behind her pleasing, fine-boned face, her figure slim and her gaze so independent and conscious-seeming; despite all that, and also despite what she knew about me, things that by the rules of courtship were surely unwise to tell, things I hardly knew myself until they appeared in her cuttlefish ink as if she was leading me by listening, leading me out of the labyrinth on a thread, so that with her I could vanquish the beast; yes, despite all that, I clenched the tube of the programme tighter in my fist and made a fast beeline around the back of the bandstand and on up to where the Robinsons were perched like gang-gangs in their geniality on the hill.

It seemed I could no sooner face her appraisal as back a winner. But, of course, from the vantage up there I could see her only too well. And not only that, Brian and Rose and Annie could as well.

'Oh look, there's Leonie and True,' Rose said, almost as soon as I'd sat down with the ticket. 'We'll have to call them up after the trot, won't we, Brian? Won't we, Wes?'

Oh why did I ever come to these fucking races, was all I could think. Cocooned in the written words of Wait-a-While, and sending them off like hidden confessions, I'd felt safe. Better than safe even. The pages were unleashing what had been crammed in me for so long, my shadows lightened into words and then packages of words, each word a bead of sweat from the pores of my skin, carrying salt and poison. It had been a purification without a reckoning, until now.

As the horses and sulkies gathered out on the back straight for the beginning of the trot, Leonie and Uncle True stood down on the rail in front of the TTC steward, both with field glasses raised. They were serious about the race, as was everyone else about me. Perhaps, I thought, Lascelles and I were the only ones on the whole track with other things on our minds. A library and a reading room, romantic mercy. I stared with naked eyes at her dress fluttering and buckling in the pent up pre-race breeze. By pairing myself with Lascelles even the delivered phrase – *I will love you with the power of two men* – seemed as ridiculous as his memorial. Was I too a gusher, a believer, a Pollyanna, a trafficker in hope? Lascelles could be forgiven at least for his altruistic intentions. But I, no, I was irredeemable. A man who war had whittled back to a skeleton key and who still couldn't find the right door.

Half an hour earlier I would have shucked this off and turned to the race and the Robinsons with a serendipitous irony. But now it was difficult, with her standing down there in front of me.

Vaguely, faintly, I felt a butting, a tapping on my leg just above the knee, a goat's timeless persistence on a slope above the Libyan Sea. I turned, Rose was leaning across her husband, her purple eye make-up, bright lipstick and the wide planking of her teeth all giving her a ghoulish look as she smiled. 'They're about to go, Wes. But they needn't bother. I've got full faith.'

I stared at Rose Robinson as if she was a plaster duck. It could all have taken place on a sideboard. With human figurines, model rails. Tissue paper and green paint for the track. A tousle-haired little boy barracking beside. His horses like charms. The free world.

And then I was nodding with the recognition, re-rolling my programme to emphasise how ready I was for the victory to come. As far as Rose was concerned, we had bonded.

With a shot fired, the trot commenced, six runners, all in a bunch with wheels glazing in motion. I looked out, eyes raised to the middle distance. It was easy. All I had to do was lower them to see her. And lift them up again to the wild spaces of the sky.

The crowd were aroused as the runners passed us for the first time, the sound of the hooves and the jockeys' encouragements barely audible through the excitement. Our Bonny Cologne was in the box seat on the rails, one behind and with a full lap of the track to find his way clear. As the clump went rattling by, I couldn't resist. She let the binoculars fall to the side and called out to the race with a curl of hand around her mouth. Uncle True beside her took a deep slug, the close range of the race freeing him up from having to look through the glasses. I remember thinking how impossible it would be to train the binoculars on the pack of sulkies and drink from a bottle at the same time.

'A perfect sit,' was how Brian Robinson described Bonny Cologne's going, and I had to agree. But I wondered which horse, if any, she was on. Combray, perhaps, or the Mower. She seemed definitely to be barracking for someone.

As the horses came out of the back straight for a second time, Brian and Rose, both with glasses trained, couldn't help but commentate the race. Coming round the turn it was clear that Bonny Cologne needed some luck. The Mower was in front on the rails and didn't look like budging. The pace was naturally quickening.

At the furlong mark, I watched as True lowered his binoculars again to raise the bottle, and Leonie began to bounce a little on her feet. Rose called: 'He's clear!' and Brian muttered quietly: 'There it is.' The Mower had seemed to step aside out of some purely polite impulse and Bonny Cologne was left with only grass between himself and the post. He shot clear, with Combray and a grey horse whose name I don't remember following. But Bonny Cologne had the sit all along and clearly now would not be beaten. I lowered my eyes again to see Leonie no longer bouncing on her toes. I reckoned she was on the Mower. Uncle True leant over and gave her a cuddle as Bonny Cologne flashed by the post and I was accosted with the Robinsons' celebrations.

'War or not, Wes,' shrilled Rose, leaning over Brian to plant a kiss on my cheek, 'you're my bloody hero now! What *nous*! What a great win!'

I took the slaps on the back, the offers of crème de cacao from the basket. But all the while my eyes were trained on the uncle and his niece on the aftermath rails.

When she finally turned from the track, sighing for her defeat, our eyes met. It was only then that I smiled without actually deciding to, it was only then I felt I'd finally had a win.

~

It wasn't long until Uncle True and Leonie were climbing the hill to join our group. Halfway up True noticed me sitting there with the Robinsons for the first time and called my name enthusiastically. 'Wesley! Number one on the gurry! Fell asleep at tea, didn't I? Bloody typical.'

I stood up to shake his liver-spotted hand as they arrived at our perch. His thanks were appreciated, if nothing else they broke the ice.

'Leonie reckons you gurried like a Fermoy by the end of the day,' he went on. 'Filthy work, ain't it, guts and grease and oil, feathers stuck all over ya, but that's what ya said, weren't it? Leonie? You said Wes here was a professional.'

She stood beside her uncle in the grassy makeshift aisle between the seats. 'Well, I don't know if I went quite that far,' she said, 'but, yes, Wesley was a great help in getting those birds ready for the plane.'

'Squab in aspic,' I said, looking down at my feet.

Uncle True let out a snort so boisterous it required a wipe of his suit-cuff across his nose. 'Yes, yes, yes!' he cried. 'For the Yankee cousins. To thank 'em for helpin' us out in ya stoush. The Septics'd believe anything these days.'

'Did you back the winner, True?' asked Brian, lighting his meer-schaum. 'Coz we did. Bonny Cologne, you little ripper. Thanks to Wes.'

Everyone laughed, all eyes on me. The newcomer made welcome, the digger with the ghosts in his kitchen. But the benefits of their kind natures would have been lost to me if it wasn't for the presence of her. With her I could bask a bit. I felt in fact as if I almost glowed.

'I did back it, yessir,' True replied, with a twang of his father's brogue. 'But the girl here missed out.'

'I backed the Moorcroft's horse,' Leonie said. 'The Mower. I've ridden that old thing myself and was led to believe —'

'Led to believe in bulldust!' Uncle True said plainly.

'Well come and sit here with us,' Rose said. 'There's room and we'll have a good look at the next.'

~

We eased our way through the crowd, the banjo and tuba thankfully filling any awkward pause there might have been, as she boldly stepped ahead to lead me, as she had been doing ever since we met. This was her demesne, her people, her race meet on a rock in the ocean. She'd long ago accepted and improvised her role. She also, as I'd already seen, had a secret disdain for mown grass, for cleared landscapes and all the appurtenances and imitative foibles of an anxious society. So she led me through that crowd with something patrician about her, with a subtle scorn in her step, and the way she shouldered through, as if the deeper task of the day was just to humour this child-like annual display, had me pick up the feeling that we were a pair in that deeper task, to front the torrid face of reality head-on, without sentiment, without a need for trivial pheasant hunts, or the monotone of farms.

I still felt unsure but was swept along anyway. Every family's roots on the island were known and Leonie, with old Nat the whaler still recognisable in her slightly ski-jump nose and Fermoy blue eyes, was allowed her independence. The crowd parted before us as we came towards the bookie, people muttering hellos to her which she very sweetly returned, but no one was in any doubt about the strength of the woman.

The next being the King Island Cup, the main race on the mongrel card of gallops and trots, the queue for Dawson's tickets and odds and brisk surliness was long. We took our place and, relaxed by the letters DAWSON on the familiar polished leather of the bookie's bag, I swung from inside to out and simply thanked her in a safe, sardonic tone for being our pilot through the throng.

'They're a funny mob,' she said, smiling in reply. 'They'd eat you alive given the chance but scatter like kicked dogs if you make yourself plain.'

'You do that?'

'Well, it's not as though I try. But I'm known. Half of them think I'm mad, I s'pose, especially for staying with Dad, the other half quite like me. Like Brian and Rose. They sympathise. They've got hearts that wake up every morning with the rest of their bodies. A lot of the people you can see here have battened down long ago. That's why I don't mind Lascelles.'

'And what about me?'

The words came out like a squirt of ink, before I could do anything at all about it. I couldn't throw my hand out to clutch them back as they went. It was too late. Something was happening to me. I felt like I had no guard anymore, no protection against exposure. It was the writing that had done it. And she didn't bat an eye.

'Well, I want to know what happened when you left the monastery.'

This was confusing. Was her opinion of me to be conditional on such information?

'Yes, but you also need to tell me how you got that black eye.'

We might as well have been deep in shrubbery at that point, shrouded and sheltered, inured to the winds by flaky paperbarks, a candle flame cupped in a scented protective hand. The band plucked on, not forty yards from where we stood in the queue, people darting and cajoling each other all about, but we knew nothing of it. We had decamped to the truth of the matter. 'Society' was finally, as I'd long wished, in suspension.

She looked straight into me then, and said: 'You don't have an opinion on how I got it?'

'I've no right.'

'You back horses?'

'That's all a parade.'

'So you don't like to guess.'

'Sometimes. But nowadays . . . well, you can read. Nowadays I prefer to know.'

'When it counts.'

'Yair.'

'Me also.'

'I know.'

I fished out my cigarettes, lit one, offered her one, which she refused, and then stood as if waiting for a train.

In my bottomless vulnerability what I wanted her to say was whether she trusted me, whether she would let down her guard. Would that be dependent on what happened after I left Agio Dormiton? I wondered. Could it be as simple as what I'd done for the rest of the war?

There were two strands that needed braiding: *one for who you are, the other for what you'll become.*

I let it be.

~

By the time we got back to our seats on the hill the horses were on the line and the population of the island, bar the infirm and the reluctant, was poised. It was only seconds later that the starter gun was fired and the horses sprung forward out on the back straight with a cry from the crowd and all field glasses trained. I looked across Brian, Rose and True and saw her profile, her elbows crooked, the binoculars up to her eyes. The things we don't see, I thought to myself. Things in the distance brought suddenly close. She was a woman watching a horse race. On an island. That was all, but there was so much more.

It was a two mile race and, as they came down past us the first time, they were in a long ragged line. True's tip, New Moon, was in the lead, mine, King Ballyee, was midfield and running rough, and Hatstand, who Leonie had chosen on account of it not being local, was already sweaty at the tail of the field. In short, none of them looked like winning. But by the time they'd galloped away from us and far out along the back straight New Moon had settled into a steady clip and was stretching his lead. As they came round the turn to head for home, the grey was doing it easy and eight lengths out in front. No one else looked like catching him.

And so it was that Leonie's Uncle True had the biggest win by far he'd ever had on the King Island Cup. Dawson set New Moon at 25–1 and by the time Leonie and I had got to him there'd been no takers and he'd drifted to thirties. And that's the odds True got him on, the fist of coins he'd poured into Leonie's hand amounting to over four pounds, which he'd instructed to be outlaid on the nose. He'd won over a hundred, which made a week's worth of catching, gurrying and packing muttonbirds look like punishment for some prior will. True had struck gold, from memory his winnings were even greater than the prize money for the winning horse.

Immediately he was on his feet demanding the betting ticket from his niece, who admittedly seemed rather reluctant to hand it over. She knew him well. One hundred pounds in the hands of True could lead absolutely anywhere. But what choice did she have? I could see the hypotheticals racing behind her eyes before she coughed up, rising from her pew to accompany him down to Dawson and whatever lay beyond.

King Ballyee was apt. Not only had my former lustre as a judge of horseflesh suddenly vanished in the eyes of Annie and Rose, but now I was losing Leonie to her chaperoning duties as well. With True now set for a hundred pound spree I feared she'd never return. For god's sake he could buy the whole of Surprise Bay with that type of money, but everyone knew he wasn't about to. At the very best the windfall would be a sinecure for twelve months or so, allowing him to sleep late in the house at Yellow Rock, drink hard, set his nets, and drive his already wiry body into the ground. There'd be no need for industrious ventures with deadlines such as the Moynihan job. He could relax, and that, by the look on Leonie's face as she moved to follow him down off the hill, was a worry.

She didn't even look at me as she went off in pursuit of the cock-a-hoop True, not even a glance did she give as she passed right by my seat. We had come so close, in our frank exchange, but once again I felt thwarted.

For even on this island, the simplicity of being was tangled in the difficult knots of family and society I'd determined to be free of. I had come here to let my own knots stew, but it would take more than the amorality of gales, and the careless brutalities of stinging southern sleet, to wear away what held me. It would take another person. The love of another person.

All I could ask for, in that moment as she hurried off in her assidu-ous love of True, was to be assisted in my new helplessness. I could sense my salvation out there. This time it wasn't an ambition of a boy who was otherwise good with machines, this time it was real and the heart was the only equipment I had an interest in.

The afternoon scattered then, Brian and Rose and Annie leaving their perch on the hill to socialise amongst the increasingly shickered throng gathered in front of the podium for the cup presentation. I sat alone, conspicuous to no one but myself, wondering if I should stay or go.

The presentations were made and afterwards Lascelles was given the podium for a brief spruik on his mission, to weighty applause. As he spoke he caught sight of me alone, like a sad bird of prey on the hill. I saw his shoulder ride up in momentary tension but he brought it down. And soon he was stepping off his soapbox and back onto the grass, with drunks and sentimentals and Presbyterians no doubt chucking coins into his bucket. I thought how much he would have liked at that moment to be on the right side of True. It amused me that the man with the freshest cache of money in his pockets on the track thought the memorial cause a dodgy one. But nevertheless, Lascelles had a crowd around him and was not short of takers.

Before anyone was ready, the next trot was due, the starter's gun fired, and the Robinsons did not return to their seats. This suited me now, and if anyone was wondering, I'm sure they could put my solitude down to the drink and, therefore, an inability to walk. I watched the rest of the island descend that way, the loosening of annual ties, the staining of frocks; one bloke, whose name I didn't know but who I recognised from shopping in Currie, taking it upon himself to piss on the hallowed finishing post. Which only brought sniggers from those around, even from the steward who by this time had a beer glass in his hand. I saw the Robinsons, their heads back in laughter, Rose beginning to lean heavily on Brian's arm, and as the runners for the second last race of the day – all of whom had run before in earlier events – lined up on the back straight, I saw True and Leonie talking to the musicians by the bandstand. When the race commenced True looked to the track and Leonie turned to look opposite, directly at me. She smiled, and in the most unexpected of gestures, held up two fingers in the Victory sign. Then she turned her head to starboard, said something to her uncle, who seemed to take no notice, and slowly she began walking away from him and through the shambolic crowd towards me.

She arrived in the seat to the sound of thundering hooves and immediately took my hand in hers.

'When I was a kid,' she said, 'after the first war, the north of this island was full with diggers granted settler's land wandering about the roads. They used to give me things, Egyptian coins, bottle tops, cigarette cards, lollies. My old man warned me off 'em but Uncle True used to say the things they gave were for all the children they'd seen die. One day he said this in front of Dad, who told him to shut up, that he was talkin' nonsense, that the war was between soldiers not civilians. Obviously he was saying it to shelter me. But True pressed on and explained himself. "I don't mean little kids like her, Nat, I mean the innocence the war has taken away." Nat went straight out the kitchen door. And I was left there, with True. He made me put those bottle tops and cards and coins and things on the kitchen table and tell him about them, which was my favourite and so on. By the time Dad came back in from outside we'd polished off a tin of biscuits and catalogued the things from the soldiers and put them in the tin. Uncle True got up and kissed me and left through the kitchen door without saying a word.'

She stopped there and let go of my hand. We looked out at the race. She had begun again, like back at the ten sheoaks, to tell her tale. As the horses straggled towards the finishing post for the sixth time that day we saw True down below, ripping up his betting ticket and throwing it

on the ground in disgust. He took a long draught of his beer and gesticu-
lated at the musicians. Then Leonie said: 'I hope he lost the bloody lot.'

~

Later on in the evening light I rode in the tray of the Robinsons' Dodge
as it gurgled slowly across the middle of the island, down the paperbark
chutes of the road back east. In the cabin they were shoved in four
abreast: Brian at the wheel, Annie next to him, portly Rose beside her
slim sister, and Leonie on the other side. Three of them drunk and
perfectly happy with the day's events. The other a little worried on at
least a couple of counts.

The plan was for them to drop me off first at Wait-a-While and then
to roll the truck down into Naracoopa where they'd turn north and take
Leonie most of the way home. As the truck bumped along I thought
about an alternative to this plan. Was she wondering about it too? After
all it would save the merry driver the added journey. If they didn't have
to go up north they would get home before dark, which was a good idea
given the truck had only one headlight working. But there was no way
of being discreet.

Stymied, I leant back against a bag of spuds and watched the colours
of the browsing pheasants on the roadside recede before me in the Cup
Day dusk. As we rumbled along I saw the blocks of cows, the up-tailed
turkeys, even caught sight of the Currie–Naracoopa telephone wire
from time to time, strung and hooped from tree to tree, wound round
the top branches, its long irregular loops crossing the island like some
continuous airborne script.

Funny thing was, in considering the possibilities I'd neglected the
most obvious one. To be indiscreet. The truck crested and rounded

the curve approaching my turn-off, and Brian ground down through the gears till we came to a halt under a panel-slapping profusion of mirror bush. The island etiquette had won me over. I jumped down from the tray and looked in through the open driver's window to say goodbye.

Yes, I agreed, a great day was had. No, I concurred, I couldn't believe that True Fermoy could be that tinny. And thank you, I said, as Rose handed over a bundle of leftover scones wrapped in a *One in–All in* tea towel.

'Cheerio, then,' I said, 'bye for now, and thanks.' Whilst trying too hard not to look. Brian shoved the big old gearstick into position and gave me a smile. I watched in a painful grimace, but waving, as they bluesmoked back onto the road.

Just before they descended over the crest to leave the sky and begin the roll down to Naracoopa I saw a movement. The drunken wheels ceased to roll, a black oblong flung out from the side of the truck, and she stepped out onto the road.

She straightened her clothes, dusting herself down, as the truck moved slowly away. Then one red brake light appeared on the verge of the long descent. She heard the engine temper, turned towards it, and then waved it on. The Dodge remained at a standstill. All currents of the island seemed to pause. Then finally the gears ground again in the clear acoustic of evening and the Robinsons began to disappear over the hill.

Four

Catch Me Alive

XXVIII

WHEN I LEFT AGIO DORMITON THAT MORNING I COULD SEE THE criss-crossing options laid out, the pale clay paths ribboning the slopes of the descent in front of me. But strangely, I felt I couldn't miss. The lie of the land, my course to the south, like everything else in the amoral universe, seemed suddenly very simple. One path might be more exposed than the other but in the end how was I to know? The very nature of the sweat coming through my pores seemed already transformed by the pulling of the trigger. I no longer stank with fear. I was no longer unhinged by shock.

As I set off down the slope I did not care anymore for a reckoning of sources. In the end nothing was proved by where you were from, what your name was, nor what you claimed your cause to be: an Orthodox monk meditating on the death of Christ's mother; a British archaeologist finding wisdom in an ancient shard; an Aussie digger calling a spade a spade. Not to mention an RN admiral running a tight ship in defence of the free world. Even the dead virgin herself, with her unconditional compassion, was someone I might meet on the road.

I wore remnants of at least three uniforms: *pallikari* bog-catchers, an Englishman's car-coat, my dog tags hidden in the hair of my chest. But they couldn't claim me now. Not even as some kind of unofficial Australian mongrel. The motley garb was more than emblematic and I was beyond it all, with only the sea ahead of me. I had travelled inward and far.

By lunchtime, with the travel all downhill and winding forever across the spiny slopes, and hairpinning down through country parched from the sun reflecting off the far sheet of saltwater and belted dry by the Libyan sea winds, and all alone with not even a goat by the roadside and no vultures in the sky, I got to rummaging quite differently through my condition. Perhaps I was simply refreshed by the reflections brought on by finally walking again after the long period of stillness. Either way, it was as I came traipsing down the zigzagging track, with orange rocks on my high side and the dramatic cut of the Arvi gorge looming against the sea and sky below, that I arrived at an unexpected and liberating notion.

When our mum was dying, it was Vern who was bundled up beside her in the bed. I understood now how that saved him from being boiled down to just another wiry countryman. In the mornings he and I would walk the track round the lakeshore to the school, our pockets stuffed with knucklebones and slingshots, as if nothing out of the ordinary was going on, as if our house hadn't become like a hole in the daylight. But I could smell her on him even out there in all that air. He carried her with him wherever he went. We'd return after school, do our jobs under Dad's instructions, and after tea the situation would deepen. I'd be allowed to sit on her bed and chat about the day. But every night through that long year it was the same. Baby's bedtime would come, I'd get a loving kiss on the cheek and have to leave her. I'd go blinking into the light of the kitchen and he would disappear through the door

I'd emerged from. Leaving me alone, with Dad and the smell of lamb's fry on the stove.

Sometimes she'd heft herself up out of the blankets and I'd hear her going over to the piano. I'd duck outside, around through the laundry and listen breathless from out under the verandah, estranged from the thick interior of her dying, listening not so much to the notes she played – those surging runs from the airs of Moore she loved so much – but to the high aether of the notes, the echoes ringing in the painted eaves of the dark room. At the touch of the soft hammers on the strings I saw stars ignite in the night sky. Those high sounds became proof of another existence to me; it was nothing that you could write on paper but without the echoes the air would have been strung tight, clipped as a train ticket. This was my mother in the music, this was her solution to the unsolvable mystery: her slow death in our growing lives.

Gradually through that year she became more echo than music, her body thinning amongst the fug of the sheets and eventually tapering like the light effects on the lake at dusk.

This is what Vern had absorbed in the bed. Her wishing him close was his real education. The poems he got interested in after she was gone: the Brooke, the Byron, the John Shaw Neilson, were his stars in the eaves. And even more telling was the womanly sweat of her armpits, her whispering, the smell of iodine on the blankets, the liquid music of her bedpan in the cold hours of the night, the old Tipperary mottoes she mumbled as together they awoke, the mother and child, at dawn by the lake.

This is what I had mistakenly thought it was my duty to deny. That real power manifests not in the note but in the echo, in the presence of death in the room of life, in the spirit of a woman staying alive in the growing identity of a boy.

This was Vern's fullness, what gave him his fearlessness. What sent him up onto those broken rafters of Iraklio on the night of the evacuation.

Our mother's truth. As the precious sky above our lake was torn apart and opened. And she ascended into heaven. This is why I felt left behind.

~

There were no villages on the dusty road I'd taken, no *kaphenois,* not even a roadside shrine. I was glad I'd had the presence of mind to take the food from Agio Dormiton. Eventually I clambered up a small cutting off the road, sat under a rare shady tree and ate. I scanned the sky through the branches, slurped on the messy juice of a marrow and kept an ear out for engines or warning sounds on the track below.

It was the absence of anything but blueness overhead and the utter silence of those deserted slopes that I remember most. Even through the mozzled shade of the tree the sun was warm and though the slope itself was scrabbly and harsh, with each passing minute I could feel my muscles thawing and the tissues of my flesh softening.

We had no need to ask where our mother's knowledge and beauty came from, she was always telling us: the cool black soil, the lava crumble, the loamy guzzles and dry rises of stone and bracken, the plains of fescue and turkey bustards round the lakes. In the sagging iron bed, as Vern had imbibed her tales and absorbed the pictures, I'd felt locked out in a streaky place resembling the lake when the water dried up. Marooned, with Dad's dudgeon. Poor Dad. The bastard. He stalled, he wouldn't cry, and expected me to be the same. In the end I reckon he was only half human from trying so hard. Shrill as fence-wire in a northerly. Then silent as the volcano. I lay back under the tree and sighed a thawing sigh.

Later that day, on the winding downward march, Ken Callinan came into my head. The Ken we knew before his face fell half off. He was the salt in the soup, Ken Cal, such a good bloke to have around. He stood square on the ground, the duty came natural to him, he had no trouble walking in the nation's shoes, had no desire to be anyone else, any better or worse. Or so it seemed. But in that courtyard, under the moist sponge in Adrasteia's hand, I remember the moment. When his struggle to speak, his need to stem the flow of blood with words and my attempts to keep the parts of his face and head together so that he could do so, so that he could live and be heard, was superseded. His eyes began to stare as if at some puzzle back inside himself, a puzzle resolving. Was he listening to the music? Seeing stars come to life in the eaves?

We leant in close to him and there were no longer ranks or reveille, no definitions of Private Kenneth Callinan. We felt it, Adrasteia and I, this thing beyond names, and what's stranger is we knew it well too, as if beforehand.

And then he was gone. Ken Cal. And after one of those deep and holy pauses that if you're lucky follows death, the horns of Jericho started screaming again, our hands went to our ears, time and the battle carried us on. Now on the road above Arvi I knew that that was what was worth telling, the only thing I could tell Ken's dad about, what I'd recount to his mother and sisters too, on the mint settee in Newcastle. If only I could find the words. For how he came into his fullness.

~

By dusk I'd noticed the brush of the mountainous slopes giving way to olive groves again and reckoned by this alone that, despite the zigzags, I was more than halfway down. I'd still not seen a living soul, and from side to side I'd tacked all day, alert to all possibilities, in keeping with the revolutions of my mind. My feet were sore, from not having walked for so long, and after making the decision not to continue through the night I grew instantly rather weary. I looked around for a place to prop, somewhere level and hidden, to eat again, and sleep.

I wandered on slowly, past sprays of rockrose in the cuttings of the track, squinting into the thick shade of the olives, and thinking I might even chance upon a wayside chapel, some star of the sea. I thought of the monk. His body would have gone cold by now. The terraces of Agio Dormiton would be dead quiet. The bell would be still. Not for the first time that day I marvelled at my lack of remorse. Not even a twinge. Perhaps I was no longer human after all? It was hard to tell, being so far out on my own.

But no, it couldn't be. I felt strong, strangely complete, and felt my life so keenly. More keenly than I ever had. It wasn't the taste of Andreas' blood I had in my mouth but the taste of my own self-creation.

We live in our natures, as beasts and by rote until this moment comes. For many it arrives at the point of death, when death, as it seemed to do for Ken Cal, appears like a new sunrise. But for others I believe the moment sidles up in the midst of living. That's when a morality is born rather than inherited, when it takes its place in harmony not with duty but with freedom.

XXIX

THOSE FIRST FEW NIGHTS WITH LEONIE AT WAIT-A-WHILE I WAS aware of her listening out, for a footfall outside the hut, a human movement, even perhaps the loading of a gun. I held her in my arms imagining all types of stereotypic chivalries I could perform, but I never said a word about them and in the end nothing of the kind was required. Nat Fermoy never came near the place.

It wasn't in her nature to abandon her father completely, an old man now, in an empty farmhouse, surrounded by scrimshaw ghosts and tragic memories. Once a week she'd cycle off to take him food, she'd cook him a steak, she said, fry him a fish, run his clothes through the mangle and hang them out to dry, on condition that he never said a word, ever again, either about the past or the future. One word, she told him, one whining bleat or recrimination, and she'd be out of there, never to return.

She told me things in that first summer of our love, about her growing up, her roamings alone amongst the boxthorns, the way he used to keep her locked up and scared. But it wasn't until later, until we'd moved down here to Naracoopa, that I found out the worst of it, and that, ironically enough, was all due to our deepening friendship with Lascelles.

It had taken Lascelles years to finally cobble the money together to have the Memorial Reading Room built. It still stands today, a humble enough structure on the slope there in Currie, but nicely built by the Sanders twins from Surprise Bay. John Sanders had helped me out with this and that when I was building the hut at Wait-a-While and so eventually, after Leonie had stayed put with me and the time came for us to move down the hill for a fresh start near the water, it was he that we asked to do the job. By that stage it was 1951 I believe, the year before they finally built the memorial, and it was Lascelles' visit out to our new place that convinced him that the time was right to finally get cracking. The problem was that, despite all his fundraising efforts, he and his committee had still fallen short of the required mark. But, after seeing what the Sanders boys had done here for us, and having come to feel quite a deal of personal pressure that the unconventional nature of the memorial he was advocating was the sole reason for the delay, Lascelles decided to take a personal loan of eight hundred pounds to get things over the line.

Like everyone on the island, Leonie and I had watched the fundraising campaign from the outset, but now, as Lascelles took us into his confidence about the loan, we sat back to marvel at the courage of his convictions. The committee he'd formed at the outset had had countless blues over the journey, many defections and attempted coups, but no one had been able to divert Lascelles from the path. In the end I would have to say that, despite his extreme eggheadedness, his social awkwardness, and the touch of the otherworldly that he had about him, Lascelles turned out to be a damned convincing negotiator.

'What on earth is wrong with erecting another plinth,' was the common cry, 'it would cost less and be in step with every other memorial around Australia.'

'But no,' Lascelles would calmly say in the monthly meetings held in the hall, 'can we not offer our diggers more than a mere symbol of our respect? Can't we offer them, in the difficult years of their resettlement, not only a roof over their head but a path to healing, to happiness?'

In the end it was the island's taste for practical improvisation that helped get Lascelles' unusual notion over the line. We are an island after all, an outlier to the mainstream, and though the very fact of our separation can lead to an anxious kind of conformism at times, for the most part, through basic necessity, we end up doing things pretty much our own way.

Lascelles had already accumulated a vast amount of books, clippings, unit histories, and other military documentation, even before the Memorial Reading Room was built. The stories written about me by the journalist fella Noonan were part of this collection, the rest of which Leonie and I saw with our own eyes when, after he had visited our place and made his decision, he requested we visit his house just up the hill from the PO to help confirm to his father that the Sanders twins would be the right choice to build the memorial.

By this stage, and certainly under Leonie's influence, my position on Lascelles had already softened somewhat. I was learning to tolerate his company, just so long as he didn't harass me about where I'd been, what I'd done, what I'd seen. Deeper down though, I already harboured a silent store of sympathy for the man. I knew what he'd done for me, even if I didn't have the wherewithal to admit it. And the fact that he still felt the need to get his father's approval before proceeding with what he considered to be his national duty amused me greatly at the time.

We knocked on the door that day, sat at the kitchen table with his old dad, Kenneth, who seemed rather a different man at home, without his green post office visor. He had just been for his constitutional swim under the Currie lighthouse, I remember, and his white hair was swept with quite a salty flourish to one side of his narrow head. The elder Lascelles was always very taciturn in the PO but he seemed quite enlivened by our visit to his home and, after approving without hesitation our reckonings regarding the Sanders brothers, he even opened up a little about his prior life in Melbourne, when John was a boy and Mrs Lascelles was still about.

I sensed a certain loneliness about the Lascelles house as old Kenneth spoke about their golden days on Port Phillip Bay. The father and son were both far from your common knockabout types, and neither of them had what you'd call the common touch. They were thinkers, not eccentric as such, but outsiders just the same.

Eventually, after polishing off a sherry with his father, we were ushered keenly by the younger Lascelles down a hallway towards his den at the back of the house, which was positively stuffed with papers and books and whatnot, all to do with the war. I had just expected a quick cup of tea and a chat, I hadn't expected to be exposed to all that and felt immediately as if I'd walked into some kind of trap. Leonie however quietly pinched me before I could even develop a scowl. Of course Lascelles' purpose was not to trap me in his lair but merely to demonstrate how urgent he felt the need for the building of the Memorial Reading Room was. Well, I could certainly see what he meant. You could hardly move in that little den of his, and on the way home Leonie and I spoke of our astonishment at the dedication of his mission.

'If it was me,' I remember saying, 'I'd collect Phantom comics and be done with it. The info'd be about as trustworthy, and a hell of a lot cheaper.'

Leonie laughed. 'That's all very well,' she said, 'but what if old Ken doesn't agree?'

The joke had a bit of extra bite coming from her, who'd only recently begun to throw off the shackles of her own widowed father.

~

Contrary to what some people think, Leonie and I had made our decision to move from Wait-a-While even before things were taken out of our hands by it burning down. But up it went the old place, with my few remaining possessions, my furniture and clothes, my dad's tobacco case, Vern's copy of Epictetus, and all bar one of the packages I'd written to Leonie. That last one, the one I'd written but never had to send – not until Lascelles passed on and we buried him at Wait-a-While – was still in the pocket of my overcoat, hanging on a hook in the bicycle shed near the hut, where Brian Robinson used to keep his hay.

It was a hole rusted through the old kero tin flue that officially set the place on fire but I often wonder if that old hut of hessian and newsprint actually made its own mind up after all. It was almost as if the joists and bush-jambs of Wait-a-While had overheard us discussing the move and had taken it as either an insult or with humble acceptance of the end of the road. Well, I could at least say the hut had been my second skin and confidante, until Leonie moved in and it came to personify an isolation I was learning to outgrow.

To be honest though, I've never entirely outgrown that isolation, and nor has she. The solitude that descends upon a person when they are divided from their mother at birth is a condition that, in both of our lives, and for different reasons, has managed to prevail. It would be true to say that in the first months of her shacking up with me at Wait-a-While we had some difficulty being together. And not just because old Nat was thunderstruck that she'd gone. If, in fact, it was the case that the old hut was eavesdropping on our new arrangement then it might have come to the conclusion we were being a bit gruff with each other as we moved about the house. A bit short. Insensitive, perhaps. Though really, it wasn't like that. Quite the opposite. After spending our whole lives apart we found our way of coming together mainly through silence. By quietly looking each other in the eye, and knowing all that had gone before. We still had things to tell, of course, but this time we could say them not with pen and ink, or buttery shortbread and kindling, but by the fire we shared outside the hut at night, sitting on the brow of the hill under the stars, with our pent-up feelings set free and the violence of the sea well below us.

After we'd moved down the hill, Lascelles took to visiting us more often, mainly on Sundays. He was experiencing a great mixture of emotions now that his memorial idea had finally become concrete. On the one hand, he was more inspired than ever by actually having the building in existence, but, on the other, he had to face the daily feeling of deflation at the obvious lack of interest in the reading room on behalf of the island SS.

I for one found it considerably easier to be with Lascelles now the building was out of the way. I'd hear the high note of his Velocette coming down the hill of a Sunday and actually be happy that he was on his way. Leonie and I would have a ploughman's lunch prepared, or a casserole in winter, and then the three of us would go fishing together on the jetty, or we'd drive up to Sea Elephant and walk leisurely out over the mudflats to the river mouth. We enjoyed many easy Sundays staying out right into the dusk, looking for remains of the old hunter's shacks from way back in the 1800s, chatting about local affairs, Leonie's growing interest in the plants unique to King, books we were reading, and inevitably too about the war. Or should I say, Lascelles would talk about the war. He still got barely a word out of me on the subject, though I remember us talking at length one windy day at the Blowhole about the fall of Singapore, a subject I knew nothing whatsoever about, having been incommunicado on the Cretan massifs at the time that it happened, and incurious since I'd returned. Leonie seemed to know a bit about it though and Lascelles lent me an article on the subject, which in fact I read with great interest. But if he ever dared to take things further, to probe into the enigmas of my own war, I always gave him short shrift. I still felt raw enough about it all that what I had written in the pages to Leonie could only be entrusted on the true proviso of love. And even though Lascelles was becoming my most trusted male companion on the island I would not, at that time, have gone so far as to describe what ran between us as love.

~

We had not yet put the phone on here at Naracoopa in those days so, despite the increasing use of cars on the island, communication could be difficult. One Sunday I was holed up in bed with a bad cold when we heard the Velocette whining down the hill. There'd been no easy way of letting Lascelles know that I'd come down with something the night before and not to come out on his weekly visit. So on he came, with a bag of peaches and nectarines from his father's garden, only to find me out of action. After a cup of tea and a brief discussion, he and Leonie decided to make up a picnic and go off on their own in search of fish.

It was a nothingish kind of day, cloudy, with a light September wind, and as she described it to me later, the words just started coming out of her mouth before she really knew what was happening.

They were on the northern side of the jetty, with the usual three or four cormorants perched alongside, and that lightest of southerlies behind them. Councillor Island was in view, as well as the beach, its white streak running all the way up to the high hummocks of Cowper Point in the distance. They had always been tender with each other, Leonie and Lascelles, going right back to when I first arrived, and, as she said, it can get very pleasant and deep-feeling out on that jetty on a calm day when there's no fish biting.

Lascelles was describing to her a rare visitor who'd turned up at the reading room a couple of days previous. When the man, who Lascelles had never seen before, expressed surprise at the extent of the collection of books and documents assembled there, Lascelles had taken it upon himself to expound his theory about the benefits of time spent in meditation, with books and writing materials, for those who've experienced the traumas of war. At this the man slumped heavily down into one of the chairs provided, muttering something about hailing from a long way away, from Queensland, from right up the top above Cairns. And what brings you to King Island? Lascelles had asked. But the man did not answer. He had gone beyond answering. Instead he sat motionless, with a blank face, until quietly he began to cry.

As Lascelles said to Leonie, he didn't know where to look, it was so unexpected for a grown man to do such a thing. But there they were, the tears slipping freely down the man's face and him not even reaching for his handkerchief as they did so.

Lascelles tried to comfort the man and eventually left the room to make him a cuppa from the urn. But by the time he came back the man was gone. Must have just slipped out the side door, Lascelles said, otherwise I would have seen him go out through the foyer from the kitchen.

On the jetty there were no bites on the ends of their lines, the water was a calm blue skin, but in the telling of this strange encounter Leonie could sense that Lascelles had become quite het up. He had such a sincere and caring soul, Lascelles, but also of course that racing mind. He began to speculate as to how he could locate the crying man from Queensland, how he could help him, and whether or not Leonie had any idea who he might be or what boat he came in on. She could see his distress, he was shaking his head and going over all the possibilities of who the man was. Before long she felt that, in his agitation, Lascelles too might even begin to cry.

And so it was that, by way of helping him, she told Lascelles a story of her own. The story of the glowing coals. When she told me about it later she said it was just an instinctual thing, ostensibly to steady Lascelles' ship, to break his fixation on the crying man who, she had suddenly presumed, represented to Lascelles the grief he felt for his own dead mother.

You see. We were all motherless, all three of us, right through those growing days of our friendship.

But it was more than that too, Wes, she said. It was the jetty, you know, the calm sea, the slow waves with the kelp beneath. I've always loved Naracoopa since I was a girl and now, finally, I was here. Living here, you know. With you. I felt safe, maybe for the first time, happy and safe. And with that feeling the time had come to tell it.

~

Amongst the anguish of her girlhood, the dark rooms of her father's house, his bullish paddocks, the estrangement between him and her Uncle True, there had been one day that she had blacked out, one day that was worse than all the rest. Her father could be perfectly kind to her, in keeping with the absence in their lives, but at other times it was all well beyond his control. He had locked her up, yes;

beaten her, yes, even as an adult; and now she interrupted Lascelles to tell him this, as they sat with their rods alongside the cormorants of the jetty.

'But the worst,' she said, in an almost-whisper that would have been barely audible if the sea had not been so tranquil, 'was when he went and saw the fortune teller down at Grassy.'

She took a deep breath as it came back to her. After all those years. 'For a time he used to hear horses every night,' she told him, 'and I'd hear him yelling them away in his dreams. I knew they were horses because he'd call out and sometimes I was so terrified that I would even go into his room and light the lamp to wake him, and he would talk breathlessly about them. "They're coming round the lagoon," he'd say, "coming over the hill. They're thundering for us," he'd say, quite out of breath, *"thundering."*

'It was around that time we had a visit on the island from a fella calling himself Genghis, who had advertised in the paper before he arrived, calling himself a faith healer and a fortune teller. From time to time we'd get these kind of visitors on King, no different really from a visit from a barber from Tassie or the dentist with his foot-operated drill. Anyway, without my knowing, Dad went off on the pony and trap to see this Genghis down at Grassy, where he'd set himself up with a small sign and a table outside the bar there.

'Then one day, not long after, I'd got it into my mind to head off to school – which I didn't always do but this day, for some reason, I wanted to – and Dad wouldn't let me. He'd been up early and had a raging fire going in the kitchen. It wasn't even that cold. I remember I was dressing for school when he came into my bedroom and told me I wasn't to go. I asked why not and he said he had a very important job for me. I asked him what it was and he said he'd tell me soon enough, and then went back out into the kitchen.

'I was miserable as it was and so I crawled back into my bed and got under the blankets. I was lying there, contemplating jumping out the window, when he called my name. It was too late. I didn't move. So he came in and silently, without a word, lifted me up out of the bed in his arms. He carried me to the kitchen where I saw he'd cleared away the table and chairs from their usual position on the floor and in their place he'd shovelled hot coals from the stove, laying them out on a spot on the wooden floor. I remember seeing the soot-handled shovel standing beside.

'"What are you doing, Da, you'll burn the house down," I cried. I thought rightly that he'd gone balmy, and was wriggling to get free. But he just strode straight over to the glowing coals and, without so much as a word, began to lay me down upon them.

'I screamed, and screamed again, but he held me there, my own father, held me fast, forcing me down onto them on my back, saying it was the only way, the way to make things right, and that I was a good girl and would I just do this last thing for him, to cure us all as Genghis said, or some such thing . . .

'I screamed and screamed, from the pain and the heat but more the terror of it all, the madness, the look in his face as he did what the faith healer had instructed.

'I must have fainted then because the next I knew I was in the washhouse, with Uncle True beside me, swabbing my back and legs.

'"It's all right, girlie," he said, "I've got you now, just in the nick of time. It's all right, girlie."

'As it turns out, I was lucky. True just happened to have come over that morning, and he'd just arrived, only seconds before I went out. He could hardly imagine the scene he found as he burst through the back door but, as he said, all my screaming had saved me because he was only planning to get a roll of eight-gauge from the shed. He and Nat weren't talking by then and he'd never even planned to come up to the house till he heard my cries.'

Leonie fell silent on the jetty. Lascelles turned to look at her, as she pulled her beanie close round her ears and stared out towards Councillor Island. Eventually she confessed that until that moment she'd blacked the whole thing out. In sympathy he said he could well understand why. For how, after all, do we speak the unspeakable, even to ourselves?

It was Leonie who started crying then, but gently, her tears rolling slowly like the sea below. Uncle True had never told a soul about what had happened and that, of course, was a terrible secret he chose to carry. For months, nearly a year afterward, she had chosen not to have anything to do with him and stayed well clear of the old Fermoy house, despite him having saved her. And when she finally did start turning up back at Yellow Rock, the fact that he'd never reported Nat and had left her living with him alone never even entered her conscious mind. It was just her life, she said, her motherless family, the world of those two womanless brothers on her grandfather's island.

I knew as soon as they returned from the jetty that day that something had passed between them. But I didn't know what. I was feeling a little better for the rest I'd had and volunteered to cook us some eggs for tea. We ate them with lemon whiskey and beans and we laughed and played cards and ate chocolate until well past midnight. He was actually a great mimic Lascelles and when he was relaxed could really be quite funny.

I had not been privy to what had passed between the two of them on the jetty but nevertheless, as we farewelled Lascelles at the gate, I felt that something had deepened, that he had, from that moment on, become an indispensable stitch in the fabric of our destiny.

XXX

THAT NIGHT IN THE OLIVES TREES ABOVE ARVI I DREAMT OF A stagnant pool covered with algae. My father stood beside it, like a sentry, as if he was somehow in charge of it. Amongst the algae, on the thick slimy surface of the pool, Andreas' body lay floating. Slowly, with encouragement from a stick my father held in his hand, it began to turn over in the water until finally I was looking at the monk's face. His mouth was slack but his eyes, even in death, seemed to peer straight into me.

I woke from this dream just on first light, with a bad feeling, my new-found fullness gone, and, from under the branches where I lay, the silhouette of the high walls of the gorge in the distance below stood like an enormous stone vice against a wheat-sheaf sky. Still quite exhausted, I sank immediately back into sleep and when I woke again it must have been quite late. I felt refreshed, as I had the day before, and resolved to get on my way.

After an hour or two I was below the treeline and could no longer see the sea. But I could smell the salt strongly now, and felt the sharp contrast of energies the world takes on at its shorelines. In a field by the roadside I sighted an old chair standing alone, its stuffing spilt. Then I saw people for the first time since leaving the monastery: a family, grandmother and children included, tilling bushy rows of wind-stunted beans. I was tempted to acknowledge their presence with a nod or a wave, as much out of politeness as any attempt to maintain my disguise, but when they just stared at me I found it unnerving and thought better of it. I set my eyes back on the track and walked on.

A mile or so further and the road grew sandy, it ran level and parallel with the shore in a westerly direction to what I presumed would be the village of Arvi, which I'd decided, from the scraps of information about the south coast that I'd picked up along the way, was the place where I would be most likely to find a boat. I wondered, really for the first time since leaving Agio Dormiton, how it all would work for me there. How would I set about making the right connection to get me onto a boat? I felt little anxiety about the outcome, as if it was myself who had died with those shots from Spenser's revolver, as if I was wandering the coast like some unassailable ghost.

Eventually I emerged out of shrubbery right up against the beach, and walked for a time listening to the regular dump of the waves against foreign-looking ash-coloured sand. Out over the water, the sky too had an ashen tint, the horizon towards Africa seemed dirty and sullied, and I guessed why. Something to do with the combinations of wind and war.

My first impulse was to scan the water for boats, but I saw nothing. My eyes fell back to the deserted road and I continued. After another mile or two, and just as I was feeling that the south coast was almost devoid of human activity, I found myself standing in front of a small taverna.

The slanting roof of this rubbly hovel would have been barely six feet from the ground. I noticed two more buildings just like it further down the street, one with rush chairs out the front, and another two buildings even further along past that. The empty chairs all faced the empty shore, as if waiting for something that might never come, or as if the sea was a stage for favourite stories to be enacted upon, when and if its audience finally arrived. The ashen sky became a grey proscenium, and the whole scene was dwarfed by the towering massif I'd descended from. I felt like I'd stumbled into the strangest, saddest, village on earth.

Two men came out onto the covered terrace of the taverna, talking like fellow townsfolk do the whole world over, about some important local issue no doubt, some person's foible or small-time scandal in their midst. I could tell by the familiarity of the way they were enjoying their chat that they weren't discussing anything as incomprehensible as the war.

They must have noticed me standing out on the road between the terrace and the beach but they betrayed no sign of it. I listened to them speak, noted the familiar tones, the pleasure they took in disagreeing. The taller of the two men was dressed in a decidedly untypical way – in fact it was the first time in my life that I had seen a pair of the American-style denim jeans that became so popular after the war. Above the jeans he wore a dusty but nevertheless impressive houndstooth jacket, with a schoolmaster's patches on its elbows, and in the breast pocket of this jacket hung a pair of steel-rimmed reflective sunglasses, which, like the jeans, seemed a great novelty to me in those days before I'd had anything to do with the Yanks.

The worldliness of this character was the last thing I'd expected to find, and although his get-up could quite reasonably have given me cause for optimism, the sheer difference of it made me windy just the same. I s'pose I felt by now that no one on Crete was exactly as they appeared. There was no reason why this bloke should be the exception.

His friend, dressed in the dark duds and shirt of an ordinary villager, showed no obvious deference towards the man in the worldly clothes and I would've bet they'd known each other all their lives. Even so, it was the unlikeliness of the tall man's garb that I couldn't trust and I turned and walked back the way I'd come, hoping that they would continue to ignore me in the midst of their conversation.

I walked fast to the east till I felt clear of the village. I slowed, looked back over my shoulder onto the dry lonely road, and figured I was safe.

Up on the rising slopes a few miles further along, I noticed the high cut of the gorge. I realised by its distance, and by one or two remarks of Andreas' that had led me to believe the little port of Arvi was almost directly below the rocky cut, that the tiny settlement I had just encountered was not Arvi at all. I decided that it was a stroke of luck that I'd turned on my heel, and I resolved to keep going east, with the epic walls of the gorge as my bearing, in the hope that there was some turn-off from the road I had missed coming down that would cut across the lower slopes and lead me to the village of Arvi, where I hoped I stood some kind of chance of finding a boat.

But when the road eventually took its turn away from the water and started gently to climb again back into the hills, I began to doubt myself. If I'd not seen a turn-off coming down why on earth would one magically appear going up the other way? Sure enough though, before too long a narrow turn-off did appear, an even rougher donkey road tilting sideways across the downslopes in the direction of what I imagined to be the open throat of the gorge.

And so I went on, all that day, on what turned out to be a rigmarole of a track, trudging this way and that, first back up the slope then switching down through hairpin bends and dry-locked gullies, some of which were brief but all of which were unpleasant, cut off as they were from the distant hiss of the sea's motion and therefore laden with an eerie silence.

It was in one of these gullies that I thought I'd come to a hopeless dead end. An enclosed and lonely kind of place, its heavy silence was only sliced with dry reeds rustling occasionally, as if from thirst. At my feet, white skeletons were scattered everywhere – the gully seemed to double as a seabird cemetery – and my boots crunched through these discards as I moved along, frail limbs strewn by vultures or by bleached eddies of the wind. I had no choice but to stop and eat amongst them, feeling suddenly low again, without much energy to continue. I stood chewing, in a rotten mood under the sun, until I could stand it no more. I raised my face to the sky as if to make my final plea and, as it happened, sighted a glancing meander of the track some thirty yards ahead that I hadn't seen before. Immensely relieved, I went bashing through the hip-high reeds right away, until once again I was treading over the rise and could sight the water, hugging the hill's parched mouldings arcing east.

I expected to be below the gorge by nightfall and thus to have worked out whether my reckonings of the whereabouts of the village were true, but no such luck. When night came I fell exhausted into a shallow cave on a south-facing hill, worried now that I was stuck in a donkey-track version of the Minoan labyrinth and would never arrive at Arvi. All through the day, the orange clay of the path had taunted me, the bearings of the gorge walls shifting in their proximity, first looming close up as a sure thing, then disappearing altogether behind the hill I toiled around, until when they reappeared they seemed more distant than ever. Whether it was tricks of the ashen sea-light, or illusions of the salt haze which hovered above the track, I still don't know, but I was tested all that long day through.

Such is the power of our expectations, I s'pose, the way they have of lifting our spirits or disappointing them. Whatever the case, as I rested later, with the car-coat wrapped tight around me in the tiny cave, I felt myself calming down a little at the thought of all I'd been dished up and all I'd survived, and how I'd seen not one bit of it coming. Not one bit.

So the next morning, which dawned even warmer than the day before but with that ashen murk disappeared from the sky above the sea, I set out with the gorge of Arvi not so much as a landmark of my destination but as a reminder. It was Vern himself, who with notions of the mythic past, had cast his mind towards a glorious future, encouraged by all he'd read in Pommy books lionising the Greeks, and by Tiny Freyberg and his fluttering Union Jack, and in a deeper sense bolstered from above and below by the fighting spirit of our mum. But perhaps it was precisely this imagining of a great future that had so disillusioned him in the end. I promised myself that I would only proceed step by step, *patousia me patousia,* and what appeared as my right the day before I accepted now as only my aspiration.

XXXI

IN MY RECURRING DREAM LASCELLES AND I ARE WALKING ALONG A beach. He is talking, attempting to ferret info out of me, about what happened before we ended up out here, washed up on this island. His mood is urgent but it's not so much the words he says but the looks he gives me. The concentration in his eyes.

What are the griefs you've felt, they ask, what are the horrors you've seen?

I walk along in silence for a long time. We go right around the island in fact, for what seems like days, along the sand and over the bluffs and capes, past the shipwrecks and along the abandoned kelp tracks. The wind blows then stills, he walks beside me, but he doesn't look straight ahead, he's never watching where he's going, he's always looking across at me. I want to say only one thing, to tell him to watch out, that he might trip over, but I don't. I don't say a word.

Eventually we make it all the way around the island, right back to the same beach where we started, but when we get there we simply continue. We carry on walking. And it's then that I begin to speak.

I could tell you, I say, how I endured frostbite and burning sun, I could tell you about the fleas, the screaming Stukas and the blood, the violence of women and priests, and how I stayed in the battle long after it had passed, long after the grey ships had come and let down their scramble nets to take us away. I could describe how, in fact, the battle was far from over at that point, how it never ends, and how I slowly came to realise that, and how I then assembled a new face, with new eyes, a new uniform, a uniform built from the inside out, a ragtag uniform of the nation of the free man, the improvised fighter for freedom.

I could tell you of the consequences of this new uniform too, what it meant in the realities of the occupation, the reckless deeds I performed, as my brother had before me, the 'heroism' entailed. And I could tell you how this heroism was actually something more akin to what you'd told me about the Japanese. The way they are prepared to die. In order to live more fully.

But really, I say, as we walk on, none of that would tell you anything. None of it would tell you anything at all.

He looks at me, perplexed, even a little horrified. Over the water a sea eagle circles. A dolphin with a child on its back pushes through the waves.

What I really want, I say then, is for you to tell me. About how your mother died. So that then you can see where it is we are going. We have been travelling round and round in circles all along. Only when you see that, Lascelles, I say, finally, can we be friends.

XXXII

I T WAS LUNCHTIME AS I CAME INTO THE VILLAGE – I COULD TELL THAT
not only by my gurgling guts but by the smell of cooking wafting out
onto the road as I entered. A few tidy buildings fronted the water, and a
little further along I could see two or three masts and the coloured bulk
of a couple of caiques straining at their moorings.

It felt unlikely that any German or Italian presence would be in such
a remote area but of course I couldn't entirely trust such a feeling. If
what happened next was to take place as I planned – a berth on some
seaworthy local boat, or even on one of the RN subs which Spenser's
mates on the wireless from Cairo had months ago mentioned would
be searching the south coast – I had to proceed with my wits about
me, and with any western district wool well and truly removed from
my eyes.

So I trod into the village with great caution. However, just as it had
been at the Kavroulakis villa, so it was again. The combination of a
Cretan woman and the taste of chicken saw me drop my guard, though
this time the woman was neither young nor lithe, but stout, in her
eighties, and the chook was already plucked and cooked.

She came scuttling out into the road as I approached, ushering me with vigorous arms into the front downstairs room of a tall rough-plastered building, as if I was the chook rather than the hungry stranger. Her name was Maria she told me and within a few minutes she had me seated at a wooden table in the dark but refreshingly cool room, with a plate of hot steaming chicken and potatoes set in front of me.

At first I didn't know where to look and, against the growls of my stomach, feigned a firm reluctance. But the sight and smell of the food was too much and, negotiating a temporary surrender with myself, I tucked in, while the black widow, satisfied she'd snared her catch, disappeared through a doorway back into her kitchen.

I sat at the table, looking straight out through a pair of open double doors, down a broken lane silent with sleeping dogs, onto the grey beach and milky blue water of the sea. I ate quickly, huffing through my nose at the pleasure of the food's taste and heat. When I had finished everything on my plate I sat motionless for a long time, *non compos mentis* after what had been a two-day march across the unforgiving coastal slopes.

Eventually Maria appeared again from the kitchen with coffee and freshly baked bread. She set it down in place of the empty plate, which she removed to a sideboard on the wall, and then sat down opposite me.

'English, *ne*?'

'No, no. *Ohi*.'

'*Ohi*? *Ne*, you English soldier.'

My motley costume quite obviously didn't cut the mustard here, my Greek was limited, so I came right out with it.

'Australian. *Ine* Australian soldier. I need a boat.'

'*Australien. Ne, ne*.'

'I need a boat.'

'*Kaiki*?'

'*Ne*, a caique, or bigger.'

I stretched an imaginary accordion with my hands, not sure of the word. Maria nodded, smiling with intelligent, almond-shaped eyes. She clapped her brown hands with enthusiasm.

'*Kaiki*,' she repeated. '*O hios mou. Kremeethia mas.*'

I looked at her, none the wiser.

'*Ne, ne, kaiki*,' she stressed, nodding again, full of earnestness. '*O hios mou. To kaiki tou kremeethia mas.*'

'Your son? He has a boat?'

'*Ne, ne. O hios mou. Kaiki kremeethia mas.*'

I nodded approvingly and she rose from the table, picking up my dirty plate from the sideboard with one hand and motioning with the other for me to stay put while she went off, presumably to find her son.

~

Alone now on the chair in the black widow's front room I slumped with a sigh and waited. Perhaps, after so much varying fortune, it was the almost childlike hospitality of certain Cretans that in the end made the greatest impression on me, an impression as indelible as the war itself, for it is certainly true that the two opposing principles: destruction and mercy, are on Crete like the separate braids of a single unbreakable twine. I sat at the table and gave thanks for the welcoming of strangers, reflecting also how this could never be entirely removed from the fear of annihilation. It is in fact a response to annihilation, the best possible response, being both incomparably dignified and strategically practical, for when the day comes for a god to turn up in your own small village, you can bet your bottom dollar he'll seem like a stranger.

As I sat at the table waiting for Maria to return with her son it was Tassos and Adrasteia that my mind kept returning to. They too were a twining braid, the uncle and the niece, welcoming us as they did into the heart of their house but alert always to their own immediate purpose. Tassos and Adrasteia lived as if all the untidy parables of history were bound into their flesh, as if every day was the subject of a *mantinades*, every second a chosen word, every minute a familiar melody, every hour a recurring verse, sung or unsung. We would all amount to something, our life is a story we must be proud to tell. When all is done and dusted, I wondered, was this purpose mine as well? Not to die like Vern but to follow the unbreakable braid made from destruction and mercy to the heart of the labyrinth, to slay the beast and then to live to tell the tale? Is that what Tassos and Adrasteia understood, in a way I could never have? Was that a wisdom they were holding as if in safekeeping for me, in safekeeping perhaps for the entire world?

After all, what was I fighting for? My father's farm? Or was there something before all that, something as ancient as our childhood's volcano, something frightening but as ordinary as a lemon, which justified their derailing me on the night of the evacuation?

I stared past the sleeping dogs to the sea at the end of the lane. My mother's face came once more to my mind, so clearly now, more clearly than it had for years. I saw her lovely brown eyes, the tawny flecks within them, and in that light I saw the way she had sacrificed me, the way she had sacrificed her love for me, so that her husband would have a companion through the trials of his grief. He wouldn't be alone. None of us would, if Mum had her way.

It was a flawed decision, an impossible situation. We could not all of us sleep in her bed. Only the little one, only the baby.

By the time Maria had returned from searching for her son my tears had dried. The western light was slanting across the dogs in the lane. I had been sitting alone at the table with a glass of water in front of me for hours.

XXXIII

IT WAS A FEW YEARS AFTER WE MOVED HERE TO NARACOOPA THAT Leonie really started to immerse herself in what is endemic to King. The island celery, the gale-shaped succulents, the wild herbs, the subspecies which have evolved in isolation since the inundation of Bass Strait waters some twelve thousand years ago cut the place off from the mainland. She had an image in her mind of the place before the farms, before the sealers and the skin trade, before the European grass seeds floated up from the shipwrecks, before the abattoirs and before her father's bulls. The gashes being dozed through the centre of the island for the SS houses only encouraged this vision in her. We had the right amount of land, she told me, in the right spot, and she showed me an engraving a French naturalist made on Napoleon's ship the *Geographe*, when it moored here in Naracoopa in 1802. Towering blackwoods flourished right down to the shore, in a way that is hardly imaginable today.

Because of the money I'd inherited from the family farm, because of her skill with vegetables and fish, and all the good water here, she had no need to work at the co-op anymore, and having made the break from Nat she had no desire to either. So she began to fossick and search, combing the capes and lagoon lands again as she had as a girl, but this time in search of small tinctures of a past that she was convinced would refresh the future. She set out every which way on those daily field trips, and not always alone, often in fact accompanied by myself, and sometimes, on Sundays, by Lascelles, who could see the merits in her project, intellectually at least, even if he was not the most intrepid of explorers. I think he enjoyed the break from his own preoccupations though, from working the PO and manning the reading room, though it has to be said that Leonie kept the two of us well and truly busy on these forays, digging up roots, bagging plant samples, keeping our eyes peeled for what she may miss. Which in truth was very little.

She brought the handful of old cages she'd got from the Robinsons down to the house too, as with the steady increase of vehicles on the island the rate of injured animals was growing enormously. It was not so much the deaths that affected Leonie – in fact, she has been known to scoop up freshly killed wallabies from the roadside and butcher them up for a stew that very same evening – but the woundings and shudderings and pain. The suffering.

I look out through the desk window on the thatch of groundcovers she has created, the spurge and the cudweed, the wort and spinach, the bushy blackwoods waving gently in the wind along the southern perimeter, the little birds that have discovered us here over the years since the war due to the unexpected resurrection of the local plants they prefer. It occurs to me that these local restorations are Leonie's own version of this very text, the tiny plants the grammatical units in her own living statement on the nature of life, loss and recovery.

And so I recall the most important conversation of all we had with Lascelles on those field trips in search of the old flora. It was Leonie that teased it out of him, the confession of what a wrench it had been to be dragged as a teenager from the mainland to help his father run the PO out here. How at sea he felt about both his mother's disappearance and his father's grief. For, as it turns out, she had not died at all, Mrs Lascelles. She had shot through with another man, without explanation, and without so much as a goodbye to her gifted and extremely sensitive teenage son.

They had arrived on King in '37, the fragile father and son, and like some common species of periwinkle Lascelles had gone straight into his shell. The relocation was a much needed fresh start for the father but, initially at least, not the son. He had been a popular member of a chess club back in Sandringham, he was a keen scout, he had a small but loyal group of like-minded friends who he now felt in exile from. So straightaway he associated the island with the winds of disorientation, and yearned to leave, but he also felt dreadfully beholden, and so was devastated at the ill-timing of the war when it came. If he had been a little older, or even had a little more gumption, been a bit more capable of a larrikin's lie about his age, he could have escaped from his plight into a uniform. But no, he was who he was: intelligent, scrupulous, reflective, full of integrity, anxious, and paralysed by the double dislocation he'd endured, first from his mother and then from the world that he knew.

We were sitting in the field under the pines by the small lagoon at Pearshape as he spoke of this. I picked at the cheese and peanuts of our picnic, drank a beer, and said not a word. Not a word about the mother I had lost, not a word about the duty I'd felt to my own dad. Not a word about the damage that had been done, the things we had in common.

Later on that night, after the Velocette had whined its way up the hill to cross the island back to Currie, Leonie said to me when we were getting ready for bed:

'You know, Wes, I'd never realised. Not until today. He sympathises so much with what you blokes went through because of what he was going through himself. His thing about the war has nothing really to do with the fact that he just missed out.'

The potency of Leonie's words hung in the bedroom long after we turned off the light. We lay there the two of us, hand in hand, listening to the frogs, the wind and sea, and thinking I'm sure the same thoughts. That none of us have eyes in the back of our heads or a clear view into our own being. And that this was the deep unsolvable knot, the true labyrinth, not so much a tangible thing but a feeling thing, a thinking thing, a darkness interweaving with the light.

Lascelles and Leonie and I were just different facets of the same refracting shard. It was only I that was the returned soldier, only I that could command the official sympathy and the national applause, but we were all in the same situation. We were islands of the same archipelago, adrift in a sea of unknowing.

~

The following Sunday after the one by the lagoon at Pearshape, Lascelles' father had taken ill and was admitted to the hospital. Needless to say, Lascelles didn't make it out to us that week but by the next Sunday when he did come I'd already made up my mind.

We had a normal enough day out at Sea Elephant, gathering bait from the mudflats there and enjoying each other's company. But when we made it back to the house and were sitting in the dining room with cups of tea and scones I began casually enough.

I was sitting up at the kitchen table, the newspaper spread in front of me. Lascelles was on the couch with his pipe and a book. Leonie was standing, with her hair cut newly short, by the window as if in anticipation, as if she already knew, as if she could already read the situation, staring out onto her garden and the sea.

'You know,' I said. 'There's an article here in the paper, about whether or not cats can swim. I saw cats on a beach once. Lots of them. Back in '42.'

There was a pause, outside not a breath of wind.

'Yairs, I was on the south coast of Crete. In a village I didn't know the name of. I was alone. I'd had an awful time and was waiting for a boat to get me off and back to my unit in Egypt.'

Leonie remained motionless by the window. It was as if she, like the ocean outside, was holding her breath. On the couch Lascelles didn't dare look up, or puff on his pipe, or even move.

XXXIV

S HE CAME WITH A YOUNGER WOMAN, AND A SMALL GIRL, ALSO A TORTOISE-
shell kitten. The girl played with the kitten on the floor while Maria
and her daughter-in-law, Athina, a blonde woman of about thirty with a
large gap between the two front teeth of her smile, sat down at the table
to say that the son could not be found. Athina had better English than
Maria and she said the word had been put out and that I should wait
with them until the following day when she was sure her husband would
come. She told me with a fond smirk that this husband of hers could not
sit still, he had been in America she said, before the war, in Chicago. She
pronounced it *Chicagee*. He had made money yes, but he could not sit still.

'So he will come tomorrow,' Athina said, and then, in a lowered voice,
'his English is good and he knows what to do.'

I was shown upstairs to a small room with a painted stone floor,
a divan, a mirror on the wall above a single rush chair, and a painted
blue window with a view of the sea. Maria set a pottery jug of water on
a low table beside the bed alongside a wooden cup. She unlatched the
window, pushed it out and the sound of the sea flooded in. Then she
smiled graciously and left.

Only a few minutes later I heard voices and Athina and the girl came up the stairs to tell me where I could wash. The kitten ran in between their legs where they stood in the doorway and flipped itself onto the divan. Athina laughed and the girl, Zoe, threw herself after the kitten and swept it into her thin arms.

'*Efharisto*,' I said. 'Does it have a name?'

But Zoe was too shy to answer. She stood up from the divan with the kitten writhing in her arms and went to stand behind her mother's skirts.

'The cat has no name yet,' Athina explained, laughing. 'Maybe tomorrow. If my husband comes, we will name her.'

I nodded. Athina told me what the washing arrangements were and that the washtub was behind her mother-in-law's kitchen downstairs. We stood in silence for a brief, awkward moment.

'Athina,' I said. 'Is it safe for me here to wash in the sea? To swim, is there any danger?'

'Danger?' She clicked her tongue knowingly. 'Italians, no. Not yet,' she said. 'They are only near . . . up there.' She tossed her head back, towards the massif. 'But Germans will come.'

'Yes. I see,' I replied, thinking she'd misunderstood the question.

'But danger from the sea?' she went on. 'Yes, so it is best for you to swim today.'

'It is?'

'Yes. Tomorrow there will be white lambs.'

'White lambs?'

'*Ne.* On the water. The wind is coming.'

'Uh, I see. Thank you, Athina. *Efharisto*, Zoe.'

The little girl dug deep into her mother's folds and the kitten squirmed. Laughing again, Athina prised herself free of the two of them and said goodbye with the smiling gap in her teeth. I was left in the room alone.

$\sim$

On the grey sand there were many cats, some patting at the waves with their paws, some just slinking about in the salt hiss. Others went running along the beach with smiles on their faces, like I'd never seen cats run before, they were more like dogs in fact, and had an air of perfect ease and happiness about them.

There was no one else on the beach bar the cats and an old fella laying out nets down near the moorings. Even so, I felt conspicuous as I unwrapped the cummerbund of my costume and stripped off to my underwear. If nothing else my dog tags were a dead giveaway and for the first time in over two years I pulled them free of my neck and over my head, and quickly tucked them away amongst the pile of clothes.

The ashen sand was like coarse dark screenings once you were on it. The waves were small but dumping and hard to negotiate. It took me a while but eventually I got out beyond them where the milky water went slack.

I stood with water shoulder high and looked back on the village: just a sparse gathering of buildings with what looked like a small quarry on a hill behind, surrounded by sun-bleached grass and bare rock, purple thistleheads, and eventually the sage-green groves leading back up to the towering slopes. I could see no sign of the walls of the gorge however, and realised that I wasn't even sure whether this village I'd struck upon was Arvi at all. It wouldn't matter, as long as Maria's son could do something for me.

From where I stood in the water I could still see snow high up on the top of the massif and now at the sight of it I became suddenly stupefied by how Andreas had invented his version of John Pendlebury in an attempt to capitalise on my disillusion. I shuddered, chilled to the bone by how elaborate human subterfuge could be. Then my thoughts jerked, not from the memory of the shots ringing out in the monastery, but from Simmo, whose hacked-at carcass would no doubt be shredded now by the vultures. I'd slaughtered beasts on Corangamite from the age of twelve, sheep and chooks and rabbits, skinks and fish even earlier than that, and went most days to school with dried blood between my fingers. But none of them had been a friend like him. From the sea in front of the village that freezing mill at the top of the island felt about as far away as the moon. But also so close.

I turned away from the land with a grimace and, lying on my back to float on the water, looked up to see, like a broken wafer of ice, the daylight moon propped on the air in the silence of the sky.

I closed my eyes, heard the metallic sparks of the underwater, the fire in the sea, as the currents edged above my ears. I had thoughts of the layout of the ship. Rivets, tight metal corridors, hard steps and mountings. The spaces of its going down. And down it went, again, for the millionth time since May, away and forever . . .

~

The next day rose windless, despite Athina's prediction of white lambs. I awoke to an empty house but to talking in the lane below. I knew that in all likelihood I would be the subject of the discussion, the stranger who'd come from the battle in search of a *kaiki*. All it would take would be one treasonous bastard to get on the end of such chat and I'd be stuffed. Inexplicably though, I felt no tension at the thought. I lay back on my pillows, sipping at the water Athina had left by my cot, staring through the window at the perfect sky. Before long I had drifted back to sleep, dreaming of Sarah Murtagh with a gap in her teeth, swimming in the Libyan sea.

When I woke later and went downstairs I found that in the place of Athina's 'white lambs' the outside of the house was being whitewashed for Easter. Old Maria and a paper-thin younger man, another of her sons, were hard at it in the lane. At the sight of me the widow dropped what she was doing and once again ushered me back inside, urging me to sit again at the table and calling in a bright shriek for Athina as she hurried back towards the kitchen.

Soon an omelette was brought, more bread, an orange juice, and Athina was sitting opposite me, explaining how she'd still not heard from her husband.

'But we will protect you,' she said. 'We will protect you . . . and one day soon he will come.'

One day soon . . .

Was it just her English or was I a chance to be stuck in this village for weeks? The Maori in the bathtub came to mind, how he'd been happily holed up and how the same fate may now be awaiting me. At least in my case I knew, however, that the man from Chicagee wasn't that far away. I had seen him, hadn't I, with my own eyes, deep in conversation near that hovel when I first descended to the coast? And anyway, if it came to it, there were boats down along the beach at the moorings, there'd be comings and goings. I wasn't high and dry in a fastness of the hills.

Athina left me alone and I polished off the omelette and bread. Then sipped at the juice. What would be my plan? How long would I wait for the man from Chicagee to show up? One day? A week? These were the thoughts in my head as, for the first time in months, I took out my army diary and began to write a few things down.

Out in the lane, I could hear the whitewash being slopped on as I scribbled away. No matter what happened, this was going to be a different Easter to the last one we'd had up at Vevi. From the kitchen Athina reappeared, put down a coffee and took away my empty plate. I wrote:

It's a part of me now, the constant change. Those classical yarns they made us learn by rote at school, which V took upon himself back on the lake, have finally been digested. Perhaps after all it's just my fate to quietly understand, not to wear my knowledge like a crown. I live not in peace but in my own skin.

XXXV

O VER A LONG SOUTHERN WINTER OF SUNDAYS I TOLD LASCELLES THE whole story. Not, as I said to him, the story you will read elsewhere, in books like that bloke Noonan's, not the story about the two and a half years I spent half-wild with fearlessness, making life hell for the Germans from the strongholds in the hills, driving them mad in tandem with the SOE and the *andartes* networks. Not that story, nor about how we were finally picked up in early '45, semi-mythical figures by then, in an RN sub off the south coast at Lendas; how we were slapped on the back, fed cocoa and sandwiches, and then eventually pardoned back in Alex for all our primitive excesses, our all-it-takes methods of subterfuge and survival. No, not that story of derring-do, but what came before.

When he was finally able to believe his luck that I was actually talking, Lascelles was enormously respectful. But the sad thing is I never told him how grateful I was to him. For that day years before, back in the hotel, when he proposed his theory about my aching tooth. He had loosened the bitterness in me but how could I suggest that he himself had ignored his own pain in order to lessen the likes of my own?

Yes, as it turns out that was harder for me to say than anything else in the end, though I do like to think that he understood that by filling him in I was also expressing my gratitude.

Even so, I would have liked to be able to actually return the favour, to actually say the words while he was alive, rather than to rely on interpretation and implication.

Leonie of course didn't necessarily need to hear it all again. She was glad nevertheless that I had made the decision and on the Sunday I told him about the snipping of Spenser's moustache in the cave above Tzermiado I remember her saying to Lascelles that it was just a shame it wasn't all still in writing, so he could place it in his archive as a kind of number one ticketholder of the stories that he stored there. When she said this a little light came on in my mind. But I said nothing at the time, and what with one thing and another it's taken me till now, with Lascelles six foot under on Wait-a-While, to get it all down on paper at last.

~

Like old Nat Fermoy and Patsy Ballyhoura, who bunkered down amongst the westerlies at Yellow Rock without so much as a promissory note for the land, it never seemed to worry anyone on King when Leonie and I shacked up without a wedding certificate. By the 1950s, with a new wind blowing, people in Currie or Grassy were even referring occasionally to Leonie as my wife, so glad were they that she had finally escaped from her father's perpetual storm cloud. They sensed, partly it has to be said from gossip and innuendo, how much effort that would have taken, and perhaps they reasoned that a coupling such as ours demanded more than the usual commitment, official, ceremonious, or otherwise.

It has done me no harm on the island to be hitched to its favourite child. My early identity as the flinty recluse began gradually to change into something with the glowing hint of salvation about it. Like the next-day light on the western spits after a genuine dune-lashing storm. There was a view that somehow I had saved Leonie from Nat but also there was a decided feeling, I think, that she had saved me. People became cheerier when I bumped into them and, as if by reflection, I became a little more agreeable to them too. And as the years rolled by the chances of any off-the-cuff remark to do with the war lessened, and therefore, from my point of view, so did the social risk of blowing my top.

At about the time I started relating my story to Lascelles, Leonie and I had taken to getting out a bit more, going to the odd footy match, and now and then to see a special visitor spruik in town. It was a benefit I didn't see coming, but with my saying my piece, Lascelles'd got a new purposefulness about him with respect to the memorial, an extra relish that finally seemed to be bearing some fruit. I don't know if they ever knew that he financed the completion of the reading room with his own money but, whatever the case, people on the island, some of the SS included, suddenly seemed to take a bit of an interest in his collection, and at some point around that time he even had a letter from the national president of the RSL, who'd heard about his work, and seemed more than impressed. A few years later Lascelles was invited as a kind of advisor to the national shrine in Canberra when they were reorganising the archive of family documents to do with the war and I ribbed the hell out of him about it. Leonie and I were both very happy for him though, and he knew that, I think, despite the jibes.

It was during those years that Lascelles became somewhat of a celebrity on the island, insofar as his name occasionally popped up in the pages of the mainland or Tasmanian press, either as a correspondent or as someone whose opinion was worth quoting on the subject of military history or commemoration. He had also become the popular mainstay of the island Literary & Debating Society, who began conducting their meetings from the Memorial Reading Room. Very occasionally Leonie and I would venture over to attend one of these gatherings. One I remember was to do with the writings of George Bernard Shaw, a subject which caused some earnest debate between the Presbyterians and the Catholics; and another talk was on the Hungarian Revolution. This Hungarian meeting was noteworthy, being spiced up by the attendance of a solo Yugoslavian sailor, who was moored in Currie harbour at the time and who, despite his pretty rough English, walked up and over the hill to contribute plenty of interesting information to the debate. Not all of it was anti-communist either, so that was one of the more controversial evenings held by the society.

Leonie knew better than to suggest that I, given my Catholic education and my love of reading, could contribute a little more than I was to this Literary & Debating Society. But when Lascelles informed us one Sunday that they had a man coming over from Melbourne to give a talk on underwater archaeology, with particular reference to Greece and the Mediterranean, she really had to bite her tongue. I felt the question hanging in the air, as Lascelles spoke of how interesting the talk would be. Apparently they had discovered ships from the Bronze Age under the sea near Crete, he said. And, more recently of course, there were important discoveries being made about ships that went down during the war, some of which there'd been no record of until now. Of course he knew better by then than to push for my attendance but I could feel nevertheless that that was what he hoped for. Which even then, even that late in the day, made my hackles rise. Because the implication was that I should attend. Would I or wouldn't I come along, he seemed to be asking. Definitely not, was my silent answer. I think of that incident now as a relapse of sorts but even so I am overwhelmed by my own weakness. We have to work at being human, don't we?

Why, in the end, couldn't I have gone? I could have broached the subject with this visiting expert, perhaps I could have even initiated some investigation into the whereabouts of certain soldiers lost on the HMS *Imperial* when it was sunk by its own navy on 29 May 1941.

Alas, even then, with my new sociability, and with all I had got off my chest to Leonie and then to Lascelles, I could not face exposing my story to such a public arena. Leave me alone, I wanted to cry out, all over again. Just leave me alone.

It was still a raw nerve that had been touched, an underwater nerve that I'll never entirely be rid of I'm sure. And as I went walking out to the jetty on my own that night I remember sighing deeply at the truth that no matter how far out you go, no matter how many miles from the scenes of your distress, even if you settle at the other end of the earth, the ghosts that trouble you will always be there. Like the moon and stars in the sky.

As it turns out the visit from the marine archaeologist was cancelled due to his plane not being able to take off from Essendon in high winds. It was never rescheduled. But it was not long after that when, perhaps needing to further shore up my defences, or better put, needing to quarry the last vestiges of bitterness from my trembling soul, I proposed to Leonie and she accepted my hand in marriage.

XXXVI

WHEN I HAD BEEN IN MARIA'S HOUSE FOR OVER A WEEK AND THE man from Chicagee still hadn't shown, late one afternoon I climbed up the stairs at the back of the kitchen to take a nap. Through the open window of my room the sea breeze had a soothing quality about it, a light feathering of the skin that seemed to penetrate deep into me. I recalled the same sensation from Iraklio before the brollies. I slept easy.

When I woke the breeze had dropped and it felt like it was getting on to evening. I got a little shock as I stood looking at myself in the mirror that hung over the bed. Once again I looked different. Had my eyes become less green in the last few months? It certainly seemed that way. There were the faintest flecks now, of the brown like Mum's. Perhaps this was hazel, I wondered.

On my way downstairs I could hear Zoe and the kitten playing in the yard. Athina was bent over in the open door of Maria's oven. She straightened up as she heard me, turned, her cheeks flushed from the heat. Smiling apologetically, she raised her palms upwards in a gesture of no luck. Well, at least not yet.

'And the white lambs?' I asked, a little in jest.

She laughed, showing the gap again between her teeth. 'Tomorrow,' she said. 'It will all come tomorrow.'

Wandering down past the sleeping dogs, I made my way back onto the beach. I stood marvelling at the cats on the sand again as I slowly stripped off and left my clothes in a pile.

Out past the dumpers I floated on my back, feeling the currents on my skin, smelling the salt, listening again to the underwater in my ears. I looked straight up at the sky: it was pale, pale as a candle with the day's tapering off. I closed my eyes.

I drifted, past the jagged curtain of blood falling amongst the oleanders in the lane above the Kavroulakis villa, past the jolting of the monk's body as slugs from Spenser's revolver threw him back and back again into that bed on the third terrace. Where was the revolver? I wondered briefly. Amongst my clothes. Was it safe? Abruptly, I tipped myself upright in the sea, looked back at the beach, scanned for the pile, found it, and remembered. My dog tags I'd hidden there, the revolver was in the room, with my kit. I scanned the buildings now until I recognised the one. The tall one, Maria's, its front wall half whitewashed, with lilacs blooming beside my open window on the upper story.

It was too late now. Too late to do anything. And so I thought fondly of the little girl, Zoe, and the kitten, the one without the name, the gap in Athina's teeth . . .

I leant back, floating again, reassured. Went through that gap in her teeth and saw the mirror image of my old eyes, my mother's eyes. Just because the damage has occurred do we have to make it our only caper? Can we not believe again, for the first time in fact, that what has happened can be redeemed?

I was an ordinary man, cut adrift in the weight of life, but I could feel my buoyancy as I floated there, my body light on the water at last.

I was in no need of a boat, not yet, and I had the first glimmers of understanding of what my fighting would be all about. An island should not be stolen, nor could it ever float away. And I? I would do things my own way. I would not be transformed into breathless myth, not like Pendlebury, not like Vern.

XXXVII

W

E DIDN'T WANT A LOT OF FUSS ON THE DAY, NOR COULD WE HAVE mustered it. But she was, of course, in a lot of people's minds, a pride of the island, and thus it seemed only right to allow them to pay their respects.

So we arranged to have a little service in the church in Currie, with Don Lawson the priest flown over from Smithton in Tassie to officiate. But as the day approached a couple of questions loomed large. Firstly, whether or not Nat Fermoy would be invited. Leonie hadn't even mentioned this issue until I brought it up when things were getting close and we were driving across the island to speak to the church secretary, Eveline Aspinall, about the proceedings. Leonie's reaction was firm and instant. She would continue to take him food and wash his clothes but her father would not be there on the day.

Uncle True, however, was not such a clear-cut issue. Since Leonie's retrieval of the memory of what her father had done to her, she hadn't been able to bring herself to go see True. It was not that she resented the fact that he'd held this information close to his chest all these years, leaving her in that house and in danger as a child, it was more that she didn't want to embarrass him. But she wanted him at the wedding, she said, in fact she wanted him to give her away.

We agreed that I would go and see him. I turned up at the old house at Yellow Rock one Tuesday morning with the weather beating a harry from the south pole, the wind and swell absolutely castigating the spits and beaches. The house was battened fast, a round-shouldered timber creature with its head down, and when I knocked on the door I had to hold onto the jamb so as not to be blown over. I half expected no one to answer, such was the noise in the sky and the corresponding shut-away feeling the old Fermoy shack had about it.

But sure enough the door did open and there stood True, in a faded flannelette shirt and workpants, his white hair sticking out at all angles, with an empty kitchen pot in his hand. Without saying hello he gestured me in quickly out of the wind and shut the door behind us.

The shack was sealed tight and immediately the volume of the world was reduced to just the quiet hum of a fridge.

We greeted each other now that it was safe enough to do so and True ushered me into the large westerly room where once I had watched him nod off into his toddy after a long day's gurrying. I found the room as shining and spick as it had always been, its old sheoak timbers glowing brown and the kitchen still tightly organised as a ship's. Once again the contrast of this houseproudness with the dishevelled state of True himself was startling.

It seemed that despite the hour – roughly ten o'clock in the morning – he had already availed himself of a claret or two. I couldn't remember him ever drinking anything but rum but the evidence was plain now, the drinker's disciplines had disassembled, the half-finished bottle of plonk was on the table.

We sat down and he offered me one. 'Would you take a drink, Wesley?' he said. 'We can toast your courage.'

His mouth curled in amusement, his eyes laden with the layers of the joke.

'I will have a splash, True,' I replied. 'But not if you persist with being a smartarse about it.'

The old bloke smiled broadly and got up to fetch me a glass. As he shuffled back across the glowing boards, polishing the glass with a tea towel, he said: 'Aw but seriously. I've no trouble with ya pinchin' my niece. I only wished I saw the two of you more often.'

He poured the glass with the steady hand of mid morning.

'Yair, well, we don't get over this side too often, True. Need a bloody suit of armour to live over here.'

He told me that that's what his brother Nat always reckoned.

I sipped at the claret and, as True started to speak at length about the art of living on the west side, I wondered how on earth I was gonna broach the subject. Not so much of the wedding but of what came before.

I listened as he rambled on about what he'd learnt from Harry Grave, a hunter who lived further up the west coast when he was a boy. Eventually, when a gap appeared in his talk, I skirted round the main issue of why it was me sitting at the table and not his niece, and just invited him straight out.

'She wants you to give her away,' I told him. 'At our wedding. Her father won't be there.'

True brought his fingers to his lips. He toyed with them there for a good while. He took another sip of the claret. Then he grimaced like he had a stitch and shook his head.

'No,' he said. 'I couldn't do it.'

'Why not?'

'Just . . . couldn't.'

I took a breath. I waited. Slowly I began to hear the roar of the wind outside above the hum of the fridge.

'Well actually, True,' I said at last, 'There's no one else. She wants it to be you. And she's done enough time fending for herself on this island. I reckon she needs an elbow to lean on as she comes down the aisle. What do you think her mother would say?'

I don't know what got into me. I just blurted that question out as if it wasn't my body the words were coming from. I was as shocked as he was.

Perhaps his hackles did rise for a second at this interloper telling him what's what about poor beautiful Alma Burrows who'd birthed the child and died in the very room we sat. But immediately they went down again. He gave me a strange look, a sizing look, he was taking fresh stock of me and I saw in his face the notion arrive that a soldier like me must have done some pretty terrible things while I was away, some ruthless things a long, long way from home, some things that couldn't have been avoided and that needed being done.

It was respect I saw in those old rheumy eyes, and for once it was of some use to me. He got the picture. I wouldn't be sitting in his kitchen speaking on behalf of his dead sister-in-law unless I meant business.

~

The day of the wedding itself was unusually picturesque. A day for real estate salesmen and postcard makers. Even the west coast was blithe and royal blue, the water rolling gently up to paddocks that looked like the fairways of a links golf course. If you didn't know better you would have thought the whole place had its best duds on for the occasion.

Lascelles was my best man but his main and rather daunting job was to make sure True got to the church in one piece. 'I don't care if you forget the ring,' I told him. 'Just so long as her uncle's waiting for her on the steps when she arrives.'

Rose Robinson was the maid of honour, the eldest the island had ever known. Certainly the first one to use a stick. But despite her grey curls she seemed as sweetly innocent as any of them that day. She cried all the way through the service too and people told me later she was bawling even when Leonie and her first arrived at the church in the back of Bill Murray's convertible.

I stood alone at the head of the aisle with only Don Lawson, the priest, for company. He was a good bloke, Don. We talked about how smooth his flight was in from Smithton, and he told me how the pilot had said the weather was that calm he could have landed on the church spire. 'A great day to get married anyway, Wesley. The gods are shining on you today.'

I'll always remember that comment from Don Lawson, the way he used the plural *gods* like that, and with him meant to be officiating as a monotheist priest and all.

We weren't too long chatting at the top of the aisle before I heard the whine of Lascelles' Velocette outside and heard the sound of him and True talking as they stepped up into the porch of the church. They sounded like they were getting on fine. I was safe. Any minute now she would clap eyes on her troubled old uncle and the two of them would be walking arm in arm towards me. I had never given any thought to marriage or a wedding day but as I stood there with Don Lawson arranging his vestments beside me I felt that such a ceremony had its role to play. Well, maybe not for everyone but at least in our case.

She came down the aisle that day, and dressed in white, her hair cut short and her eyes with that wise old smirk about them. We kissed in public, would you believe, and when the service was over we went as arranged to the pub for a meal in the dining room. No speeches allowed. Our stipulation. To save any awkwardness.

As for a honeymoon, well, we thought briefly about Melbourne but didn't bother, though I'd say we've had the longest one ever here at Naracoopa. We've waged our wars all right, achieved some moments of peace, and we travel on knowing full well that the world will also travel on, far beyond us, and that like the Bass Strait weather it will have no influence or regard to any children of ours. Problems hover above us for a time but like the lenticular the next moment we look up and they have gone.

I leave the breakfast table of a morning and know that this is right. That we have more than enough living to reflect upon. And Leonie, in her garden slicker the colour of the red heath, and her worn-out gloves, with plant samples trailing from her pockets, takes her cup and plate to the sink as I go, and calls after me, only half in jest: 'It can never be true as the original, you know, never as true as the pages you wrote in my cuddle-ink.'

I take the path to the bungalow. Pen in hand. She may indeed be right but I console myself that neither Lascelles, nor any of the future visitors to his Memorial Reading Room, where today I will deposit this manuscript into the safe hands of the archive, will ever be any the wiser.